MILTON'S ELEMENTS

Cordelia Strube

Coach House Press
Toronto

Coach House Press
50 Prince Arthur Avenue, Suite 107
Toronto, Canada
M5R 1B5

FIRST EDITION
1 3 5 7 9 10 8 6 4 2
Published in Canada 1995
Published in the United States 1995
Printed in Canada

Published with the assistance of the Canada Council,
the Ontario Arts Council, the Department of Canadian
Heritage and the Ontario Publishing Centre.

Canadian Cataloguing in Publication Data
Strube, Cordelia, 1960-
Milton's Elements
ISBN 0-88910-477-8
1.Title.

PS8587.T78M5 1995   C813'.54   C95-930766-4
PR9199.3.S77M5 1995

Our torments also may in length of time
Become our elements
—John Milton, *Paradise Lost*

ONE

Milton sits in traffic picking his nose. Before, he'd worry about other drivers seeing him. He'd have his finger up a nostril then remember he was in public and quickly withdraw it, pretending to scratch his nose. Now he doesn't care. He picks in plain view, rolls the boogers into balls and flicks them out the window, sometimes hitting the other cars. It's a gesture of defiance.

Lately he's been thinking about killing people. He pictures his arm encased in steel jutting out from his shoulder, Robo-cop-style, his metallic fist shattering noses and cheek-bones, mashing brains to pulp. He hears necks snap, watches bodies keel over backwards, hears skulls splat against the concrete. As he steps over the bodies, he feels exalted, free, powerful.

This fantasy lasts for six to ten seconds while he's stopped at a light or waiting in line at a bank machine, moments when he has no choice but to think. He wonders if this means he could kill people.

He doubts it, since he can't even kill bugs. When Judith spots a bug in the house and asks him to get rid of it, he finds a piece of paper, places it in front of the bug and waits patiently for the bug to crawl onto it. Then he carries it outside wondering how the bug feels while it's being transported through the air. He worries that it becomes disoriented when it's shunted onto the damp grass after it's been snuggling up to broadloom. Judith tells him bugs don't have brains, just antennae. She tells him it probably takes the bug a millionth of a second to figure out it's in the backyard and not the living-room. She says it's no sweat to the bug. Milton doesn't argue with her; he's aware that most humans think bugs don't have brains.

He wonders why, in his killing fantasy, the faces never belong to anyone he knows. It seems to him that the fantasy would be therapeutic if the heads belonged to people who get up his nose. Munroe, for example, or Aiken. The two of them were drunk again last night. Aiken was trying to cram a twelve-foot flatbed into an eight-foot freight elevator. Munroe was throwing rubber disks around, and one hit Milton's shoulder. Every payday they get stoned out of their minds and mess around in the plant. Milton suspects that Nelson, the supervisor, knows what's going on but doesn't report it because he doesn't want trouble. Milton would report it only he's scared to lose his job. He has a feeling that one of these days a rubber disk is going to hit him in the temple and kill him. He has no problem with this if death is instantaneous. He just doesn't want to become a vegetable like his dad.

He suspects that part of the reason that he fantasizes about smashing people's heads is that the killing resolves something. In real life he never resolves anything. Judith says she feels like they're hanging on to the planet by a tiny thread that could easily break.

He almost wishes she would leave. When he comes home, she jumps on him. All he wants to do is watch TV, even though he hates what it's doing to his head; even though his thoughts are starting to look like TV commercials. When he considers spending his savings on a vacation, he pictures the empty, glistening beaches in the commercials. He tries to place himself and Judith in the picture, but it falls apart. The truth of it is, he hates getting sand in his shorts, and Judith won't wear a bathing suit because she has stretch marks from when she had Ariel.

He wishes she'd quit worrying about him not having any friends. She thinks you're not normal unless you have friends. He claims that Winnie's his friend.

'Winnie's retarded,' she points out.

'He's got a job, he can't be that retarded.'

'It doesn't take brains to wash floors.'

Winnie lives two doors down with his mother. He has a wide, flat face, pimples and eyes that almost cross. On his time off he wears a black satin cowboy-shirt with gold piping, and rhinestone buttons. Judith says he has the worst body odour of any human she has ever met, as well as 'halitosis'. Milton doesn't smell it. He likes Winnie. 'You like him because you can push him around,' Judith tells him. Milton doesn't disagree with her. He doesn't see what's wrong with having a friend who doesn't argue with you. Judith seems to think friendships have to be confrontational. She's always trying to find the 'honesty' in people, insisting on 'truthful' relationships. She goes through friends like panty-hose. For days he'll hear about how 'interesting' or how 'aware' a person is, and they'll start showing up at the house; then suddenly they'll vanish, and Judith will stop talking about them. He'll be sitting with her quietly after dinner, and she'll complain that they don't know anybody. He'll say, 'What happened to what's her name?'

'I don't know.'

'Why don't you call her?'

'I don't think it's a good idea.'

'Why not?'

'I don't think she really likes me. I mean, she doesn't really know me.'

Since Ariel died, Judith seems to think that nobody really likes her. She tells Milton he's the only one who really knows her and likes her anyway. This may be true, but it gets tiring, knowing her. She can't stand him not knowing everything, including details of personal hygiene. Conversely, she wants to know everything about him. He can't even close the bathroom door on her. The truth of it is, he doesn't want her to know everything about him. She even asked him when he masturbated. He didn't like how she presumed that he did.

He didn't think it was something they should talk about. In his opinion, there are things better left unsaid. His killing fantasies for example. No doubt she'd find significance in his killing fantasies and connect them to Ariel's death. She believes in the after-life and spirits inhabiting human bodies. She's been seeing a 'Trance-Channeller' to talk about Ariel. The 'Channeller' explained to her that Ariel's soul only needed the three and a half years of Ariel's life to learn what it had to learn. Now the soul is flitting around looking for another body to inhabit so it can move to another plane and learn some more. Milton has no problem with Judith imagining Ariel's soul continuing on if that makes it all easier for her. He just doesn't want to hear about it. But Judith calmly insists that at some point he'll feel 'ready', and they'll be able to talk about the accident together. But Milton can't see that happening, sees no point in it. He knows Judith will want to discuss the significance of Ariel being crushed by a TV because she's already told him she thinks it's significant.

'Significant to what?' he asked.

'I'm not sure. The effect of TV on us maybe, the hold it has on us. I mean you know we haven't exactly stopped watching it. You'd think we would have.'

They did stop for a while, since the TV was ruined. But the evenings seemed so endless and empty. Then Winnie started coming over, distracting them with his chatter about the CD player he wants to buy and the party he's going to have. He's been planning to have a party since they've known him. Milton suspects that Winnie puts off the party because he's afraid nobody will come.

So when Sears had a sale Milton bought the new TV. He didn't put it where the old one had been but in the bedroom on his dresser at the end of the bed. He lies with his hands behind his head watching it, hardly noticing the difference between the shows and the commercials. When Judith sorts laundry on the bed she says, 'Why are you watching the comercials? Use the thing.' She gropes around the bed until she finds the remote control, then flicks through the channels looking for a show. Milton figures by the time she finds a show the commercials are over anyway. Before Ariel died this bothered him. Now it makes no difference.

He can't believe she doesn't blame him for not being there to stop the TV from falling. He was supposed to be watching her. Judith was washing her hair. Judith has an alibi.

Often he tries to piece together the picture of his tiny daughter pulling the TV down on herself. But he can't. Where did she find the strength? What did she pull on? The volume dial? The power button? He didn't think she could reach up that high.

At least Judith tried to do CPR on her. He just stood there, numb. He didn't even think to call an ambulance until he realized that Judith was screaming at him to dial 911. Ariel was dead before they got to the hospital. Crush injuries.

For seven months he has been waiting for Judith to blame him. But he knows she won't. She's not that kind of person.

TWO

'I'm really weirded out about the leaves falling off the trees,' Judith says.

'Why?' He tears some chicken off a wing with his teeth.

'It just seems harder this year.'

Milton nods and glances out the window. The neighbour's cat is sitting on the fence staring at him. Milton scowls at it. It stares back. He hates cats because nothing gets to them. The world could end, and there'd still be cats, sitting around staring.

Judith pushes her plate away. 'You know what happened with Dr. Moriarty today?'

Ariel always used to say 'You know what happened?' It drove Milton crazy because even when he asked 'No, what happened?', she'd repeat 'You know what happened?' He knew she was stalling, that she'd only spoken up to get his attention, that really she had nothing to say.

'What happened with Dr. Moriarty?' he asks. Dr. Moriarty is

the name of the spirit that the Chaneller becomes when he goes into a trance. Judith says he talks like Laurence Olivier.

She plays with the string on the blind. 'He says I have to forgive more.'

Milton stands and rips some paper-towel from the holder to wipe his hands.

Judith winds the string around her finger. 'It's weird because I thought I had forgiven.'

Milton wipes his mouth, steps on the pedal of the trash-can to flip up the lid, then drops the piece of paper-towel into it.

Judith leans her elbows on the table, cradling her face in her hands. 'Dr. Moriarty says you can never forgive enough. But he says you can't forgive others until you forgive yourself.'

He can hardly remember when Judith didn't talk like this, when he wasn't uncomfortable around her, preparing to ward off her subliminal messages. 'I thought you were working today,' he says.

'Marty asked me to switch shifts with her.'

He starts to clear the plates.

'I know you don't believe in it,' she says, 'but I really think that's good advice. For anybody, not just us.'

He shrugs and piles the dishes in the sink then turns the taps on full blast hoping to drown out any further attempts at conversation.

'He says everybody has a right to be happy,' she continues, raising her voice. 'Regardless.'

'Regardless of what?'

'Of anything. What happens to us. We don't have to be unhappy for the rest of our lives if we choose not to be. It's our choice.'

They've had sex twice since the accident. It felt mechanical, as though they were doing it because they thought they should.

'What are you waiting for, Milton? I feel like you're waiting for something.'

'I'm not waiting for anything.'

'John Lennon said life happens while you make plans.'

He hates it when she quotes John Lennon. 'I'm not making plans.'

'Well, something's going on, and I'm not a part of it.'

'Nothing's going on. I hate my job; what else is new.'

She stands and leans on the counter watching him scrub a plate with a J-cloth. 'You hate everything. That's all I ever hear from you. You never have a good thing to say about anybody or any thing. I feel like you don't feel or hear or see anything any more.'

He rinses the plate and places it carefully in the rack. 'And all I ever hear from you is what you're feeling.'

'You don't think feelings are important?'

'I think people make up feelings so they have something to talk about. It's like, if you don't have a feeling, there's something wrong with you. Well, a lot of the time I'm not feeling anything, so maybe there is something wrong with me, maybe you should find a guy who has feelings.'

'Everybody has feelings.'

'Not me. I can go for days without feeling a thing.'

'You're just protecting yourself.'

'What's wrong with that?'

'What's wrong is that you're horrible to be around.'

He would like to smash a plate right now. But she might laugh at him, and he'd have to clean it up. 'So leave,' he tells her, 'I'm not stopping you.'

'Is that what you want?'

All of a sudden he imagines the place without her: cobwebs clinging to corners, doors creaking, torn curtains billowing through broken windows even though the windows have blinds. 'No.'

'Well, I don't like it like this. Things can't go on like this.' She picks up what's left of the chicken and wraps it briskly in tin foil. 'Maybe we should try to have another one.'

'No.'

'What do you mean "no"? You can't just say "no".'

He scrubs at the roasting pan with steel wool. 'Not now.'

'So when?'

He feels her staring at him, waiting, cradling the wrapped carcass in her arms. 'I don't know,' he mumbles.

'Why don't you just be honest and say you don't want another one, ever. You want to go on pedestalizing Ariel until the day you die.'

He's never heard her use the word pedestalizing before and

14

suspects she got it from Dr. Moriarty.

She yanks open the fridge door and stuffs the chicken in on top of other leftovers. 'Well, I do happen to want another one, so that's a problem for us isn't it?'

'Nothing's a problem unless you make it a problem.'

'You always try to make it sound like I'm inventing the problem.'

'I don't see that there's a problem. I think it's normal to want to wait. How do you think her soul would feel if we had another one right away?'

'You don't give a shit about her soul, and anyway it's not exactly "right away". Besides, who knows if we can have another one.' It took them three years to conceive. She had 'hostile mucus' that paralysed his sperm. Finally he had to 'produce' sperm so that a doctor could inject it directly into her uterus. It has always disturbed Milton that Ariel was immaculately conceived.

He shakes water off his hands. 'I think a period of grieving is appropriate.'

'Is that what you're doing, grieving?'

'Well I'm not exactly rejoicing, am I?'

'There, you see, you can't even say the word "grieving" without that snarky tone.'

Winnie's doughy, squashed face appears in the window. He waves, disappears from view, then comes through the back door. 'Great,' Judith mutters.

'Hi, guys,' Winnie says.

'How goes it, Win?' Milton asks.

'I went to see the car show. Are there some cars there I wouldn't mind.'

'Fast?'

'Yeah. And computerized. It's like, all you do is steer.'

Judith grabs a cloth and starts to dry the dishes. 'Have you eaten, Winnie? There's some chicken.'

'No thanks. I had a burger.'

'Your mum's not too happy about you eating burgers all the time.'

Winnie fingers one of his rhinestone buttons. 'What she don't know won't hurt her.'

'Looks like you're putting on a pound or two there though, Win,' Milton says, pointing at Winnie's bloated waistline.

'So? Who'm I supposed to save it for?'

'Where do you pick up language like that?' Judith asks.

Winnie drops his chin into his chest. 'Sorry. I'm sorry.'

'Don't give him a hard time,' Milton says.

'I'm not giving him a hard time. I'm asking a question.'

'You're making him feel bad.'

'I am not. Am I making you feel bad, Winnie?'

Winnie shakes his head, fingering the end of his nose.

'You make him self-conscious,' Milton explains.

'Would you quit protecting him? What is this? Am I in the way here? Would you rather be alone with Winnie?'

'Don't go on about it,' Milton grumbles.

'You'll do anything except face the truth. You'll even house-clean. I've been wondering how come you've been helping out so much. It's just so you don't have to face me.'

'So you don't want me to houseclean?'

'Of course I want you to houseclean.'

'I can houseclean,' Winnie offers. 'At work we've got this chemical cleaner. You should see what it does to carpets. Grease ... even dog do.'

Milton grips Judith's elbow. 'I don't think this is the time to talk about this.'

'No time's the right time. You know what, Milton?' She throws the towel on the table. 'I'm never going to talk about it again. You're going to have to talk about it.' She snatches her jacket off the back of a chair.

'Where are you going?'

'I need a walk.'

He glances at his watch. 'It's late.' Two weeks ago a sixty-three-year-old nun was raped and sodomized three blocks away.

She looks at him. 'Do you want to come with me?'

'I'm pretty tired,' he says, hoping she'll change her mind.

'Alright then.' She leaves, slamming the door. Milton leans his hands against the sink and stares at the dish-water.

'Is she pissed at me?' Winnie asks.

'No,' Milton replies, already worried about her. The rapist told the nun she reminded him of his mother.

The worst part about it is that he has no feeling when he looks at her. Nothing ties him to her. He's not sure anything ever did. Except Ariel. So why stay together? Wouldn't it be easier if they were apart?

'I wish I had a girlfriend,' Winnie says.

Milton pulls the plug, the drain gurgles. 'You can get one, Win, you just got to spruce yourself up a bit, maybe take a shower.'

'If I have a party, do you know any girls that would come?'

Milton sees a bug on the floor, a centipede. 'Not right off the top, but I'll think about it.' Slowly the centipede crawls towards his foot. He wonders where she's gone at this time of night, if he should go looking for her, if that's what she wants. He can't even figure out what she wants. He almost wishes she'd stay away, find herself a guy with feelings who knows what she wants. But then he'd be alone, really alone with the absence of Ariel, and he doesn't want that either. He doesn't know what he wants. He lifts up his boot and holds it over the centipede.

'Don't kill it!' Winnie squeals.

'It's just a bug,' Milton says and crushes it.

THREE

He tries not to worry about her. Lying on the bed, he watches a TV movie about an abused wife and wonders why he has never hit Judith. It seems his entire life he has wanted to smash things or people, but he never has. When men smash things on TV, he empathizes with them even though he knows they're just actors. He respects them for having the guts to break a chair. In real life, Milton knows that if he broke a chair no one would respect him. They would despise him for losing control and expect him to pay for the chair.

The husband hits the wife, calls her 'slut' and 'bitch' then says he's sorry. The wife sits down on the bed; the husband drops to his knees burying his face in her lap. The wife does nothing, only stares at the back of his head.

Milton feels badly about the centipede. It was a stupid thing to do. When he wiped it off the floor with a Kleenex he realized it wasn't completely dead. A few of its legs were still twitching. He had to crush it between his fingers to put it out of its misery. He hated the way it felt, the way it crunched.

He wonders if the feeling he has that there is no justice in the world is common to all men. He doubts it. The politicians and corporation heads can't be too worried about justice: Munroe and Aiken, sucking back beers: they can't be too concerned.

'What are you thinking about?' Judith asks, standing in the doorway.

He considers jumping up and hugging her but worries that she will take this to mean she won the argument. Although he can't remember what the argument was about. 'I didn't hear you come in,' he says.

'Well no, you've got the TV on.'

He doesn't turn it off; if he turns it off she'll talk. She talks anyway. 'I was watching all the little kids out with their parents choosing Hallowe'en pumpkins. They're so serious about it. The kids. It's like, it's so important to them. I was practically bawling, watching them.'

He closes his eyes hoping she'll see that he's tired and leave him alone.

'I have the feeling,' she continues, 'that you think I don't grieve because I don't cry all the time. I think you resent me for wanting to get on with my life.' She sits on the edge of the bed and pulls at a loose thread on the comforter. 'Milton, I miss her all the time. Not a second goes by when I don't miss her.'

'I know.' Milton opens his eyes and stares at the TV. A greaser in a leather jacket slides a beer down the bar to a pretty blonde who catches it and smiles.

Judith doesn't watch the TV. She looks at the floor. 'I'm going to say something pretty awful now, but I have to say it.' Often she prefaces statements in this manner, giving him time to worry about what it is she has to say and why she has to say it now. She leans forward and turns the TV off by pressing the power button. He continues to stare at the blank screen. 'I think,' she says, 'you feel guilty because you're not grieving enough. I think you're scared to get on with your life because you think you're a shit for letting your daughter die and not suffering for it. I think you want to suffer but can't. So you act like you're suffering but really you're just thinking about those jerks at work, or what you're having for dinner or something.'

He lies inert, stunned that she could think so little of him, scared that there's truth in what she's saying and that, now that she's pointed it out, he has no choice but to live with it.

'What am I supposed to say to that?' he asks.

'Nothing. I just had to say it.'

'How can you stand to live with me if you think that?'

'Because I forgive you. I just think you should be aware of it. There's no point in torturing yourself because you're not feeling the pain you think you should be feeling. It doesn't make you a better person or anything.'

He stares glumly at his feet then wiggles his toes slightly. She watches him for a moment then leans forward abruptly and turns the TV back on.

'I didn't ask you to do that,' he says.

'It fills the air, Milton.' She stands wearily and pulls her night-gown from the closet. 'I'm going to sleep in her room.'

She often sleeps on the narrow bed in Ariel's room. He has never asked why because he doesn't want to hear about Ariel's spirit flitting around.

''Night,' he says.

She nods and is gone, and he feels nothing. Lately, more and more layers seem to be forming between himself and the world: insulation. He has no problem with this.

FOUR

Those people who say they have no regrets, he doesn't believe them. He regrets every dumb move he's ever made. It seems to him he's never done anything for a good reason. He's never thought a whole lot about anything, never planned; he's just gone ahead and done it, to get by. And mostly he's hurt people doing it. If you're going to hurt people, build an empire, make a fortune, don't just sit around earning enough cash to keep you going. He might be able to have some self-respect if he were rich and famous. On 'Entertainment Tonight', a movie director said you have to hurt people to get to the top and stay there. Milton respected the movie director for having the guts to hurt people. The movie director understood that he wouldn't be liked; he understood that this was the price of greatness. Einstein said all great men face opposition. Well, Milton hasn't done anything great, and still nobody likes him. People he meets for the first time don't like him. They turn their backs on him and start conversations with other people. Judith says he has a sour face, that no matter what he's thinking he always looks miserable and mean. He hasn't noticed this. The only face he sees is the one in the mirror, and it doesn't look sour. Tired maybe, bored maybe but not mean.

He dreamt last night that he was having a piss at a urinal. Beside him, an old man was having trouble unzipping his fly. He kept fumbling with it, but he couldn't get it down. Finally he pissed his pants. Milton could see the dark patches spreading down the old man's crotch and pant leg. He felt badly for the old guy but couldn't think of what to say, so he zipped up his own fly and left without a word. Milton thinks about the dream while he is waiting outside Nelson's office. Nelson locks his door when he goes to the can because he's afraid one of the workers will steal the junk on his desk or his London Fog trench coat. When he finally shows up he's chewing on a Swiss Roll and has chocolate in the corners of his mouth. 'What's up?' he asks, unlocking his door. Milton follows him inside inhaling the stench of Nelson's cologne. Milton stands uneasily, not knowing what to do with his hands. He wishes he'd brought his clipboard so he'd have something to hang onto. He clasps his hands in front of him.

'There's something going on on the floor that I think you should know about,' he says.

Nelson stuffs the rest of the Swiss Roll in his mouth, tosses the wrapper in his waste-basket then wipes his mouth with a Kleenex. 'What's that?'

'Munroe and Aiken are drinking on the job.'

Nelson doesn't look at him. Instead he pulls open a desk drawer stuffed with invoices. 'How do you know, have you seen them?'

'It's not hard to tell. They goof off. It's dangerous.'

Nelson nods. 'Well, thanks for bringing this to my attention, Milt.'

'Somebody's going to get hurt one of these days. They throw equipment around.'

'I'll have a word with them. Anything else?' He squints up at him. Milton imagines driving a nail into his bald head, blood spurting out, Nelson's eyeballs rolling upwards.

'No.'

'Good. Well, you take it easy, Milton. Don't work too hard.'

Staring at the coffee-machine, Milton is amazed that he's reported on Munroe and Aiken. He presses the cream-and-sugar button and waits for his cup to fill. He'd expected to feel different afterward—relieved maybe, noble maybe—but all he feels is scared.

~

He watches Judith unpack groceries. It disturbed him how, after Ariel died, they never seemed to need anything; he never had to make a rush to the corner-store for milk or juice or bread. Sometimes he goes anyway, just for something to do.

'I reported on Munroe and Aiken.'

She looks at him then opens the carton of eggs and studies them to make sure none are cracked. 'Do you feel good about it?'

'I don't feel anything.'

'So why did you do it?'

'I don't know.' He watches her open the fridge and set the eggs one by one into the egg tray. 'Maybe I thought it would impress you.'

'Why would it impress me?'

'Because I told the truth.'

She unwraps a pack of cigarettes, pulls one out and lights it. She quit smoking when she got pregnant and never started again because she believed it would affect Ariel's brain cells.

He nods at the cigarettes. 'That's really intelligent.'

'So what did Nelson say when you told him?'

'Nothing much. He didn't look surprised. I guess he knows.'

Judith searches the cupboard above the sink for an ashtray, finds one, sets it on the table and sits, heaving a big sigh.

'What's that for?' Milton asks.

'I'm just tired. I was reading this article about stress, how you get headaches from it. It's a biological thing that goes on.' She flicks ash into the ashtray. 'It said ninety percent of illnesses are because of stress. It said stress equals change and that, in the twentieth century, we've lived through more change than anybody in any other century. So it's no wonder we're all stressed out.'

He understands that this is leading somewhere, that momentarily she will point out the significance of this information; how it pertains to their lives. He considers making a rush for the bathroom or the TV but feels that this would be too obvious. He massages the bridge of his nose with his fingers, hoping to appear pensive.

'Milton, what if I met someone else?'

For an instant it feels as though she has jerked the chair out from under him. 'Did you meet someone else?'

'I don't know.'

He isn't sure he wants to know what this means, so he doesn't ask.

'You remember that guy Terry?' She inhales on her cigarette then exhales slowly. 'He was at the Christmas party last year.' He does remember. Terry wore a leather vest; his hair was long and greasy. He slobbered over Judith, got her drinks, laughed a lot, touched her arm. 'Well ...' Judith stares at the cigarette between her fingers, 'he keeps talking about how he wants kids and a home life and all that.'

'So?'

'I just think it's weird. I mean I think he's trying to tell me something.'

'So go with him, if that's what you want.'

'I didn't say I wanted to.'

'I think he's an asshole.'

'You think everybody's an asshole.' She flicks her cigarette at the ashtray. 'Anyway, he's coming over later.'

'Tonight? What for?'

'To visit, what do you think? You'll probably be watching TV anyway.'

It sickens him that she would invite this goof into their home and pretend they're just having a chat when really she's considering making a run for his sperm. He can't believe she really wants to get pregnant again. With Ariel, she sat around for months with her hands on her expanding stomach staring blankly into space. He'd worry about her and ask if she was all right. 'Sure,' she'd say. 'It just feels so different. There's no way to describe it.' She napped for two and three hours a day then woke up and stared at her stomach in the mirror. She seemed possessed, controlled by some unknown force. He felt something growing between them; he knew that things would never be the same, that this creature in her womb would take her away from him. Her eyes grew glassy; her conversation, disjointed. When he lost patience with her, she tried to explain that the baby was always on her mind, that she couldn't think straight because of what was going on inside her. He wished she were happy. He'd heard that some women blossom during pregnancy, soften, but Judith grew cold and withdrawn. For months she felt nauseated at all times of the day. Brown blotches grew on her face, and veins appeared on her legs. It shocked him to see her bum flatten and sag, her breasts grow to the size of melons. He no longer recognized her body, it was as if another woman were occupying his bed. Not wanting her to think he no longer desired her, he tried making love to her, but she wouldn't let him. She said that everything hurt. When the company wouldn't give her maternity leave, she quit. It seemed to him that all she did was sleep, stare at her belly and cry. When they had to cut her open, he knew he'd been right about the creature destroying them. She told him not to watch the surgery because it would only upset him. He paced the waiting-room furious at God or whoever for allowing them to cut her open. He was told the baby was trying to make it down the birth canal feet first. Why? he wanted to know. The doctor shrugged and said, 'These things happen, the baby settles in one position and stays there.' When he saw the creature flat on its back in the hospital crib, he was stunned by the helplessness of it. It lay stranded, clenching its fingers, squeezing its eyes closed, determined not to see, not to face the world. He'd expected it to have powers, to stare out at him from tiny, black, alien eyes. But this baby's eyes were blue, and when it looked at him it seemed not to see him. For months he felt anxious while holding it, aware that he could easily break its neck, crack its skull. Judith laughed at him, said that babies were much tougher than anyone thought. She'd hold Ariel upside down, and the baby would get the goofiest grin on her face. 'See,' Judith would say, 'she likes it.' Gradually he began to pick her up. Judith said that when Ariel cried it was because she sensed his nervousness, that she was happiest when you weren't worrying about her. Judith never let her dwell on a fall or a bumped head but distracted her with toys or goofy faces. When Milton was looking after Ariel and she cried, he wanted to cry with her, understood her despair at being born. He didn't think it was fair that she had no say in the matter.

Then he began to see himself in Ariel, as she grew older and more cautious, reserved, always braced to fend off her gregarious mother. This distressed Milton; he didn't want her to look like him, be like him. Watching her kneeling on the floor, intently filling in her colouring book, he didn't think he could stand to see her learn what he had learned, to watch the blue eyes harden and the tiny shoulders hunch against the onslaught of human ignorance. He couldn't tell Judith any of this. Judith believed she was watching a brand new human form; that Ariel could be whatever she wanted to be. She tried to instil in Ariel a sense of endless possibility, but he could see that the child only humoured her mother, allowing her to believe that she believed, all the while knowing that ahead was an endless struggle for approval, love, self-respect and money.

Not long before she died they were walking in the park when she asked him to carry her on his shoulders. He said, 'Why don't you carry me for a change?' and slid his legs over her shoulders so that she was standing between his feet. He had meant to tease her, but she panicked and cried, 'Carry *me*, Daddy, carry *me!*' The despair in her voice caused his throat to contract and his eyes to water.

Immediately he bent down, picked her up and slid her onto his shoulders. As he felt her little hands gripping his forehead, he knew that he had lost her trust by inadvertently forcing her to take responsibility. He was convinced that she was born fearing what was ahead and that she wanted to put it off as long as possible, wanted to be a child for as long as possible. Which is why he is so confused about her death and can't grieve like any ordinary, devoted father would. He can't help feeling that Ariel made it happen. Not that she committed suicide but that somehow she willed it to happen. Never in his life has he heard of a child being crushed by a television. Last week, in the paper, there was a story about a child being mauled by dogs. The week before a child was abducted and murdered. They get hit by cars, fall into lakes, but they don't pull TV sets down on themselves.

~

He turns the TV up so that he doesn't have to listen to them laughing. But he strains to hear them anyway. Judith's laugh sounds unfamiliar, stagey, ha ha ha. Normally Judith doesn't laugh; instead, a corner of her mouth jerks up, and she snorts. He wonders if she's hoping to make him jealous by laughing, wonders if he is jealous or if it's just that he can't take his wife partying with another man. It shouldn't bother him. If he loved his wife and knew that she loved him, it wouldn't bother him. On TV, Bruce Willis said he doesn't get upset when Demi does love scenes with other guys. Terry's talking about the special effects in some movie he saw, describing how they burnt the guy's face off. 'Gross!' Judith says. Terry explains that really the stuntman is wearing a mask and doesn't feel a thing. He says Judith should go see the latest Terminator movie because of the special effects; everything's done by computer. Then they talk more quietly so Milton can't hear them, even with the volume turned down. He decides to get a Coke.

'Milton, good to see you,' Terry in his leather vest says, offering his hand. Milton pretends not to notice it and opens the fridge.

'There's no Coke left,' he mumbles.

'I didn't buy any,' Judith says. 'I was reading this article that said there's seven teaspoonfuls of sugar in one can of Coke.'

'Not to mention the caffeine,' Terry adds.

Judith nods. 'It's like injecting poison into your veins.'

Milton tries to think of an excuse to stay in the kitchen. He takes a glass from the cupboard and runs the tap, holding a finger under it as though he were waiting for the water to cool.

'Since when do you drink water?' Judith asks.

'I'm thirsty. There's no Coke.'

'So, go to the store.'

He doesn't respond but fills his glass then holds it to his lips and drinks hoping to look as though he's enjoying it, although really he hates drinking water. He downs the whole glass then sets it on the counter and belches to annoy Judith.

'Charming,' she comments.

'Anybody being laid off where you are, Milton?' Terry asks.

'They're talking about it.'

'We've lost seventy-eight with this restructuring. They're even looking at cutting management positions.'

'What about you?'

'Well I'm senior, you know.'

Milton nods and starts to refill his glass.

'I can't believe you're drinking water,' Judith says.

'You're always telling me I should, to detoxify or whatever.'

Judith turns her back on him, grabbing the string on the blind and twisting it.

'It's rough times for everybody these days,' Terry adds.

Judith abruptly pulls out the other chair to rest her feet on it. Terry shifts his coffee-cup back and forth a couple of inches on the table. Milton imagines yanking the cup from his grasp and smashing it into his messy, stinking, greasy hair. Terry looks up at him then at Judith. 'You know that guy who won the forty-seven million? He was found dead in a trash-can.'

'Was he murdered?' Judith asks.

'They didn't say. It was in the paper. It just said he was crushed.'

Milton burps, not on purpose this time but because all the water has made him feel like throwing up. 'Maybe the garbage-men tossed him into the truck, and he got compressed.'

'Very funny,' Judith comments, and he realizes she hasn't done the ha ha ha laugh since he came into the kitchen. And she's got her feet up on the chair so he can't sit down.

'What's on TV?' she asks.

'Not much.'

Terry shakes his head. 'You know, I can't even watch it anymore. There's not one good show on. I watch the news and maybe a National Geographic special once in a while, but that's it.'

'I like animal shows,' Judith remarks.

Is this her idea of conversation? Is this what she wants from him? Maybe they should start watching 'Sesame Street' together so they can discuss the letter of the day. Milton remembers the night she called him a social cripple. They'd been at her mother's and he hadn't said a word all evening, hadn't needed to. Judith insisted that the only reason everybody else did the talking was that he wouldn't. Milton wonders what it would be like to be in a room with people and not have to talk. You could just sit there, looking at each other.

He always feels he has to talk and hates it, hates the crap that spills out of his mouth like 'Can you believe this weather?' or 'Boy, is the traffic bad.'

He sees Winnie's face squashed against the window. Judith follows his stare. 'Oh my god,' she mutters. 'Every night this week.'

Winnie pushes open the door. 'Hi, guys.'

'Hi, Win,' Milton says, 'how's it going?'

'Some man threw a lady's baby out the window. Mom says women shouldn't have babies unless they have husbands.'

'What man, Win?'

'Some guy in a van. They were driving. The baby got run over, but it's in the hospital.'

Judith grabs her coffee-cup and pushes past Milton to rinse it in the sink.

'Winnie, this is Terry,' Milton says. 'Terry, this is Winnie.'

'Hey,' Winnie offers Terry his hand. They shake. 'Isn't that something, though?' Winnie asks. 'Throwing a baby out a window? He must've been really steamed.'

'It is interesting, Win,' Milton assures him, 'but it's not really the kind of news you want to spread, you know. I mean, it's not great news.'

Winnie fingers the end of his nose. 'I'm sorry.'

'Now you're making him feel bad,' Judith says, taking plates from the dish-rack and stacking them noisily in the cupboard. Milton glances at Terry who's looking at Judith as if waiting for a cue.

'So what should we talk about?' Winnie asks.

'I don't know.' Milton crosses his arms. 'The weather maybe.'

Winnie nods. 'It's been changing every time I change my underwear.'

Judith turns on Milton. 'Look, why don't you two go out for a Coke or something.'

~

Driving the Plymouth Volare that his mother sold him after the cops revoked her license, Milton feels tingling in his arms and feet. He wonders if he's having a heart attack. They say it runs in families. In one instant he could lose control and swerve into an oncoming car. Even without a heart attack he could create a disaster, the smack of colliding metal, flashing lights, sirens. In one instant he could make her sorry.

'You know why I like driving at night?' Winnie asks.

'Why?'

'Because I can see inside people's houses. I like seeing what people have. You know what Buzz told me?'

'What?' Milton wonders what they're doing right this second, probably talking about what an asshole he is.

'He's a burglar part-time,' Winnie explains. 'He drives around at night to see what people have. He says it's alright to steal from rich people because they've got insurance. He says some rich people leave their doors open just so he'll rob them, and they can buy all new stuff.' He starts to pick his nose. 'We're not insured though. I asked Mom. She said we don't have anything worth stealing.'

'I think he was yankin' your chain, Win. If Buzz was a burglar he wouldn't be telling you about it.'

'So why did he lie?'

'I don't know. For fun maybe.'

'Lying taints the soul. It's a known fact.'

'Yeah well, I'm sure he didn't mean any harm by it.'

They stop at a Coffeetime. Winnie orders a double double and a glazed chocolate. Milton has a Coke and sits at the counter watching the bubbles fizz. Beside them two young men in jeans, leather jackets and earrings debate whether or not Jesus was gay. 'He was born without semen,' one of them says.

'That doesn't necessarily mean he was gay,' the other argues. 'Maybe he was asexual.'

Milton taps Winnie's shoulder. 'Let's sit at a table.'

Outside the window on the sidewalk two prostitutes in stiletto heels and mini-skirts wait without speaking, staring hard at passing cars. A car slows, the driver's window opens, and one of the prostitutes leans towards it. When the car starts to drive off she jabs her heel into it shouting, 'Fuck you, asshole!'

It seems to Milton that he never sees anything good anymore. All he sees is scum. 'You got a booger hanging from your nose, Win.'

Winnie quickly wipes his nose with the back of his hand, looks at it then wipes it on his polyester pants. 'Do you have any brothers and sisters?'

Milton shakes the ice in his glass. 'You already asked me that.'

'I forgot what you said.'

'Yeah.'

Winnie scrapes icing off the wax paper with his finger then licks it. 'I wish I did.' A garbage truck slows down across the street. The driver leers at the prostitutes. One of them gives him the finger.

'Sometimes I get lonely,' Winnie admits.

Milton rolls an ice cube around in his mouth. 'Just because you've got brothers and sisters doesn't mean you don't get lonely.'

Winnie stirs what's left of his coffee then licks the spoon. 'You could phone them up, though. They could phone you.'

'Not if you don't like each other.'

'You'd like each other. If you were family.'

Before his brother got AIDS, Milton barely spoke to him. He'd never understood why, in their teens, they didn't do things together the way Milton thought brothers should. Leonard never allowed him into his room, which was plastered with posters of Mick Jagger; and he never gave him advice about girls. Leonard was their mother's favourite, the creative one. She bought him art supplies and referred to him as though he were a potential Picasso. But, since he got sick, he phones Milton regularly to talk about his symptoms and how, now that he's got AIDS, he understands the value of close relationships. Milton doesn't see why, just because his brother is dying, he should love him all of a sudden. He doesn't see how dying excuses a person. Leonard used to call him Stupid and Moron and Twit and Reject, used to tell him he had chimpanzee breath. For years Milton obsessively rinsed his mouth with Listerine until Judith assured him it wasn't necessary and upset the natural chemistry of the mouth. Even now, Milton sometimes doesn't say things because he's afraid of sounding stupid.

When Milton figured out that Leonard was gay it freed him. He understood that his brother had pushed him away for fear of being discovered. It didn't make him like him any better, though.

'If I have a party,' Winnie says, 'do you know some people who

31

would come?'

'How does your Mom feel about you having a party?'

'I didn't ask her.'

'Well, maybe you'd better.'

Winnie nods, looking down at the table, fingering one of his rhinestone buttons. 'You'd come though, right? With Judith?'

'Of course.'

It takes so little effort to be decent to Winnie, and it makes Milton feel as though maybe he isn't such a shit. Why can't Judith understand this?

~

She has her hair wrapped up in a towel. 'It's like living in a prison, Milton. It's like Alcatraz-time.'

'What do you expect me to say to that?'

'Nothing. Why would I suddenly expect you to say something? God forbid you should express an emotion. God forbid you should treat me like a friend instead of an enemy.'

He looks at the TV.

'If you turn that on I will scream.'

'I wasn't going to.' He sits on the edge of the bed beside her wondering if he should place his arm around her shoulders, if physical contact would help or only worsen the situation.

'Your brother called,' she says.

'What did he want?'

'He's blind in one eye.'

'Why?'

'It's part of the disease. The virus is in his brain. He says it's only a matter of time before he goes completely blind.'

'He called to tell me that?'

'I guess he wanted your sympathy. You should call him.'

'Why?'

'Milton, he's dying.'

'So?'

'You are unbelievable.' She yanks the towel off her head and starts to rub her hair dry. 'All this anger and resentment is going to poison you. Pretty soon nobody will even try to get close to you.'

'That's nothing new.'

'And why do you think that is?'

'Because I don't talk about my feelings.'

'If you could just hear yourself, you act so superior. Honestly, Milton, sometimes you're such a snob.'

'Sorry.'

'No you're not. Don't say what you don't mean.'

She hooks the towel around her neck and combs her fingers through her hair. 'I'm going to sleep in the other room. He's still driving, with one eye. If I were you, I'd be concerned.'

He'd ask why, but he doesn't want to piss her off further. He pictures Leonard with an eye-patch driving his Jeep, steering wildly. 'He should just stop driving,' he mutters.

'Well, tell him that. Let him know you care.'

Why does she assume he cares? Why does he have to care? Why are there all these stupid rules? 'Fuck' em,' he mumbles, thinking she can't hear from the hall.

'That's real constructive,' she says.

FIVE

They wrote RAT FINK on his locker and left a dead rat on the hood of the Volare. Milton carries it by the tail to the trash-can thinking there's no way he can prove he was laid off because of Munroe and Aiken. Nelson insisted it had nothing to do with them, that the orders came from higher up. He had no say; it was purely a business decision. Nelson's office stank of Chinese food. There was a packet of plum sauce and a dirty napkin on his desk. Milton thought of pushing the desk over, breaking his chair over the desk or ramming the waste-basket onto Nelson's head. But instead he sat gripping his clipboard, which he'd remembered to bring this time so he'd have something to do with his hands.

He stops at a Shell station to put some air in the tire with the slow leak. Pressing the nozzle to the stem he thinks about how he'll have to fill out applications and talk to assholes who'll treat him like there's something wrong with him because he's out of a job. They'll ask him pointed questions to determine if he's got a good attitude, i.e. can he kiss ass? He doesn't know if he can go through that again. He thinks maybe he'd rather die.

He'd like to know more about the guy who won the forty-seven million and ended up squashed in a trash-can. What was he doing around trash-cans anyway? Was he drunk? Did he tick people off by bragging about it so they beat the shit out of him? You'd think if you'd won that kind of money you'd keep quiet about it and get out of town. If you had that kind of money, you'd never have to answer to assholes again.

If he goes home he'll have to tell Judith. Instead he goes to the strip joint they went to their first New Year's Eve together. He'd wanted to buy condoms, but no drugstores were open, and he knew the strip joint had a dispenser in the can. He hadn't expected to stay, but Judith sat down at a table and stared up at a stripper dancing around in a graduation gown. Standing outside the men's room, he'd watched her order a drink from a waitress wearing only a G-string. Judith turned in her chair to watch the waitress walk away then noticed Milton looking at her and signaled for him to join her. 'What are you doing?' he asked.

'Don't you want a beer?'

'You want to stay here?'

The stripper slid out of her graduation gown and began undulating and rubbing her breasts. 'I just can't get over how ordinary their bodies are,' Judith commented. 'I mean, you know, I thought they'd have better bodies.'

The waitress brought their beers. She ignored Judith, expecting him to pay. 'No, I'll get it,' Judith said and handed the waitress some bills. The waitress's face, caked with makeup, did not move as she made change and slapped it on the table. Again Judith turned in her seat to watch her walk away. 'What a roly-poly bum,' she observed. 'Does that turn you on, Milt? Do you come here a lot?'

'Sometimes.'

'Why?'

'Something to do.'

'There's movies, though, right? Why come here?'

'I don't know.'

'I bet because it's live, and you don't have to do anything. Look at them.' She indicated the men slumped over beers and staring glumly at the stage. 'They don't look happy. Or horny even. They're just glad nobody's asking them to get it up. I bet there isn't one serious boner in the place.'

He never went back because she'd changed it for him. Before, he'd gone without thinking about it. Now he feels like just another loser ogling naked women. Women he can't touch. Women who can't hurt him.

It seems to him that Judith often forces him to think about things he'd rather not think about. She loves watching documentaries about diseases or the homeless, the starving, the disabled. He hates those shows, doesn't want to know about those people, doesn't see why he has to know or how his knowing helps anybody. Even when he doesn't watch the programs she'll bring it up later. She'll tell him about the guy with bone cancer, how courageous he was, how he had a positive attitude, how he thought of life as a stream bubbling down mountains until it flowed into the sea that was death, which was okay because it meant that when he died he became part of the whole. 'The whole what?' he'd asked.

'The whole universe. He understood that he would lose his individuality when he became part of the sea. But that was okay because the sea nurtures the streams. It's all part of the same thing.'

Milton knows she hopes to make him appreciate his own life more because he doesn't have bone cancer. It doesn't work though, he just feels sorry for the guy.

He remembers the time he saw her at the Dairy Queen. He was walking Winnie's dog and had to wait while it took a leak. Judith was sitting on a stool facing the window. If it hadn't been dark she would have seen him. He couldn't understand how she could go to the Dairy Queen so soon after Ariel's death. She spooned the ice cream slowly, deliberately, without lifting her eyes from the plastic dish. Occasionally her right foot slid off the rung of the stool, and she'd set it back on. When she finished she pushed the dish aside and rested her forehead in her hands the way she does. He waited for her to look up or move, but she didn't. He had a feeling there was a side to Judith he could never possibly know. Some other guy might be able to, some guy with feelings. But not him.

~

He can't believe Terry's there again, sitting in the kitchen talking about the special effects in some movie. 'Pretty phenomenal effects. They made you feel like you were inside the computer.'

Milton looks at Judith. 'Did you eat?'

'I was expecting you sooner. I would've made something.'

'I'm not hungry anyway.'

'Winnie was looking for you.'

'Okay, well, maybe I'll drop by there.'

'Do you want to sit down?'

This is a good sign, he thinks, she wants him to stay.

'Yeah, siddown,' Terry adds, pulling out a chair.

He tries to think of something to say to Terry besides 'Get the fuck out of my house'. Maybe he should pick up the chair and smash it over the table. 'They're saying snow flurries,' he offers but doesn't sit.

'A bit early for that isn't it?' Terry asks.

'It's because of Global Warming,' Judith explains.

Milton leans his bum against the counter and crosses his arms. 'If it's warming, how come it's so frigging cold?'

'It's the overall effect.'

It used to intimidate him that Judith seemed to know more than he did. Then he figured out that she didn't really know. She'd just skim articles in magazines for bits of information she could toss into a conversation to impress people.

'So what's new and exciting with you, Milt?' Terry asks.

'Not much. You?'

'I was just telling Judy I was out pricing cars. You would not believe what they're asking for Japanese cars these days.'

Milton tries to picture Terry naked. He takes note of his hairy forearms and neck, suspects he has hairy shoulders and a blubbery belly with black hair running from his navel to his pubes.

'A sedan with the basics costs sixteen thousand with tax. Those Japs boy, they've got us running.'

Judith stretches her leg across the floor and nudges Milton's foot. 'Mandy called. There's some crisis going on with your little sister. She had an abortion or something. Your mom's freaked and taking it out on Mandy. She says she can't take it anymore. She's scared she's going to become an elder-abuser. She wants you to go over.'

'So what am I supposed to do about it?'

'I don't know. Be a son, I guess. Help out.'

After his mother's second by-pass operation, Milton decided that he wasn't going to see her anymore, that he shouldn't have to just because he was her son. She'd had to wait two weeks for surgery because the hospital was backed up. They tied her to the bed because every time she moved she had an angina attack. They expected her to die but insisted there was nothing they could do about it because they had more urgent cases. Milton couldn't see what was more urgent than being about to die. But he didn't argue with the doctors because they intimidated him, and he assumed they knew what they were doing. His mother accused him of not caring what happened to her, even though he brought her fruit and flowers and made sure the TV was working and at the right angle. Even the nurses hated her. She kept accusing them of stealing and giving her the wrong drugs, reading the wrong charts. She demand-ed repeatedly to see her surgeon, but he was unavailable. At one point the doctors proposed moving her to another hospital. They claimed that a surgeon there specialized in the kind of by-pass she required. But Milton suspected this was a ploy to get rid of her, and since they said moving might kill her, he insisted they leave her where she was. When she was unconscious and strapped to the bed with tubes up her nose, she looked small and fragile. It shocked Milton that he'd had such violent feelings towards her. While her eyes were closed he believed that he loved her, that he could forgive her for hitting him and calling him Stupidhead and forgetting his birthday. But when she woke, stared and railed at him, he hated her all over again. Leonard visited briefly, so did Mandy and even his lit-tle sister Connie. But no one paced the hospital corridors as Milton did. He believed it would be the last thing he'd have to do for her before she died. No more would she call him to unclog her toilet or change her washers. No more would she tell him about other peo-ple's sons who became doctors and lawyers and took their mothers to Florida. He believed that if he stood by her on her death-bed, he would be absolved of the guilt he felt for hating her. On TV he'd seen dying people change, become calm, magnanimous, sobered by their impending deaths. In the scenes of reconciliation, the dying person and the loved ones hold hands and say they love each other. The changed dying person insists that the living person must go on and live life to the full. Through tears, he/she asks for forgiveness, so does the living person. Even though Milton knows that TV isn't like life, he had hoped that his mother would change; hoped for a shared moment between them, a look, a touch that would indicate that all had been forgiven. But her beady eyes only scorched him; her veiny hands only clawed him. And he saw himself as she saw him: a failure, a Stupidhead. While she was in the operating-room he wanted her to die because he couldn't stand who he became when he was around her.

But she didn't die, although her heart condition worsened, and now the artery they opened is closing again. She has as many as five small attacks a day, breaking out in a sweat and suffering pain in her chest and left arm. Mandy has taken her into her home because no one else would.

'I got laid off today,' he says. He wasn't going to tell Judith in front of Terry but decided he might as well since she was bound to tell him anyway. He waits for her to react but she only stares at him.

'Did they give a reason?' she asks.

He shrugs. 'A business decision.'

'That's unfortunate,' Terry says. 'I'm sorry.'

Judith watches him. 'How do you feel about it?'

'How do you think?'

'Do you think it was because of Munroe and Aiken?'

He shrugs. 'They were laying people off anyway.' He feels her staring at him and thinking he was stupid to have reported on Munroe and Aiken. If Terry weren't here he'd tell her she should be glad he told the truth, tell her he was just taking her advice. He could imply that it was all her doing. But with the Goof sitting right there he feels uncomfortable, afraid of looking like some loser blaming his problems on his wife. 'Anyways, I guess I should go see my sister,' he adds without looking at her because he's afraid she's pitying him. Already it feels like his problems are no longer their problems.

39

~

Most of the lights are out at Mandy's. He wonders if he should have phoned first. He didn't because, if he knew what he was in for, he wouldn't have come. He likes Mandy, thinks it's too bad she has to suffer, but then she's always suffered. He has a feeling if she wasn't suffering she wouldn't know what to do with her life.

Nobody answers the door so he lets himself in and is immediately blasted by loud rock music. He checks the living-room then walks down the hall and finds Mandy and Connie in the kitchen.

'What's with the music?' he asks.

'It's that bitch next door,' Mandy explains. 'She's brain-damaged, I swear. I ask her to turn it down because I've got an old lady in the house, and she turns it up. I went over there this afternoon and asked her really nicely, you know, explained the situation for the millionth time. She said, "I'm not turning it down because it's not loud. It's only set at two." Like, who cares what it's set at? It's too fucking loud. I swear I almost strangled her.'

'Maybe you should call the cops,' Milton suggests.

'It's not a general disturbance. You can't hear it out on the street. It's these fucking walls. They're made of cardboard. Mom's got ear plugs in, but she says they give her headaches. It says on the package you're not supposed to shove them into your ear canal, but of course she does, so I have to fish them out. A real treat let me tell you. Almost as fun as cleaning her shit off the sheets.'

Milton leans his bum against the kitchen counter. 'So things are that bad?'

'Milton, I can't even remember what my life was like before. If I had one. I'm starting to think she's evil. You know for a while there I felt sorry for her, because she has these attacks and knows that one of them is going to kill her. But now I think she's just out for revenge, but I don't know what for. Like why does she hate me? What've I ever done to her?'

'She hates us because we're not old like her,' Connie says. It's the first time she has spoken, and Milton is shocked by the venom in her voice.

He pulls up a chair and sits at the table. 'She can't hate us for that. She's our mother.'

'Anyways the point is,' Mandy continues, 'I can't look after her anymore, so either you guys do something, or she goes into a home.'

'How are we supposed to pay for it?' Milton asks.

Mandy sighs and rubs her face with her hands. 'Well, that's the problem isn't it?' She stops rubbing but keeps her hands over her face. 'Milton, I'm scared I'm going to hit her. I'm not kidding. I mean she swatted us around so much it just feels natural.' She pulls a cigarette from a pack on the table and lights it. 'She stinks of cak all the time. It's like, she doesn't know how to wipe herself anymore. I swear pretty soon I'm going to have to wash her. She hates bathing because she has trouble getting in and out of the tub. She hates doing anything that requires an effort. All she wants is to sit around watching game shows, which is fine by me, except she screams at Rory and Morty whenever they so much as open the fridge. She says they open the fridge too much.'

'Someone should gas her,' Connie says. Milton looks at her slouched in her chair with her knees hiked up against the table. The size of her breasts always surprises and embarrasses him. His little sister has the kind of breasts men whistle at in the street, talk dirty about in bars.

'So what's with you?' he asks. 'I didn't know you were pregnant.'

Mandy stares at him. 'That might be because you never call us, Milty.'

'So what happened?' He watches Connie put one of Mandy's cigarettes in her mouth and take a long time to light it. What he always forgets about her is that she lies. She can't tolerate anyone being more unfortunate than herself so she invents stories. When Leonard admitted he had AIDS, Connie claimed to have some bacterial infection. Every few weeks she'd show up at Mandy's coughing and acting as though her days were numbered. Whenever Mandy questioned her about the medical care she was receiving, Connie would insist that she hated doctors, that all they did was prescribe drugs she couldn't afford. When Mandy threatened to take her to her own GP, Connie disappeared again.

'Earth to Connie.' Mandy snaps her fingers in front of Connie's face.

Connie picks up the cigarette pack and slowly turns it over in her hands. 'I had an abortion.'

'Not exactly an abortion, dear,' Mandy adds. 'She miscarried on purpose.'

'My baby had water on the brain and spina bifida. So the doctor told me I should miscarry.'

Milton looks to Mandy for confirmation that this is true. She nods.

'What's …?'

'It's when the vertebrae don't join up,' Mandy explains.

'So was it deformed?' Milton asks.

Connie hauls on her cigarette then blows the smoke out through her nostrils. 'It was going to die anyway.'

'So Mom thinks she's a murderer,' Mandy continues. 'You know, we'd just gotten her around to accepting that Connie was going to be a single mother. Now she's a murderer, and I'm her accomplice. So she's not talking to anybody. She'd probably talk to Leonard if he'd come by, but he says he's looking too sick. He's lost forty pounds or something. There's no way she wouldn't notice.'

'He still hasn't told her?' Milton asks.

'Of course not. He wouldn't be perfect then would he?'

The last phone conversaton Milton had with Leonard lasted an hour. Leonard told him that he shit his pants in the parking lot, that he had blisters on his back, that his yeast problem was so bad he had to stick his fingers down his throat in the morning to scrape it out, that he had trouble remembering things, that the new drugs he was taking weren't helping and that he was afraid of chemotherapy. Then he started to cry. 'I can't go out anymore,' he said.

'Why not?' Milton asked.

'They know.'

'Who knows?'

'The people on the street.'

'What do they know?'

'That I'm sick. They can see it.'

'So, lots of people are sick.'

'They know I've got AIDS.'

'Leonard, there's no way they can know. You just look thinner that's all.'

'You haven't seen me lately.'

'Okay, well, what does it matter if they know you're sick?'

Milton can't understand why Leonard doesn't want anyone to know he has AIDS when he goes on about how it's nothing to be ashamed of. He would have said this, but he didn't want to upset his brother further.

'Well, what's he going to do?' Milton asks. 'Never see her again? He's not going to start looking any better.'

'Well, you talk to him,' Mandy insists. 'He just gets hysterical with me.'

Rory, Mandy's sixteen-year-old, comes into the kitchen and opens the fridge. 'Wash your hands first,' Mandy tells him.

Rory stares into the fridge. 'They aren't dirty.'

'They're filthy, you've been crawling around under cars again.'

'It's ingrained oil; they just look dirty.'

Mandy rolls her eyes and smokes. Rory pulls out a package of individually wrapped cheese slices. He leans against the fridge, peeling and eating the slices one after another, then dropping the plastic wrappings on the counter.

'Put the plastic in the garbage,' Mandy tells him.

'I will. Where's Dad?'

'How should I know? He doesn't report to me where he is.'

'I saw him go into the Black Swan,' Rory says.

'So if you know, don't ask me.'

'Didn't he have a job interview?'

'I don't know, why don't you ask him? Lay off me, Rory, I've had a shitbag of a day, and I don't need you nagging at me.'

Rory bunches up the plastic wrappings and drops them in the trash-can. 'I just thought you might know where your husband is.'

'Well, I don't, okay? Now would you go do homework or something. Your aunt's upset.'

'What happened?' he asks.

'None of your business.'

It always shocks Milton how like his mother Mandy has become. He'd warn her, but he knows it's too late. He suspects that people turn into their parents no matter how hard they fight to be themselves. He believes that, like his father, he will suffer a stroke, then become obese and imbecilic: unable to dress, eat, walk or shit on his own. Towards the end, his father reminded him of a beached whale, groaning and heaving. To his mother's credit, she never deserted him but cared for him as you would a child. Mandy always says she was a better mother to her husband than to her children.

They hear the shuffle of slippers, and his mother appears. 'What's going on in here?' she demands. 'Some kind of party? You keep opening and closing the fridge; I thought for sure you must have company.'

Mandy stares at her. 'Mother, he opened the fridge once.'

Mare rubs her abdomen through her house-coat. She does this habitually now. No one knows why, since she claims to feel no pain in her abdomen.

'Hello, Ma,' Milton says, hoping to sound as though he doesn't hate her.

Mare turns to look at him and clasps a hand over her chest, exaggerating her surprise. 'Well, look who's here? To what do we owe this honour?'

'He came to see you,' Mandy tells her.

'When I'm in bed?'

'I thought you'd still be up,' Milton lies.

Mare's eyes shift around the room then fix on the clock above the table. She squints at it. 'What time is it?'

'I would've come earlier, but I got held up.' Milton hates how he makes up excuses around her.

'Yes, yes.' Mare waves her hand dismissively then turns a half circle as though unsure of her next move.

'Do you want to sit down?' Mandy asks.

'Why would I want to do that? All you want me to do is sit down. You'd like it if I stayed in that room all day. Maybe you should tie me to the bed. You could just close the door and forget about me.'

Mandy sighs. 'Mother, if you get excited you only hurt yourself.'

'So what's wrong with that? Don't pretend you're not waiting for it. You think I don't know what's going on here.'

Mandy pulls a cardigan from the back of a chair and wraps it around Mare's shoulders. They all watch apprehensively as Mare shuffles towards the window and jerks back the curtain. 'Is it snowing? They said it was snowing.'

The front door opens and heavy footsteps approach. Seth, very wide and square but softening, stands in the doorway, surprised to see such a family gathering. 'Well, hello,' he offers. 'The gang's all here.'

Mandy stares at him, crossing her arms. 'You seem cheerful.'

'Shouldn't I be? Would you prefer for me to be sad?' He enunciates carefully. Already Milton can smell the beer.

'Did you see about that job?' Mandy asks.

He holds up his hand like a traffic cop. 'Don't start.'

'You know what I can't figure out,' Mandy says, 'is how you can always afford beers.'

Seth nudges Rory out of the way, opens the fridge and pulls out what's left of the cheese slices.

'You're buying beers,' Mandy continues, 'while I'm walking past the meat counter without looking because I'm scared I'll start crying because I can't afford to feed my boys.'

'Oh now don't overdo it.' A cheese slice slips from his grasp. 'Shit.' He bends down to pick it up.

'So what am I supposed to do, Seth?' Mandy throws up her hands. 'Tell me what I'm supposed to do? Work nights? Leave my mother alone in the house with the boys?'

'Leave me out of it,' Mare insists.

Seth folds the cheese slice in half and eats it. 'I don't think we should talk about this now.'

'In front of my family you mean. Why not? Don't you think they have a right to know what a fuck-up I married?'

'Okay, so leave me. I'm a loser. I can't feed my own kids.'

'Oh, stop it, the two of you.' Mare waves her hand. 'You're giving me a headache.'

Mandy clamps her hands on her hips. 'Oh, well, excuse us. This only happens to be our own home. I think we have a right to argue in our own home.'

'I should get going anyways,' Milton mumbles, getting up.

Mandy points at him. 'Oh no you don't. You're not leaving

until we work something out.'

'Dad?' Rory asks, 'Carlos said he'd let me have the Mazda for two-fifty.'

Seth nods. 'Sounds good.'

Mandy throws up her hands again. 'Are you crazy? He doesn't even have a license yet. I'm sick to death of hearing about that stupid Mazda. Nobody's getting any Mazda.'

'Mum, we need a car, and Carlos is practically giving it to me.'

'What do we need a car for? So you can cruise around getting into even more trouble?'

'He'll learn responsibility,' Seth points out.

'Oh, you mean like you did. Forget it. Out of the question.'

'Mandy?' Milton interjects. 'Do you think maybe we could take a walk or something, get some air? I need some air.'

She stares at him as though she'd forgotten he was there. 'Fine, let's do that.'

He takes her to a Chinese restaurant. They sit across from each other beside a velvet painting of a pagoda. Mandy touches the plastic roses in the white vase on the table. 'They're coated in grease.'

Milton's hands stick to the plastic table-cloth. He folds them in his lap. 'We'll just have a coffee or something.'

Mandy stares at the vase, shaking her head. 'I'm just sick and tired of everybody expecting me to do everything.'

'Then don't do it. I mean, maybe if you stop doing everything other people will do something.'

'Oh, yeah, like you're going to look after Mother? You know I was the only one who got her a birthday gift?'

He'd ask if she wants a medal, but he doesn't want to tick her off because she might dump Mare on him. 'Well, you're doing a great job,' he offers, 'looking after her.'

'You're just saying that so you won't have to do anything about it.'

He avoids her eyes, pretending to look at the menu. 'So what's the story with the Mazda?'

'Rory's turning into a juvenile delinquent in front of our very eyes, but Seth can't see it.'

'He seems like a good enough kid.'

'He's keeps getting suspended. He threw a chair at a teacher who told him he was stupid.'

'No kidding, he threw a chair?'

'Yeah, it only hit her leg. Seth says I treat Rory like he's stupid. I only treat him like he's stupid when he acts stupid.'

Milton absently taps a corner of the menu against his chin. 'I think some people act stupid when they're treated like they're stupid.'

'I don't treat him like he's stupid.'

Milton closes the menu. 'You just said you treat him like he's stupid when he acts stupid.'

'Yeah, when he acts stupid. That doesn't mean I think he's stupid.'

Milton nods and flicks his fingers against the menu. 'Maybe he's got a learning disability. I saw this show about it. I think maybe I'm learning-disabled. You know that problem I have with reading?'

'That's dyslexia.'

'Well, maybe Rory has something like that. They said a lot of learning-disabled kids get into trouble because it's the only thing they're good at. Maybe you should get him tested.'

They order two beers from a bald black waitress. Milton wonders how she shaves the back of her head and around her ears without cutting herself. He pictures bits of bloody Kleenex stuck all over her scalp. 'Albert Einstein was learning-disabled,' he remarks. 'He flunked all kinds of stuff. And Winston Churchill. There's special classes they can go to.'

Mandy straightens a corner of the table-cloth. 'I think he's just lazy.'

'That's what everybody thinks, so the kids turn into juvenile delinquents.' He remembers having to stand by his desk in class because he couldn't spell or pronounce words exactly right. All the other kids were sitting, staring at him, whispering 'reeetard'. His fourth-grade teacher told him he'd have to carry her in a sack over his shoulder because he didn't use his own brain and would need her to tell him what to do. She was a dried-up troll of a woman with dyed red hair cinched into a bun. She'd taught Leonard before him, and she kept saying, 'Who could have guessed you were brothers?'

When he had to do assignments Leonard had done, she'd point out how Leonard's were superior. Milton hated her scrunched up little face and would have liked to have thrown a chair at her. He admires Rory for actually throwing the chair. 'He's got guts anyway,' he comments, 'to throw the chair.'

'Violence doesn't take brains. It doesn't take guts to shoot people. Any dirtbag off the street can do it.' The bald waitress brings them their beers. Mandy drinks from the bottle. 'I just wish he'd think about somebody besides himself for a change, it's always "me, me, me, what can I get for nothing." It makes me sick.'

'Maybe he learnt it from us.'

'Speak for yourself. I'm always doing stuff for people.'

He'd like to say, 'Yeah and you never let them forget it.' But he doesn't because he doesn't want to tick her off. He's noticed that the people who help out or who give to charity want everybody to know about it. Nelson sends twenty dollars a month to a little African kid and brags about it to everybody in the plant. 'For what you spend on coffee,' he tells them, 'you could be giving a child an education.' Milton wonders if Nelson thinks sending twenty bucks a month to Africa excuses him for being a prick.

'What have you ever done for this family?' Mandy asks.

'Nothing. I didn't say I did.'

'Do you think that's right?'

He shrugs. 'I don't know. What's right?'

'Don't you feel even a little guilty about me having to look after Mother?'

'It's your choice,' he says, realizing he sounds like Judith talking about 'choosing to be happy'.

Mandy slams her hands on the table. 'That's crap, somebody has to do it. What are we going to do, leave her on the street?'

Milton blows on his half-empty beer-bottle making a hollow sound. 'Maybe she'd die if we left her alone. That's what the Japs used to do; they'd take the old people up in the mountains and leave them there to die.'

'Oh Milton, for chrissakes, grow up. Be responsible for a change. I've been easy on you because of Ariel, but I think it's about time you took part in this family.'

'I just think we'd all be happier if we didn't live as long.' Milton rolls the bottle between his palms. 'I mean, who wants to get operated on and take pills and shit their pants. Pretty soon she's going to have to wear a diaper, you know. They make them for old people. Who wants that? I'd rather be dead.'

'Well, Milton, let's just hope you still feel that way when you're old and there's nobody around to look after you.' She starts to peel the label off her bottle. He realizes that she will sulk if he doesn't say something. When she was eighteen and he was eleven she would sulk if he didn't fetch things for her: her hairbrush, a magazine, a Coke. He was the only family member she could push around, and when he rebelled, she wouldn't speak to him for days. He hated it and realized that she was the only family member who ever talked to him. Leonard was busy with his art projects, Connie with her Barbies, and their mother with their father. Milton began to obey Mandy just so she would talk to him.

'So what do you want me to do?' he asks.

'Take either Connie or Mother off my hands. I can't cope with both of them.'

'Connie can look after herself.'

'No, she can't. She's a liar. Half the time I don't think she even knows what's real and what isn't. She steals my clothes and says they're hers.'

'Your clothes fit her?'

'Thank you, Milton. Thank you very much. You try having kids and see how your body holds up.'

He hadn't meant to insult her; it's just that she looks about twice Connie's size, except for her chest, of course. 'No, I mean it's just …'

'I know what you mean, forget about it.' Mandy finishes her beer. 'The thing is, I think she believes half the stuff she makes up. She should be seeing a shrink.'

Milton has a problem with shrinks. Right after Ariel died, he and Judith went to see one who pulled at the hairs growing out of a mole on his cheek. The habit drove Milton crazy, but he didn't feel it was his place to tell the doctor to stop. It didn't bother Judith; she told the doctor all about her dreams and feelings. The doctor listened, pulling on his mole hairs. He asked Milton questions about feelings that Milton had trouble answering because he couldn't describe his feelings without sounding stupid. The psychiatrist suggested that Milton was passive because he'd had an 'absentee father' and lacked a strong role model. He told Milton he had to make an effort to express his emotions to Judith more clearly. Milton knew this already because he heard it from Judith all the time. They stopped seeing the shrink because Judith said she was falling in love with him. 'Well, not exactly falling in love,' she explained. 'It's transference.'

'What's transference?' Milton asked.

'It's when you project emotions onto people. It happens a lot with psychiatrists because they don't say much, but when they do it's like they're seeing right into you. They're really listening to you.'

'They're paid to listen.'

'Trust you to make it sound negative.'

Mandy rests the back of her head against the banquette. 'Remember how Connie always wanted to see if your G.I. Joe had a penis?' He nods. 'There's something wrong with her, I swear. I don't know if she's one of those sex addicts or what. She says she's going to night school to learn air-traffic controlling, but I don't believe her.'

'What's she do for money?'

Mandy raises her eyebrows. 'Well that's a question, isn't it?'

'I thought she was waitressing or something.'

'Try calling her where she works. They've never heard of her.'

Milton raises an eyebrow, hoping to suggest that he appreciates the gravity of the situation. At the entrance to the kitchen, the waitress is demonstrating a funky dance step to an East Indian cook.

Mandy rubs her face. 'And Seth is acting weird with her around. He comes out of the bathroom with just a towel on and walks around the house pretending to be looking for cigarettes. He's too fat to cover up with a towel, and half the time his dong is hanging out. I don't know what he's trying to prove.'

It shocks Milton to hear Mandy speak so bluntly; he feels himself blush. Fortunately she still has her hands over her face so she can't see him. The cook attempts to follow the waitress's dance steps, but he stumbles. She punches his shoulder jocularly and laughs. He grins and wipes the sweat off his face with his apron. When Milton looks back at Mandy, she still has her hands over her face. 'You okay?' he asks.

'Don't you wish we had a normal family? I mean everything's so fucked up with this family. We can't even die properly. First of all Dad becomes a vegetable and takes forever to die, now Mom. And god knows what's going to happen with Leonard.'

'People have to die,' Milton points out. 'Especially old people.'

'Well, I know that. It's just always so messy with us.'

Milton knows what she means. On TV nobody shits their pants. They become pale and develop dark shadows under their eyes, but nobody has to put diapers on them and bathe and feed them. On TV, when they get strokes, they become paralyzed in one arm and have difficulty speaking. They don't become fat and groan and drool. Even though he knows TV isn't like life, he can't help wondering if his father was a uniquely revolting case.

'Maybe that's the way it is in real life,' he suggests. 'Messy.'

Mandy has peeled most of the label off the bottle. 'God knows what's going to happen to us. Kids don't care about anybody but themselves anymore. I can't see Rory taking me in. That whole thing about having kids so they'll look after you when you're old? Forget that.' She stares morosely at the bottle.

'Well, I wouldn't worry about it,' Milton says, although when he sees an old man hunched against the wind, creeping along the sidewalk, he remembers that this will happen to him, and he, too, worries. A ninety-five-pound old lady was mugged in the cemetery by a two-hundred-and-forty-pound man. He pushed her over and snatched her purse. Knowing that he will become weak and defenseless frightens Milton. He hopes to die before then, instantaneously, in a car crash, hit from the side so he doesn't see it coming.

It also worries him that at the present time he is relatively young and able-bodied and supposed to be having the best years of his life.

'I hate every frigging thing about getting older,' Mandy says, 'every frigging thing, my flab, my arthritis, there's no pay off.'

He tries to think of something to say that will console her. He pictures the plump, white-haired, rosy-cheeked granny in the commercial for long-distance calls. The granny answers the phone, smiles and says, 'Grandpa and I were just thinking about you.' Milton can't see Mandy getting rosy-cheeked or phoned by her grandchildren, if she ever has any. He can only see her slowly but surely turning into Mare.

When she takes her hands away from her face to rummage in her handbag for her purse, he sees what might be tears on her cheeks. He isn't sure, though, and he doesn't want to make a fool of himself by trying to comfort her if she isn't really crying.

He pulls out his wallet. 'I'll pay for this.'

'Thank you.' It sounds so formal when she says it, as though they'd only just met. He wishes he could say something that would bring her closer to him. He helps her on with her coat. 'Thank you,' she says again, and he feels that, as with his wife, there is a side to his sister he can never possibly know. He has failed her as he has failed Judith. Maybe, as Judith says, he does have poor communication skills. He remembers the one time he ran home to Mare after being beaten up after school. She asked him what he'd done to make the other boys angry; she insisted he must have done something. He couldn't tell her that they beat him up because they thought he was a 'reeetard'. Never again did he reveal his suffering to her because he knew she would demand a reason for it—hard facts—when it seemed to him that suffering was due to indescribable elements, like looks and attitudes. He remembers the humiliation he felt in school when he was the last person chosen for gym teams. He wasn't chosen, only left over. Without words they made him feel worthless. He could never articulate his despair without sounding feeble, so he stopped trying to describe his feelings with words.

Mandy holds the door to the restaurant open for him. 'So which one are you taking?'

'Well, Judith and I aren't getting along so great right now.'

'So how do you think Seth and me are doing with them around?'

Milton zips up his combat jacket remembering the time Mare decided to wash his polar bear, and it came out yellow and smelly. When he cried, she told him to be a big boy about it. He showed the teddy to Mandy who tried to fluff it up with baby powder so that at least it wouldn't smell. The next day she brought home a red ribbon to tie around its neck.

'I'll take Connie,' he says.

SIX

Milton pulls the Volare to the side of the road.

'What are you doing?' Connie asks. She has her knees hiked up against the dash.

'Looking at the moon,' Milton explains. 'It's full.'

'Do you have to stop the car to look at it?'

He looks at her. 'Are you in some kind of hurry?'

She slides her knees off the dash, crosses her legs and stares grimly at the moon.

Most of the leaves have fallen from the trees. The naked branches form jagged black lines against the sky. Milton feels as though he's in a horror movie and wolves are about to howl. He glances at Connie whose sullen expression looks almost sexy in the moon light. He can understand why the guys go for her. 'Do you believe any of that stuff about full moons making people crazy?' he asks. She shrugs despondently. Around Connie, he becomes a talker because her brooding makes him feel as though he's trapped in a room with no air. 'I always feel different when the moon is full,' he continues. 'It feels like a whole new start of something. It's so clean-looking.' They sit in silence. A man in an Irish tweed hat who is walking an Irish setter stares in at them as he passes.

'What's his problem?' Connie asks.

'Maybe he thinks we're doing something illegal.'

'Like what?'

'I don't know.' Mandy thinks that when Connie left home she lived on the streets, took drugs and 'sucked off johns' for a living. Milton doesn't want to believe this, although he's rarely seen Connie over the past ten years and doesn't have an alternate scenario to offer.

A car passes, a gust of wind blows brown leaves onto the hood of the Volare. 'Can you see a face on the moon?' Milton asks.

'No.'

'I can. If I look long enough. There's a smile and a couple of eyes. Do you remember when you were little you used to call the stars guitars because you couldn't pronounce stars?'

'No.'

When he was eight and she was two, he loved picking her up and carrying her around. It made him feel older and important. For a year she let him, but then she wailed any time he came near her. As she grew she continued to shun him because, unlike himself, she had no difficulty finding playmates and no need for a doting older brother. Eventually she understood that he was the family joke and ignored him. He stayed away from her. Now he hardly knows her.

'So what's with you?' he asks. 'Who was the father?'

'He's dead. He died in a motorcycle accident.'

Milton reminds himself that she lies. 'When?'

'A couple of months ago.'

'How did it happen?'

'It was raining. He lost control, slammed into a truck.'

'What hospital did he go to?'

'The General.'

'What was his name?'

'Bug off, Milton.'

'Why won't you tell me his name?'

'Because it's none of your business.'

55

He knows she's lying. She won't give him a name because he could check the hospital records.

He has been trying to formulate in his mind how to tell Judith that Connie will be staying with them. Judith has never met Connie, but since Judith wants truthful relationships, he can't see them getting along.

'I was sorry when I heard what happened to your little girl,' Connie tells him. 'I would've called, but I didn't know what to say.'

'That's alright.'

'It must be hard.'

He wonders if her condolences are genuine or if she's just trying to change the subject. 'So how come you don't have a place?' he asks.

'It burnt down.'

'Oh, come on.'

'Nineteen-fourteen King Street. Go look if you don't believe me.'

'How do I know you actually lived there? Have you got some ID with the address on it?'

'Bug off, Milton. I don't have to prove myself to you.' She starts to open the car door. He grabs her arm. 'I'm sorry,' he says. 'It's just these unbelievable things keep happening to you.'

'I can't help that.'

'Well, maybe you're mixing with the wrong people.'

'I don't mix with any people. Stuff happens that's all.'

After settling Connie into the spare-room, he comes back downstairs to talk to Judith. She's in the kitchen studying her *I Ching* book. 'Okay, so who is this person?' she asks.

'My sister.'

'I realize that. What I mean is, why has she turned up all of a sudden?'

'I don't know exactly.'

'She's got body odour.'

'She does? I didn't notice.'

'Yeah, well, you've got numb nostrils. You can't even smell Winnie. I'm making hot chocolate, do you want some?'

'Please.' This is a good sign. They haven't had hot chocolate since Ariel died. Maybe this is some kind of truce. He sits at the table. 'So Terry left?'

'Yeah.'

'How old is he anyway?'

'I don't know. Early forties, why?'

'Just wondering.' What he wants to know is if she's decided to make a run for Terry, if she wants a divorce or an open marriage. She once said if he ever screwed another woman he'd better wear a condom. It had disturbed him that she would even suggest that he might 'screw' another woman. She sensed this and explained that she couldn't see two people staying interested in each other their entire lives. 'It's bound to happen to one of us sooner or later,' she said.

'What?'

'We're going to be attracted to someone else, and we'll have to decide if we're going to stay together.'

He watches her bum jiggle slightly as she whisks the milk. Does Terry dream about that bum, he wonders. Has Terry fondled it in passing? It unsettles him that something so familiar to him can cause sexual stirrings in another man. He understands why Arabs want their women covered. They don't want another guy even thinking about it.

'So how long is she staying?' Judith asks.

'I don't know. Until she can afford to move out.' He doesn't like how the conversation has veered away from Terry, but he can't ask more about him without seeming too interested. He wants her to think he doesn't take the Goof seriously.

'Okay, this is what I think,' she says, still whisking, 'and I'm just saying it. It's not a big deal; she can stay. It's just I wish you'd asked me first.'

'It was an emergency.'

'You could've called me.'

'I didn't know if you were out. You were with what's-his-name.'

'You could've tried. If I wasn't home, fine.'

'I'm sorry.' He watches her pour the milk into cups and stir in the cocoa. If Ariel were alive and in bed, it would feel cosy in the kitchen with just the two of them, the parents. Only in the last year had he begun to feel like a parent and to trust the feeling of belonging to a family. So used to being on his own, he'd felt awkward at first, unable to believe in its durability, unable to believe that anyone could regard him as a parent when he still felt like Milton. But then he started noticing other 'parents' in the supermarket: they didn't look any more like parents than he did. In fact it seemed to him that he was a better parent because Ariel didn't whine and grab at the candy bars beside the check-out counter like the other kids did. It seemed to him that maybe he wasn't setting such a bad example. He began taking pride in being a good parent, realizing that he could build himself new in her eyes. He made a point of standing straighter and shaving regularly so as not to burn her with his stubble. A feeling of responsibility gripped him, and he liked it, understood that he was on the planet to protect her. But now, sitting in the kitchen, he feels like the same old Milton, the centipede-crushing coward who lets his wife walk all over him. When she hands him the hot chocolate he grins idiotically like the doorknob on the commercial for breakfast cereal who spoons up flakes while his wife smiles because she's fooled him into eating fibre.

But the truth of it is, living like this isn't all that bad. He prefers it to talking about feelings. He's willing to grin idiotically if it will keep Judith off his back. He's even willing to listen to her talk about spirits if it will keep her from running off with the Goof. Without Judith, Ariel would really seem dead. At least Ariel's still alive in both their minds.

'I did my *I Ching* before,' she tells him. 'It talked about how repression and restraint accumulate strength. You know, I always think of holding back as being a bad thing, but I don't know. It said that with firmness and caution I can escape peril.'

He waits for her to explain the significance of this, but she doesn't. She wraps her hands around her mug and stares down at it, puckering her forehead the way she does when she's thinking. He understands why she searches for guidance from the *I Ching* and from Dr. Moriarty. Milton, too, would like some guidance, would like to believe in something, would like to believe that things happen for a reason. Downtown he has noticed a man with an emaciated, pock-marked face hovering around street-corners, clutching rosary beads, saying Hail Mary mother of God etc., over and over again. Milton suspects that counting the rosary beads keeps the man from going completely insane, keeps him connected to something. Milton would like to feel connected to something. When he watches the latest TV evangelist demanding that viewers send him money, Milton envies the believers' faith. Sending money soothes, absolves and heals them. Even though the TV evangelists usually turn out to be slimeballs, the believers continue to send money and cry Hallelujah. Milton would like to send money and feel better for it. He would like to believe that Ariel's spirit is flitting around. But he can't, and he knows that it's not because he's smarter than all the believers, or that he knows something they don't; it's that he can't suspend disbelief. He doesn't believe anything until it happens. Judith insists that he's afraid to believe because he might be disappointed. He agrees with her: why should he get all worked up about something only to have it not happen? He's seen too many cement-heads sit around waiting for things to happen that don't, then sit around moaning about it. Like why should it have happened in the first place? What made them think it would happen? It seems to him that they set themselves up for disappointment. So he tries to expect nothing.

'Maybe we should go somewhere,' Judith suggests.

'Where?'

'I don't know. Somewhere different. We should just get in the car and go.'

Milton doesn't understand why suddenly she wants to be with him when before she wanted to be with the Goof. 'It's pretty late to be driving,' he says.

'Can you not make excuses for once, can we just go for once?'

'Where do you want to go?'

She folds a dish-cloth and arranges it on the rack. 'Marty and Budro went to Niagara Falls. There's a two-night package for like a hundred bucks. I know it sounds corny, but it's supposed to be really beautiful. Marty says Germans fly over here to see it. We have to go some time. I mean it would be really dumb to go through our entire lives without seeing it.'

'Why?'

'Because it's so close and happens to be one of the wonders of the world.'

'I just don't want the car breaking down on the highway in the middle of the night.'

'We never do anything, Milton. Can't you see that? I mean we're supposed to be having a life here.'

'Do we have to go now? Maybe we can go tomorrow.'

Judith drops her face in her hands and shakes her head. 'Fine, alright, forget I said anything.'

'No, I mean if you really want to go ...'

'Forget it.'

Winnie knocks on the window then pushes the door open. 'Hi guys. Boy is my mom ever steamed. I went and did my Christmas shopping and is she steamed.'

'It's a bit early for Christmas shopping, isn't it?' Milton asks.

'There were sales on,' Winnie explains. 'You wouldn't believe what I got. A shirt for five bucks. Down at Gerrard Square. They were good deals, and now I don't have to worry about it till next year. I've just got one more to get.'

Milton watches Judith scrub the saucepan angrily. It seems to him that she has no right to be ticked off since she spent all afternoon with the Goof. If anybody should be ticked off, it's him. He pulls a chair out for Winnie. 'So why's your mother mad?'

'Because I was supposed to buy a heater. Now there's no way she's going to let me have a party. I asked her last week, and she said she'd think about it. But now there's no way.'

'Why don't you have the party here?' Judith suggests. Milton looks at her to see if she's serious.

'You mean it?' Winnie asks.

'We could use a party here,' she adds, without returning Milton's stare.

'That would be great,' Winnie says excitedly, reaching up and smoothing down the hair poking up at the back of his head. 'It would have to be BYOB.'

'Of course,' Judith agrees. 'Although maybe we could make some punch with alcool. That's not too expensive.'

Winnie eyes widen. 'You'd do that?'

'Sure.'

'We won't tell my mom. We'll say I'm over here for dinner.'

'If you like, although I always think it's best to be honest.'
'If I tell her, she won't let me come.'
'So don't tell her,' Milton says to annoy Judith.

~

Later Milton sits on the edge of the bathtub while Judith brushes her teeth. 'So what's the story with the party?' he asks.

She spits in the sink. 'Don't you think it's about time Winnie got his party?'

'Who's going to come?'

'I don't know. People he works with maybe.'

'They're all Filipino; they don't speak English.'

'Okay, well, I don't know, maybe Connie knows some people. Marty might come, and Terry.' He figured the Goof had something to do with it. They're going to flirt not only in front of him but in front of the general public. If she wants to make him jealous, she's doing it. He pictures the Goof in the leather vest laughing and joking, reaching across Judith for a drink, acting like it's only coincidental that he's rubbing his crotch against her. Milton would like to grab her throat and shake some sense into her; he imagines the feel of her neck in his hands, the soft skin, the pulsing carotid artery. He squeezes it, restricting the blood flow; her face flushes red, her eyes bulge, her mouth gapes. 'What if Winnie has a lousy time?' he asks.

'He won't have a lousy time.'

'Sure he will. He won't know anybody.' Milton has gone to a few parties in his time, mostly as Judith's escort. Always he stands alone by a wall, nursing a beer, watching people huddle in groups of three or four, glancing over each other's shoulders to see if there's someone else they'd rather talk to. Judith flits through the crowd like some kind of bee. He can see that people think she's a flake. They shake their heads and roll their eyes as she moves away, and he knows she's been mouthing off about spirits or the *I Ching* or something.

It seems to him that people at parties spend the whole night moving from room to room looking for the party.

'Who's going to talk to him?' he asks. 'He's retarded.'

'We'll warn them. We'll ask them to talk to him.'

'Great. Make him into a charity case.'

'Well, Milton, what do you suggest?'

'I suggest we forget about it. The party thing's like a religion to him. He believes it'll be heaven or something.' He knows that Winnie expects his party to be like a beer commercial filled with models with large breasts playing darts.

'I think you have to quit protecting him,' she asserts. 'His mother protects him, you protect him. The poor guy can hardly breathe.'

'I just think there's no way we can throw a party like the one he's got in mind.'

'Well, why don't we try?' She looks at him, but he looks away. 'Oh, Milton, stop being so negative.'

He would like to say, 'You just want to have a party so you can get it on with the Goof', but he realizes this would make him look small.

He knows that if the party is a disaster, Winnie will never be the same. He can't say this to Judith because she will argue that you have to take risks in life. He sees absolutely no point in taking risks in life. Sticking your head out only makes it easier for the assholes to chop it off.

Judith opens the medicine cabinet. 'I've been thinking about us.' She pulls out a strand of dental floss. 'I think we have to back off each other a bit.'

So she does want an open marriage.

'I don't mean an open marriage. I just think we have to give each other space.'

So she can screw around with the Goof.

'I don't think we need to separate,' she adds. 'Do you?' She holds the strand of dental floss taut between her index fingers and stares at him. 'Milton, do you think we should separate?'

'Why don't you just go and fuck the guy.'

'Excuse me?'

'Why don't you fuck him, just fuck him, get it over with.' He feels wonderful saying this, the words gush out of him. 'I'm sick to death of hearing about this guy. If you're so hot on him, fuck him. I don't want to hear about it.'

'I can't believe you're saying this.'

'Believe it.'

'You're acting like a total jerk.'

'Look who's talking. You were practically drooling over the guy.'

'We were having a conversation. Something you never do.'

'Oh right. Well excuse me for not wanting to talk about *Star Trek Three.*'

'I can't believe you're acting like this.'

'Well, maybe I've been a little too nice, you know, maybe I've been a little too understanding. Maybe you should just figure out what you want and not waste my time.' He likes the way this sounds: authoritative, in control. Maybe he should smash his fist into the wall. But then he'd have to plaster it. He stands, hoping to dominate her with his size.

'I don't know what's going on with you,' she remarks. 'It's like, you've chewed yourself up with hatred; you hate yourself and everybody else.'

'So, if you don't like it, leave.'

'Oh that's real constructive. Here's where you start calling me bitch and slut right? God, Milton, you really are pathetic.' She turns to the mirror and starts dental flossing, dismissing him. It seems to take forever for his fist to reach her. He can't decide where to strike, the back of her head like his mother used to do, or her shoulder, her ass. When Judith sees what he's doing and turns to block his blow, it's too late. His forearm hits her chin, causing her head to snap back and crack the mirror. Stunned, he watches her touch her lip to see if it's bleeding. The blood on her hand looks too dark. It should be bright red. He starts to reach for her hand to verify that the blood is real, but she snatches it away. 'That's it, Milton,' she says coldly. 'That's definitely it.' She pulls toilet paper from the holder and presses it against her lip, staring at him as though he were some kind of worm. 'All I can say is thank God Ariel didn't live to see this.'

He sits on the edge of the tub for a long time, listening to her move around the house. He expects her to leave immediately, but then he realizes it's late. She'll probably prop a chair against Ariel's door like the battered wife on TV. But it didn't stop the husband, he broke down the door, forced her to her knees and ground her face into the floor. Milton knows he will not do this, knows he will never hit Judith again because it has left him completely alone. He'd thought he was alone before; he didn't realize it was possible to feel more alone, didn't realize that, in spite of everything, Judith believed in him. Now she no longer believes in him. No one believes in him. Not even he himself.

He wishes he'd gone to Niagara Falls.

SEVEN

It does not please him to see Winnie and Connie in the kitchen having breakfast together.

Winnie holds up a box of cereal. 'Want some Shreddies?'

'What're you doing here so early, Win?' Milton asks. 'Don't you have to go to work?'

'It's Sunday,' Winnie reminds him.

'Oh, right.' Milton glances around for some sign of Judith. Usually she leaves a trail of rings from her glass of orange juice. 'Is Judith around?'

Connie leans back in her chair, folds her arms and crosses ler legs. She has dark sunglasses on, the wrap-around kind. He can't see her eyes. 'She said to tell you she's taking half the money out of the joint account.'

Milton tries to appear unphased. 'What's with the sunglasses?'

'My eyes are light-sensitive.'

Hoping that his sceptical expression will unsettle her, he stares at the glasses. But her face doesn't move. He starts to make coffee so he doesn't have to look at her.

'We already made it,' Winnie announces triumphantly, drumming his hands on the table. 'Connie and me were talking about the party.'

Milton realizes that he cannot possibly tell Winnie that there isn't going to be a party.

'Connie knows all kinds of people who'll come,' Winnie says. 'Girls even.'

Milton glances at Connie, but her face remains immobile, his look bouncing off the dark glasses like bullets off a bullet-proof shield. He pours coffee and leans against the counter, sipping. Outside the window, the neighbour's cat sits on the fence, staring at him.

Winnie holds up some sliced bread. 'Do you want me to make you some toast?'

'It's alright,' Milton answers. 'Thanks.'

Winnie gobbles what remains of his toast then wipes his hands on his pants. 'So we thought next Saturday night would be good. Connie says if we give her some money, she'll buy stuff for the punch.'

'Isn't that nice of her,' Milton remarks, hoping to rattle her with sarcasm since he can't do it with looks.

'I'm going to invite Angelo,' Winnie adds, 'and Buzz and Mr. Huang from work and his wife.'

'You've got jam on your chin, Win,' Milton says before he realizes how stupid this sounds.

Winnie wipes his chin with the back of his hand. 'And I'm getting paid Friday so I'm going to buy Doritos and Cheese Doodles and stuff.' He licks the jam off his hand.

Milton watches him. 'Did you tell your mom?'

'No way. I'm not telling her. It's okay if I say I'm having dinner here, isn't it?' He looks plaintively at Milton who has no choice but to nod. He curses Judith for getting him into this, curses her for not even leaving a note. The wife should leave a note. This way he has no idea where she is or if she'll ever be back. He checked the closet as soon as he woke and saw that she hadn't taken all her clothes. He remembers a TV movie where a guy burnt his wife's clothes after he found out she'd been sleeping with an airline pilot. He piled the clothes in the driveway, even the mink coat he gave her, and poured gasoline over them. The neighbours came out and watched, shaking their heads.

'Since Judith isn't here,' Winnie says, 'can Coco come in?' Judith never allows the dog in the house because it always humps her legs.

'Sure,' Milton agrees wearily, thinking that maybe he should just go back to bed. Except he wouldn't be able to sleep. Unless he had some pills. He's always wondered how people get them without a prescription. Winnie opens the back door for Coco who jumps on him then hurries over to sniff Milton's crotch. He tries to push the dog's snout away from his privates. 'Get out-a-here. God, Winnie, teach your dog some manners.'

'No Coco!' Winnie says, deepening his voice, but Coco continues to shove his snout into Milton's groin. Milton resents the attention drawn to his crotch. Even his little sister seems to be staring at it. 'Oh for god's sake, get him off me, or he goes.'

'Comere, Coco,' Winnie commands in the deep voice, then he grabs the dog's collar and drags him back to the table. 'Now sit.' The dog's tail wags, thwacking the table, causing the plates to rattle. 'Sit. I said sit. Sit!' He presses his hand on the dog's rump. Coco finally sits. 'Good boy.'

Milton forces himself to stare into Connie's glasses. 'So what are you doing today, looking for work?'

'It's Sunday.'

'Oh, right.' Does it ever bug him that his little sister can make him feel like a jerk.

'Did you know,' Winnie offers, 'that Connie has a photographic memory?'

'Is that right?' Milton asks doubtfully. Coco starts for him again, but Winnie grabs his collar.

'We thought ...' Winnie looks at Connie then back at Milton, 'that maybe we could all go to the zoo. Since it's Sunday. There's a McDonald's; maybe we could eat there.'

'I thought your mom said you were eating too many burgers?'

'I'll tell her I had Filet-O-Fish.'

Milton wonders why he finds it so hard to deny Winnie anything when he can hit his own wife. Maybe it's because he knows he can push Winnie around. He doesn't know he can push Judith around so he keeps testing to see if he can shake her up, break her down. If she ever does crumble, he plans to be there for her. She'll weep and he'll take her in his arms. He'll tell her everything's going to be alright. He remembers the scene in Gone With the Wind when Rhett shows up and Scarlett throws herself on him, just hangs on to him with tears streaming down her face. He loves how Clark Gable just smiles to himself, like he knew all along that Scarlett was going to give in to him.

'So can we go to the zoo?' Winnie asks.

'Sure.'

~

All three of them sit in the front seat of the Volare. Milton keeps his right elbow tucked into his side hoping to avoid touching Connie's breasts. It doesn't work though, every time he turns left she leans into him. She feels spongey and hot, and she smells like clothes that have been lying around in a damp basement.

'Look out!' Winnie squeals.

A drunk stands in the middle of the busy street halting traffic. Drivers attempt to pull around him, but he lunges at them. 'Come on!' he taunts, 'Come on!' His sagging grey overcoat swings back and forth as, twisting and turning, he charges at the cars. When Milton honks, the man throws himself on the hood of the Volare, hammering on it. 'Fuck you!' he shouts, 'Fuck you, asshole!' He tries to stare at Milton, but he seems unable to focus. His eyes roll back down to the hood of the car, which he continues to pummel, screaming 'Fuck you, asshole'. It shocks Milton that the man is close to his own age; he only looks older from a distance because of the stooped shoulders, ragged hair and beard. What did the man do before he became a bum? Milton wonders. What happened that made him give up? By now several cars are honking, but the man seems not to hear. Milton steps out of the Volare and tries to get the man's attention. 'Okay, buddy,' he cautions, 'take it easy.' The man's eyes roll before he is able to focus, but when he does, Milton wishes he'd stayed in the car. Staring into the drunk's spinning black eyes, he understands blind hatred. He sees that the drunk would like to kill him, would like to see him suffer, would like to pour acid over him and watch him burn. Milton wants to explain that he, too, is miserable; that he's lost his job, his wife, his child. He, too, is an outcast. When the drunk takes a swipe at him, Milton grabs his arm and escorts him to the sidewalk. 'Take it easy, buddy,' he repeats. But the drunk has slid back into his own private hell and pays no attention to him as he grumbles about fucking assholes. Milton pulls out his wallet and offers him a five-dollar bill. The drunk snatches it and backs off quickly as though he were afraid that Milton might take it back. Watching him lurch down the street, Milton wonders how he'll keep off the street himself now that he's out of a job, a wife and a child. There must be some comfort in poisoning your mind with alcohol, eliminating your peripheral vision, seeing only that you have been wronged. In Milton's mind there is always doubt. He always suspects that he has done something to deserve being treated like shit. As much as he calls them all assholes, he fears that he himself is an asshole. He almost envies the drunk for cutting himself loose, for having the guts to face the traffic head on. The drunk does not value his life. Milton thinks this could be an asset, this could be the ultimate weapon.

'Boy oh boy,' Winnie comments when Milton gets back in the car. 'Was he crazy or what? You were brave, Milt. I wouldn't've picked a fight with him.'

Milton knows that people are only brave when they're cornered and have no choice but to fight back.

When he woke this morning, for about two seconds, he thought last night was a dream. After he remembered that he had actually hit Judith he wanted to crawl under the bed and die. After twenty minutes of listening intently, he suspected that she was gone and felt relieved that he wouldn't have to face her. He prayed to God or whoever that Judith wouldn't tell anyone. But already he feels that everyone knows. That they can see in his face that he's a loser who takes it out on his wife.

At work Munroe and Aiken talk about men who are 'pussy-whipped', which means men who phone their wives to tell them they're going to be late; men who buy groceries, help with the house cleaning or make an effort to spend weekends with the family. Milton knows that he's been labelled 'pussy-whipped'. He tries not to mind, but he does. And sometimes, when Judith asks him to do things like vacuum or the laundry, he tells her 'no' just to prove to himself that he isn't pussy-whipped. He knows this isn't rational, that any decent human being doesn't expect another human being to do all the cleaning, cooking and grocery shopping. Even so, while he separates the whites from the colours or kneels on the floor shoving the vacuum nozzle under the couch, he feels pussy-whipped and hates her for it.

~

Winnie leans over the railing above the seals' pool. 'If you could be any animal you wanted,' he asks, 'what would you be?'

Connie flicks ash from her cigarette onto the pavement. 'One that dumb fucks don't kill.'

'Like what, though?' Winnie persists.

Milton watches a seal slide down the rocks on his belly and splash into the water.

'Not a seal, that's for sure,' Connie says. 'Dumb fucks club them to death.'

Winnie wipes his nose. 'What about a lion? Or a tiger?'

'Yeah and get shot by some jerk on safari.'

'What about a bat? Everybody's scared of bats, and they only go out at night.'

Connie adjusts the glasses over her nose. 'Too fucking ugly.'

'What about you, Win?' Milton asks, hoping to lighten things up. 'What would you be?'

'I wouldn't mind being a gorilla. Nobody bugs them. If they did, the gorillas would tear them to bits.'

Milton doesn't think caging animals just so cementheads can gawk at them is fair. He tries to imagine what it would be like to travel the same route day after day without variation, knowing that you can't go beyond a certain point. Then he realizes that he himself travels the same route day after day without variation. He drives to work and home again, sometimes stopping for gas or groceries. He's in a cage; only, unlike the animals, he can't count on food being delivered and no predators attacking him. If he weren't a loser he'd bust out, start a new life, get an education and become a financier or a pharmacist. Although, how would he write the exams when he can't even read? Besides, going back to school costs money. Staring at the 'Do not feed the animals' sign he realizes that, as Judith says, he can always find excuses. She used to suggest they drive to Nova Scotia or Maine, but he always said they couldn't afford it, or he couldn't take time off work. He hasn't been out of the city since they went to Buffalo before Ariel was born. Judith wanted to shop at the malls there. They spent two days buying baby things and sheets and towels. Judith kept pressing him for his opinion, but he told her to get whatever she wanted. Irritated by what she called his 'lack of interest' she ran up six hundred dollars on his credit card. They had a fight in the pink and green motel room. She claimed that he wasn't participating, that he resented her for having the baby and was shutting her out on purpose to make her feel guilty for getting pregnant. She wouldn't believe that his feet were tired or that the flourescent mall lighting had given him a headache. The motel mattress was soft and sagged in the middle. Judith clung to her side of the bed so she wouldn't roll into him. Milton swore to himself he'd never go to a mall again. He has, though, but always knowing exactly what he wants and where to find it. He hates not knowing exactly where he's going. Maybe he'd be better off in a cage.

'What about you, Milt?' Winnie asks, unwrapping a stick of gum. 'What animal would you be?'

'When I was little, I used to like wolverines.'

'What are they?'

'They're like wolves only fiercer.'

'Hunh.' Winnie considers this while crumpling his gum wrapper.

'I'm bored,' Connie announces. 'Let's eat.'

~

Screaming, squealing children race around the tables ignoring their distracted parents' efforts to quiet them.

Winnie lifts the bun off his Big Mac and scrutinizes it. 'I found a piece of bone in one of these once.'

Milton feels a headache coming on and stares down at his burger with little appetite. Connie eats her fries one by one, dipping them in ketchup. She looks almost like a little sister again, and he feels brotherly towards her. 'Your fries okay?' he asks.

'Yeah, why?'

'Just wondering.' It would be nice if they could have an ordinary conversation like a normal brother and sister. He pictures another commercial for long-distance calls, sees the 'sister' answering the phone and jumping for joy when she realizes it's her brother.

'So what've you been up to these last ten years?' Milton asks. Connie pokes a fry into the ketchup. 'You didn't want to go to college or anything?'

'How was I supposed to pay for it?'

'I don't know,' Milton says. 'People work their way through college, waitress or whatever.'

'Did you?'

'No, but I wasn't good at school. You were pretty smart, as I remember.'

'It sucked.'

Milton feels his face twitch. It's been happening more lately, one side of his mouth jerking up slightly.

'School's boring,' Winnie offers. 'You don't learn anything in school. Buzz said he should've quit in grade eight. He said all he did in school was check out what the other guys were wearing and try and look like them.' Milton remembers begging Mare for a pair of Levis because all the other boys had them. But she would only buy him flannels. Connie jabs at the ice in her coke with the straw.

'So, you been working?' Milton asks.

'Off and on.'

'Doing what?'

'I really don't need you interrogating me.'

'Well, don't you think we should get to know each other a little? Since we're related? And since you're staying in my house?'

'Oh, don't start with the "staying in my house" bullshit. Mandy did that.'

'Okay, so what do you want me to do, ignore you?'

'That would be nice.'

Winnie glances nervously at both of them then shakes his apple turnover from the packet. 'You know why giraffes have long necks? So they can eat leaves off trees. I guess they don't like grass.' He bites the turnover. 'The other thing I was wondering is how come the chimps have no fur on their bums. You'd think they'd get cold. 'Specially if they sat down.'

Grateful for the change of subject Milton nods seriously, as though contemplating the question. 'I don't think they sit much, Win. I think they squat or hang.'

On the way home Connie insists they stop at a bar. 'Take the rod out of your ass, Milton,' she says.

'I could use a drink,' Winnie agrees.

'I don't think your mother would be too pleased,' Milton cautions.

'What she don't know won't hurt her.'

Inside the bar the waiters wear G-strings and wreaths like the ones native girls drape around tourists' necks when they visit Hawaii. The rock music blares; Milton winces. On the dance floor, men take small steps side to side, swiveling their hips. 'This is a gay bar,' Milton observes.

'Trust me, Milton, they won't come near you,' Connie assures him.

Winnie slides onto a stool and scoops a handful of popcorn from a dish on the bar. 'I like the palm trees.'

They order from the balding, bare-chested bartender who lisps. Milton has never understood why some homosexuals talk different-ly from other people. Leonard used to speak normally. The first time Milton noticed him lisping, he was describing wallpaper from one of his interior-decorating jobs. Milton wondered if he'd been to the dentist and had his mouth frozen.

'I don't mind faggots,' Winnie declares.

'Tell it to the whole bar, why don't you?' Milton mutters.

While the bartender sets beers in front of them, Milton notices that he has tiny gold loops through his nipples. He's heard that gays into s&m have their nipples and scrotums pierced. He wonders if the bartender has a pierced scrotum. Looking around the bar he realizes that these men have had their joint up some guy's ass. He tries to be open-minded about it.

'So this is where Leonard got AIDS,' Connie tells him.

'How do you know?'

'He used to hang out here.'

'That doesn't mean anything.'

She shrugs and pours beer into her glass.

'Who's got AIDS?' Winnie asks, his eyes widening.

'Our brother,' Connie says.

Winnie pulls his beer towards him as though protecting it. Shaken by the loud music, Milton sits with his shoulders hunched and his fists clenched. Connie stubs out her cigarette and slides off her stool. Milton watches her walk into the crowd of men without hesitation. He assumes she's finding the ladies' room, then he wonders if there is a ladies' room.

Winnie points at a tall man in jeans and a sweatshirt. 'That guy looks exactly like Chevy Chase.' Winnie often insists that people look exactly like other people, but they never do. 'How old is Connie?' he asks.

'Twenty-six.'

'Did you know she was raped at knife-point when she was nine?'

'She told you that?'

Winnie nods. 'She went to the circus, and some guy asked if she wanted to join and she said yes. So he got her in his car and raped her. At knife-point.'

'Win,' Milton cautions, 'don't believe everything Connie tells you, okay?'

'Why not? I like her.'

'Well, that's fine. It's just, sometimes she exaggerates, you know what I mean?'

'She said you'd say that. She says your whole family puts her down all the time and doesn't believe her. She says you don't want to believe it because you're responsible.'

'How does she figure that?'

'She says if she'd had a supportive and loving family she'd've been a totally different person.'

74

Milton can't imagine Connie saying this many words at one time. Why did she confide in Winnie? Does she think he will prove to be a useful ally?

'She has to sleep on the street in cardboard boxes,' Winnie adds, 'where any dumb fuck can get at her.' He swigs his beer. 'I think you should be nicer to her.'

This is the first time Winnie has told him what he thinks he should do. Milton doesn't like it, and he doesn't like how his little sister is seeping into his life.

'Has she got a boyfriend?' Winnie asks.

'I don't know. Probably.' He wants to discourage any hopes for future romance. He spots her in the crowd talking energetically with a man wearing a fedora. The man pinches her cheek. She pinches his, laughs, then heads back towards Milton and Winnie. Milton thinks she shouldn't wear tight pants if she doesn't want men staring at her. He's always wondered how women can complain about men staring at them when they walk around in tight jeans and T-shirts, or mini-skirts and heels. Judith tells him that women dress to please themselves, but he can't believe a person willingly wears skirts and shoes that make it hard to walk. There's a girl in shipping and receiving who wears short skirts and gets mad if the men comment on it. She struts around the plant adjusting the skirt over her ass. There's no way she can't want guys looking at her. Judith says there's a difference between looking and calling out 'nice ass'. She says, when she sees a sexy guy on the street, she doesn't call out 'nice ass' but just enjoys looking at him. She doesn't feel she has to 'objectify him'. Cat-callers are scared little men, she says, who can't accept women as whole human beings because they might blow them out of the water. Making smutty comments about women, according to Judith, is their 'last vestige of power'. Milton doesn't disagree with her; he thinks that men who cat-call are jerks. But he can't help wondering if the women wearing the clothes aren't doing a power thing: taunting the men, saying you can look but you can't have. He's never tried to date those women. He figures they're only interested in guys with money. Women have a way of summing you up, he thinks. No really gorgeous woman is going to waste time on a guy like himself. That's what bugs him about the beer commercials: all the women are gorgeous; but the guys are nerds. There's no way nerds get girls like that in real life.

Connie slides onto a stool beside him. 'So, you look depressed as usual.'

'I'm not depressed.'

'Is this place too exciting for you?'

'Yeah, right,' he says sarcastically.

She crosses her legs and stares into the crowd, jerking her foot. 'I wonder what Leonard looks like now. A friend of mine died of AIDS. He looked like a concentration-camp victim. I had to carry him around.'

'How do you mean carry him around?' Winnie asks.

'He was so weak he couldn't wash himself. I had to bathe him.'

'Oh,' Winnie says, blushing and protecting his beer again.

'His whole family deserted him,' Connie explains. 'He had nobody.'

'Except you,' Milton comments.

'You don't believe me?'

'Now why would you think that?'

'Milton, you know what your problem is? You have no faith in people. Some people think about others more than themselves. Some people actually try to obey the ten commandments. Do unto others as you would do unto yourself; love thy neighbour.' It surprises him to hear her speak so much and so quickly. Only when she prods his shoulder, forcing him to look at her, does he notice the strangeness of her eyes, the pupils spreading over the irises. 'Thou shalt not commit adultery,' she admonishes, wagging her finger at him. He doesn't know much about drug addicts, except that nothing matters to them except drugs. He saw a documentary about it. They showed a guy getting high on cocaine. Before snorting it he seemed like an okay enough guy, but as the drug took effect he started acting like a real asshole, as if he knew things nobody else did. 'It's all attitude,' Connie continues. 'People like you act like you're the only people on the planet and you're doing the rest of us a favour by letting us exist. It's people like you who start wars.' She shakes her finger at him again. 'Do unto others as you would do unto yourself. What are the other ones? I can't remember. Thou shalt not steal.' He realizes that she is possessed and that he can do nothing but stand back and let the drug take its course. Before, he was just uncomfortable around her. Now she scares him. He slides off his stool. 'Let's get going.'

'Why, you got to be somewhere?'

'I want to get back.'

'To an empty house? That's brilliant.'

'You can stay here if you want. Come on, Winnie, your mom's probably worried.' To his surprise, Winnie doesn't protest so they leave her at the bar, squinting into her cigarette smoke, trying to remember the ten commandments.

After he drops Winnie off, he gets into bed and watches a nature show about grizzly bears. A mother bear and two little ones stand in a river catching leaping salmon in their jaws. Far off, in a clearing, an old and scarred male bear lies in the grass. The narrator explains that the mother and cubs know not to disturb him; they understand that if they do, he may hurt them because the old warrior bear craves solitude. This makes sense to Milton, and he wonders why humans don't follow the bears' example. It seems to him they have a pretty good system worked out. He wouldn't mind being an old warrior bear lying around in a national park. When the phone rings it disturbs him that he hopes it's Judith. He lets it ring six times so she won't think he's sitting by the phone waiting for her call. 'Yeah,' he says, trying to sound like he's in the middle of something.

'I hit mother. Milton, are you there? It's Mandy.'

'I know.'

'She says the boys steal from her. I've had it with her. She's coming to stay with you.'

'That's not possible.'

'She's on her way over,' Mandy warns. 'I couldn't stop her. You'll have to pay for the cab.' He considers ripping the phone out of the wall, but he knows they'll get at him anyway. They can always get at him. And if he wrecks the phone he'll have to pay for it. 'That's not possible,' he repeats.

'Bullshit it's not possible. It's about time you took part in this family. I'm sick and tired of looking after everything. I've got my own problems.'

77

Hunters aim shotguns at a warrior bear no longer within the sanctuary of the National Park. They curl their fingers around triggers while the bear plods through a field. Milton wants to shout out a warning. He tries to make himself change the channel, but he just freezes, his eyes riveted to the screen. 'I can't have her here,' he insists. The rip of gunfire causes his mouth to twitch. The warrior bear stumbles, moans, crawls then lies still. The hunters swarm to him like flies to shit. Milton wants to kill them: grab their guns and blow their brains out. They examine the warrior's paws then start carving him up to preserve the fur. Milton manages to look away, searching frantically for the converter among the bedclothes.

'There was nothing I could do to stop her,' Mandy explains. 'Except tie her up. Milton, are you listening to me? I'll do what I can to help. It's not like I'm dumping her on you. It's her decision. Maybe she'll want to come back. I doubt it. I hit her. I have to live with that.' He flips to a commercial for breath mints. On a beach, tanned and shiny-muscled young men and women in bathing-suits bounce around a volleyball. One of the young women stumbles into one of the young men who prevents her from falling. He cradles her in his arms and she smiles up at him, her white teeth inches from his. 'Milton?'

'Forget about it.'

'What?'

He slams the phone down. Already he can hear his mother scratching at the door.

EIGHT

'It smells of cat pee in here,' Mare says, sniffing and squinting around the kitchen. Her eyes remind Milton of a lizard's.

'We don't have a cat.'

'Must be somebody else's then. Somebody else's must've sprayed, and it's coming in through the window.'

'The window's closed.'

'Just the same, it comes in through the cracks.' She rubs her abdomen. 'It'll take months to wear off. You'd better get some Lysol and some ammonia.'

'Right, I'll do that.' He can't smell any cat pee. 'Do you want to sit down? Do you want some tea or anything?'

'Do you have any apple juice?'

He knows he doesn't but opens the fridge for something to do. 'I guess not. I can go to the corner for some.'

'Don't bother. I'm not thirsty anyway.'

'So, is Mandy picking you up later? How're you going to get

home? I can drive you.' He acted surprised when he saw her, and he hopes that, by pretending she's just dropped by for a visit, he can propel her back to Mandy's.

'I'm not going back there,' Mare insists.

'Not right now, but later.'

'I'm never going back.'

'Did you two have a fight? That's normal. People living together always fight. It'll blow over.'

She shuffles over to the window and stares out, rubbing her abdomen again. It seems to Milton that she has shrunk since the second by-pass operation; he almost feels sorry for her. He wonders where Mandy hit her, if she's bruised and sore, if she needs medical attention.

Mare points out the window. 'There's the cat, sitting on the fence.'

'You feeling alright, Ma?'

'Why?'

'Just wondering.'

She turns abruptly and squints at him. 'Where's your wife?'

'She's ah …' He looks around as though Judith might be in the room. 'She's gone.'

'She left?'

'That's right.'

She settles on a chair. The curve of her spine forces her head down. To look at him, she juts her chin forward and peers from under her brow. If she lives much longer, he thinks, she'll become a hunchback. He straightens up himself. For years Mare told him to stand straight, so he slouched. Now every three months or so pain radiates from his lower back into his left leg, and he can do nothing but lie flat or crawl on all fours. Judith says if he doesn't start 'carrying' himself properly he'll be crippled at forty.

'So why did she leave?'

'Who?'

'Who do you think? Your wife.'

'I don't know. You'd have to ask her.'

'How can I ask her? She isn't here.'

'I don't know why she left.'

'Did you hit her?'

'Of course not.'

'Whose house is it?'

'Nobody's, we rent.' Her questioning causes his voice to rise and his muscles to tighten. No matter how many times he tells himself that she's just an old lady to be pitied, she still gets up his nose. He sighs heavily, hoping to release some of the tension gripping him.

'You must have done something to make her leave.'

'Maybe.' As usual, she assumes it's his fault. He crosses his arms, determined to say as little as possible.

'She was nice enough, as I remember. Although you hardly let me see her. I hardly saw the baby. First I heard she was born, then I heard she was dead.'

Milton opens the fridge and pulls out the only immediately edible thing in it: cottage cheese left over from Judith. He hates cottage cheese but desperately needs to avoid his mother. He turns his back to her, pretending to search the silverware drawer. After what feels like minutes he grips a fork and, still with his back to her, pries the lid off the container, sets it on the counter and jabs the fork in. It makes him think of a movie he saw where a woman jabbed a fork into a guy's neck.

'How's your job?' Mare asks.

'Alright.' The cheese fills his mouth like vomit. He tries to swallow it in one big clump, but he chokes.

'What's the matter with you?'

'Nothing.' He pounds his chest with his hand. When he was small, Mare insisted that he eat everything on his plate. He'd stuff food into his mouth, storing it in his cheeks, then he'd leave the table and spit it into the toilet. Eventually she caught him and squeezed his cheeks forcing the food onto his sweater and the floor, insisting he clean both. 'People are starving,' she told him, 'You should be ashamed of yourself.' She related, as she had many times before, the story of how during the war she had to beg the baker for stale bread; of how her father had his hand mangled at his factory job and couldn't feed his family because they didn't have unions then; of how she worked eighteen-hour days sewing ruffles on rich women's dresses then came home and cleaned because her mother couldn't kneel on her swollen legs. Milton remembers this story like a Hollywood movie. He pictures Julia Roberts playing his mother trudging through grey streets lined with the lit windows of the rich people's houses. Julia wears a threadbare suit-jacket belonging to her handless father. Shivering, she pulls the jacket tight around her and knocks timidly on the baker's door. When the baker—fat in a white apron with a shiny bald head—opens the door, she bows before him, clasping her hands as though in prayer. He sneers and tosses a bag of stale bread at her then slams the door in her face.

'You shouldn't be eating from the container anyway,' Mare advises.

One of Judith's short-term friends was a Jewish woman whose father grew up in Hungary during the war. The Nazis took his parents from him then pushed him into a truck crowded with children and drove them to the Hungarian ghetto where they were expected to die either from starvation or exposure. He told his daughter, Judith's friend, about naked bodies being stacked and left to rot. He told her about eating rats and drinking urine. Milton wondered what the father hoped to accomplish by telling his daughter this. Judith's friend said that, since she was five, she'd had nightmares of Nazis breaking into her apartment and shoving her into a truck full of naked, dead bodies. It seemed to Milton that Judith's friend wasn't a better person for hearing the stories, wasn't particularly considerate or compassionate; she was just neurotic. Milton doesn't consider himself a better person for having grown up listening to Mare's stories of poverty. He just feels guilty, for not having suffered as she has, and weak because he's had it easy and is a loser anyway.

He jams the lid back on the container. 'Well, I think maybe we should get you home. It's pretty late.'

'I'm not leaving. I'll sleep on the couch. I won't bother you. You go to bed.' She pretends to be occupied looking out the window. He realizes that he can only remove her by force. Watching her cling to the back of the chair, he prays to God or whoever that he doesn't grow old but dies instantaneously in the car crash, hit from the side so he doesn't see it coming.

'I'll make up the bed in Ariel's room,' he tells her. 'You can sleep there.'

'I'm happy on the couch.'

~

She has one of her attacks while he's helping her up the stairs. He leans against the banister, supporting her while she fumbles for her pills. He wonders if she is about to die and what he'll do with the body since it's Sunday and he can't call an undertaker. He wonders if he should cover it with plastic in case it starts to smell. 'Do you want help?' he asks, but she doesn't seem to hear him. Finally she pulls the pill-box from her cardigan pocket, opens it and pops a pill into her mouth. 'Don't fuss,' she grumbles. He helps her into Ariel's room, trying not to look at the walls that Judith painted to look like clouds. After getting his mother a glass of water he closes the door gently behind him, tiptoes down the hall and flops back on his bed. He switches on the TV. It's late, and the only things on are reruns. He flips past 'The Mod Squad,' 'Love Connection,' 'Wheel of Fortune,' a Doris Day movie and a heavily hair-sprayed man saying, 'You must say to yourself "Yes, you can work through this! Yes, you can get through this!" and it will bring you closer to Jesus Christ, you know that.' Milton flips back to 'The Mod Squad.' Sammy Davis Jr. is guest-starring. He wears apricot bell-bottoms and a matching jacket with wide lapels. He's playing a movie-star with a drinking problem. Link, the black man with the afro, is trying to help him out. Sammy sits, glass in hand, with one leg draped over the arm of the couch. Link, dressed in white bell-bottoms and a white shirt, stands very rigid, listening. It feels strange watching Sammy, knowing that he's dead. If Sammy had known he would die of cancer would he have lived differently? Would he have been in 'The Mod Squad'? Watching him so alive on the TV, Milton feels like spirits or God or whoever must feel looking down at human beings, knowing their fate. Milton wonders if even then the cancer cells were multiplying. Sammy, as the movie-star, attempts to perform his own stunt. He climbs a high tower and prepares to jump. Link finds out from Sammy's ex-wife that Sammy is suffering from a crippling disease and wants to die. Link climbs up the tower after Sammy and tells him that he has a lot to live for, that he has to make the best of what time he's got left because people are counting on him, man, especially his ex-wife. This convinces Sammy. They climb down the tower together. Milton wonders how Sammy felt when he was diagnosed with cancer; if he remembered the 'Mod Squad' episode and wanted to jump from a tower.

This whole idea of time running out gets up his nose. It seems to him that people would be a lot better off without worrying about time. It seems to him that people are slaves to their watches, always glancing down at them. He takes his off and sticks it under the bed. Now that he doesn't have to go to work, he doesn't need it. Judith talks about time running out and how they're not getting any younger. It seems to Milton if people didn't try to trap time into seconds, minutes, hours, days, months and years, they'd be a lot happier. They wouldn't have to turn thirty, wouldn't have to go to New Year's Eve parties, wouldn't have to remember wedding anniversaries. Judith has a fit when he forgets their wedding anniversary. He doesn't understand why she wants to be reminded that they're getting older and that time is running out. He doesn't like knowing how old he is and doesn't know anyone who does. Everybody worries about getting older. He tries to forget about it.

He still doesn't believe she's really gone. He thinks she's just mad at him and wants to make him miss her. He misses how it was before, but now that he's hit her, he isn't sure he wants her around reminding him that he's just another useless bastard who hits his wife.

He picks his nose, rolls the booger into a ball and flicks it on the floor. He couldn't do this with Judith around. She'd say it was gross and that his nostrils are stretching from him sticking his fingers in them all the time. 'Fuck you,' he says out loud. He's been saying it often lately, usually when he's driving. Sometimes the 'fuck you' is meant for other drivers, but usually it's more general. It occurs to him that saying 'fuck you' in the car isn't all that different from saying it out in the open like the drunk on the street.

He starts to pick his nose again.

He hates how you never know you've got it good until it's over. Looking back on the years with Judith and Ariel, he thinks they must have been the best of his life. But at the time he just felt tired, as though there were no end to chores, errands, duties. He cursed having no time to himself. Now he's got all the time in the world. It ticks him off that things only have a beginning, a middle and an end after they're over. At the time it just feels like things will stay the same forever. You get so used to it that you don't even notice if you're having a good time.

~

The TV's still on when he wakes up. He looks at his wrist to see what time it is then remembers his watch is under the bed and reaches for it. Four-thirty a.m. He wonders if Mare is making the noise, creeping around in the dark, snooping. Or maybe she's had an attack and is rolling around on the floor. Or maybe it's a burglar. He switches the light off and waits for his eyes to grow accustomed to the dark, then he moves stealthily into the hall, sees that Mare's door is closed and stops at the head of the stairs. Two figures lean over the back of the couch. He recognizes Connie but not the man. Both their pants are pulled down, and the man is entering her from behind. She seems unconcerned, leaning limply over the sofa while he thrusts into her. Milton feels an urge to vomit or shout or pull the man off her, but he can't move. He doesn't understand what's before him, if it's an act of violence, lust or business. Then he feels aroused and worries that he himself is a pervert. No decent brother gets horny watching his sister being raped. If she is being raped. Maybe she likes it doggy-style. He prefers conventional sex, or anyway he thought he did. Judith used to say that if he wanted to try something new, all he had to do was ask. But he never wanted to. With her. Not that he wanted to with anyone else. Sometimes he dreams about tying women down, but he'd never do it in real life, it might hurt them. Or they might laugh at him.

The man grunts and pulls away from Connie, hitching up his pants as he stumbles backwards, knocking over Judith's floor-lamp. 'Shit,' he grumbles, starting to pick it up.

'I'll get it,' Connie tells him. 'Just go.' As she turns, Milton backs out of sight and creeps back to his room, then crawls into bed and masturbates. Afterwards he lies in the dark feeling that he doesn't have a chance, not a chance of ever being a decent human being. This comforts him. He can succumb to the evil inside him.

The religious freak with the rosary beads had shouted out that Satan stood on the mountain and told Jesus that, if he bowed to his will, all would be his. He didn't explain why Jesus didn't take up the offer. He acted as if everybody understood that bowing to Satan was a bad idea. Milton doesn't see why, if all would be yours. He doesn't believe that all will be his now that he has bowed to Satan, but at least he doesn't have to keep trying to be decent. Maybe tomorrow he'll buy a gun and shoot holes through Munroe and Aiken. And Nelson. Maybe he'll drown his mother. Maybe he'll rape his little sister. The possibilities are endless.

~

In his dream he asks Ariel to wait outside while he uses a public washroom. When he comes out she is gone. He runs into the department store looking for her, hurrying up and down aisles, asking salespeople if they've seen her. They all shake their heads disapprovingly. He runs into the mall crowded with Christmas shoppers, but he loses his sense of direction and ends up back at the department store. He tries to find an escalator that will take him to the lower level, but they're all going up. The ceaseless flow of shoppers forces him into a corner beside a Christmas tree. He slumps against the wall understanding that he has lost his daughter, that he has failed to protect her, that he will never see her again, that he can never forgive himself. When he wakes it takes him a moment to realize that the dream is not real, that really his daughter is dead not lost.

'What are you doing in there?' Mare demands, scratching at the door. He pretends to be asleep. She opens the door and shuffles over to the bed. 'What's the matter with you?' She prods his shoulder. 'Are you sick? Milton? Get up; it's past ten. I know you're awake, your eyelids are twitching.' She starts to yank the covers off him.

'Leave me alone.' He clutches the blankets.

'Quit feeling sorry for yourself, what's the matter with you?'

'I'm tired.'

'You can't be tired; it's past ten.'

'I'm staying in bed.'

'Are you sick?' She clamps a gnarled hand on his forehead. 'You don't have a fever.'

He pushes her hand away. 'I just don't feel like getting up.'

'Oh, well, excuse me, your highness. How do you think your boss feels about you staying in bed?'

'I don't have a job.'

'What do you mean you don't have a job?'

'Oh for chrissakes, mother, would you lay off? I'm in my underwear, would you please leave? I'll get up if you leave.'

She leans over him, peering at him with her lizard eyes. Her breath smells like old meat. He has to restrain himself from sending her across the room with one blow. 'Would you please leave?'

'I'll make you some eggs.'

'Fine.'

He locks himself in the bathroom and stares at the crack in the mirror. He runs his thumb over its sharp edges thinking that maybe if he cuts himself he'll feel better, as though he'd atoned for his sins. On TV, when the wife leaves, the man drinks and gets depressed then goes out and gets laid. Milton isn't interested in getting laid. One of the nice things about being married was that he didn't have to answer to cementheads who wanted to know the last time he got laid. When you're married, people assume you're getting it at home.

Milton would never admit this to anyone, but sometimes he gets tired of being a man, tired of having to act like he knows what he's doing, tired of having to pretend he likes sports. Before Munroe and Aiken stopped talking to him, they'd ask if he'd 'watched the game last night'. He'd say 'yeah', knowing that if he didn't they'd say he was pussy-whipped. The truth of it is he thinks football is stupid. He can't see why anyone would want to watch a bunch of guys beating the shit out of each other. His father used to watch hockey, and when the Maple Leafs scored, he shouted 'He scores!' with the announcer. During a play he'd chant, 'Come on, come on!' and 'Yes!' slamming his fist into his palm. Watching hockey, his father changed: he became animated, aggressive, loud. Even though Milton was just a child, his father explained the game to him in detail. Hockey was something his father understood. It had set rules, limitations and rewards, unlike life. When Milton pictures his father prior to the stroke, he's either sitting in his armchair watching hockey or looking baffled because he was out of a job. When Mare wasn't around, he would tell Milton and Leonard that he walked off the job because his boss was an idiot.

'Are you coming down?' she calls from the bottom of the stairs.

Sometimes Milton would be woken in the night by her yelling. He could hear her calling his father useless, a failure. His father wanted to be an inventor; he tinkered in the basement with projects that never worked. Mare wanted to know why he had to be an inventor, why he couldn't be an ordinary man with an ordinary job. Why did he have to be special? Why couldn't he be grateful for what God had given him? His father said he didn't see why he should be grateful for being thrown in with a herd of sheep. He told Milton that whichever way the herd was going, he was going the other way.

Just as Milton wonders if Ariel willed herself to die so she wouldn't have to harden and suffer, he wonders if his father willed himself to have a stroke so he wouldn't have to dream and fail.

~

The scrambled eggs are like rubber, but he eats them anyway because he doesn't want to argue. Mare sits across from him, staring. Like the cat. 'Is Connie up yet?' he asks.

'Connie?'

'I guess not.'

'What's she doing here?'

'The same thing you're doing.'

'I don't want to talk to her.'

'So don't.'

'I'm becoming dead, and you'd think she'd notice? All she thinks about is herself.'

'That's all most people think about.' He looks up and can't believe that Terry is at the door. He knocks then opens it.

'Hello,' he says, looking grim.

'Did somebody die?' Milton asks.

'Pardon?'

'Forget it.'

'Aahh ...' Terry glances around the kithen then clasps his hands

together. 'Judith asked me to drop by. She needs some cooking uten-
sils. She didn't think you'd mind if she took some.'

Milton can't believe that Judith could go for this guy. His jeans
are pressed. What kind of goof irons his jeans? 'Seen any good
movies lately, Terr?' he asks. 'Seen any special effects you want to tell
us about?'

'Who're you?' Mare demands.

'I'm a friend of Judith's.'

'Who's Judith?'

Terry waits for Milton to answer. He doesn't. 'His wife,' Terry
explains.

Mare squints at him. 'She's going off with you, then?'

'No, no, I'm just doing her a favour. You know I have a car and
can collect a few things for her.' He looks at Milton. 'She thought
you might be out actually. She told me the back door's always open,
I should just come in and leave a note.'

'Leave a note,' Milton repeats.

'Yes. Explaining.'

'So where is she?' Mare asks.

'She asked me not to reveal that information.'

'She doesn't want her mail?' Mare asks.

'Aahh, I don't think she's thought about that actually.'

Milton has heard about a form of torture that involves electro-
cuting a man's balls. He wants to electrocute Terry's balls.

'So what do you say, Milt? Can I take some stuff or ...'

Milton grabs the frying pan off the stove and wields it at him.
Bits of egg fly around the kitchen. 'Get the fuck out of here.'

'It's her stuff, Milton; she paid for it.'

On TV Milton wouldn't have to hit him with the pan, Terry
would run like the coward he is. But he doesn't. He just stands there
while Milton holds the pan dripping with egg. Milton feels his arm
trembling from the weight of the cast iron. He tries to foresee what
will happen if he hits Terry on the head: will he die, will he sue him,
will he tell Judith who'll say 'That's real constructive'?

'Look, I know you've been hurt,' Terry says.

Milton's arm is burning. He realizes he must do it now or never.
If he doesn't, he'll have lost. If he does, Judith will think he's an

asshole, and if he kills Terry, he'll be thrown in jail and raped by ugly burly men with tattoos.

'What do you think you're doing?' Mare demands, reaching for the pan. He drops it. It hits the floor with a resounding clang then bounces feebly towards his mother's feet. All three of them watch until it lies still.

'Take what you want,' Milton mumbles as he grabs his jacket and his car keys. He flings open the door planning to slam it behind him, but his jacket gets caught on the latch, and he has to stop to unhook it. He slams the door anyway, hating how he can't even make a clean exit. He kicks Ariel's plastic wading pool. 'Fuck 'em!' he says.

NINE

The heater in the Volare doesn't work; he wishes he'd worn a sweater. When he was younger, he walked around in a jean jacket and sweatshirt until it snowed. Now he's always cold, and he wonders what it is about getting older that makes you need more clothes, more stuff in general. It seems to him that you're born naked and free then gradually you get loaded down with junk. You think you need the junk, that it makes your life better. You think the clothes make you look good: slimmer, sophisticated, confident. You hide behind them, hoping to fool people, but really you're just getting more and more scared inside your clothes. By the time you're old, you're so covered in clothes and junk that you don't even know who you are. You think it all means something, that it defines you, but really it's just smothering you.

He pictures Ariel's little naked body. It seemed absolutely pure to him. He hated knowing that it would lengthen and broaden, grow hairy and begin to smell.

He parks half a block away from Mr. Grocer so Judith won't see the car. A blind lady with a cane walks ahead of him. He slows his pace, not wanting to startle her. Whenever he sees a blind person he feels inferior, humbled by the courage it must take to face the world without eyes. Judith told him about a blind man who shops at the store, spending an hour feeling vegetables and fruits, discerning apples from pears, lemons from oranges, carrots from parsnips. When Judith offered to help him, he shook his head vehemently. He's very proud, Judith explained. Milton can't imagine being proud, doesn't know what he'd be proud of except when Ariel, towards the end, believed in him and would relax in his arms. He felt proud of her but also of himself. Through her eyes he could appreciate his worth. She justified his existence. Without him, she would perish. He understood that to protect her he had to work for assholes, and it didn't bother him. It disturbs him to think that he needs another child to restore this sense of purpose. It disturbs him even more to think that another child might not restore this feeling but might despise him for working for assholes, might see how scared he is inside his clothes. He doesn't want to take that chance and tells himself that a child limits a person. Suddenly you become a slave to the cause of the child. Hitler wouldn't have tried to take over the world if he'd had a child. Einstein wouldn't have come up with the Theory of Relativity. George Bernard Shaw wouldn't have written plays. This is what Milton tells himself.

He pokes his head around the corner of Mr. Grocer and sees Judith at the express cash with her back to him. He steps around the gum machines and leans against some shopping carts, watching her shuttle the groceries across the scanner with dexterity and speed. No one could possibly detect that she's left her husband and run off with another man. She holds up a jam jar, asking for a price check. A stock boy runs down an aisle to get it for her. The man with bushy eyebrows who is waiting to pay looks annoyed. He says something to Judith who shrugs and stares after the stock boy, rapping her nails on the register. Milton pictures himself pushing through the glass doors—even though they open automatically—walking to the express cash, grabbing Judith's arm and dragging her out of the store. Maybe then he takes her to a restaurant or home; or maybe they argue on the sidewalk in front of the store while customers cheer them on, taking sides. Maybe they start to fight physically, ending in a passionate embrace. The customers applaud, and he sweeps her off her feet, carrying her to the car. He likes this ending.

~

She starts the conveyor belt under his items without realizing it's him. When she reaches over to grab the Raisin Bran, she glances up and freezes. 'What are you doing here?'

'Buying food.'

'I'm sure. Milton, if you cause a scene here, I'll never forgive you.'

'I'm not causing a scene. I just came to buy food.'

She continues processing his groceries. 'I'm just checking you out like a regular customer.'

'Regular customer' makes him think of whore. He pictures her in a black garter belt and red lacey bra. She probably says to the Goof, 'If you want to try anything new all you have to do is ask.' Milton wants to hit her again. 'That's fine,' he says.

She picks up a jar of Taster's Choice. 'Since when do you drink instant coffee?'

'I just thought I'd try it.' Her lip doesn't look swollen, this pleases him. At least the whole world doesn't have to know.

'That's twenty-one ninety-three,' she tells him. 'You have to bag it yourself.'

Milton feels around in his pocket, pulls out his cash and examines it. 'I don't have enough.'

'Oh Milton, for god's sake.'

'I'm sorry. I forgot I had to pay for my mother's cab.'

Judith heaves a huge sigh and leans a hand on the cash register. 'Okay, how much have you got?'

Milton drops his money onto the conveyor belt. He can hear the customers behind him grumbling. He feels his face flush. They think he's some dumb loser who can't afford groceries.

Judith counts his cash. 'Nine fifty-three. Figure out what you want. I have to void a whole bunch of stuff now. Thanks a lot, Milton.'

Some cementhead wearing a pin that says 'Manager' leans over the register. 'What's the problem here?'

'This customer miscalculated.'

The cementhead fingers his moustache while he stares at Milton who notices hairs growing out of his nose. He tries to think of what to do that would impress Judith; maybe he should tell the guy to mind his own business, maybe he should storm out of the store.

'I'm handling it, Mr. Jacobi,' she insists, sorting through the groceries, deciding what Milton should keep. 'You don't need instant coffee.' He considers objecting, standing up for himself; but he decides against it as it will only piss her off. It seems to him he's always not saying stuff because it will piss her off. He doesn't know why he bothers, why he's here, why he cares. 'Fuck her,' he mumbles.

'Excuse me?' she says, sweeping his money off the conveyor belt.

'Nothing.'

She hands him some change. 'Bag the stuff, Milton, and get out of here. You're being a total jerk.'

The cementhead looks at Judith. 'You know this man?'

'He's leaving. Everything's fine.'

The cementhead, still fingering his moustache, stares at Milton who considers telling him that there's snot on his nose hairs. But all he says is, 'Everything's fine.'

'Next,' Judith announces loudly, without looking at him, and he realizes that he has been dismissed. He considers throwing his groceries at her or screaming 'You dumb slut!' or grabbing her arm and dragging her out of the store. But he knows it won't work. Not in real life. Not in his life. He bags his groceries and walks out of the store. It upsets him that even though he doesn't believe in spirits, he can't help worrying that maybe Ariel's flitting around thinking he's a total jerk.

Since he doesn't want to go home he decides to visit his buddy, Wayne. He and Milton worked together at a hardware store their first year out of high school. Wayne wanted to be a cop, but he didn't make it past the initial interview. Later he applied to be a fireman, but he didn't make it past that initial interview either. Milton hasn't seen Wayne in a while because he gets tired of listening to him rant about how he got ripped off and how he's going to start kicking ass. Milton can't imagine Wayne kicking ass. He's the gentlest person that Milton's ever met.

He parks the Volare and walks over to where Wayne stands on the corner, staring up the street. Wayne doesn't notice him because his peripheral vision is limited by the orange hood and peaked hat of his crossing-guard uniform. Milton taps his shoulder. 'How's it going, Wayne?'

Wayne turns and grins, revealing his missing front tooth. 'How you doin', buddy?'

'Alright.'

'It's good to see you, man. What've you been up to?'

'Not much. You?'

'I moved. Remember that dive I was in? Well, I moved into an apartment building. So far so good. Except I don't have any place to park.' He pulls a tattered Kleenex out of his pocket and wipes his nose.

'That's a drag,' Milton agrees.

'It's one big pain in the ass. I tried parking in the mall across the street, but I got a twenty-dollar ticket. So then I parked on the street and got another ticket. So I says to the super, there's empty spots behind the building, and she says she'll rent me one for a hundred bucks. Well, no way I'm paying a hundred bucks a month for parking.' A young woman in a beret starts to cross the street. Wayne hurries after her, brandishing his sign. 'Just to be safe,' he cautions, and she smiles. He returns to the curb. 'So then I says to her, nobody else is using them so why can't I until somebody else does. She says she can't do that, says she has to have one available parking spot per unit. Well I'm about ready to kick ass. I mean I don't see why I can't use them until somebody else does.'

Milton wonders if talking about kicking ass makes Wayne feel better, if he's managed to fool himself into thinking he could kick ass. It seems to Milton that if you tell yourself something long enough, you'll start to believe it. 'Maybe you should kick her ass,' Milton suggests.

'Whose?'

'Your super's.'

'It's not her fault.'

'So whose ass are you going to kick?'

'I don't know. The landlord's.'

'Is he ever around?'

'I don't know.'

'It just seems to me you get all worked up about kicking ass when there's nobody's ass to kick.'

'I don't get all worked up.'

'Sure you do. You're always talking about it.'

Wayne drops his head and kicks his Wallabee into the curb. Milton wishes he hadn't said anything. Talking about kicking ass was probably the highlight of Wayne's day and now Milton's ruined it. It seems to him he has to be so careful talking to people that he's better off not saying anything at all. He zips up his combat jacket. 'That's some wind. You must freeze out here.'

'I don't mind it,' Wayne says without looking up from the curb.

'Anyways, I should get going. Listen, I'm having a party Saturday night. You should come. Bring somebody.'

An old woman in a balding fur coat walks hesitantly towards the crosswalk. 'I've got to help this lady,' Wayne tells him. 'She has trouble stepping over the curb.' He takes her arm and gently escorts her across the street.

'I'll see you later,' Milton calls after him. He heads back to the Volare thinking that at least Wayne gets worked up about something. Milton wouldn't mind getting worked up about something, he just doesn't see the point, doesn't see how it will make any difference. He wouldn't mind getting worked up about Judith and the Goof. Any normal man would. Every day he hears about jilted husbands killing their wives. They get angry, really angry, and do something about it. He just sits back and lets it happen. Maybe that's why he's a loser: he doesn't get worked up about stuff. Often he thinks he should be feeling things, and he starts to imagine he's feeling them. He thinks about the feeling; he tries to form it in his head and send it down to his body. While he was watching Judith at the express cash, it was as if he were standing outside himself, watching himself go through the motions of the jealous husband. But really he wasn't feeling anything.

He has always known that if he really wants something he won't get it and he hopes that, by tricking himself into thinking he doesn't really want it, he'll get it. Maybe this has something to do with why he doesn't get worked up about things.

A legless man in a wheelchair rolls towards him, talking to himself. Milton averts his eyes, not wanting to stare, then remembers that the disabled want to be treated like normal people. So he looks back at the man who continues to speak emphatically into the air. It upsets Milton that the man is legless, that he has to suffer, that he has gone mad. But he doesn't get worked up about it because it won't change anything. Judith would want to talk about it, she'd say, 'Can you imagine not having any legs? How does he go to the bathroom? How does he shower? He must walk on his hands. Poor guy.' Milton tries to shake the image of the man from his mind and steps into a phone booth to look up 'guns' in the Yellow Pages. It surprises him to see a number of listings for rifles, shotguns, handguns, muzzle loaders and licences. There's even a listing for a gun store in Buffalo. He suspects he wouldn't need a licence if he bought one in Buffalo. Not that he's going to buy a gun. He just wanted to know he could if he wanted to.

~

'Oh, it's you.' Mandy steps back from the door. It surprises him to see that she's still in her bathrobe. 'Where's Mother?' she asks.

'At my place.'

'Who's looking after her?' She stares at him, pulling the belt of her bathrobe tight. 'Milton, you can't just leave her there.'

'She doesn't want me around.'

'That's not the point. She could die at any moment.'

'So let her.'

'Did she take her pill this morning?'

'I don't know. She made eggs. It's not like she's an invalid.'

'Alls I'm saying is she shouldn't be moving around a lot. The doctor says it could kill her.'

'She knows that. If she moves around a lot maybe she wants to die.'

97

'Oh Milton.'

'I think we should just leave her alone.'

'Well, fine. She's your responsibility now. So what are you doing here? You never come here.'

'I just wanted to talk.'

'About what?'

'I don't know.'

'There's no way I'm taking her back.'

'I didn't ask you to.'

She slides her hands into her pockets. 'Okay, well, Leonard's here. He's got to have a bunch more tests done, so I said I'd go with him.'

'Maybe I should come back later.'

'Don't be a pig, Milton. He wants to see you. He's always asking about you.'

When he sees Leonard at the top of the stairs he doesn't recognize him. As Connie said, he looks like a concentration-camp victim.

'Len,' Mandy says, 'Milton's here.'

'How wonderful.'

'Can you get down the stairs alright?' she asks.

'Oh, sure.' Leonard grips the banister and holds his foot tentatively over the first step. 'You two go ahead. I'll join you.'

Mandy grabs Milton's arm. 'Come on. I've made tea. He can't drink coffee.' In the kitchen she whispers while Leonard makes his way down the stairs. 'Try to act normal. His other eye's going now, too. He's really upset. So be nice to him.'

'It's so good to see you, Milton,' Leonard says. Mandy pulls out a chair for him. He sits, holding himself straight. 'Are you well?'

'Alright.' Milton notices Leonard's left eye roll away from his right.

'I've been thinking about you,' Leonard tells him.

Milton doesn't like it when people say they've been thinking about him because they never explain what they've been thinking. They leave him wondering if they were thinking about what an asshole he is. He doesn't want them thinking about him, period. It disturbs him that they can manipulate him in their minds, see him as they want to see him.

'I was thinking about our childhood,' Leonard continues. 'All of us. How we had to rely on each other.'

Milton wonders what he's talking about.

'There's something to be said for growing up parentless which, for all intents and purposes, we were. I'm not sure why we grew apart. My being gay didn't help.'

'That didn't bother us,' Mandy assures him.

'I'm sure it didn't. It was me, you see. I couldn't accept you accepting. And of course I was afraid to tell mother. I'll have to now.'

Why? Milton wants to know but doesn't ask.

'I hadn't really accepted it myself, I guess. I always wanted children, you see. I thought maybe one day I'd find a woman and start a family. I really wanted that. Although I realize now it couldn't possibly have worked. Funny how we want what we can't have when really we have so much.' Mandy puts a mug of tea in his hands. 'Thank you,' he says. 'Although I'm losing my sight I'm seeing certain things for the first time. Part of me is angry for being blind to them for so long. On the other hand, I'm just grateful for being given the chance to see. You two, for example, I'd pushed you from my mind because I was afraid to face you, to let you see who I really am.' He reaches towards them. Mandy gives him her hand and signals with her eyes for Milton to do the same. He doesn't want to hold Leonard's hand but already his brother is gripping his arm. 'I'm hoping you'll forgive me.'

'Of course we forgive you,' Mandy assures him.

Milton searches himself for a feeling. But all he can think about is how grotesque Leonard looks with his sunken skin and emaciated body. And how at certain times in your life you think other people have it made, then later something happens to them, and you're glad to be yourself. He wonders if he's secretly glad Leonard has AIDS, if he's that bad a person.

'Do you remember our sandbox?' Leonard asks. 'It wasn't even a box really, just a pile of sand.'

Milton remembers Leonard burying his cars. He had to dig them out and rinse the grit out of them. Even then they never ran smoothly again.

'We made so much from so little,' Leonard continues. 'Children do that. Then somehow we lose that ability as adults. We become greedy and stop seeing the forest for the trees.'

Milton remembers Judith asking him if he were outside a forest and had to get through it quickly, would he take the winding path through the forest or would he take a chance and cut through the trees. Milton said he'd take the path, and she'd said 'I thought so.' He could tell by the way she wouldn't look at him that he'd failed some kind of test.

'How's Connie?' Leonard asks.

'Alright,' Milton says.

'It's good of you to take her in. I've always suspected that you had a good heart. You just don't like people knowing about it. Let them know, Milton, before it's too late. The only absolute is love. If you have love, you have everything.'

Milton is pretty sure he's never loved anybody, except maybe Ariel. He's grown used to people, expected them to be there and been surprised when they weren't, like Judith. He wouldn't mind having a love affair like in the movies where they're always jumping on each other, but he can't see that happening.

'Jerry and I were very lucky,' Leonard admits. 'Perhaps that's why I let go of my family. He seemed to fulfil all my needs. Of course, when he got sick, there was no time for anything. We had to look after each other. He was always worrying about me. He worried about me more than about himself.' Leonard covers his eyes with his hand. 'I miss him so much.'

'It's okay,' Mandy says. 'You can cry with us.'

'Thank you.' His shoulders tremble slightly. 'No one can know what we went through, what we shared. I consider myself privileged to have known him.'

Milton would like to ask if he feels privileged to have AIDS, but he realizes that this would sound negative.

Leonard holds his mug with both hands and sips his tea. 'It's funny. I don't know if we would have stayed together if he hadn't gotten sick. You see, he changed when he knew he was dying, became gentler and considerate of other people. I would like to die with half the grace he did.'

Mandy told Milton that Jerry used to hit Leonard, tell him he was fat and lock him out of the apartment. Twice Leonard showed up on her doorstep crying, swearing he would never go back to Jerry. Milton wonders if Leonard has forgotten these incidents as he has the unpleasant episodes from their childhood.

'He was a very special person,' Leonard emphasizes. 'I'm sorry you never had a chance to meet him. I have a picture of him.' He pulls out his wallet and opens it to a snapshot of a man with his hair slicked back like a mafioso. 'This is before he got sick.' Milton wonders if Leonard thought Jerry was a very special person before he was dying, wonders what it is about having AIDS that glorifies people. On TV, he has seen the marches for AIDS, the AIDS benefits. He has listened to people with AIDS talk about AIDS, has listened to movie stars talk about AIDS. He remembers the TV special about the quilt. People from all over the world pieced together a quilt embroidered with the names of their loved ones who had died of AIDS. They read out their loved ones' names as though they were heroes: men who'd gone off to battle and died in combat not men who'd stuck their joints up each other's asses. Milton would like to know why nobody sews a quilt for people with cancer or for little kids with terminal diseases. What makes the guys who take it up the bum so special when they're partially responsible for getting it in the first place?

'I think I have to lie down for a bit,' Leonard tells them, 'if that's alright.'

'Of course,' Mandy agrees. 'Do you want to go upstairs?'

'The couch is fine.' He stands, leaning on the back of the chair like an old man.

'Do you want help?' she asks.

'I'm fine.'

She pours more tea, and when Leonard is out of sight, she glares at Milton. 'You could be a little more giving.'

'What do you mean?'

'You know what I mean.'

'I listened to him. That's all he wants.'

'I think he wants a little more than that.'

'Like what?'

'He's our brother.'

'He's got it all worked out. If I say anything it'll just throw him off. Let him think we're the Waltons if he wants.'

'Somewhere inside you, Milty, there is a feeling person. I know it because I've seen it. You've just locked it away because of Ariel.'

Milton wants to throw a chair again. He wishes she'd quit bringing up Ariel. She has no right to bring up Ariel. He stares at the floor because he's afraid that if he looks at her, he'll call her a dumb bitch who doesn't know what she's talking about.

'What is it?' Mandy asks.

'Mouse shit.'

'Where?'

'Under the cabinet.'

'Great, like I don't have enough problems.'

'Well, I'd better be going.'

'I'll pack some of Mother's things for you.'

Leonard appears to be asleep when he leaves. Milton's glad he doesn't have to think of something meaningful to say.

~

It seems to him that the day is taking forever. He doesn't know why he wants it to end since it means he has to return home to his mother and Connie. He pictures Connie with the man, the curve of her ass. He's never been with a woman with a great ass and would like to have seen her breasts. Maybe she'll start turning tricks regularly in the living-room, and he'll be able to watch. It doesn't seem unnatural since he watches sex on TV all the time. He and Judith have lain on the bed night after night watching other people have sex. On the rare occasions when they did copulate, he felt clumsy, unable to operate smoothly like the men on TV. Judith didn't act like the women on TV either, groaning ecstatically and crying 'Yes, yes!' He's always feared that he isn't good in bed. To him sex is an endurance test: can he make her come, can he hold off ejaculation until she comes? If he can't, can he sustain an erection until she comes. Afterwards, can he stay awake long enough to reassure her with tender hugs and kisses so she won't think he's insensitive. Then there's the problem of being too sensitive. Before Judith, he had a one-night stand with a woman whose car he jump-started. She invited him to her place for a drink. In the light of her apartment he realized that she was older than he'd thought. Grey roots showed under her yellow hair. He could see she wanted him and enjoyed being an object of desire. But once they were in bed it became clear that he disappointed her because she kept insisting he not be afraid to hurt her. He tried to hurt her, tried to remember things Mickey Rourke did to Kim Basinger in *Nine and a Half Weeks,* but his mind went blank. Half-way through she got up and poured herself another drink, leaving him in a tangle of bedclothes.

He prefers watching sex on TV.

~

He goes to McDonald's and finds Winnie eating a Big Mac while he studies a flyer from Radio Shack. 'Hi, Win.'

'What're you doing here?'

'You told me your lunch is at one.'

'That's right.'

'So I thought I'd drop by.'

'Is Connie here?'

'No.'

'There's a girl at work I invited to the party. She said she'd try and make it. I invited Mr. Huang and his wife, and Angelo.'

'That's good.'

'Who are you inviting?'

'Ah ... I don't know yet.'

'You must know somebody.'

'Sure, I just haven't got around to it.' The truth of it is, he doesn't know anybody, and he wonders how this came about. How any human being can not know anybody, except his wife. 'I invited my buddy, Wayne,' he offers.

'We need girls.'

'Yeah, well, Connie said she knew some, didn't she?'

Winnie nods. 'I've got a cold. I hope I'm better by the weekend. I'm taking pills. I hope they work. I'll take more later. Is Judith coming?'

'I doubt it.'

'She still steamed?'

'You could try dropping by the store and inviting her.' He knows that if Winnie invites her, she won't be able to say no.

'Okay.'

'Tell her you need her to bring some of that punch she was talking about.'

'Okay.'

'Listen, Win, don't be disappointed if not too many girls show up, alright? I mean you don't need a girl. Lots of guys don't have girls.'

'Most do. Mr. Huang has Mrs. Huang. Angelo has Maria, and Buzz has Nancy.'

'Yeah, but they don't have to have them. I mean I don't exactly have Judith at the moment, and you don't see me crying about it.'

'Why not?'

Milton shrugs, stalling. 'Because I don't need her really. I like being single. There's all kinds of stuff you can do that you wouldn't be able to do if you had a girl.'

'Like what?'

'I don't know. All the stuff you do. You don't have to check with anybody. You just do what you want.'

Winnie fingers the end of his nose. 'I'd still like one though.'

'Sure, just don't think it's the be all and end all. I mean there's more to life than girls.'

Winnie looks down at the Radio Shack flyer again. 'Why don't you think any girls will come?'

'I didn't say that. I just said don't count on too many coming. Since we don't know any.' Already he can see that he has ruined the party for Winnie. Once again words have betrayed him. 'Maybe lots will come, who knows?'

Winnie arranges his burger wrappings on his tray and picks it up. 'It's alright if they don't.' He carries the tray to the waste receptacle, pushes the garbage through the flap, then returns to Milton, wiping his hands on his pants. 'Anyway, I got to get back to work, or Mr. Huang will be pissed.'

'If you want, drop by later.'

'Okay.'

Milton doesn't move from his plastic chair because he can't think of where to go. As usual he feels dirty and mean. He should have left Winnie alone, should have left Wayne alone. He thinks he's doing them a favour, but all he does is bring them down.

He looks at his wrist then up at the clock above the menu. Only twenty minutes have passed. It occurs to him that it's possible he could live another fifty years. The thought of filling all those minutes depresses him. He really wouldn't mind dying young, so long as it was in the car crash. At least then he wouldn't have to answer to assholes and worry about growing old and shitting his pants. It seems to him life is too long anyway. You spend thirty years thinking things are going to get better, then suddenly you're looking at forty wondering what went wrong. Judith read somewhere that most people accomplish their greatest work before forty. He's got seven years left. If nothing happens, he might as well be dead. Since he isn't necessary. Now that Ariel's gone.

TEN

When he comes in the back door, Connie is waving a knife over Mare's head. 'Give it to me,' Mare shouts, trying to grab it.

'What's going on here?' Milton demands.

'She's trying to kill me,' Mare says.

Connie drops the knife to the floor. 'If I was, I would've by now.'

Milton snatches up the knife. 'So what were you doing?'

'Joking around.' She has her dark glasses on.

'She's evil,' Mare insists.

'Okay, Ma, maybe you should go upstairs and take a nap.'

'She's trying to kill me. I don't want her here.'

'I don't want you here either,' Connie argues, 'and I got here first.'

'That's enough now,' Milton says.

'A rat-faced hag is what you are,' Connie taunts.

Milton moves between them. 'Ma, let me help you upstairs.'

Mare waves him away. 'I'm cooking fish-sticks.'

'I ate already,' Milton tells her. 'You should get some rest.'

'I'm sick of resting. All you people want me to do is rest. I may as well be dead.'

He can see sweat on her forehead. He puts his arm firmly around her waist almost hoisting her out of the room. She smells bad, and he suspects she's shit her pants. 'Maybe you'd better have a bath.'

'I don't want a bath.'

'Okay, well, do you want to watch TV? You can sit in my room and watch TV.' She'll stink up his bed, but he can't think of an alternative. 'Sit in my room, and I'll make you some tea.'

~

In the kitchen Connie sits eating corn niblets from a can.

'So what were you trying to prove?' Milton asks.

'You don't like her either.'

'Yeah but I wouldn't kill her.'

'Why not? She's waiting for it.'

He looks in the fridge so he doesn't have to look at her. 'What do you need those glasses for? It's night.'

'The fluorescents hurt my eyes.'

He would like to tell her to stop lying, but he knows this will only start an argument. 'Maybe you should go see a shrink or something. That's what Mandy said.'

'Maybe you should go see a shrink.'

'There's nothing wrong with me.'

'You think watching your sister get fucked up the ass is normal?'

Suddenly he feels naked and that his penis has shriveled to the size of a worm. He closes the fridge. 'You're disgusting.'

'I'm disgusting. At least I don't get off watching other people.'

'I was trying to figure out if you were in trouble.'

Connie smirks and picks up a corn niblet between her fingers. He feels as though he is the corn niblet, as though he's in one of those movies about shrinking people. She could crush him between her fingers, gnash him between her teeth. He can't even look at her.

'It's alright, Milton. All men are perverts. Being my brother doesn't make you any different.'

107

Suddenly short of breath he leans against the fridge. His arm tingles. He wonders if he's going to die and if she'll care. He pictures himself gasping, clutching his chest and sliding down the fridge to the floor while Connie jumps up, holding her hands over her mouth and saying 'Oh, my god.' She drops to her knees and leans over him, cradling his head in her arms. 'I'm sorry,' she says over and over while her breasts brush his cheeks.

'There's something wrong with the toilet,' she tells him. 'I think she put something down it. Her dirty underwear.'

He closes his eyes trying to connect the person in his kitchen with the little sister he remembers.

'Don't make a big deal out of it,' she adds, 'just get a plunger.'

He watches her mashing niblets between her fingers. 'What's happened to you?'

'What's happened to you?'

Staring into the black holes of her eyes, he realizes that something has happened to him. There was a time he wanted to be an ambulance driver. Now he's a pervert who watches his sister get 'fucked up the ass'. He hates how he became this person without even knowing it.

Her fake gold bangles jangle as she stands and slides into her jean jacket. It seems to him that if she bent over, her jeans would split. His mouth twitches. 'Why do you wear pants like that?' he demands, surprised at the harshness of his voice.

'Like what?'

'Crawling up your ass like that.'

'Why do you notice?'

He tries to glare at her, but the dark glasses defeat him. 'Where are you going?'

She has her hand on the doorknob. 'I have to meet somebody.'

He tries to think of a way to stop her. Otherwise it will mean that even his little sister can walk all over him. 'If you go now, don't come back.' He's seen men say this in movies.

'See you later, Milton.'

She leaves and it feels as if the floor's caving in. He clings to the fridge, bashes his forehead against it. And then Ariel's fluttering above him. He runs into the living-room and dives onto the couch.

He pushes his face hard into a cushion, squashing his eyeballs, but it doesn't help, she flutters over his shoulder. He rolls onto his back and kicks the air. 'Fuck off,' he shouts, not believing it's Ariel but some evil spirit using Ariel's image. He jumps up and swipes at it with his arms.

'What's going on down there?' Mare calls from the top of the stairs.

'Nothing.'

And it's gone.

~

He dreams that he is trudging through a snowstorm, trying to remember where he parked the car. He's left the motor running to keep Ariel warm. Walking down street after street he becomes confused, unable to remember which streets he's already walked. Lights are on in the houses, but he doesn't seek help because he fears the people inside will think he's an idiot to have lost track of his car and his child. The cold bites his face, his fingers, his toes. He begins to understand that he will perish. But he forges on, determined to die searching. His lungs begin to burn from inhaling the icy wind; frost forms on his nose hairs and eyebrows. He pictures Ariel coughing, beating her little fists against her car-seat. Or maybe she doesn't realize that she is inhaling poisonous fumes but accepts death peacefully, like sleep, trusting that her father will return for her.

Mare prods his shoulder. 'Wake up, there's a burglar in the house.' Only half-conscious it takes him a moment to realize that she's holding a gun.

'What are you doing with that?'

'What do you think? Come on.'

'Call the cops if you think there's a burglar.'

'They don't do anything.'

She yanks on his arm.

'Let me put some pants on.' He tries to shake her off, but she clings to him.

'You don't need pants. Come on, he'll get away.' She pulls him into the hall. 'Listen,' she whispers. They stop still. He hears someone in the kitchen.

'It's probably Connie,' he says.

'Then why hasn't she turned the light on?'

'Maybe she didn't want to wake us up.'

'Come on.' She starts for the stairs.

'Ma, give me the gun, I'll do it.' He takes the gun, surprised by the weight of it.

'Just scare him with it. Don't kill him.'

He moves stealthily to the kitchen, flicks on the overhead light and sees Judith who stares at the gun wearing an expression he has never seen before; her mouth gapes and her eyes bulge. He continues to point the gun at her, enjoying her terror. 'What are you doing here?' he demands.

'Picking up the stuff I paid for.'

'It's a bit tacky creeping around at night, don't you think?' The gun sends power-surges up his arm and into his body. Even though he's in his underpants he feels invincible.

'Where did you get the gun?' she asks.

'I don't see how that's any of your business.' He senses her fear diminishing so he jabs the gun into the air threateningly. 'Sit down,' he commands.

'Oh, Milton, for god's sake.'

'Sit down!' His chest resonates with power. The hairs on his legs stand up, suddenly alert, alive, like antennae.

'Milton?' Mare calls from the stairs.

'Everything's fine,' he shouts. 'Go to bed.'

'Is he gone?'

'Yes.'

'Who are you talking to?' He can hear her coming down the stairs and panics.

'Go to bed!' he almost screams, aware that when his mother appears the spell will be broken. She pokes her head through the doorway squinting into the light and then at Judith.

'Who are you?' she asks.

'His wife.'

'So why are you pointing the gun at her?' She grabs Milton's forearm and snatches the gun. 'What are you doing here, young lady?'

110

'Picking up my stuff. I knew if I came in the daytime, Milton would cause a scene.'

'So get your things and go,' Mare tells her. 'Milton, don't be an idiot, put some pants on and help her. The sooner it's over with, the better.'

~

It's when she's packing the last of her underwear that he begs her to stay. He's not sure why except that he feels that, if she leaves, he'll stop breathing.

'Give me a reason to stay,' she says.

He tries to think of one but can't, tries to remember what men say on TV to keep their wives from leaving. 'I love you.'

'If I believed that I wouldn't be doing this.'

Still in his briefs he feels cold suddenly, and can't stop shivering.

'I hope you don't mind me taking the toaster,' she says. 'I know it was meant for both of us.'

'That's okay.'

He searches his mind for words to stop her. Words that will cause them to make wild, passionate love. She picks up a lacey camisole he bought her one Valentine's Day. She never wore it, said it wasn't her style. He'd bought it because one of the guys at work bought one for his wife and said she'd liked it because it made her feel sexy. Judith drops the camisole back in the drawer and closes it.

'I'm leaving you the TV even though we both paid for it.'

He reaches up from the bed and touches her bum. He's not sure why.

'What are you doing?' she asks.

'Nothing.' The guy at work who bought the camisole said that he and his wife sometimes covered themselves with whipped cream when they did it. Milton couldn't get excited about this, although the other guys listening seemed to think it was a good idea. Maybe he should have suggested whipped cream to Judith. Maybe he should have expressed a need. She's always said he doesn't seem to need her, need anybody. All he needs, she says, is a TV.

'I need you,' he says.

'Oh, Milton, don't be a dink.' She twist-ties the garbage bags filled with her clothes.

'It's true.'

'You can't just say things and expect people to believe you. I mean, sometimes I feel like you say things just because you think you're supposed to. You can't do that your whole life, I mean some time you're going to have to say what you mean.'

What if he isn't sure what he means?

'It's like you're trying to be somebody else,' she explains, 'and I don't happen to like that person.'

'Which person?'

'The person who points a gun at me and hits me, that person.'

'Oh.'

'Do you like that person?'

Milton shrugs.

'I think he's a total jerk. I miss the other person. But I've been thinking about it and maybe I made up the other person. Maybe he never existed. Maybe you are a total jerk.' He examines an ingrown hair on his thigh because he can't think of what to say. 'What do you think?' she asks.

'About what?'

'Which person you are.'

'I don't know. Maybe both.'

She sighs heavily and picks up her bags.

'How are you going to carry those?' he asks.

'Terry's waiting in the car.'

Immediately he tries to think of where he put the gun, then he remembers that his mother took it.

'Don't do anything stupid,' Judith warns him.

From his window he watches her get into Terry's new Honda. The Goof doesn't even get out of the car; he just pulls the bags in and stuffs them in the back seat. It pleases Milton to think that Terry's scared he'll get swatted by a frying pan.

He sits on the edge of the bed trying to free the ingrown hair, thinking that it's not fair that she's giving him a hard time because he doesn't say what he means. It seems to him nobody says what they mean. People talk behind each other's backs all the time then greet

112

each other with shit-eating grins.

He remembers an article Judith read to him about a couple who formed a suicide pact because they didn't want to grow old. The man shot the wife then his Pekinese dogs then stuck the shotgun in his own mouth and blew his head off. It said in the article the couple bragged about being rich when really they were poor. It said they were very proud and didn't want anyone to know that they weren't successful. Milton can relate to this; he doesn't want anyone to know that he's a failure. Part of the reason he doesn't have any friends is that he hates people knowing about his life. If he were a success he'd probably have lots of friends; they'd go golfing and talk about the stock market or whatever. As it is he wants to be alone with his failure. At least then he can contain it, prevent it from spreading into other people's lives and mouths. 'Poor Milton, his daughter was crushed by a TV. Poor Milton, he got laid off. Poor Milton, his wife left him'. The truth of it is, they don't really feel sorry for him; they just talk about him to make themselves feel better. Compared to him they aren't doing so badly.

Maybe after Ariel died he should have shot Judith and himself. Maybe, in a way, that would have been a happy ending.

He hears his mother shuffling down the hall and covers himself with the blankets.

'Everything alright here?' she asks.

'Yeah, fine. Go to bed, Ma.'

'I was in bed. I got up to see how you were.'

'I'm fine.'

'You don't look it.'

'Well, I am.'

'What happened between you two?'

'Nothing. It's over that's all.'

She rubs her abdomen. 'Quit feeling sorry for yourself.'

'I'm not.'

'You can't go blaming other people for your troubles.'

'I don't.'

'Nobody likes a complainer.'

'Ma, I want to get some sleep.'

'You've got no reason to complain.'

'I'm not. Goodnight.' He switches off the light, pulls the covers over his shoulders and waits for her to leave. After the door closes he switches on the TV and sees disabled children lined up in wheelchairs singing John Lennon's 'Imagine'. One of the little girls breathes through a device implanted in her throat. One of the little boys has withered arms and legs. Another's arms and legs are strapped to his chair, and his head jerks repeatedly. Milton tries to watch their pathetic rendering of the song; he feels that he should—that he owes it to the suffering children—but he can't. It horrifies him. He changes channels. A large-breasted girl in spandex sits on exercise equipment, puckering her lips as she exhales. Her midriff is exposed, her cleavage visible. 'Only twenty minutes a day,' a male voice announces, 'and you can lose those unsightly bulges.' Milton wonders where she lives, if she's married, if she takes it up the ass. He flicks to a James Bond movie. Sean Connery in a toupee is being seduced by a blonde in a mini-skirt. Judith hates James Bond movies because of their violence and what she calls their treatment of women. James Bond, she says, screws at least one woman per movie who usually turns out to be the bad guy. Even if the woman turns out to be a good guy there's no way James Bond ever considers making a commitment to her. He doesn't even seem all that interested in sex; the women have to fawn all over him before he condescends to poke them. What does this tell people who watch the movies? Judith asks before providing the answer. It tells them women are disposable, that you can't trust them, that you can fuck them if they really want it but make a quick exit. Judith was thrilled when they discovered that one of the James Bond women was a man. 'There you go,' she said, 'Men don't want women, they want men with plastic boobs and cunts.'

All this bores Milton. He likes James Bond movies. At the moment James is about to be sliced in half by a laser beam. When Milton tells Judith that guys don't take James Bond seriously—it's just entertainment—Judith scowls and says it's inside his head even though he won't admit it. Inside his head, he wants to be James Bond and have guns and transsexuals, tailored suits and fancy cars. Inside his head, real life will always be a disappointment. Milton doesn't disagree with her. He wouldn't mind being James Bond or at least Sean Connery. It seems to him Sean Connery can't have too much to worry about. All he has to do is play heroes in movies, and everybody idolizes him. He doesn't have to do anything in real life except spend his money. He could even beat his wife, and people would still think he's a hero so long as he played good guys in movies.

He hears the front door open, then heavy and uneven footsteps up the stairs and into the bathroom. He assumes it's Connie and hopes she won't be long because he needs to pee. He hears the toilet flush then the taps running. He hasn't heard her close the bathroom door so he can't be sure she has finished. He waits for as long as possible because he doesn't want to see her. Finally, without turning on the light, he creeps down the hall to the bathroom. Before he can back out he sees her sitting on the toilet. 'Oh, sorry,' he mutters, 'it's just I have to ...' She doesn't respond. He turns on the light. She squeezes her eyes shut and holds her hands over her face. Her scalp is bleeding.

He stares at her. 'What happened to you?'

She shakes her head sluggishly, and he realizes that she's either seriously wounded or drunk.

'What happened?' he asks again, but she ignores him. She slouches forward, propping her elbows on her knees and her head in her hands. Abruptly, she slides to the floor, leans over the toilet and vomits. He can see that a patch of her hair is caked with blood.

'You should go to the hospital,' he says.

She slumps back against the wall. Milton flushes the toilet then folds toilet paper into a wad and presses it against the head wound, relieved to see that it seems superficial. She tries to push him away but throws up again, on the floor. Milton wipes her mouth then slides his hands under her arms, lifts her up and carries her to her bedroom. While he's pulling off her shoes he sees that her fly is undone and that she's not wearing underwear. Pulling the blankets over her he has a feeling she really was raped this time and wonders what kind of sick man does this to a woman. He's never been able to understand it. When he hears about women being raped and beaten—often murdered—in underground parking lots, in parks, in their apartments, he can't understand it, loathes the men who do it, wants to shoot their balls off, wants them to suffer as he knows the women must suffer. He can't imagine ripping off a woman's clothes, restraining her, forcing himself inside her, ignoring her screams, relishing her terror then strangling her or stabbing her or smashing her skull with a tire iron. He can't imagine why anyone would do this. Then he remembers that he hit his wife. And for that brief moment, believed she deserved it.

ELEVEN

'If we buy some chicken,' Mare tells him, leaning over the meats, 'I'll
do Shake 'n' Bake.'

'Whatever.' Milton peers around the toilet paper display to see
if Judith has noticed him. If she has, she isn't showing it. She continues scanning groceries and shoving them down the conveyor belt.
He wants her to notice him so that he can ignore her.

'What's the matter with you?' Mare demands.

'Nothing.'

'Have you got butter?'

'I think so.'

'Yes or no?'

'Yes.' She's always demanded 'yes or no', would not accept 'I'm
not sure' or 'maybe'. Under pressure he would venture a definitive
answer that would inevitably turn out to be wrong.

'How about tuna?' she asks, already reaching for it. She knows
he hates tuna. Before school she'd ask him what he wanted in his

sandwiches. He'd say baloney and would look forward to the sandwiches all morning only to discover that she'd put in tuna.

She drops a tin of corned beef into the cart. 'What's wrong with Connie this morning?'

'I guess she slept in.' He did check in on her, to make sure she was breathing. He dreamed that she had been pulled out of a lake dead, white and puffy.

'Ma, I've been meaning to tell you, I'm having a party this weekend.'

'Why?'

'For a friend of mine. Anyway, I have to buy a bunch of stuff for it, so you just keep doing your regular shopping, and I'll go get some Coke and stuff.'

Even though he walks by her checkout, Judith doesn't notice him. He lingers by the detergents resisting an urge to pick his nose in case she does see him. It takes him a moment to realize that the two men ten feet away, conferring over garbage bags, are Munroe and Aiken. Unsure if they've seen him, he pretends to remember something he needs from another aisle and abruptly turns away. It disgusts him that he doesn't have the guts to walk up to them and spit in their faces. Instead he lurks by the potato chips, hoping they'll leave without seeing him.

'What's the matter with you?' Mare demands, startling him.

'Nothing.'

'Let's get going, I need to sit down.'

'Wait a minute.'

'I can't wait a minute.'

He grabs some chips. 'Let me get some Coke. You go get in line.'

Fortunately Munroe and Aiken aren't at the carbonated drinks. Milton collects several bottles then returns to his mother, disappointed to see that she hasn't chosen Judith's checkout. Munroe is at Judith's checkout apparently joking with her because he's smirking. Judith just stares at him, waiting for him to pay. Milton remembers that she doesn't know who Munroe is, has only heard about him but never seen him.

'Well look who it isn't.' Aiken steps around Milton. 'Munroe, look who's here.' Munroe turns and stares at Milton, so does Judith.

'Hey, Milt,' Munroe calls.

'Would you pay, please,' Judith says loudly.

'We've been missing you at work, Milt,' Munroe continues. 'We don't have anybody to kick around anymore.'

'Who are these men?' Mare demands.

Milton imagines smashing his Coke bottles over their heads or grabbing their ears and bashing their heads together even though they're bigger than he is. He remembers Al Pacino in *Sea of Love* attacking men bigger than he is. Milton feels like Al Pacino, tells himself if he wasn't holding the bottles—and if Judith wasn't watching—he'd give them what for. Causing a scene now will only upset Judith. She'll call the cementhead manager who'll have them all arrested.

'Pay or I'll call the manager,' Judith warns.

Munroe takes out some cash. 'Don't get excited, sweetheart.'

'Don't call me sweetheart.'

'Don't call her sweetheart,' Milton says.

On the news, they said killer whales at an aquarium drowned a woman by pinning her to the bottom of the tank. Some people think the whales should be shot. Milton thinks it's unfair that the whales are trapped in tanks. If some dumb human jumps into the only territory they have left, he figures the whales have every right to kill her. It seems to him, watching Munroe pester his wife, he has every right to kill him. He starts for him, but his mother grabs his arm. 'Don't be foolish,' she chides. But he shakes her off and strides towards Judith's checkout. 'Leave her alone,' he commands.

'Milton, for god's sake,' Judith pleads.

'What's your problem?' Munroe asks, already bagging his groceries.

'That's my wife,' Milton says.

Munroe looks at Judith then back at Milton. 'Well, isn't that special.'

'Leave her alone,' Milton repeats.

'He isn't bothering me, Milton. Would you just go?'

But Milton feels that he's on a roll, that momentarily Munroe will be out cold on the floor. Momentarily, music will surge, Ariel will flutter over his shoulder, and he will feel vindicated.

119

'Milton, you're being a total jerk.'

His Robocop arm stiffens preparing to smash Munroe's face, but Judith jumps out from behind her cash register. The force required to prevent his fist from striking her causes him to fall backwards, knocking down the blind man who has just finished packing his groceries. His bags of fruit and vegetables break as he crashes to the floor; oranges, lemons, apples and pears roll in all directions. 'Oh, my god,' Judith gasps, rushing over to him.

'Now look what you've done,' Mare says.

Judith leans over the blind man. 'Are you hurt, sir?' He flails his arms, making it impossible for her to touch him.

Munroe winks at Milton. 'Good going, Milt.'

The blind man, on all fours, begins to grope around the floor for his fruit. Judith, panicked and confused, grips her forehead with her hands. 'Sir, we'll get you some new fruit.' The blind man crawls along the floor, stuffing the fruit in the pockets of his sagging duffle coat. Frustrated, Judith turns and runs at Milton, kicking his shins. 'Get out! I want you out!' He can't believe she's kicking him: she's not a violent person. 'Get out, Milton! I want you out, I mean it!' He'd like to move, but he can't; it's as though he's hip-deep in mud.

Munroe collects his bags and joins Aiken who's been buying cigarettes. They both wave. 'Catch you later, Milty.'

The blind man, having filled his pockets, slowly pulls himself off the floor, then stands helpless without his cane. Milton wants to find it for him, but Judith won't stop kicking him. 'Get out!' she screams. Why doesn't the blind man say something, yell at him, swear at him? He just stands there mute, with his arms held out and his palms facing open like Jesus. Milton wants to help him, has to help him, but Judith with a vice grip yanks him towards the door. He can't stand it, can't stand how this woman is preventing him from redeeming himself. Heat blasts through him, and he breaks free of her, causing her to fall into the gum machines. The blind man covers his eyes—why, when he can't see? He begins to waver side to side as though dancing. Mare slowly approaches him, says something Milton can't hear, then takes the man's hand. She guides him to a bench and sits him down. 'I'm sorry!' Milton shouts as though the man is deaf as well as blind. 'I'm sorry!' Around him stockboys in green jackets, hopping like toads, gather the remaining fruit. Milton tries to cry, feels that if he could cry something would be released in him. But it's as though the tears have crystallized around his tonsils. He feels them cutting into his throat and pictures a scene from a movie where a woman threw a glass at a man, slitting open his carotid artery, causing blood to gush over his white shirt. The man tried to stop the blood with his hands, but it spurted through his fingers. He fell to the floor, rolled his eyes, gasped and died. Holding his hands over his own throat, Milton notices for the first time the slits of eyes and mouths around him, the hatred. Not only does he hit his wife, but he knocks over blind people. Judith's eyes are also slits. Clearly she has nothing to say to him, or what she has to say is beyond words. He leans against the counter, covering his face with his hands, hiding.

~

'That was decent of them,' Mare comments, 'not to press charges.'

He wanted them to press charges, wanted to take the stand. On the stand he could tell the truth, and they would have to listen. On TV when people take the stand they break down and cry, and everyone understands. Sometimes the accused exchanges long glances with the accuser. If Milton could exchange long glances with Judith, she would forgive him, would see that he meant well, that he'd only wanted to protect her from those bastards.

Mare spits on a Kleenex and rubs at something on the windshield. 'What kind of person would cut his tongue out, that's what I want to know. Imagine robbing a blind man? The police said there's a group of boys out mutilating seniors. They offer them a choice of cutting off a finger, an ear or their tongues. They say they want to leave the old people something to remember them by.'

'Let's not talk about it.'

'You shouldn't go leaving me alone in the house.'

'I won't.'

'You say that now.'

'I won't!'

Mare feels around in her purse and pulls out a hard candy. The sound of the cellophane paper crackling as she unwraps it causes Milton's mouth to twitch. Sucking on the candy she says, 'I can't imagine he asked to have his tongue cut out. They probably just took advantage of him because he was blind.'

'I really don't want to talk about it.' There is no question in his mind that now would be a good time to ram the car into a tree.

'You have to talk about it,' she persists. 'These things happen.'

He looks for a tree but sees only bodies and trash-cans, mail-boxes and newspaper dispensers.

'Who were those men, anyway?' she asks.

He needs a wide tree, a tall tree with no bodies around it.

'Those men you were fighting with. Who were they? Milton?'

'The guys that got me fired.'

'How do you know they got you fired?' She sucks loudly on the candy. 'What did you do to make them get you fired?'

He pictures the tree, thick and craggy, dependable. He turns up a residential street.

She crumples the cellophane wrapping into a tiny ball and stuffs it in the ashtray on the dash. 'You must've done something.'

'Forget about it.' They're probably guzzling beers right this second, laughing at him. He tells himself not to care. There's an old man out there without eyes or a tongue.

'That house is on fire,' Mare observes.

'What?'

She points through the windshield at a smoking, asphalt-sided house. 'It looks abandoned.'

Milton jams on his breaks and flings open his door.

'What do you think you're doing? Milton, don't be a fool.'

He runs across the lawn, stumbles, falls to his knees, gets up. The front door sticks. He kicks it open and lunges into the hall. The smoke gags him, but he forces himself to take deep breaths. His lungs and eyes burn. He feels exuberant, free, because he will die a hero. A man who risked his life to rescue an innocent trapped in flames. He drops to the floor jubilant because he has found a way out, has made a clean exit. He rolls onto his back and laughs while smoke tears stream down his cheeks. Where's Ariel? He's doing it for her. He's going to take care of her now. Where is she? She should be here, loving him, trusting him, thanking him. It angers him that she's not here. Maybe she sees through him. Maybe she thinks he's being a total jerk, posing as a hero when really he's just scared, scared of Judith, of the blind man, of Munroe and Aiken, of his mother, of Connie, of Leonard, of the slits of eyes and mouths. He rolls onto his stomach and bashes his forehead into the floor. Where is she? she should be here. He hears sirens. 'Please …' he mutters but the words scorch his throat. Real tears pour from his eyes, and he sobs so hard that he feels as though he'll cough up his heart. Only then does he see the feet. Small feet in black high-topped sneakers, boy's feet. He reaches towards them, wraps his hands around the ankles and pulls. 'Jesus christ,' he says. It's a body. There's a body in here. 'Jesus fucking christ,' he mutters and forces himself to his knees to take a better look. It's a girl, a teenager, unconscious, her sandy hair falling over her face. She could be Ariel, Ariel older. It's not fair that she looks like Ariel. He crawls towards her, gasping, sweat dripping from his forehead, stinging his eyes. Flames lurch towards him from the living-room. The sirens move closer. 'It's not fair,' he mutters, wrapping an arm around her waist then crawling towards the front door dragging her with him. He's afraid she's dead, that he's too late, that while he was rolling around in self-destruction this girl was dying. The tears and smoke make it impossible to see. He stays close to the wall groping, like the blind man, towards the sirens.

On the lawn firemen clamp oxygen masks over their faces. Cool air inflates him. He pushes the device away because he wants to see the girl. On his knees he stares down at her, watching her eyelids flicker. A fireman touches his shoulder, 'Take it easy, buddy.' Milton nods obediently because he's afraid they'll take her away from him. 'Do you know this girl?' the fireman asks. Milton nods and gently carresses her cheek with the back of his hand. The hair on his fingers feels coarse against her young skin. She blinks then looks through him as Ariel did on the day she was born. The fireman takes the mask off her face. The Ariel blue of her eyes pains Milton. He tries to smile. 'Who are you?' she asks.

'A friend.'

She stares at him, and he wonders how he must look to her: sweaty, bug-eyed, a maniac. 'I wanted to die,' she murmurs and closes her eyes. He clenches grass between his fingers, ripping it from the ground. The fireman gently grips him by the shoulders. Milton knows he has no choice but to let her go.

TWELVE

'So everybody's saying you're a hero,' Wayne tells him, smelling of alcohol. He's wearing one of the party hats Judith brought. Judith hasn't spoken to Milton all evening. The Goof has been hanging around her like a bodyguard.

Milton sips his beer. 'Who's everybody?'

'I don't know. Everybody who saw the paper.'

The headline read 'Jobless Man Rescues Streetgirl From Raging Inferno'. Milton doesn't know how they found out he was jobless when all he said was 'no comment'.

'On "Rescue 911",' Wayne continues, 'this guy rescued a little girl hanging off a chairlift. The guy said nothing in his life could ever touch the feeling he had saving that little girl's life. He said it was a life-changing experience.' Wayne waits for a response from Milton. When he doesn't get one, he looks into the crowd. 'Who're those Chinese people anyway?'

'Mr. and Mrs. Huang. They're friends of Winnie's.'

Wayne appears thoughtful, as though this information takes a moment to sink in. 'Anyways, I bet you could pick up a chick or two if you went down to the Duke's and talked about it. I was talking to this one girl. I says you were my buddy. She'd never heard of you so I told her, I says you risked your life to save a girl from burning alive, and the chick says "Wow", just like that, she says "Wow". And that's with just me telling the story, imagine if you told it. She was no woof either. Anyways, she wanted to know what you were like so I says you're a man of few words.' He nudges Milton with his elbow. 'You like that? "A man of few words"? Anyways, so she says she'd love to know what you were thinking in the burning building, so I says I'd try to get you down to the bar so you could tell her in person.'

Milton doesn't know what he was thinking in the burning building. He knows only that for once in his life he felt no doubt.

'How 'bout it, Milt? In way of celebration, we could maybe go down there next Saturday?'

'I can't leave my mother.'

'Even for a couple of hours?'

Milton shakes his head and pretends to sort through his tapes. Try as he might, he can't forget the girl. Her face keeps floating to the surface of his thoughts, her features merging with Ariel's. So far Buzz and Nancy, Angelo and Maria, and Mr. and Mrs. Huang have all congratulated him on the rescue. They appeared humble before him, insisting that they would never have the courage to rush into a burning building. Maria kissed him on the lips. Buzz said he didn't know Milton had it in him. Mr. Huang shook his hand and introduced Milton to his wife as though he were royalty. Nancy, who Milton thought was attractive until she quit smoking and gained thirty pounds, insisted that there aren't many men like Milton around. Milton said little during all of this; he only wondered if they would still think him courageous if they knew the girl was committing suicide. Or that he was committing suicide.

Wayne pulls out Bruce Springsteen's *Born in the USA* tape. 'This is good. Play this.' Milton inserts the tape. He used to like Bruce Springsteen, when he looked normal, before he got into body building. Now it gets up Milton's nose that Springsteen sings about the working class when he's rolling around in dough himself.

Wayne plays air guitar and sings along with Bruce, wincing during a high note.

Milton leans against the wall thinking that, as usual, he feels uncomfortable in his own home. He looks around at Connie's friends, with their pierced ears and patchy hair, who've horked back all the chips and cheese balls that Milton and Winnie set out in bowls. A guy with his hair shaved in rows knocked over some cheese balls and didn't clean them up. Patches of orange have spread on the broadloom where people have ground the cheese balls underfoot. Connie said she'd invite girls. Milton realizes that some of these people with pierced ears must be female, but he wouldn't want to venture a guess which ones. Two of them sit on the floor with their legs intertwined on the exact spot Ariel died. They have their arms wrapped around each other's necks and keep poking their tongues into each other's mouths and ears.

Milton has lost sight of Winnie and is afraid to find him; afraid that he will be a crumpled mass of disappointment. All afternoon he ran around the house tidying and talking about the music they should play. Finally Milton sent him out to get ice. When he came back, the first of Connie's guests had arrived. Winnie greeted them enthusiastically and offered them chips and punch. They responded in monosyllables, but Winnie didn't seem to mind. When he asked who their favourite band was, they couldn't think of one. So Winnie explained at length why nobody could beat the Stones. Milton left when the guest with one side of her head shaved mentioned that Mick Jagger had been discovered in bed with David Bowie.

'If it was me,' Wayne continues, still playing air guitar. 'I mean if I was you, I'd take advantage of this opportunity. Maybe you could get a job with the fire department, now that they've seen you've got the stuff. It can't hurt to try. Once you're in with them, boy, you've got a job for life. Once you're in with them they'll loan you twenty-five G's just like that.' He snaps his fingers.

Last night Milton dreamt that he'd told Ariel he had a present for her when he didn't. As she walked towards him cautiously, hopefully, he tried desperately to think of something to give her. Before he had to admit he had nothing he woke, sweating. Then he dreamt he saw the girl from the fire on a park bench. As he hurried towards her, he realized that her wrists were dripping with blood. He woke from this dream feeling Ariel stroking his forehead, comforting him. Then he remembered she was dead and wondered if it was her spirit. He switched the lights on and sat very still waiting for the spirit to materialize. He challenged the spirit, saying if it was Ariel, it would have the guts to show itself. Nothing happened except that the tick of the clock and the sounds of the house creaking and cars passing began to reverberate in his head.

More than anything he wants to know how someone so young could want to die. He hopes that, by rescuing her, he has given her a new lease on life, that before she lost consciousness, her life flashed before her eyes and she realized that she wanted to live. He hopes that she has decided to get off the streets, find a decent job and live a normal life. Maybe she is grateful to Milton. Maybe she's searching for him as he is for her, and they are destined to meet and share their newly discovered passion for life. On TV, a disillusioned Vietnam vet and a foul-mouthed teenage prostitute got trapped in a car crushed by a collapsing motorway during an earthquake. She'd been hitch-hiking, and he'd just picked her up. During the hours they spent together—faced with the possibility of being flattened by concrete—they exchanged life stories. It showed flashbacks of when he was tortured by gooks, and she was beaten by pimps. By the end of the movie they realized that, in spite of everything, they really wanted to live. When a rescue team finally freed them, a crowd had gathered, cheering the hooker and the vet. Milton liked this ending and wouldn't mind something like this happening to him and the girl. But he can't see it. If she hasn't killed herself by now she's probably planning to. Only this time it won't be a burning house but something less visible, something she can do in a dark corner of the city, unnoticed by passers-by.

All he can think about is saving her. He has this idea that, if he can save her, he can save himself.

The fire department gave him the name of the social worker supposedly in touch with the girl, but the social worker hadn't heard from her. When she asked Milton why he wanted to make contact with 'Teresa', he couldn't think of a good answer. Finally he said, 'To see if she's alright.' After a long pause in which Milton stared at the plant on her desk and the social worker tapped her chin with her pencil, she suggested he look for Teresa in the donut shop at Queen and McCaul. She also warned him that he should be aware that she sniffs a litre of glue a day. Milton has spent the last two days in and out of that donut shop, but he hasn't seen her. He wonders how it's possible to sniff a litre of glue a day. She must spend hours with her face in a plastic bag.

'Have you seen Ellie yet?' Wayne asks.

'Who?'

'Ellie. From school? You took her to the prom.'

'What's she doing here?'

'She read about you in the paper. She wanted to come.'

'You're friends with her?'

'We met at the reunion that you were too snot-faced to come to.'

Wayne made Milton take Ellie to the prom. She was friends with Wayne's girlfriend. Milton hadn't intended to go to the prom, claimed that he thought it was stupid, although really he was just scared to ask anyone in case they said no. Ellie wore a lilac dress that was loose around the bust and too long. Each time she tripped she'd apologize to Milton. 'It's okay,' he said repeatedly. Because everyone else stayed up all night, so did Milton and Ellie. They parked her father's car on the lakeshore to watch the sun rise like the other kids. When she asked him if he wanted a blow job he said nothing because he felt embarrassed. She took this to mean 'yes', unzipped his fly and bent her head down. He didn't stop her because he'd never had a blow job, had heard about them and knew they were supposed to be great. But it just felt awkward having his penis in this girl's mouth. He couldn't get hard and was afraid she'd tell everybody, and they'd declare him a fag. He concentrated on getting hard, tried to imagine that Ellie was Bridgit Bardot, but it didn't work. It began to feel like she'd suck his penis right off. Finally he pushed her away and said it was all right. 'What's wrong?' she asked.

'It's alright,' he repeated. He could tell from her desolate expression that she thought she'd failed. He didn't tell her otherwise, hoped that if she believed she'd failed she wouldn't tell everybody he couldn't get hard.

'Forget about it,' he said, staring at the crushed roses on the corsage Wayne had forced him to buy her. She started to cry and confessed that she was afraid of going all the way, that she'd do anything else but was afraid of getting pregnant. Milton didn't admit that he'd had no intentions of going all the way or that he'd never been all the way, because she'd think he was a fag. So he said nothing, only shifted his stare to the pink spreading above the water. 'I'm sorry,' she said, sniffling. At that moment Milton wanted to hit her, to make her stop crying, apologizing, saying anything, doing anything. He wanted to get out and walk. But then everybody in the other cars would see that they weren't getting it on. 'Let's just sit here,' he told her. And they did, until daylight obliterated the drama of prom night and cars began to pull out of the parking lot. Driving her home, he turned the radio on and listened to love songs interspersed with traffic and weather reports. He said he'd call her, but he never did, and he always pretended not to see her in the school corridors.

'What's she doing here?' he asks again.

'She wanted to see you.'

'Why?'

'For old times' sake, I guess. I don't know. Anyways, there's something you should know about her.'

'What?'

'She's got multiple sclerosis.'

Milton doesn't know what multiple sclerosis is exactly except that it's some horrible, incurable disease.

'She can hardly walk,' Wayne explains. 'Pretty soon she'll be in a wheelchair.'

There are incidents in Milton's life that he would like to forget; hitting Judith for example or forcing himself on Meredith Warner because he'd wanted to get his 'first time' over with or aiming spitballs at Ralph the midget because everybody else was doing it. Milton has been cruel in his time, and he hopes that, by forgetting the people, he can forget the cruelty. But now one of his victims has turned up in his house.

'Anyways, she doesn't like it when people feel sorry for her,' Wayne cautions. 'So act normal. I mean as far as she's concerned she's not sick. That's what she says. She thinks she's going to walk again.'

Milton doesn't want to see her, doesn't want to be reminded. He feels guilty, as though he started her disabling process by humiliating her, by allowing her to believe she gave lousy blow jobs. It would have been so easy to tell the truth. He crippled her. You only get one chance at the truth, Judith says. After that you can't expect them to believe you. Like Ariel, after admitting he has no present. Things can never be the same.

'Okay so who is this girl you rescued?' Judith asks. He can tell from the way she says 'rescued' that she doesn't believe it.

'Some street kid.'

'How did you know she was in the house?'

'I didn't.'

'So why did you go in?'

'I thought there might be somebody inside.'

Judith raises her eyebrows, looking skeptical.

Waiting around for Teresa in the donut shop, Milton had been forced to listen to pop music. Every song was about loving someone. The singers sounded so sure they loved whoever they were singing about. Looking at Judith, Milton wishes he was sure he loved her. One guy was singing about if you're happier in another man's arms run to him. Another guy was singing about how he'd do anything to get the girl back if only she'd give him half a chance. Milton wanted to kick in the speakers to stop the songs from invading his mind and making him feel like a loser because he didn't love somebody like the guys singing the songs did. It seems to Milton there's no way a person can figure out what he's feeling when there's always some joker on the radio singing about what he's feeling.

'So where's the Goof?' he asks.

'The who?'

'What's-his-face. Your bodyguard. He must've gone for a piss.'

'That's really mature.'

'Well he's been sticking to you like glue.'

'He's concerned about me. With good reason don't you think? Considering you've hit me and threatened to kill me?'

'I didn't threaten to kill you.'

'So what were you doing pointing a gun at me?'

'I thought you were a robber.'

'Even after you turned the lights on?'

'You shouldn't have been snooping around anyway.'

'Milton, can't you see how you do that? You turn things around so you can blame me for your fuckups.'

'Why didn't you call first?'

'Because I wanted to make it easier.'

'So you come snooping around at night terrifying my mother.'

Judith sighs heavily and leans against the wall, crossing her arms. 'Let's not fight, okay? I don't want to fight. I came over here to have a civilized conversation.'

Two nights ago Milton dreamt that he and Judith were still together. She told him that she'd slept with her aerobics instructor. She said it as though it was a perfectly normal thing to do. He waited for her to express remorse, or guilt, but all she did was laundry. He can't remember how it happened, but suddenly he was holding her by the ankles and wrists and swinging her around like a sack of potatoes. He started bashing her into the floor, but she became amorphous, boneless. He kept slamming her into the concrete, terrified that he would kill her but angry that the beating was having no effect.

'So,' she continues, 'did you really save this girl, or were you looking after your own ass, and she just happened to be there?'

'If I was looking after my own ass I wouldn't go into a burning building would I?'

'That all depends.'

'On what?'

'On your intentions.'

'What's that supposed to mean?' He pretends to be preoccupied with the tapes so he doesn't have to look at her.

'Milton, if you kill yourself, I'll never forgive you.'

'Who said anything about killing myself?' He hates how she thinks she knows everything.

'Just don't, okay?' He can't believe she's touching his arm. How dare she touch his arm when she's touching the Goof. 'I'm not kidding, Milton. I couldn't stand it. I'm begging you, okay? Promise?'

He moves away from her, forcing her to drop her hand. He knows that by not responding, by not even looking at her, he will defeat her. He stares down at the box of tapes, absently scuffing it with his boot.

'Hello, Milton,' Terry says. 'Congratulations on your heroism.'

'Why don't you go fuck yourself.'

'Oh, Milton, for god's sake,' Judith pleads.

'I was hoping we could at least be civil with each other,' Terry says, 'for Judith's sake.'

Milton ignores him then stares at Judith, wishing he had dark glasses, like Connie's, so she couldn't see his eyes. If she couldn't see his eyes, he could scare her. 'If there's anything you want here,' he says, hoping to sound menacing, 'you'd better take it now.'

'I'll take it when I want it.'

'Well, don't say I didn't warn you.'

There's no way anybody's going to call him pussy-whipped.

'If you so much as raise a finger against me,' she warns, 'I'll call the cops.'

He can't believe that only a week ago they were drinking hot chocolate together. Now it feels like they wouldn't mind bashing in each other's teeth, gouging out each other's eyes.

'Cops don't do shit.' He doesn't usually use language like this. Again he's on the outside looking in, tossing himself words to try out for effect.

'Don't try to scare me,' Judith says.

'Maybe you two should talk in the morning,' Terry suggests. 'When you're both sober.'

Milton leans into him. 'Don't tell me what to do, asshole.' He'd like to grab his collar and lift him up like they do on TV, but Terry's wearing a V-neck sweat shirt. 'Listen to me asshole,' Milton tells him, stressing the 's's in ass, 'if you so much as lay a finger on my wife, I'll blow your balls off.' He emphasizes the 'b's in blow and balls and Terry steps back, bumping into the floor-lamp which Judith steadies. Then she plants herself between the two of them and jabs her palm into Milton's chest, almost winding him.

'You know what happens to little kids who get pushed around?' she demands. 'They push littler kids around. Munroe and Aiken push you around so you pick on Terry, the only decent man I've ever met.'

She smells different, of perfume. She doesn't wear perfume.

'Take a good look at yourself, Milton,' she says. 'You've got problems.'

'I don't have problems. You've got problems.'

'The only problem I have is you.'

'Your daughter's only been dead seven months, and you're out screwing this doorknob.'

'For your information, we're not "screwing" because I haven't felt ready for it.' She leans in so close to him that her breath burns his face. 'But now I feel ready for it. So go ahead and kill yourself for all I care. Do us all a favour.' She grabs Terry's arm and leads him out the front door. For a brief second Milton panics, believing he'll never see her again, that she actually is walking out of his life. But then it doesn't feel like any of this is really happening. He looks around to see if anyone else has witnessed the exchange. If it really was happening, they'd all be staring at him. He remembers Cheryl Ladd and Kris Kristofferson arguing. She told him to go to hell, and people stared at her. Then Cheryl got tears in her eyes and said 'you bastard'. Milton wouldn't mind if Judith got tears in her eyes and said 'you bastard'. He could put his arms around her like Kris did. If she got tears in her eyes, he'd know she loved him.

He presses his face against the window, cupping his hands around his eyes so he can see into the night. Judith stands by the car, resting her hands on the roof and her forehead on her hands. Terry puts his arm around her shoulders, bobbing his head up and down as he talks. He pulls Judith away from the car and wraps his arms around her. She rests her forehead against his shoulder, letting her arms hang limp at her sides.

'Fuck 'em,' Milton says, turning abruptly from the window and nearly knocking down a woman with emaciated legs, pushing a metal walker. 'Sorry,' he mutters.

'That's alright.'

He tries not to stare. Her knees cave inward, her feet drag along the floor, her shoulders hunch from the effort it takes to shift the walker. She moves slowly, like a crab; first the walker, then her feet. Milton feels cornered.

'Remember me?' she asks. 'I'm Ellie, from high-school days.

We went to the prom together.'

He considers pretending not to remember then realizes this would only humiliate her more. 'How are you?' he asks, immediately regretting the question, realizing that she can't possibly be fine.

'I'm fine,' she says. 'I read about your act of heroism.'

The skin on her neck looks like leather that's been left in the rain and dried. She's his age. Her skin shouldn't look like this.

She leans heavily on the walker. 'I have a story to tell you. It's a sad story, but I'd like to tell it to you so that you can understand how you've helped me.' He notices that her right hand seems locked into a fist. She grips the walker between her thumb and curled fingers. 'I had a cat,' she begins, 'that I loved very much. I found her at the SPCA. Her previous owner had starved her then slit her throat and placed food in front of her. Fortunately, the neigbours followed her path of blood and found her and called the SPCA. When I adopted her, she was very frightened and mistrustful. For months she wouldn't come near me. I could feel her watching me, but she wouldn't approach. The SPCA only let me take her on the condition that I wouldn't let her outside. As I spend most of my time inside, this was no hardship for me. But the cat must have missed the outdoors because she always made a dash for the door when I was coming or going.'

Milton wonders why she's telling him this, if multiple sclerosis affects the brain.

'One day the cat got out, and as I am unable to run, I couldn't catch her. My neighbours were good enough to make a superficial search, but no one had the time to scout the entire building. It was assumed that the cat would return home. I really need to sit down.'

'What?'

'I need to sit. Could you pull a chair over for me?'

'Sure.' He does, and she slowly lowers herself into it.

'That evening my cat was found in one of the dryers. Someone had pushed her into a dryer and turned it on. I am told it was very bloody and that her paws were burned.'

Milton wants to be affected by this story, but all he can see is a cartoon cat going around and around in a dryer, its eyes bulging, its hair standing on end.

'I can't understand this about people,' Ellie continues, covering the fisted right hand in her lap with her left. 'I have to believe that we aren't born evil, that basically we are good and that the hardships of time can make us evil. I've tried very hard to understand what would make someone torture a cat, what would drive a person to that. But I can't.' She looks at Milton as though expecting an answer. He thinks about the neighbour's cat, staring at him. He wouldn't mind somebody tossing it into a dryer.

'Anyway,' she adds, 'then I read about you, and it restored my faith in humankind.' She uses her hands to pull her left leg closer to her right then grips the armrests and pushes herself further back in the chair. Milton looks away, not wanting to stare. He can't imagine not being able to move his legs. 'I can't do much now,' she says, 'which means I spend a fair amount of time thinking, and some of that time is spent rehashing old times. For the most part, I think about how lucky I was to be free of illness and how I didn't know it. But I also think about the people I've misjudged or wronged in some way. And always I want to make amends. I feel that if I can free my conscience, I can free my body. So when I read about you I tried to remember you, and what I had done to make you dislike me so much.' She stares at him. He shifts his weight from one foot to the other. 'Why didn't you like me, Milton? Don't be afraid of insulting me.'

'I liked you.'

'No, you didn't.'

'I didn't know you. Except for that night.'

'You knew me from school.'

'Yeah, but I didn't really know you. I mean you were Wayne's girlfriend's friend.' Milton is sick of dying people. All they want to do is have meaningful conversations.

'What I've been discovering more and more,' she explains, 'is that I don't like the people who I'm afraid don't like me. Did you think I didn't like you?'

'No.'

'Were you afraid I wouldn't like you because you couldn't get an erection?'

He glances around to see if anyone has heard. 'No,' he mutters.

136

She continues to stare at him, like his mother, like Connie, like Judith, like the cat. 'I don't know what you want from me,' he blurts out. He'd like to kick her chair over, make her stop talking at him. He can't stand how nice she is, how saintly she is. If it was him who was crippled, he'd be pissed. There's no way he'd sit around worrying about the pus bags in his life who ticked him off.

'Alright,' she assures him. 'That's fine. You don't have to say anything. Just let me say that I like you, and I admire you very much for risking your life for someone else's.'

He shrugs, thinking that maybe if enough people think he's a hero he will become a hero. Just as when everybody thought he was a loser he became a loser. The problem is it just feels like he knows something they don't and that, if he wants to stay a hero, he'd better keep his mouth shut. He wonders if all heros feel this way. JFK for example. He kept quiet about being a sex addict. Rock Hudson kept quiet about having AIDS, John Lennon about being anorexic. It makes sense that all heros have something to hide since they're only human. This is how Milton justifies not telling the truth. It seems to him that, as Winnie would say, what they don't know won't hurt them, and he might as well enjoy the glory while it lasts. Except it doesn't feel like glory. He wonders if soldiers who get awarded medals feel glorified or if they see the suffering of their victims over and over in their heads. In his own mind Milton sees the girl's face over and over and hears her saying she wanted to die.

'So Milton,' Ellie concludes, offering her normal hand. 'It's an honour to know you.'

He'd always thought that if everybody respected him, he'd respect himself. But all he feels is dirty.

'Same here.' Her hand feels like driftwood. 'Can I get you anything? Some punch or anything?'

'No, thanks.'

'Okay, well, I have to go upstairs and check on my mother. She's sick.'

'You do that.'

He climbs the stairs, feeling her staring at him, feeling as though she'll never move from the chair but will sit there hunched like a gargoyle, watching him, judging him, forever.

His mother sits on the end of the bed, her face inches from the TV.

'You shouldn't sit so close,' Milton tells her.

'I can't see. Who are those people?'

'What people?'

'Don't be a smarty. The people in this house.'

'They're friends of Connie's.'

'That slut.'

'She's your daughter. I don't think you should go calling her a slut.'

'She's not my daughter.'

'Whose then?'

'She's adopted.'

'Yeah, right.' He kicks one of his sneakers under the bed.

'It's true.'

'She even looks like you.'

'She does not.'

'If she's adopted, why didn't you mention it before?'

'I did. Nobody listens. You're all just letting me die, letting me be dead.'

Milton pretends to be engrossed in the TV. 'So what are you watching?'

'I want those people out.'

'They'll be going soon.'

'An old woman can't sleep in this house.'

'It won't happen again.'

The phone rings. It's Winnie's mother wanting to know why he isn't home yet. She threatens to come and get him if he isn't home shortly. Milton says Winnie went out for Coke and will be back soon.

Mare shuffles over to the door and peers out. 'They're still in there.'

'Who?'

'In the toilet. They've been in there for hours, and I need to go.'

'How do you know someone's in there? Maybe they left and closed the door.'

'You go see.'

He pushes open the bathroom door and switches on the light.

'There's no one in here.'

'There was before. There's always somebody in the bathroom in this house. I'm sick to death of it.'

'Do you want me to get you anything? Juice or anything?'

'Why would I want juice?'

'I don't know. I just thought maybe you'd be thirsty, stuck up here.'

'Maybe you want to poison me. I wrote in my will I want an autopsy, so don't think you can get away with it. I wouldn't put it past that sister of yours.'

'I thought you said you had to go.'

'That's no business of yours.' She shuffles into the bathroom, rubbing her abdomen. 'I want those people out.' She closes the door, and he walks down the hall thinking that maybe, in Ariel's room, he can find some peace. He switches on the light revealing Winnie flat on his back on the bed with his pants down and Connie giving him a hand job. Winnie lets out a yelp when he sees Milton, but Connie seems unphased.

'What the hell do you think you're doing?' Milton demands.

'Lighten up,' Connie tells him. 'It's his birthday.'

'Get off him!' Milton grabs her arm, pulling her off the bed. Winnie groans and rolls onto his side, pulling his knees into his stomach.

'What's the problem?' Connie asks. 'It's not like I'm raping him. He's still a virgin if that's what you're worried about.'

'You're disgusting.'

'He wanted it.'

Winnie sobs. 'I'm sorry, Milton.'

'What the hell got into you?' Milton asks.

'Great,' Connie says, 'so now you're going to make him feel guilty about having normal sexual urges. That's brilliant.'

'Shut up.'

'You're such a fucking hypocrite. Maybe I should've invited you to watch.'

Winnie sobs louder. Milton leans over him and shakes his shoulder. 'Pull your pants up.'

'I'm sorry, Milton,' he whimpers.

'What's the fucking problem here?' Connie demands. 'The guy's almost thirty years old. He can look after himself. Don't you think it's about time he didn't have to jerk off by himself?'

'You're disgusting.'

'I'm disgusting? You're just pissed off because I didn't offer to do you.' She stares at him. He can't decide what to do: hit her, strangle her, walk out? The clouds painted on the walls are spinning. 'Is that the problem, big brother? Will that get you through your little mid-life thing? Because I've just about had it with your fucking little temper tantrums.' She's talking so fast Milton thinks she must be coked out. As she gets off the bed her breasts bounce at him under her T-shirt. 'Is that the problem? You're jealous because I didn't offer to jerk you off? Or suck you off, is that what you want? Because I don't mind doing it. It makes no difference to me.' Abruptly she cups her hands over his balls and begins to massage. It sickens him to feel blood rushing to his groin. He slaps her hand away, trying to think of something to say that will humiliate her as she has humiliated him. But all he can think about is how disgusting he is to have been aroused by his sister. 'You're disgusting,' he repeats.

'Oh, Milton, take the rod out of your ass.'

'I've got to get home,' Winnie howls, still on the bed struggling to pull up his trousers.

Connie turns to him. 'Winnie, you've got nothing to be ashamed of. Don't let a repressed asshole like Milton make you feel bad. Repressed assholes always try to bring you down.'

Milton grips her arm and pulls her towards the door. 'Just get out.'

'Don't you want to hit me or anything? Like you hit your wife? Or maybe you want to look at my tits.' She pulls up her T-shirt and her breasts lurch at him, the nipples brown and hard. 'You're all such a bunch of fucking fakes.' She yanks her T-shirt back down. 'Winnie at least isn't afraid to admit what he wants. Although, now that you're doing a number on him he'll probably be repressed for life.'

'I don't want you in my house.'

'Fine. I don't want to be in your fucking house, with your fucking hangups and your fucking mother. I'd rather be on the street where assholes like you can't do control numbers on me. I thought maybe it would be nice to live with my big brother. But all I got was another pervert staring at me.'

Milton's mouth twitches. He covers it with his hand.

'I would've thought you of all people would get off my case,' she adds. 'How would you feel if everybody acted like your daughter dying didn't matter? My baby died, and you all act like it never happened, like she deserved to die because I'm a bad person. Who's to say who's a bad person? Just because I didn't get some shit job and marry some dumb fuck who hits me, the rest of you act like there's something wrong with me.'

'You lie,' Milton manages to interject.

'Who says? Mandy? The hag? You all want to believe I lie because you can't handle what's happened to me. You're thinking, where were you the last ten years, how could you let this happen to your little sister? Well let me tell you something, brother, if I'd had a decent family, I wouldn't be the fuckup I am today.'

Milton remembers Judith accusing him of turning things around so that he can blame her for his fuckups. He thinks maybe she has a point.

'But at least I know I'm a fuckup.' Connie tucks her T-shirt into her jeans. 'The rest of you act like your shit doesn't smell. The truth is your heads are so far up your own assholes you think smelling shit is normal. Winnie, I'm leaving. Don't feel bad, okay? You didn't do anything wrong. Don't let this control freak do a number on you.'

'Get out, and take your friends with you,' Milton tells her.

'They're not my friends. They're kids who don't have anywhere to go. You tell them to get out.' She flings the door open revealing Mare hovering in the hallway.

'What's going on here?' she demands.

'Nothing,' Connie says, 'I'm leaving.'

'Just as well.' Mare rubs her abdomen. Milton hears Connie run down the stairs. He wishes he could play back the past few minutes so that he can understand them.

'Mother, go back to my room.'

She squints at Ariel's bed. 'Who's that?'

'Just Winnie.'

'Is he sick?'

'No.'

'Too much drinking.'

'No, everything's fine. Just go watch TV.'

'Some friends you have,' she comments. 'You can always tell a person by the company he keeps.'

'Would you just leave please?'

'Throw cold water on him.' She waves her hand dismissively and starts down the hall.

Milton closes the door and looks at Winnie who still doesn't have his pants back on.

'Stand up to do that,' Milton advises. Winnie does, meekly, with his head bowed. Perspiration stains the armpits of his cowboy shirt.

'She made me do it,' he mumbles.

'Don't go blaming her for it.'

Milton can't get over Connie calling him a control freak. He hates control freaks, like Munroe and Aiken. Or the sleazebag politicians and corporation heads. They're always out to control people's minds. But he, Milton, doesn't do that. He keeps to himself, lets the assholes do what they want. He wasn't trying to control Connie; he just wanted to make sure she didn't end up dead in an alley somewhere. Or Judith, he wasn't trying to control her; he just didn't want her on his case all the time. Or Ellie, he didn't ask her to give him a blow job. If she hadn't gone down on him, he wouldn't have had to lie to her. It seems to him it's the women who are the control freaks. They're always talking at him or shaking their tits at him. And they're always doing it because they want something. Never just to have a good time.

'I'm really sorry, Milton,' Winnie murmurs.

'Forget about it.'

Judith told Milton he likes Winnie because he can push him around. She said he couldn't push Munroe and Aiken around so he pushed Terry around. So maybe he is a control freak. Except he has no control. Judith walked out on him; Connie walked out on him. Maybe you don't have to be in control to be a control freak. Maybe you can make yourself crazy trying to be in control. Maybe, if he had control, he'd turn into a slimeball like Munroe and Aiken:

leaving rats on peoples' cars.

'I did a bad thing,' Winnie admits. 'If Mum finds out she's going to kill me.'

'Your mum's not going to find out, and you didn't do a bad thing.'

'My soul's tainted.'

'Your soul's fine.'

~

In the kitchen Wayne, slurring now, is talking to Buzz about his bank charging him twice in one year for his safety deposit box. 'So I says no way am I paying you another cent. I says you assholes with your computers try to rip off guys like me, but no way you're going to get away with it this time. So they say do I have a receipt and I says no fucking way, I just moved and there's no fucking way I'm going to empty all my stuff to look for it. I says they should have it in their computers, and if they don't, I'm going to start kicking ass.'

'You said that?' Buzz asks dubiously, scratching his armpit.

'Damn right.'

'So what'd they say?'

'They said they'd look into it.'

Milton scoops up the last of some potato chips in a bowl. 'Why don't you just forget about it?'

Wayne looks at him. 'What?'

'You're not going to get it if you don't have the receipt, so why make yourself crazy?'

'Those assholes make big money shafting guys like us.'

'So what are you going to do?' Milton asks. 'Sue them?'

'I might.'

'I'd just forget about it.' Milton brushes the salt from the chips off his hands.

'Bullshit you would. You'd want to nail those bastards.'

'No, I wouldn't.' Milton pushes open the back door and walks out onto the grass. It seems to him a person can spend a lot of time being ticked off. The truth of it is, none of it matters, because you could be dying. Or crippled. It seems to him that everybody's dying or crippled. Or blind. It seems to him a miracle that he's not dying or crippled or blind. When Judith talks about living in the present, because you may not be here tomorrow, he argues that the present sucks, he'd rather live somewhere else. But maybe it's possible to live in the present without feeling like it's really happening. When he watches people being killed on TV he has to remind himself that it's not really happening. When he watches people being killed on the news he has to remind himself that it is really happening. What if he quit reminding himself one way or the other? Maybe he already has. Maybe that's why he has no feelings. And maybe, now that Judith isn't around to nag him, he shouldn't worry about it. If he had feelings he might go around sawing off people's heads. Maybe he should count himself lucky.

He hears screams inside the house and runs in to find his mother at the top of the stairs brandishing her gun.

'I want you people out,' she shouts. 'Freeloaders is what you are.' She stumbles, leans against the wall and slumps to the floor. He takes the stairs two at a time then squats beside her, trying to find her pills in her housecoat. When he can't, he grabs her wrist and feels for a pulse, wondering if he should do CPR on her. The course was compulsory at work, but he suspects it's easier to do on a dummy than on your mother. He slides his hands under her arms and stretches her out on the floor then tilts her head back, pinching her nose between his fingers. Looking down at her lizard eyes and papery lips he thinks there's no way he's going to be able to put his mouth on hers. He presses his ear to her chest, listening for a heart beat, but all he can hear is his own heart thundering in his skull. 'Jesus christ,' he mutters, pulling her chin down to open the air passage. Her mouth gapes at him, blackened with fillings, her grey tongue lolling to one side. He inhales, leaning back to avoid her old meat smell, then fits his mouth over hers and exhales. Immediately she coughs up remnants of Kraft dinner. He leans back, wiping his face, and sees Connie's guests—the ones that didn't run—staring at him.

~

He sits on the bed waiting for his mother to regain full consciousness.

144

'What are you staring at?' she asks.

'Are you alright?'

'Did I have an attack?'

'I don't know, maybe you just fainted.'

She pulls her housecoat tight around her neck. 'I'm sick to death of this. I might as well be dead.'

It relieves him to see that she doesn't remember the CPR or anyway, isn't going to mention it.

'Did they leave?' she asks.

'Some of them.'

'I want them out.'

'They're homeless.'

'So am I, and do you see me sponging off strangers?'

'You're not homeless.'

'You don't want me here.'

He doesn't argue. Sees no point in it.

'You have no idea how you treat me. You think I have no feelings.' She snatches a Kleenex from the bedside table and wipes her nose. Tears catch in the wrinkles around her eyes. He wonders if she's crying or just reacting to the attack.

'Anyways,' he warns, 'you shouldn't go waving that gun around.'

'What am I supposed to do? You saw what happened to the blind man.'

'Have you got a permit for it?'

'That's no business of yours.'

'If you don't have a permit you could get arrested.'

'So?'

'You can't go around threatening to kill people. I mean sometime you might have to do it. And then you'll have to go to jail.'

She folds her hands on her stomach. 'I'd hide the gun.'

'The cops will find it.'

'They never find anything.

'They find people all the time.'

'They never find anybody,' she insists. 'All they do is eat donuts. I hate them. If they find me, I'll blow my brains out right in front of them. Old people get mugged every day, and you think they do anything about it? We might as well be dead.'

'It's against the law.'

'Okay, if you're such a smarty, tell me how I'm supposed to protect myself, an old woman. You tell me what to do, and I'll do it.'

Give up and die, he thinks. What's the point of going around scared all the time, hating all the time? In his head he hears Judith saying 'You hate everything and everybody'. On TV, a woman who had cancer cured herself by meditating and learning to love herself. The shrink with the hairy mole told Milton he had to love himself before he could love Judith. Milton can't see how a person can love himself when he knows every dirty, stinking thing about himself.

So what's his mother got to live for, when she hates everything and everybody? And herself.

'Maybe you should just let whatever happens, happen,' he suggests. 'I mean you can't go around scared all the time.'

'Easy for you to say.' She wipes the tears off her cheeks. 'If I had a decent son, he'd look after me.'

He thinks of Connie saying, if she'd had a decent family, she wouldn't be the fuckup she is today. It seems to him everybody's got a story. And nobody wants to hear it.

'Maybe you should call Leonard,' he suggests.

'Leonard has a career to worry about.'

Milton suspects she knows that Leonard's a fag but won't admit it. 'Anyways, you're alright now. You should try to get some sleep.'

'I didn't ask to come here.'

'I know.' She looks pathetic to him, dried up and abandoned, beyond repair. All she can hope for is to die peacefully in her sleep. All he can hope for is to die quickly in a car crash, hit from the side so he doesn't see it coming.

He understands that this is no way to live.

He tucks the covers around her. 'Go to sleep now.'

'I raised four kids on my own.'

'I know.'

'You'd think the least you could do is make sure I don't get murdered.'

'I won't let that happen.'

'You say that now.'

'I won't.'

And he wonders if he did save her life, if she'd needed the jump-start of his breath. Either way it doesn't matter because the fact is, he did try. He didn't let her die, even though he doesn't like her. This comforts him.

'Sleep tight,' he says.

'Are you going to bed now, too?'

Ariel always asked that, anxiously, as though afraid of sleeping while he was awake because she might miss something.

'I'm going to clean up a bit first.'

'I'll make eggs in the morning.'

'Okay.'

He closes the door to his daughter's room carefully, as though his daughter were in it. The familiar but forgotten action sends a message to his brain, and he can smell her, feel her, hear her short breaths signaling sleep. It's not fair that he didn't know that her little body contained his life, that there was no point to anything without her. If he'd known, he would have been more careful. He should have been more careful. He shouldn't have let her out of his sight. For an instant, he feels her hugging his leg and hiding her face in his thigh the way she did when strangers remarked on how pretty she was. He reaches down to cup the back of her head to comfort her then realizes that she isn't there, never will be there, ever again. Suddenly it feels as though his ribs are cutting into his lungs. He sits on the stairs, gasping, choking then slams his forehead into his knees. Pain shoots into his neck. His eyes leak hot water, scalding his face. Then there's a girl with a nose ring in front of him patting his foot, reminding him of the millions of times he lifted Ariel up so that she could touch the toe of the Timothy Eaton statue. He told her it would bring good luck. Everybody always says touching Timothy Eaton's toe brings good luck. The toe is shiny from everybody touching it.

He couldn't cry at the funeral. Couldn't cry in front of his wife. Now he's crying in front of a stranger with a nose ring. Again he slams his forehead into his knees. He's too fucking late. Always too late.

THIRTEEN

It's while he's bent over scrubbing the cheese balls out of the broad-loom that his back goes out. He gasps, falls to his knees then freezes, telling himself not to panic but to breath normally and crawl towards the couch. But each time he inches his left knee forward, the pain shoots from his lower back, across his buttock into his leg.

'What's going on down here?' Mare asks, gripping the banister, taking the stairs one at a time.

'Nothing. What are you doing up?'

'What do you mean what am I doing up? It's almost noon.' She peers at him. 'Your back hurting?'

'Yes.'

'That's because you're getting old. It only gets worse.'

After hiding Mare's gun under his mattress this morning, Milton decided it was time to make a fresh start now that Judith was gone. He decided he would try to be a decent human being. He phoned Winnie to apologize, but Winnie's mother said he was sick.

He fed the last of Connie's guests Cheerios, told them that if they wanted to stay longer they could. But they seemed eager to be on their way. Milton couldn't determine if they left because they didn't want to be in a house with a crazy old lady with a gun or because they didn't want to be in a house with him with a gun. He wanted to explain that he wasn't a bad person, that they could relax, that he empathized with the homeless, could even see how he himself could be homeless. But they didn't seem to want to talk to him, only to each other about people who weren't present. The girl with the nose ring described another girl as a cock-sucking bitch. It surprised Milton to hear such language from the girl because she'd touched his toe; but he didn't comment, not wanting to intrude. It saddened him that the teenagers treated him like just another right-wing ass-hole who thinks the homeless get what they deserve. While he was in the shower, planning his fresh start, he'd even considered taking some of them in permanently. He imagined them looking up to him, seeking his guidance as though he were an older brother. On TV, an ex-con took in some street kids, and they became one happy family. Milton had hoped that, once he'd earned their trust, the teenagers would introduce him to Teresa, tell her, 'This guy's alright. He saved his mother's life and gave us food and shelter.' But when he asked if any of them knew her, they stared at him as though he were a pervert, some guy who chases and molests defenceless street girls. He realized that they had an idea of him he couldn't control; that they wanted to believe he was a right-wing asshole because it gave them someone to blame.

'Put heat on it,' Mare tells him. 'Have you got a heating pad?'

'You're not supposed to put heat on it.'

'Who says?'

'Judith. Her chiro told her.'

'They don't know anything. All they do is take your money and crack your bones so you keep coming back. Howdy Wilson went to a chiropractor for years then found out he had cancer. Now he has to use a bag.'

All his life his mother has spoken at length to Milton about people he doesn't know.

'Norman Glerup got prostate cancer,' she elaborates. 'They

cleaned him right up, cut everything off. Imagine that. Now he has to use a bag.'

Milton, propping his elbows on the couch, begins to pull himself onto it. 'You could be worse off,' she adds. 'You shouldn't complain.'

All his life his mother has told him that he could be worse off, he shouldn't complain.

He has one knee on the couch when the phone rings.

'Cancer's getting everybody,' Mare concludes. 'It's the poisons in the atmosphere.'

'Pass me the phone?' he asks. 'Can you please pass it to me?'

'Miriam Weskel got kidney cancer, and they put her on drugs that bloated her right up. You wouldn't recognize her.'

With the other knee still on the floor, he edges along the couch to reach the phone.

'I saw her on the street,' Mare continues, 'and I didn't recognize her. She said hello, and I thought it was my memory again, then she said her name, and I couldn't believe it. She was always so petite and feminine. Now she's a tub. You wouldn't believe it.'

The pain stabs him as he picks up the receiver.

'Milton ...?' Mandy asks. 'Is that you?'

'Yeah.'

'We've got a problem. Leonard's blind in both eyes.'

He pulls his other knee onto the couch. 'So?'

'So we have to take care of him.'

'I've got Mother here.'

Mare squints at him. 'Who're you talking to?'

Mandy pauses. He can tell she's inhaling on a cigarette. 'I realize that,' she admits, 'but I've got enough problems. The landlord's told us that if we leave at the end of the month he'll forget about the six months we owe. Otherwise he's taking us to court. There's no point in getting Leonard settled here if we're just going to have to move him. I know you've got room, Milton. Connie told me what happened.'

He wonders what Connie told her, if she explained that she was masturbating his friend.

Mare approaches him. 'Who're you talking to?'

'Mandy.'

'Oh, her.' She starts arranging cushions around him.

'We can't talk with her there,' Mandy tells him. 'Can you come over?'

'My back's out. I can't move.'

'Did you take some aspirin?'

'No.'

'I'll come over. I've got some Tylenol with codeine left over from when Rory had his wisdoms out.'

Mare prods his shoulder. 'What does she want?'

'She's coming over.'

'I don't want to see her.'

'Then stay in your room.'

'You kick me around like old shoes.'

He hangs up. Mare lifts his head and shoves a cushion under his neck. 'Christ, Mother, would you just leave me alone.'

'Don't swear. Did you have a bowel movement today?'

'No.'

'You should have a bowel movement every day.'

'I usually do.' His mouth twitches.

'Have you got any Metamucil?'she asks.

'No.'

'You should have a tablespoon of Metamucil every day.'

'I'm sure I will have a bowel movement.'

'You get back pain when you're constipated. It builds up and puts pressure on your nerves.'

'Mother, I'm just going to lie here, alright? Just let me lie here. You should call your doctor and tell him you had an attack last night. Maybe you should go see him.'

'He doesn't know anything.'

'Well, then you should rest.'

'I'm sick to death of resting. All you people want me to do is rest. I might as well be dead.'

~

Mandy hands him three Tylenol No. 3s and a glass of water. 'I'm taking four of these a day now.'

151

He knows that if he asks why, she'll explain how hard her life is, so he doesn't.

'Maybe you should sit up to take them,' she suggests.

'I can't move.'

'So lift your head.'

One pill sticks in his throat. He gulps more water to wash it down then looks at Rory slouching by the front door. 'Rory, how's it going?'

The boy shrugs. 'Alright.'

Mandy takes the glass from Milton. 'Rory, why don't you go see Gramma?'

'Why?'

'Because I want to talk to Uncle Milton.'

Rory, his shoulders slumped, his pony tail hanging limp, reluctantly climbs the stairs.

'So, have you thought about Leonard?' Mandy asks. Milton shakes his head. 'He was crying on the phone,' she adds. 'He can't afford a seeing-eye dog.'

'I thought he was making good money.'

'He hasn't worked in seven months. He says they don't want him back. Especially now that he's blind.'

Milton slowly bends one knee and rests his foot flat on the couch. 'He shouldn't have quit in the first place.'

'They "advised" him to take time off, it wasn't like he wanted to. He says they just didn't want him around because they thought he'd scare off clients.'

'They were probably right.'

'Trust you to side with them.'

'Well would you want some guy who looks like a concentration-camp victim decorating your house?'

'He doesn't do houses,' Mandy reminds him. 'He does hotels.'

Milton bends his other knee.

'I think you'd better improve your attitude, Milton, before he gets here.'

Milton likes how nobody's asked him how he feels about sharing his house with a person that's got AIDS. All Leonard has to do is cut himself shaving and the virus will be all over the bathroom. He

152

says none of this because he knows Mandy will think him selfish. Instead he adjusts a cushion behind his head. 'So how am I supposed to look after him?'

'I'll help.'

'You won't be here.'

'Well, that's the other thing.'

'What?'

'If we have to get out by the end of the month … I mean maybe by some miracle Seth will get a job, and we won't have to.' She sits on the couch beside Milton's feet, gripping her handbag in her lap. 'But if we do, I was hoping you could put us up for awhile.'

'There's no room.'

'Just me and the boys. They can sleep on the floor, and I don't mind going in with Mother. I'll buy a piece of foam and stick it on the floor.' She stares at her handbag, fingering the buckle, scratches her nose nervously, then goes back to the buckle. He has never seen her speechless before, and it disturbs him. For years he has listened to her complain, knowing that she expects nothing from him, will be able to cope, will continue to oversee her small empire of husband and boys and, lately, mother. But now she's looking to him for help, and he doesn't feel strong enough. Yesterday he saw an injured pigeon on the street desperately flapping its wings, trying to escape traffic. Milton stood watching, thinking that maybe he should help, at least move it onto the sidewalk. But he was scared it would contaminate him. People always say that pigeons carry diseases. So he left the pigeon to be mashed by cars. Later he wondered who decided that pigeons were contaminated: did they know it for a fact, or did they just make it up? He can't see how moving the pigeon off the road would have contaminated him. It seems to him there's all kinds of things he doesn't do because people say he shouldn't.

He's too scared to help a pigeon; he can't see how he's supposed to help his brother.

'I'm going to apply for welfare,' she informs him. 'I'm going to tell them I'm divorcing Seth.'

'Are you?'

She shakes her head. 'I can't afford a lawyer. But there's no way I'm going to go on living with him. He keeps saying he's going to go to AA, but he never does. He says he doesn't need it; he can take care of the problem himself. Well, that's crap.' She pulls out her cigarettes. 'So now he's trying to make me feel guilty for leaving, like I'm copping out. He's the one doing the drinking. If that isn't copping out, I don't know what is. The really sick part is, I do feel guilty. Like maybe I'm impossible to live with. He's always saying it. He says he drinks because I make him crazy. I say I'm crazy because he drinks.' She lights up. 'I swear to god, sometimes when we're fighting I see myself, it's like I'm watching myself, and I hate it. I hate what happens to me around him. It's not fair to the boys, seeing me like that. Seeing him like that. If he comes home at all it's with a twelvepack. By eleven o'clock he's drunk every beer; just sitting there, vegging out.' She inhales heavily on her cigarette. 'I'm back to a pack a day now.'

'You can't go blaming him for that,' Milton says.

'Oh no? You try living with a drunk ...'

Milton knows that if he doesn't interrupt she'll go on about what a bastard Seth is and how he ruined her life. 'You can stay here,' he concedes. 'If you quit smoking.'

She stares at him as though he'd just asked for a million dollars. 'That's not fair.'

'You smoke a pack a day because he makes you crazy. So, if he's not around, you won't have to.' He likes how he has taken a stand.

'What's it matter to you if I smoke?'

'I don't want smoke in here.' This isn't true. He doesn't care about smoke. The truth is he doesn't want his sister dead. He's not sure why, since he hardly ever sees her. And when he does, she gets up his nose.

'Alright,' she agrees. 'I'll smoke in the back yard.'

He shakes his head. 'You have to quit cold turkey.'

'What's it to you if I smoke outside?'

He realizes that he has to admit that he cares about her and tries out different ways to say it in his head: 'Because I love you' or 'Because you're all I've got left'. Instead he says, 'I don't want you dead.'

'Well, thank you so much for your concern.' She hauls on her cigarette and looks around for an ashtray.

'In the dishrack.'

While she's gone, he remembers a dream he had last night in which he was trying to climb a cliff face that kept crumbling beneath him. Looking down at Judith struggling below him, he'd realized she wouldn't make it and that, for him to survive, he would have to leave her behind.

Mandy comes back with the ashtray and balances it on the arm of the easy-chair. 'So do you think Judith is ever coming back?'

'No.' He has never said this out loud, and the finality of it shocks him. He wishes he could strike it from the record like a judge. He's always wondered how the jury's supposed to forget something that's been said. When Judith used to say something he didn't fully understand he'd ask, 'What?' and she'd say, 'Forget it.' He couldn't forget it. He'd keep asking what she meant until he figured out she'd say 'Forget it' just to make him feel like an asshole who doesn't understand anything.

'I'm sorry,' Mandy says.

'About what?' How much longer, Milton wonders, will Judith be inside his head.

'About Judith.'

He doesn't want Mandy to feel sorry for him. If he weren't forced to lie on his back he'd leave before she starts saying 'maybe it's for the best'. Immobility has made him realize how often he leaves uncomfortable situations. He hears Judith say, 'You keep walking away from everything, and pretty soon you'll have nowhere to go.' He couldn't follow her logic. As it was, when he left he had nowhere to go, just out into the city, always knowing that on his return she would act like he wasn't there.

'Maybe it's a good thing,' Mandy tells him. 'I don't know how a couple is supposed to recover from losing a child.'

Mare and Rory appear at the top of the stairs. 'What's the matter with this boy? All he talks about is cars.'

'There's nothing the matter with him,' Mandy insists.

'What kind of job have you done raising this boy when all he talks about is cars?' She prods Rory's arm. 'Why don't you learn about computers?'

'Mother, leave him alone. He didn't have to come and visit you.'

155

'Why did he? I didn't ask him. All he talks about is cars.'

'He happens to be a talented mechanic.'

'How's he supposed to support you in your old age with that?' Mare leans on Rory's arm as they start down the stairs. 'All I asked was that one of my children look after me, and what happens? They can't even look after themselves, not one of them.'

'Except Leonard,' Milton reminds her, knowing she won't respond because it would mean she'd have to admit that her favourite son never visits her.

'That reminds me,' Mandy says. 'Mum, Leonard's coming to stay with Milton.'

Mare squints at her. 'What are you talking about?'

'He's sick, and he needs someone to look after him.'

Mare hesitates then shakes her head as though denying this information. Suddenly she yanks on Rory's ponytail. 'What do you need that for?'

He shrinks away from her. 'I like it.'

'What do you want to look like a girl for?'

'Lots of boys wear ponytails, Mother,' Mandy says.

'He looks like a girl.'

Mandy sighs. 'Rory, why don't you take Gramma for a walk.'

'I don't want to go for a walk.' Mare rubs her abdomen.

'The doctor said you should.'

'He doesn't know anything.'

Mandy takes some money out of her wallet. 'Just go to the corner and back. Buy some lemon loaf or cookies or something.' She hands the money to Rory. 'And pick me up some smokes. Mum, where's your coat?'

After she ushers them out, Mandy flops back into the easychair. 'You can always get her out with sugar. Lemon loaf is her favourite.' She pulls out another cigarette. 'So anyway, I told Leonard I'd talk to you then go pick him up. He says I might as well use his Jeep since he can't. Is that alright with you?'

Milton shrugs. It makes no difference to him because he's decided he's not going to be here. As soon as his back is better, he's going to find Teresa, and they're going to go away somewhere. He's going to look after her, protect her, make sure no slimeballs

156

get anywhere near her.

'That's really decent of you, Milton,' Mandy says. 'Leonard was worried. I told him, Milton's changed since his tragedy. He's much more understanding.'

Milton doesn't mind her thinking this, even if it isn't true.

'So I have another favour to ask.' She lights another cigarette. 'It's about Rory.'

Milton rubs his hands over his face, remembering that he hasn't shaved. Sliding his right hand down his neck he feels a lump.

Mandy inhales deeply. 'Remember, how I got him a Big Brother?'

Milton shakes his head still feeling the lump. It's hard, about the size of a chick pea.

'When he was seven I got him a Big Brother because I could see that Seth wasn't going to take him to a ball game or anything, and I thought that was important for a little boy.' She flicks ash into the ashtray. 'Anyways I never liked Ryan; there was something weird about him. But Rory seemed to like him, and I had enough problems looking after Morty with work and that.'

At this moment it makes perfect sense to Milton that the chick pea will grow to the size of a grapefruit and kill him.

'Anyways,' Mandy continues, 'it turns out this guy Ryan is suspected of molesting Little Brothers. Milton, are you listening?'

It makes perfect sense, now that he doesn't have anything to live for. Maybe this is the way to go. Nobody gives you a hard time when you're dying. Nobody expects anything from you. Except that you die. He knows for a fact it gets pretty boring if you don't. His father didn't die when he was supposed to, and everybody got sick of him.

'So,' Mandy says, 'I asked Rory if Ryan had ever done anything to him, and he said he didn't think so. That was two months ago. So Monday night, another Big Brother calls me and tells me that Rory told him he was molested.'

Milton decides he won't tell anybody. He'll just wait until they notice the grapefruit, then he'll shrug it off like it's no big deal.

'So I asked Rory again if Ryan sexually abused him, and he said "not exactly". Now what am I supposed to make of that? Milton?'

Except, if he dies, what happens to Teresa? If he doesn't save her, she'll go ahead and kill herself. He looks at Mandy and realizes that she's waiting for him to say something. 'Maybe he didn't exactly sexually abuse him,' he offers.

'Well, what did he do then? He must've done something. So I said, if he so much as touched you where you didn't want him to, I want to press charges. I said, if he's done it to you, you can bet he's doing it to other Little Brothers, and for their sakes, you'd better report it. So right away, Rory's acting like nothing happened.'

'Maybe it didn't.'

'Then why would he go and tell another Big Brother it did?'

Milton shrugs. 'For attention?'

'Rory wouldn't do that.'

Milton isn't sure if it's the codeine or knowing that he is about to die that has calmed him. But he feels good, sinking into the couch, now that he no longer has to worry about the rest of his life. Maybe, when he tells Teresa, she'll want to look after him. He'll get thinner and thinner, and she'll grow to love him. She'll even want to give him her young body, but he won't take it. He'll tell her to save it for the right man. 'Someone your own age,' he'll say, 'who has the rest of his life to share with you.' He'll be strong, like in the movie about the sculptor who was dying but who fell in love with a volunteer nurse. His hair fell out, and he couldn't move, but she loved him anyway. Milton wouldn't mind something like this happening.

'Milton, I need you to talk to him. He won't talk to me and god knows Seth isn't any help. When I told him, he said Rory's old enough to work it out on his own. That may be so but if Rory doesn't stand up and say something, Ryan's going to keep on molesting Little Brothers.'

'You don't know for a fact that he has been.'

'I've always known there was something weird about him.'

Milton presses on his lump. 'Then why did you let him look after Rory?'

'What was I supposed to do? I didn't have a car or any money. I couldn't take him to the movies or the zoo. You try raising two kids on your own.'

Again Milton sees his mother in his sister and wonders how long it will be before Mandy starts getting heart trouble. 'What do you want me to say to him?' he asks.

'Tell him it's not his fault Ryan's a pervert. And that he owes it to the other Little Brothers to do something about it. I don't want my son growing up with a guilty conscience.'

Milton takes his hand away from his lump. 'What makes you think he's going to want to talk to me about it?'

'He likes you. I think he tries to be like you. Laid back. He's always telling me I get hysterical.'

Rory thinks he's laid back; Connie thinks he's repressed; Judith thinks he has no feelings; Mare thinks he feels sorry for himself. Wayne thinks he'd want to nail the bastards; Ellie thinks he's a hero; Munroe and Aiken think he's pussy-whipped; the homeless think he's a right-wing asshole. Milton can't see how a person is supposed to know who he is when everybody's always telling him about it. He remembers Sammy Davis Jr. singing 'I gotta be me'. He'd envied Sammy for being sure of who he was and feeling he had to be himself. It made sense since he was rich and famous. Anybody who's rich and famous would feel they had to be themselves. But Milton has never felt that he's gotta be himself, he'd much rather be someone else, Bruce Willis or somebody.

Mandy kicks off her shoes. 'So are you going to tell me what happened with Connie?'

He watched a show once about AA. One of the alcoholics said that he was afraid to face himself, but that when he stopped drinking and got to know himself, it wasn't so bad. Milton can't get excited about knowing himself. He thinks again about the woman who cured herself of cancer by loving herself, and the shrink with the hairy mole telling him he had to love himself before he could love Judith. It seems to him everybody's going on about loving themselves before they can love anybody else whereas, it seems to Milton, it works the other way around. Loving his daughter made him feel good about himself. He didn't have to think about loving himself. He was so filled with love for her it spilled over onto himself. He thinks sitting around worrying about loving yourself could make a person crazy. Maybe if people worried less about loving themselves, and loved somebody else for a change, there wouldn't be wars and pollution.

So why couldn't he love Judith?

'Milton, are you stoned?'

He looks at his sister, with her cigarette, her creased brow, her thinning lips, and he tries to love her.

'I used to get stoned by them,' she admits. 'But now I'm used to them. The only problem with codeine is it constipates you.' She massages one of her feet. 'Anyways, Connie told me you came on to her. I didn't believe her because she's always saying guys come on to her. She said Seth tried to rape her. She said she was on the couch reading, and he asked her to feel how stiff his dick was. I don't believe it. I've never seen her read in my life.'

He wanted to love Judith. He just wasn't comfortable around her. It was like every word he said was wrong before he even said it.

Rory pushes open the door for Mare who's clutching her lemon loaf. She shuffles across the floor and peers at Milton. 'Where's my gun?'

He's been waiting for her to bring this up. 'In a safe place.'

'Mother,' Mandy chides, 'have you been bringing that gun out again?'

'It's my gun. I want it.'

'I'll give it to you later,' Milton tells her.

'I want it now.'

Mandy winks at Milton. 'Seth took her bullets.'

'I've got plenty of bullets,' Mare declares. 'I want it back. I paid for it.'

'Where'd you buy it is what I want to know,' Mandy says.

'That's no business of yours. I'm not eating till I get it.'

Mandy shrugs. 'Suit yourself.'

'I have to go find it,' Milton interjects, 'and my back's out. As soon as I'm feeling better I'll get it for you.'

'You say that now.'

'I will.'

'You take advantage of me because I'm old.'

Gripping her lemon loaf she reminds him of a rat sitting on its haunches clutching a piece of cheese. He tries to love her.

'A woman shot her mother then her budgie then herself,' she tells them.

'What woman?' Mandy asks.

Mare shakes her finger at them. 'So don't go getting any ideas. I'll kill myself before I let any of you kill me.'

'Why did she kill her mother?' Rory asks.

'How should I know?'

'Maybe because she got sick of looking after her,' Mandy suggests.

Mare turns on her. 'You don't know how you treat me. You think I have no feelings.'

'Alright, Mum, just cool it, okay? I was just kidding.'

Mare heads towards the stairs with her loaf. 'I'm sick to death of everybody killing old people. You wait till you're old. You think it's not going to happen to you. Well let me tell you something, you don't know anything. When you're old and people take advantage of you, you won't be such a bunch of smarties.'

'Mum,' Mandy interjects, 'why don't you cut up that loaf, and we'll all have some.'

Mare begins the climb upstairs. 'Nobody's getting any loaf until I find my gun. You think I'll forget about it. Well, let me tell you something, I paid good money for that gun, and I want it back. You won't protect me, so I'll protect myself.'

Mandy looks at Milton, rolls her eyes then stubs out her cigarette and pulls out another one. Rory leans against the wall flipping through a *Life* magazine left behind by Judith. Milton attempts to roll onto his side but, feeling a twinge, decides to stay on his back.

'So Rory,' Mandy begins, 'I thought you might want to talk to Uncle Milton about Ryan.'

'Why?'

'For another person's opinion.'

'I don't need another person's opinion.' He doesn't look up from the magazine.

'You told me you couldn't decide what to do.'

'There's nothing to decide.'

'Of course there is,' Mandy persists. 'You have to decide if you're going to press charges.'

'What am I supposed to charge him with?'

'Sexual abuse.'

'He didn't sexually abuse me.'

Mandy picks her cigarette up from the ashtray and holds it between her fingers, staring at it. 'That's not what you told Bob Metner.'

'What did he say I said?'

'He said you told him Ryan masturbated you.'

'Oh, Mum.' He stares down at the magazine.

'Well, is it true or not?'

Milton wonders why Mandy asked him to speak to Rory when she's doing all the talking.

'Is it true or not?' she repeats.

Rory tosses the magazine onto the coffee-table. 'It only happened once. It wasn't like he had his hands all over me.'

'Once is enough. What exactly did he do to you, Rory? Tell me the truth.'

'It's not important. It's not like it's screwed me up for life or anything.'

'If it's not important, you can tell us about it.'

Milton wonders if Mandy loves Rory and, if she does, why she's pushing him around when she knows from experience that being pushed around only makes a person feel like they can never do anything right, like they might as well give up and die. He tries to get up. 'Maybe you two want to talk about this in private.'

'Rory, if it's no big deal,' she insists, 'why can't you tell us about it?'

'The guy jerked off with me, that's all.'

'Did he touch you?'

'Maybe once.'

'Well then, you should press charges.'

'Maybe,' Milton interjects, 'you should let him decide that for himself.'

'He won't decide; he'll let it ride like everything else. At some point he's going to have to learn that there's other people in this world, and he can't just go around looking out for number one all the time.'

'Well, maybe this isn't that "point",' Milton suggests. 'Maybe you should just let this one go.'

'And let Ryan abuse a whole bunch more Little Brothers?'

'You don't know that he does,' Rory emphasizes. 'You don't know anything. You act like you know everything, and you don't know a fucking thing.'

'Don't swear.'

'You're just like Gramma. You put her down all the time for wanting everything her own way, but you're just like her.'

'You have to learn responsibility.'

He shakes his head and starts for the door. 'I can't even talk to you.'

'Don't walk away from it, Rory,' she warns. 'You can't do that your whole life.'

He turns on her, his face flushed. 'You press charges if it's so important to you.'

'You know I can't do that.'

'You just want to be famous,' he says, his voice rising. 'You don't give a shit about the Little Brothers. You just want to be the mother that found out. The mother that stood behind her son. The mother that turned in Ryan Melanson.'

'How dare you say that!'

'So then forget about it if it's not important to you. It's my business. It has nothing to do with you. I won't be home for dinner.' He leaves, slamming the door. She sighs heavily and slumps back into her seat.

'You see why I smoke?'

Milton circles his lump with his index finger. 'He's got a point, though.'

'He's not old enough to understand the consequences of his actions. I don't want him turning twenty-one and feeling guilty because he was too selfish to press charges.'

It seems to Milton people call other people selfish when the other people don't do what they tell them.

'I think,' he says, 'if you keep giving him a hard time, there's no way he's going to press charges.'

'I'm not giving him a hard time.'

Milton thinks that if there were hidden cameras that taped people in domestic situations it would help to clarify things. The argument could be played back, and people could see exactly what was said.

'I wasn't giving him a hard time,' she repeats. 'I'm sick and tired of him letting things go all the time. He's never going to get anywhere if he doesn't start taking a stand once in a while. It's his dad that did it; watching his dad slouch through life and get away with it.'

Milton can see how Rory might start drinking and end up with a pudgy wife who'll look after him and complain about him until she can't stand him anymore. Then she'll go live with her brother who'll get a fatal disease and turn into a vegetable.

'I should have left him years ago,' Mandy says. 'I swear, if I had a daughter I'd tell her never marry a guy who's got big ideas. Marry a garbage-man for all I care, just make sure he isn't too stuck up to do an honest day's work.'

Again Milton hears his mother in his sister. And here he is—already a vegetable like his dad—unable to move, escape. He pictures a mouse in a maze, scurrying around and around, always ending up in the same place. What's the point in moving?

'How's your back?' she asks.

'The same.'

'You should put ice on it.'

'No, I'm alright,' he says, knowing that it will make no difference, that in moments his sister will be shoving ice under him. And like the mouse, he will surrender, exhausted.

FOURTEEN

When Mandy holds the front door open for Leonard, Milton, still on the couch, glances over. He avoids looking at Leonard's eyes because he's afraid both will be rolling around. Instead he looks at Leonard's denim shirt and notices that it's buttoned one button-hole off.

'Do you want to sit down, Len?' Mandy asks.

'Is Milton here?'

'Yes.'

Leonard turns slightly, facing away from Milton. 'Hi, Milton. I'm sorry to hear about your back.'

Mandy stares at Milton. 'Leonard doesn't know where we are unless we say something.' She waves her hand, cuing Milton to speak but he doesn't know what he's supposed to say, 'I'm sorry that you're dying'?

'I'm sorry about your eyes,' he offers.

Mandy gives him a can't-you-do-better-than-that look. 'We

brought Chinese food. Maybe we should eat it in here then nobody has to move.' She leads Leonard to the easy-chair and sits him down. 'It's in the Jeep. I'll go get it.'

Milton stares at the floor-lamp trying to think of something to say to Leonard. He wonders if he should mention his lump, if the fact that he too could be dying will give them something to talk about.

'I don't feel very good about showing up on your doorstep like this,' Leonard admits.

'That's alright.'

'I really appreciate it. I'll try to keep out of your way.'

'Don't worry about it.'

Mandy bustles in with the food. 'Okay, I'm going to put it on plates for you guys, and you're going to go at it with your fingers. Is Mother here?'

'Upstairs.'

'Does she know I'm here?' Leonard asks, suddenly anxious.

'I don't know.' Milton tries not to stare at Leonard groping around on his plate, discerning ribs from pineapple chicken balls. Mandy waves her hand to get Milton's attention then mouths 'Don't stare.' Milton mouths back 'He can't see.' She frowns.

'So we're going to put Leonard's things in storage,' she explains.

Leonard tears open a packet of plum sauce with his teeth. 'Not right away. I mean there's still a chance I'll be going back there.' Mandy looks at Milton and shakes her head gloomily.

'As soon as I get control of this blind thing,' Leonard adds. 'They still have my last month's rent.' He squeezes plum sauce over his egg roll. Some drips onto his jeans, but he doesn't seem to notice. 'I can still see the outlines of things at close range. I just need time to adjust.' When he bites the egg roll bean sprouts fall onto the broadloom.

'Of course you do,' Mandy agrees then looks at Milton, mouthing something he can't understand.

'It's been the hardest thing so far,' Leonard admits, 'going blind.'

'You just need time to adjust,' Mandy repeats.

'That's right.' Leonard puts his egg roll down and bends his

166

head over his plate.

'Do you want a napkin?' Mandy asks.

'Please.' She hands him one, and he wipes his hands. 'I'm afraid I'm not feeling terribly hungry.'

'That's okay.'

As he puts his plate down carefully on the floor, soya sauce spills onto the broadloom. 'I really can't believe that I won't be able to see any of you again.' He shakes his head and rubs his eyes with his fingers. 'I refuse to believe that.'

'Maybe they'll come up with a cure,' Mandy offers then looks at Milton and frantically signals something that he can't understand.

Leonard gasps. 'I forgot to water my plants again. That's the sixth day in a row.' He begins to shift around on his chair as though tied to it with rope. 'I really can't stand the idea of my plants dying.'

'I'll bring them tomorrow,' Mandy assures him.

'Will that be okay, Milton?' Leonard asks. 'The Hibiscus is flowering now.'

'Sure.' Milton wonders how he knows it's flowering when he can't see.

'You're a good soul, thank you.'

'See, Len, I told you he'd changed.'

Leonard smiles weakly and wipes his mouth with a napkin. 'Did they give us any fortune cookies?'

Mandy looks in the bag. 'Yeah.' She pulls out some cookies wrapped in cellophane. 'Do you want to pick one?' Leonard nods. She holds the packet in front of him then places his hand on it. It amazes Milton that she knows what to do, as though she's looked after blind people her entire life. He can't see himself looking after Leonard, leading him around the house, putting his hands on door-knobs and faucets, buttering his toast. Suddenly he recognizes the value of his sister.

Leonard cracks open his cookie then hands Mandy the fortune. 'You'll have to read it for me.'

Mandy studies the slip of paper. 'Why is it all so hard? Because that's the way it's good.' She hands it back to him. 'I don't know about that.'

'What about you, Milton?' Leonards asks. 'You choose one.'

167

Mandy holds the bag out to Milton who reluctantly takes a cookie, breaks it and unravels the fortune. The print is tiny and the words scrunched together. He doesn't want Leonard to know he has trouble reading so he makes one up. 'You stand to make great fortune.'

'I always get that,' Mandy says. 'They're always telling me my personal finances are going to improve.' She bites a cookie, pulls out the fortune and reads: 'So many itch for what they want but are unwilling to scratch for it.'

Leonard nods. 'Well, that's certainly true.'

Leonard has said that Milton has an aptitude for finding dead end jobs, that Milton attracts tragedy, that Milton has a loser mentality. Milton knows this because Mandy has told him. Staring at his sickly brother, Milton wonders how he's supposed to forget all the shitty things Leonard has said about him.

'Milton, there's another thing,' Mandy says.

He looks at her.

'Can Leonard bring his cat?'

Milton pictures a dryer, Leonard's cat in a dryer. How is he supposed to say no? If he says no, everybody will say he's selfish. 'Fuck 'em,' he mumbles.

'Pardon?' Mandy asks.

'Are you allergic to cats?' Leonard asks.

'No. I just hate them.'

'Oh.' Leonard tightens his grip on his crumpled napkin.

Mandy waves her hand trying to get Milton's attention, but he pretends to be dozing off. 'Why do you hate them?' she asks finally.

'They smell.'

'Well mine's been neutered,' Leonard offers hopefully.

That's all Milton needs: a cat with no balls sitting around staring at him.

'I think,' Mandy persists, 'that you can make an exception in this case. I mean it is Leonard's cat.'

'Actually it was Jerry's cat. I promised to look after him.'

Milton wonders what it is about being blind that opens people's faces. Suddenly their emotions are in plain view. It's as though they think that since they can't see you, you can't see them. Leonard looks as though he'll burst into tears if Milton refuses to take his cat.

'Please?' Leonard asks. 'He's not like other cats. He thinks he's human.'

Milton has never understood why people think it's great when their pets think they're human. It seems to him dogs should think they're dogs, and cats should think they're cats. 'You can keep it in your room.'

'Oh thanks, Milt. Thanks a lot. I really appreciate it.'

Never in a million years would Milton have expected his brother to suck up to him. It seems to him that it should make him feel good—like he's getting his own back—but all he feels is sick. He's always wondered how politicians can switch alliances, suddenly be best pals with some tyrant just because he's got oil. Watching news footage of politicians shaking hands repeatedly and smiling for the cameras, he has wondered if somehow they've forgotten their differences, somehow forgotten that the tyrant orders people killed and tortured. Otherwise, how can they live with themselves? Maybe Leonard has forgotten their past history, maybe the virus has erased it from his brain. Otherwise how can he stand sucking up to his loser brother? How can he live with himself?

'I need to use the washroom,' Leonard says.

Mandy gets up and takes his hand. 'Come on, I'll show you.' She leads him to the stairs. 'Okay, here's the first step,' she cautions. Tentatively, Leonard lifts his foot and sets it on the stair. They make slow progress, and Milton wonders what gets his brother out of bed in the morning.

When Mandy comes back down she stares sternly at him. 'I would have thought you could be nicer about the cat.'

'I don't see why, just because he's dying, I have to look after his cat. Like how's he supposed to change the litter box when he can't even see? It's me that's going to have to do it.'

'I'll do it when I move in.'

He doesn't like how all these people are moving in on him, but he can't think of how to stop it.

'I could be dying myself,' he says.

'What?'

'I might be sick myself.'

'How do you mean?'

'I've got a lump.'

She stares at him. 'Where?'

'On my neck.'

She peers at him, just like their mother. 'I can't see it.'

He fondles it. 'I can feel it.'

She sits on the couch beside him and puts her fingers over his. 'Let me feel.'

'It's sore.' He takes his hand away. 'Can you feel it?'

'Yeah.' She feels the other side of his neck. 'You've got one here, too.'

'You're kidding.' Now he knows he's dying.

'Those are lymph nodes, Milton. Everybody has them.'

'It's swollen, though.'

'Probably from you squeezing it all the time. Or sometimes they get swollen if you have a big zit on your face, or a cut or something. Did you cut yourself shaving?'

He feels like a fool. He knew he shouldn't have said anything. 'What do you know about lymph nodes?'

'When Rory got mono, they got swollen. Maybe you're getting mono. I doubt it. Quit squeezing it, and it'll stop hurting.'

Milton feels very tired suddenly, realizing that it's possible he may live for many more years.

Mare squints at them from the top of the stairs. 'Who's in the bathroom?'

'Leonard,' Mandy says.

'Who?'

'Leonard.'

Mare rubs her abdomen. 'It is not.'

Mandy sighs. 'Fine, alright, it's some complete stranger off the street who came in to use Milton's toilet.'

'Don't be a smarty with me.'

Leonard, feeling his way along the wall, looms over her. 'Hello, Mother.'

She turns and stares up at him. 'You're not Leonard.'

'I'm afraid I am.'

170

She looks back at Mandy then at Milton. 'You all think you can play games with me because I'm old.'

'Mother,' Mandy explains, 'that is Leonard. He's sick so he looks a little different.'

'I'm not talking to you.' She starts down the hall. 'You don't know what you're talking about. I'm sick to death of all the people in this house. An old woman can't even use the toilet.' She slams the bathroom door behind her.

Leonard, stunned, wavers at the top of the stairs.

'Don't move,' Mandy warns, hurrying up to him and taking his hand. 'Alright, first step.'

'I guess I should have expected something like this,' he murmurs. 'Maybe it's better she thinks I'm somebody else.'

'No way,' Milton says, surprising himself. It's just that he doesn't want to live with the legend of Leonard his entire life. He wants his mother to know the truth, wants her to be devastated, wants her to come crawling to him, begging forgiveness for neglecting him all these years. He wants to be appreciated finally. He says none of this because they will think him small.

Mandy looks at him. 'What do you mean "no way"?'

Milton crosses his arms. 'I don't think it's right.'

'Since when are you concerned with what's right?'

'So what happens if he dies and she asks about him?'

'We'll say he's on business.'

'No,' Leonard interjects. 'Milton's right.' He sits on one of the stairs and drops his head.

Milton isn't sure that he is right; he thinks that if he were what Judith calls a mature human being he wouldn't care what his mother thinks. Judith says you can never please your parents so don't even try.

'Maybe I'm wrong,' Milton concedes.

Leonard shakes his head. 'No, I think you're right. He rests his forehead in his hands. 'She should know.'

Milton has a feeling he's started something that will only cause harm. As usual he shouldn't have said anything.

~

Mandy sets Leonard up to rest in the spare room then goes home after advising Milton to leave Mare alone in her room. Once he's taken more Tylenol No. 3, Milton feels able to stand and decides to visit Winnie to apologize.

'What do you want?' Winnie's mother asks, barely opening the door. She's almost bald and looks like ET except that her eyes are mean.

Milton holds out a bag of caramels. 'I brought Winnie some candy,'

'I'll give them to him.'

'Please, can I just see him for a minute?'

'If I'd known what was going on, I would have called the police.'

Milton hears him behind the door whispering. When Winnie comes out, he's still in his pajamas and robe. 'She says we can talk for five minutes out here.'

'What did you tell her about last night?'

'Nothing. Just that we were partying.'

'You shouldn't have told her that.'

'She'd've found out anyway. She always does.'

Winnie's dog, Coco, slips past the door and lies at Winnie's feet, groaning.

'So are you really sick?' Milton asks.

'I don't know. I don't feel too good.' He pets Coco's head.

'You didn't do anything wrong.'

'Then how come you got so mad?'

'I think I was mad at myself.' Milton leans against the railing. 'I get mad when I do something stupid.'

'Then you shouldn't go getting mad at other people.'

'No.'

Coco groans again and rolls onto his back, holding his feet in the air. 'What's his problem?' Milton asks.

'He thinks he's pregnant. Mom's cat got pregnant and really depressed, so Coco is too.'

Milton nods as though this makes perfect sense.

'You shouldn't go shouting at people,' Winnie says.

'No.' Long-haired teenagers drive by in a Camaro with the

radio blaring. 'Assholes,' Milton mutters.

Winnie tightens his bathrobe belt. 'Did Connie come back?'

'No.'

'Are you going to let her?'

'I guess.' Milton glances around and sees Winnie's mother watching from the window. 'So did you go to church this morning?'

'She said I didn't deserve to.' Winnie rubs Coco's belly with his foot. 'Milton, do you think I'm retarded?'

'No.'

'Sometimes I worry that I come across really retarded.'

'You don't.'

'Mum says I'd better learn to look after myself because she won't be around forever.'

'You can always ask me if you've got a problem.'

'Thanks.' Winnie's mother raps on the window with her knuckles. 'I guess I better go.'

'Come by later if you want.'

'Does Connie think I'm retarded?'

'I don't know.'

Winnie fingers the end of his nose. 'Can you ask her?'

'If I see her.'

Winnie's mother holds the door open for him. 'Okay, so I guess I'll see you later then.' He goes inside.

Milton can't get over how he thinks he's doing somebody a favour then it turns out he's doing the exact opposite. If he hadn't had a party for Winnie, none of this would have happened. Judith wouldn't have told him to die for all she cared; Connie wouldn't have walked out; Mare wouldn't have had a heart attack. If he hadn't tried to save Teresa, she wouldn't be back on the street.

A little boy limps by on a shiny plastic leg. Milton wonders what happened to his real leg, and where his parents are. Why aren't they with him, protecting him? If he was Milton's son, he'd protect him. He wouldn't let him out of his sight. Then Milton remembers that every person he has tried to protect, he has ended up hurting.

He waves at the boy. 'How you doing?'

'Alright,' the boy replies, and Milton believes he means it. Even though he's got a plastic leg, he's all right. Without him. Maybe

Teresa's better off without him. Or maybe she's dead already, and her soul's flitting around looking for a new body to inhabit. He holds his breath, wondering how long it will take to suffocate himself by not breathing. He sits on Winnie's steps clamping his mouth shut and pinching his nose. It begins to feel as though his eyeballs will pop out. He remembers a movie in which a guy got electrocuted. His eyeballs popped out, then blood gushed from his empty sockets and his brain started seeping out. While his eardrums swell, Milton imagines the horror of the people who discover his body, then he pictures Judith hearing about it and kneeling at his grave crying, realizing that she loved him all along and won't ever be able to love the Goof.

'What do you think you're doing?' Winnie's mother demands, shaking his shoulder. He gasps and air invades his lungs. 'Go home now,' she tells him, 'or I'll call the police.' She shoves him again. 'Go on, go home.'

He does because he can't think where else to go.

FIFTEEN

He can hear his mother in the kitchen frying hamburger steak. He tries to sneak up to his room.

'There's somebody in the bathroom,' she calls after him, shuffling to the foot of the stairs. 'They've been in there for hours.'

'It's Leonard.'

'Who?'

'Leonard.'

She rubs her abdomen.

'Did you knock?' he asks.

'Why would I knock when I know there's someone in there?'

Milton walks down the hall and knocks on the bathroom door. 'Leonard?'

'Is that you, Milton?'

'Yeah.'

'I can't get out of the tub. I'm sorry, I shouldn't have locked the door. Don't worry about me. If it's alright with you, I'll just stay here until I get some strength back. I'll have to wait a while I think. I may have broken a toe, it's swelling pretty badly.'

'You can't just stay there,' Milton says.

'I've drained the water, I'll be fine. I'm just sorry to inconvenience you and Mother.'

Mare hobbles up the stairs. 'Who's in there?'

'Leonard.'

'Tell him to get out.'

'He can't get out.'

'What's the matter with him?'

'He's sick.'

Mare's eyes shift from the bathroom door to the floor then back to the door.

'Your steak's burning,' Milton tells her.

'Is Mother there?' Leonard asks.

Milton looks at her. 'Yeah.'

'I'm sorry, Mother. I should be out in half an hour or so.'

'Leonard,' Milton warns, 'I'm going to break open the door.'

'You don't need to do that.'

Milton tries to force it open with his shoulder like the cops on TV, but it doesn't budge, and he hurts his arm. He tries kicking it but hurts his foot. He goes outside and sets his aluminum ladder against the side of the house. He begins climbing, realizing that the Tylenol No.3 is making him dizzy. Mare hovers below, insisting that he quit trying to be a hero and call the fire department. The window sticks, and when he tries to lever it open, the ladder shudders beneath him. Finally he wedges his shoulder under the window-frame. With one leg in, he pries it open enough to slide inside. He turns to Leonard and sees blood smeared all over his face.

'You didn't have to do this, Milton.'

'What happened to your face?'

'Nothing.'

'There's blood on it.'

'There is?' Leonard feels his face. 'I must have cut myself shaving. I shave in the bath now, you see. It's easier. I guess I should stop shaving. It's just, I hate facial hair.'

Naked, Leonard looks even more like a concentration-camp

victim. Milton remembers the Nazi news footage of the decomposing corpses being bulldozed into pits. He represses an urge to vomit.

'I'm sorry about all this,' Leonard says.

'Maybe you'd better wash your face.' Milton doesn't want to touch Leonard's blood—even though he knows he can't get AIDS from just touching it. Leonard reaches forward, feeling for the taps then rinsing his face.

'Is it off?' he asks.

'Yeah.' It isn't, but Milton can't see how a little blood can contaminate him. He remembers the pigeon dying because he was too scared to touch it. He grips Leonard's wrists and tries to pull him up, but his legs buckle beneath him causing him to slide back into the tub.

Leonard rubs his eyes with his fingers. 'This has never happened before. I don't understand what's going on.'

'You're just tired, that's all.' Milton tries not to look at Leonard's emaciated body. Instead he studies the mildew growing on the grout around the tub.

'I'm so scared,' Leonard admits, shaking his head. 'I really want to be brave. I saw this AIDS special.' He scratches the slight scab forming over his shaving cut, making himself bleed again. 'One of them had outlived three of his lovers and now it was his turn. He didn't cry or scream.' He leans his elbow against the tub and his cheek against his hand, smearing the blood. 'I cry and scream all the time.'

'That's okay,' Milton assures him.

'I want to know what I did to deserve this. I know I'm supposed to be past this. I'm supposed to find spiritual strength or something but I can't. I'm angry. I want to know what I did.' He moves his hand to his forehead leaving a trail of blood across his cheekbone and temple. 'Jerry was promiscuous at least. I fell in love once, that was it.'

Milton wonders if he should tell him that he has spent seven months trying to find a reason for his daughter's death. He hesitates because he has a feeling Leonard isn't interested. Milton leans over him, expecting him to smell like a rotten corpse, but he doesn't. 'Put your arms around my neck.' Leonard holds out his arms. Milton guides them to his neck then slides his hands under Leonard's legs.

But when he tries to lift him, his back sends jolts through him. He releases Leonard as gently as possible then sits back on the toilet.

'What's wrong?' Leonard asks.

'My back.'

'Oh, of course. I'm sorry. Milton, don't worry about me. Go lie down. I'll be alright, really, just hand me some towels so I can make myself more comfortable.'

'I'm not leaving you here.' He pulls the towels off the rack and hands them to Leonard wondering if he can get AIDS from sharing towels. Then he feels like scum for even thinking it.

'Stay with me then.' Leonard arranges the towels around him. 'Not too many people keep me company these days.'

This doesn't surprise Milton since all Leonard talks about is himself and dying. It occurs to him that all Leonard has ever talked about is himself and whatever he is currently doing.

Leonard pats his face dry with one of the towels. 'I'm glad you're here. I've been trying very hard not to panic. You see, this happens quite often now. I find myself in a situation I can't handle, and I panic. It's useless and I despair and begin to hate healthy people, and God who I don't believe in anyway. And it all ends up back inside me. I can feel it making me sicker. And even though I know it's destructive, I keep doing it.' He reaches forward and gingerly touches his swollen toe. 'The thing is, I think I did the same thing when I was healthy. Only it wasn't healthy people I hated, it was people more successful than I was. So I don't think I've changed very much. Usually people change when they're dying. They become courageous and philosophical. I just go on being a coward and hating.'

'I think you've changed,' Milton offers.

'How?'

'You're not as snotty.'

'Yes, well, becoming dependant on others means you can't afford to be snotty.'

'Even though secretly you hate them.'

Mare pounds at the door. 'What's going on in there?'

Milton leans forward and unlocks it. She pushes it open and squints at Leonard.

'Hello again, Mother.' He adjusts the towels over his legs to make certain his groin is covered. 'Yes, this is me, and I have AIDS.'

'What?'

'I've got AIDS. I didn't tell you before because I didn't want to upset you.'

Milton waits for her to be devastated, but all she does is blink her lizard eyes and tighten her papery lips. Suddenly she turns on him. 'What do you think you're doing?'

'My back's hurting; I'm resting. In a minute I'll lift him up and get him into bed.' He notices that she smells of urine.

'Mother,' Leonard persists, 'did you hear me? I said I've got AIDS.'

'I heard you.'

'Doesn't that mean anything to you?'

She rubs her abdomen. 'Why would it mean anything to me?'

'Because I'm your son.'

'You're not my son.' She turns and leaves, slamming the door behind her.

Leonard leans back in the tub. Milton stares at his blank eyes, trying to determine what he's feeling, but he can see nothing. It's as though he's vacated his body.

'She knows it's me, doesn't she?' Leonard asks finally.

'Yeah.'

Leonard nods then resumes his motionless state for what seems to Milton a long time. The toilet-seat cover is making his bum sore, and he wonders if he should try again to move Leonard. Then it occurs to him that Leonard might be unconscious or even dead. 'Leonard?'

'Yes?'

'Maybe we should try and move you again.'

Leonard nods slowly. 'Jerry's mum said the worst thing that can happen to a mother is to outlive her children.'

Milton, uncertain how to respond to this statement, watches a spider crawling towards the medicine cabinet.

'Do you think she ever loved us?' Leonard asks.

'She loved you.'

'Only when I was doing what she wanted.' He slides down in the tub, crossing his arms over his chest. 'For the longest time, I couldn't accept that she didn't love us. I mean we are of her; she made us; the mother-child bond has to be there.'

Milton doesn't see why, since he's always hearing about mothers dropping their babies into garbage-pails or the lake, or just letting them starve to death. He doesn't say this to Leonard because he doesn't want to depress him further. 'Maybe she does love us,' he suggests, 'in her own way.'

Leonard buries his face in a towel.

'Or maybe she's just scared,' Milton adds. 'Of you being sick.'

'We're all scared,' Leonard says bitterly. 'That's no excuse.' He folds and unfolds a corner of the towel. 'Jerry was so brave, but I won't be able to stand it. Milton, please don't send me back to the hospital. If I die here, you and Mandy can give me morphine. Milton, would you do that? Let me die here?'

Milton doesn't want his brother's rotting corpse in his house and doesn't like how—just because Leonard is dying—everybody has to forget about their own lives and worry about his. But he feels guilty for thinking this, for being bored listening to him and for wanting a grilled-cheese sandwich. He knows people aren't supposed to eat when their loved ones are dying. They're supposed to crowd around the bed, hanging onto every word the dying person says. Some of them cry. Milton feels guilty for not wanting to do any of this. 'You can stay here,' he says.

'Oh, thank you, Milt. Mandy's right, you have changed.'

Milton doesn't believe Leonard really thinks this, now that he knows Leonard is only nice to people he depends on. 'Okay, here we go.' Milton slides his arms under him again. When he lifts Leonard, he feels a twinge, but once he's standing, the pain lessens, and he carries him into the spare room. On the bed, with the covers pulled up around his neck, Leonard looks very small and defenceless. Milton feels sorry for him and wonders if he regrets taking it up the bum, if he thinks it was worth it. On one show about AIDS, one of the men said that the two years he spent with his dying lover—who had given him AIDS—were better than twenty years other people spend together. Milton wondered how the man knew this since he hadn't spent twenty years with anyone. He claimed that he and his lover shared more love in those two years than other people share in a lifetime and that the happiest days of his life were the last three days of his lover's life when he sat by his hospital bed. The dying man made it sound like you couldn't really love unless you were dying, and Milton wondered if this was true.

'Thanks again,' Leonard says.

'You don't have to keep thanking me.'

'I want to; I mean it. You didn't have to do this.'

Milton can't see that he had any choice. But, now that he's doing it, it's not so bad; at least he doesn't have to go around feeling guilty because he's not doing it. The same with taking in his mother and sister. This way he doesn't owe them anything.

Leonard tilts his face towards him. 'What are you going to do now?'

'Make a grilled-cheese sandwich.'

'Oh good. I'm glad.'

But Milton knows he's just saying this to keep on his good side. Switching off the light he realizes he has power and that, if he wants, he can mistreat his brother as his brother has mistreated him. But he no longer wants to, and he thinks it's sad that his brother had to get a fatal disease before he could stop hating him. He wonders if his mother is going to have to die before he can stop hating her. Or anybody for that matter: Munroe and Aiken, the Goof. Does everybody have to get sick and kick off before he can forget about them? Or love them? It seems to him there has to be a way of imagining they're dying even if they aren't. Judith always says that when you apply for a job, and the interviewer is giving you a hard time, just imagine him naked. Maybe imagining people dead is better. Dead they can't hurt you, and they say one in ten people gets cancer so they could be dying without knowing it. He could be dying without knowing it.

~

He lies in bed eating his grilled-cheese sandwich, watching a nature show about the Arctic. A mother polar bear breaks open her den under the snow and three cubs tumble out, white, fluffy and confused. They bump into each other and into their mother who rolls around in the snow. Not far off is a male polar bear. The narrator explains that the mother has to keep watch over her cubs otherwise the male bear will eat them. Milton can't understand why God or whoever would make it so that male polar bears eat their young. Judith always talks about the harmony of nature and how humans are screwing it up, but Milton can't see the harmony in bears eating their cubs. Nor can he see the sense in seagulls eating other birds' babies and stealing other birds' fish. Who eats the seagulls' babies? Who steals their fish? Judith always talks about how you get what you give, but Milton thinks that's crap. Nobody gets the seagulls. A mother polar bear slips into the water and stealthily glides towards a fat seal basking in the sun. Milton doesn't want the roly-poly seal, with its gentle eyes, to get killed. Seals don't hurt anybody, they feed off gunge under the ice. Why can't the bear eat some seagulls? The seal, still unaware of the bear, rubs its face with its flippers as though it's trying to wake up. Milton knows that momentarily blood will spurt, and the poor, dopey seal will be dead. He considers changing the channel then decides he must accept the seal's death as part of life. At least it won't grow old and mangy like Milton's mother. Then he remembers the gun and feels for it under his mattress. When he can't find it, he gets down on his hands and knees to make a proper search. Realizing it's not there he panics, wondering what she's done with it. He sits on his heels and looks back at the tv. The seal lies in a pool of blood while the polar bear tears off chunks of its skin.

It had to happen.

He's not going to take the gun away from her again. It's her gun. If she kills somebody, even himself, that's her problem. It makes no difference to him. Since everybody's dying anyway.

The gulls swoop down and pick at the seal's bones.

SIXTEEN

At first Milton thinks the man wearing the baseball cap is an under-cover cop about to arrest him for concealing an illegal weapon. But then he notices the camera on the shoulder of the bearded man behind him.

'We're from CKGY-TV,' the man in the baseball cap explains. 'We wondered if you would mind talking with us.'

'About what?'

'The rescue.'

Milton nods at the camera. 'Is that on?'

'Does it bother you?'

He shrugs. Mandy, who has been arranging Leonard's plants around the living-room, stops behind him in the doorway.

'Who are these guys, Milt?'

'TV people.'

'Is this your wife?' the baseball cap asks.

'I'm his sister. Is this "Candid Camera" or something?'

183

'No, Ma'am,' the baseball cap replies. 'We just want to talk to Milton about rescuing the girl from the fire.'

Milton stares hard into the black eye of the camera. 'I have nothing to say.'

Mandy pokes him. 'Of course you do. My brother's always putting himself down. It's a family trait.'

Milton feels the camera sucking up his face, his confusion. He doesn't want the whole world to see him like this. 'Turn it off,' he commands.

'Alright.' The baseball cap signals something to the bearded man. 'Look, Milton, we're on your side here. You did something great, and we want you to be remembered for it.' A girl, carrying a clipboard, bustles up the steps and whispers something in the baseball cap's ear. He nods then looks back at Milton. 'Listen, if you want us to go, we'll go, but I think you should know that Teresa's in the car, and she wants to meet you.'

'Who's Teresa?' Mandy asks.

'The girl he rescued.'

'Why doesn't she come out?' Milton asks although suddenly he's afraid to meet her, afraid she won't like him, will think he's ugly and stupid. Maybe she remembers him differently from what he is, maybe she thinks he's handsome and heroic.

'We asked her not to come out until we'd spoken to you,' the baseball cap explains. 'We're hoping to film your reunion.'

The sun glints off the car's windows making it impossible for Milton to see inside. He wonders if Teresa is looking at him, already disappointed. 'We don't even know each other,' Milton says.

'That's the point,' the baseball cap responds.

Mandy prods Milton's shoulder. 'My brother's a very quiet person. Everybody thinks he hates them, but really he's just shy.'

'Do you mind if we come in for a few minutes?' the baseball cap asks.

'Of course not.' Mandy nudges Milton aside and opens the door wide. 'Listen, if you want news stories this is the place for it. My brother's got AIDS, and I'm homeless.'

Milton can't believe she's talking like this. He wants to shut her up but can't think how with all these people around.

'Milton has AIDS?' The baseball cap's eyebrows shoot up his forehead.

'No, my other brother. And my sister is a street prostitute.'

'You don't know that,' Milton argues.

'So what is she?' Mandy demands. 'A nun?'

Milton has a feeling the camera is still on because the bearded man hasn't stopped aiming it at him. He turns his back to it and looks out the window at the car. He hasn't even showered or shaved. If he'd known this was going to happen he would have worn his clean jeans.

'And my son,' Mandy adds, 'is a victim of sexual abuse. But I can't really talk about that without his permission. All I can say is that the people you least expect turn out to be the child molesters.'

Milton turns on her. 'Would you shut up?' He pictures himself as he must look through the camera lense with his messy hair, his plaid shirt worn at the collar and cuffs—a loser. He doesn't know what to do with his hands; he tries pointing a finger at Mandy. 'You don't even know what you're talking about.' He stops pointing but leaves his hand suspended in the air. It feels weighted, clumsy; with the whole world watching.

Mare appears at the top of the stairs. 'What's going on down there?'

'They want Milton to be on TV,' Mandy explains.

'Who wants what?' Her eyes shift from Mandy to the baseball cap to Milton to the bearded man. 'Who are you?'

'Are you Milton's mother?' the baseball cap asks.

'Who wants to know?'

'We're doing a news report about the street girl Milton rescued.'

She squints. 'Milton what?'

Milton's mouth twitches. He grabs the baseball cap's arm. 'Just go get her,' he mumbles. The baseball cap nods to the girl with the clipboard who hurries out. 'Mother, go back to bed.'

'I'm not going anywhere. Who are these people? All day long people come and go in this house.'

Milton flops down on the couch. Leonard's ball-less cat climbs onto his lap and licks his hand. Roughly Milton pushes it off then realizes that this too will be revealed to the world. The world will think he's cruel to animals. Suddenly every move he makes feels wrong. He'd like to scratch his nose but worries that this will make him look nervous or shifty. He'd like to check to make sure his fly is up, but he doesn't want the whole world looking at his crotch.

He feels trapped inside a TV.

~

She doesn't look anything like Ariel, and Milton fears that they found the wrong girl, that this is an imposter, some girl who wants to be famous.

'Why don't you both sit on the couch,' the baseball cap suggests.

'I don't know if this is her,' Milton says.

'Ah ... it is, Milton,' the baseball cap assures him.

The girl looks at him. 'You don't recognize me?' Even her voice sounds different; older. Then he notices the black high-topped sneakers.

'I guess I do,' Milton admits.

'So, Teresa,' the baseball cap asks, 'how do you feel now that you've met your rescuer?'

'Alright.'

Milton gets the impression that the baseball cap is waiting for her to say more, but she doesn't. 'What about you, Milton?'

He shrugs. 'The same.'

'Milton,' the baseball cap continues, 'did you know that Teresa was trying to commit suicide?'

'Not until later.'

'Did this shock you?'

'Well yeah. I mean, she's so young.'

'I tried to do it when I was nine,' Teresa offers.

'Why?' Milton asks, suddenly annoyed with her.

'Because my dad kept raping me.' She says this simply, without resentment, and Milton can see how being raped by your dad could make a person want to die.

'So what stopped him?'

'Nothing. I left.'

'Did your mother know?' the baseball cap asks.

186

'Sure. She didn't mind. It kept him off her.' Again she speaks without malice, as though relating someone else's story. Milton wonders if the glue has numbed her brain.

'Why did you try to kill yourself this time?' the baseball cap asks.

Her eyes drift around the room. 'I get tired of finding places to sleep.'

'But you'd found the house,' the baseball cap points out. 'Couldn't you have slept in the house?'

'Someone would've chased me out.'

'You don't know that,' Milton argues. 'Maybe someone would have found you and given you a place to stay. You never know what can happen.' Leonard's cat jumps on Teresa's lap, and she pets it. 'I just don't think,' Milton continues, 'you should go around killing yourself just because you've got nowhere to sleep. I mean it's not like you're going to be homeless forever.'

She looks at him. 'How do you know?' Her eyes are paler than Ariel's, and watery, even though she's not crying.

Then he remembers that Connie is back on the street. 'I just don't think you should go around killing yourself until you're older.'

'Why, Milton?' the baseball cap asks. 'At what age is it alright to kill yourself?'

'When you know things are only going to get worse.'

'I know that now,' Teresa says.

'You can't know that now,' Milton insists.

Teresa looks at him. 'You think you know that.'

'What?'

'That's why you came into the fire.'

Avoiding her eyes he rolls up his sleeves, wondering how she knows he was trying to kill himself. He remembers a movie about a ghost inhabiting a woman's body. The woman's husband couldn't understand how all of a sudden she knew things about him he'd never told her. Milton wonders if Ariel's spirit is inhabiting Teresa's body and speaking to him.

'Is that right, Milton?' the baseball cap asks. 'Were you attempting suicide yourself?'

If he lies everybody will go on thinking he's a hero. If he tells the truth they'll know he's just another doorknob trying to kill himself. Maybe Ariel's spirit is challenging him to speak the truth.

'Milton,' the baseball cap persists, 'were you attempting suicide when you ran into the burning house?'

Suddenly he wants the whole world to know. He's sick of trying to please everybody. Even when they think he's a hero he still feels like a loser. He wants to spit in their faces. Wants them to see that they made a hero out of a loser, see that it makes no difference who he is. They made him up and now they want him to be Bruce Willis or somebody. 'Fuck' em,' he grumbles.

'Pardon,' the baseball cap says.

'Yeah, I was trying to kill myself.'

'Can you tell us why?'

'Because I didn't want to live.'

Leonard's screams stun everyone in the room except Mandy. 'Sometimes he screams when he wakes up,' she explains. 'He told me he dreams he's healthy then wakes up and remembers. I'll go see if he wants anything.'

Mare, for no reason that Milton can understand, has been quiet for the last twenty minutes. She stands, clutching her abdomen, staring at Leonard's door. They all hear him sobbing and Mandy trying to console him.

'You alright, Mother?' Milton asks, but she doesn't respond, only shuffles down the hall to her room and closes the door.

'Is he going to be alright?' the baseball cap inquires.

'He's dying,' Milton points out.

Nobody says anything. Milton looks at the girl.

He still wants to save her and tries to remember what the Vietnam vet said to the high-school-drop-out-hooker that made her believe that life was worth living: something about apple pie, how if he didn't get crushed by the concrete the first thing he was going to do was have a piece of hot apple pie with ice cream. The hooker said she'd go with him. But Milton has no pie in the house and can't think what to offer the girl. She just seems like a lump to him. There's no life in her. She might as well be dead.

Like himself.

He can't stand it, can't stand being dead. 'I just think,' he adds, 'you shouldn't go around killing yourself when you've got a whole life ahead of you.' He can't understand why he wants to hit her when she's homeless, a glue addict and a victim of sexual abuse. He should feel sorry for her. His mouth twitches again, and he covers it with his hand. He's angry with the girl for wasting her body. Ariel's spirit is flitting around without a body. Leonard's is rotting.

At least Milton and the girl still have their bodies.

He looks into her watery eyes hoping to find something to hang onto, but there's nothing there. She's already gone. When she kills her body, no one will notice. They'll step over it in the street. The other day Milton stepped over a body and only later wondered if the man had been dead. He sees bodies in the street all the time and tries not to look at them, tries to believe that they have nothing to do with him, that it's the world's fault. The world let the teenagers cut out the blind man's tongue, let Connie become a drug addict, let Teresa's father rape her. The world took away Milton's job and his wife. He stares menacingly into the camera at the world, but all he sees is himself huddled on his couch in his plaid shirt and dirty jeans.

~

As the baseball cap and crew leave, Milton offers Teresa a baloney sandwich because he doesn't want her to go in case Ariel's spirit is inside her.

'Do you think they'll show us on TV?' she asks.

'I don't know. I didn't get the feeling he thought we were all that great.'

'We should've cried,' she says. 'They always show people who cry.'

'I think he expected us to be happy to see each other.'

Teresa picks up a pickle and looks at it. 'I never feel sorry for the people who cry. I think they cry on purpose, because they're on TV.'

Milton sips his coke then stares at the can in his hand, slowly turning it around. 'So how did you know I was trying to kill myself?'

'You couldn't have known I was there.'

Milton sees her point and feels stupid for even thinking about spirits. 'Are you sorry I rescued you?'

She wipes mayonnaise from her mouth with her fingers. 'I

don't think about it.'

He hands her a piece of paper-towel. 'Are you going to do it again?'

'I don't know.' She wipes her mouth with the towel.

Milton flicks a piece of baloney rind off the table. 'It just does-n't seem right that we're trying to kill ourselves when my brother's dying.'

Teresa finishes her sandwich leaving the bread crusts on her plate. Milton wonders how a homeless person can be picky about crusts.

'It just seems to me,' he continues, 'we should count ourselves lucky to be alive. I mean I'm sorry about your dad, but people get over that, you know. I mean, there's people you can talk to, profes-sional people.' He thinks about the shrink with the hairy mole and wonders why he's saying these things when he doesn't believe them.

'Do you feel lucky?' she asks.

'Sure.'

He knows she doesn't believe him, and he avoids her eyes by rapping his empty coke can against the edge of the table.

'If you feel lucky, you have no right to kill yourself.' She stands and pulls her fake fur jacket off the back of the chair.

'You can stay here,' Milton offers.

'No thanks.'

He knows that she wants to get away from him so she can sniff more glue.

She opens the back door. 'Thanks for everything.'

'Sure,' he says, although he knows she doesn't mean it.

Just once he would like things to turn out the way he'd hoped. Then, if it happened once, it might happen again, and he could have hope for the future. He sits listening to the hum of the fridge won-dering what he's supposed to do now that he can't save Teresa. Even though he knows that he's wasting his body—that he can't remain dead like Teresa—he can't think of a reason to live. He knows that if he was a decent person he'd go and feed the hungry in Ethiopia.

Leonard's cat jumps onto his lap, and Milton doesn't push it off. He's not sure why. It's just that he knows that horrible things have happened to it. First of all it had its balls cut off, then Jerry had it de-clawed so it wouldn't tear up the furniture, then they wouldn't let it outside. Milton feels sorry for the cat and wonders if this feeling of pity can be extended to humans. Maybe if he imagines horrible things happening to humans who rape their daughters or who cut out blind men's tongues or who leave rats on people's cars, he won't want to kill them. He'll just feel sorry for them.

Mandy comes downstairs and sits, sighing heavily. 'I think he's really sick. I mean I think he's got pneumonia. I think he could be dying.' She leans her elbows on the table, burying her face in her hands. 'I shouldn't have moved him. I should've just stayed with him.'

'You couldn't do that. You have a family.'

'Half the time they don't notice I'm there.'

'If anybody should feel bad it's me.'

She pulls a cigarette from her pack. 'He told me you rescued him from the bathtub. It meant a lot to him. He knows you don't like him.'

Milton is no longer sure he doesn't like Leonard but he says nothing. The cat purrs in his lap.

'What happened between him and mother?' Mandy asks.

'She told him he's not her son.'

'That cow.'

'He didn't seem to mind all that much.'

'Of course he minds. Why do you think he's so sick all of a sudden?'

'I think sitting in a cold bathtub didn't help.'

Mandy lights the cigarette. 'I think all those drugs he's taking are doing sweet fuck-all. If he doesn't get better soon, we're going to have to take him to the hospital.'

'He doesn't want to go.'

'I know, but who's supposed to look after him?'

'They won't look after him in the hospital,' Milton points out. 'A woman at work got pneumonia, and they left her in the corridor for five days. Her husband put a baseball cap over her face to block out the fluorescents.'

'Okay, well then, are you going to clean up his shit and vomit? He's that sick, Milt.'

'He wasn't that sick yesterday.'

'Yeah, well he is now. The blotches on his legs are worse.'

'What are those anyway?'

'Cancer. The whole body breaks down, right. It's not just his lungs.' She inhales on her cigarette. 'It seems to me the morphine's making him sicker, but there's no way he won't take it. I think he's addicted.'

'Well, I wouldn't worry about that.'

She flicks her cigarette at the ashtray. 'He thought I was Mother.'

'What did he say?'

'Something about not waiting up for him.' She sighs again. 'I swear, just when you think things can't get shittier something shittier happens.'

Judith has said repeatedly that Milton expects the worst so it happens. He used to think maybe she had a point but not anymore. He didn't expect any of this to happen. He remembers Connie saying when he asked why terrible things kept happening to her, 'Stuff happens, that's all.' He didn't believe her. But now he has a feeling that a lot of what she said was true. Which is why she hates everybody.

'I have to get home,' Mandy says. 'I gave him a sponge bath and changed his sheets, but you're going to have to keep checking on him. His drugs are on the dresser. Read the instructions. Sometimes he forgets he's already taken them. He's not supposed to have morphine more than every four hours. I gave him a dose a couple of hours ago so see how it goes. Just give him a teaspoonful. I'll call his doctor when I get home.'

'What about Mother?' he asks.

'She'll come out when she's ready.'

He doesn't want Mandy to go because he's scared of being alone in the house with two sick people. He doesn't say this because she'll think he's being immature.

On his bed, watching 'Star Trek', he has a feeling he should check on Leonard. But he doesn't because he's afraid of what he'll find. Instead he stares at Dr. Spock and Captain Kirk watching a grotesque blob on a rock. When Captain Kirk points his laser gun at the blob, it starts to heave and smoke, oozing black liquid. Spock stands very still, clutching his forehead, trying to interpret what the blob wants. He explains that the blob is in pain and is trying to tell them something. Finally the blob shifts off the rock revealing the words 'Not Kill' carved in the stone.

After ten minutes, Milton forces himself to go down the hall. He notices light under Mare's closed door. He hasn't seen her since Leonard screamed, and he wonders what she's doing late at night in her room. He knocks on her door. 'Ma, there's nobody around so you can fix yourself something to eat.' She doesn't respond, and he assumes she's either asleep or sulking.

Leonard's room smells bad so Milton holds his breath as he switches on the light. His brother is choking. Milton tries to sit him up, but Leonard twists away from him, gasping.

'Leonard,' Milton says, trying to sound in control. 'Calm down.'

'I can't breathe,' Leonard whispers.

'Breathe through your nose.' Milton holds Leonard's head against his stomach to stop him from moving. 'Open your mouth,' he says, but Leonard doesn't. Milton pulls down on his jaw and sees that his mouth is clogged with white goo. He thinks of the blob oozing black liquid. 'I'm going to put my fingers in your mouth,' he explains. In the CPR course they learned how to dig food out of a choking person's mouth. The thought of shoving his fingers down somebody's throat had revolted Milton. He'd felt certain that, if he happened to run into a choking person, he'd let somebody else stick their fingers in the person's mouth. But now there is nobody else. Holding Leonard's jaw open, he digs out the white stuff with his index and middle finger. It feels like cottage cheese. He scoops out as much as possible then drops it in the bowl of applesauce Leonard hasn't touched. 'Try to breath through your nose,' Milton repeats. Once he has cleared as much of the white stuff as possible, he holds a glass of water to Leonard's lips. 'It's just water,' he assures him, remembering that his brother can't see. Wiping his hand on his jeans, he wonders if he can get AIDS from the white stuff then hates himself for even thinking about it.

'I'm sorry,' Leonard whimpers, gripping Milton's thigh with one hand. 'I'm sorry.'

'Don't be sorry.'

'Usually I wake up before it gets this bad.'

'What is it?'

'It's yeast. It's worse after I've been asleep because it gets a chance to grow.'

Milton doesn't understand this disease that has attacked his brother mercilessly, blinding him, choking him, rupturing his skin. Watching his father die had been different. They'd expected that one day his heart would stop and he'd be dead. He was a vegetable so Milton didn't think he suffered. Leonard's suffering scares him and makes him feel useless.

'Please don't leave,' Leonard murmurs.

'I won't.' Sitting on the edge of the bed so that his brother can hang onto him, Milton feels as though he'll never get out of this dark and diseased room. 'Is Mother here?' Leonard asks.

'No.'

'Don't tell anybody I'm dying.'

'I won't.' Milton wonders how Leonard can think that anybody doesn't know.

Leonard pulls the sheets around his neck. 'I don't want to upset her.'

'Don't worry about it.'

Milton wonders if he should remind Leonard that Mare has decided that he isn't her son, that her real son is busy becoming a famous hotel decorator. But then it occurs to him that maybe Leonard needs to believe he has a loving mother, that it doesn't matter that he's as good as dead to her because in his own mind she loves him. Lots of people think other people love them when they don't. The weirdo who camped out in John Lennon's yard, for example. He believed that John Lennon was singing to him on all his albums. When Lennon said he wasn't singing to anyone in particular, that sometimes—when he was singing—he was thinking about what a good shit he'd had that morning, Milton could see that the weirdo was disappointed. It would have been better if he'd never met John Lennon. That way he could have gone on loving him and imagining his love returned. Maybe that's the best way to love, in your head, without ever really knowing the person. That way you're in control. Milton was all set to love Teresa, but she turned out to be a gluehead.

It would have been better if he'd never met her. Then he could have believed in her. Maybe that's why people believe in God, because they'll never meet him and be disappointed.

Leonard tightens his grip on Milton's arm. 'I'm sorry it's so revolting.'

'It's alright.'

'It must smell horrible in here. I was sick earlier. Mandy said she put a bucket out for me but I couldn't find it.'

Milton pulls the bucket out from under the bed. 'It's here. Where were you sick?'

Leonard points to the floor on the other side of the bed.

'I'll clean it up,' Milton tells him.

'I'm sorry.'

'Forget about it.'

While mopping the floor, Milton notices how raspy Leonard's breathing has become and wonders if he should offer him more drugs.

'A friend of Jerry's,' Leonard says, 'didn't have anybody to look after him. When he couldn't move at all he called an ambulance and they dropped him off the stretcher. He was skin and bone and they just let him roll off.'

'Nobody's putting you on a stretcher.'

Leonard's blank eyes begin to water. 'I'm not ready to die.'

Milton pulls some Kleenex out of the box on the bedside table and presses it into Leonard's hands.

'You're supposed to go through these stages,' Leonard explains, wiping his eyes, 'and end up accepting death. But I just go on being scared.' He sobs. 'I hate it. I mean I keep hoping one morning I'll wake up and feel courageous, but it doesn't happen.' He starts coughing. 'On TV they all find this inner peace.'

'Maybe they're just saying that because they're on TV,' Milton offers. 'I mean, you wouldn't want to look scared on TV.'

'Do you think?'

'Sure. People that cry on TV want you to feel sorry for them. But people with AIDS want you to think they're heroes for not crying about it. I bet as soon as they're not on TV they cry just like you do.'

'Thanks for saying that.'

'If I were you I'd cry.' Milton realizes that this is the first time

195

he has said something to Leonard that he really means. It feels good, as though clean air has filled his lungs. 'I wouldn't go worrying about how other people die,' he adds.

'Just like you shouldn't worry about how other people live.'

'That's right,' Milton agrees, although he does worry about how other people live, and it bugs him that most of them are having a better time than he is. It doesn't seem fair to him that they get to have nice cars and houses and happy marriages with children.

Leonard closes his eyes and presses the Kleenex against them. 'Milton?'

'Yeah?'

'Can you give me some morphine?'

~

When Leonard finally dozes off, Milton goes downstairs and discovers his mother in the kitchen, standing on a chair brushing the ceiling with a broom.

'What are you doing?' he asks.

'Putting the spiders out.'

He grips the back of the chair, steadying it. 'You could hurt yourself climbing on chairs.'

'There's too many spiders in this house.'

He helps her off the chair and watches her shake the broom out the back door. 'Maybe you should eat something,' he suggests. 'Are you hungry?'

'I ate already.'

He sees no trace of food and thinks she's lying: really she's staying up to find out about Leonard, but she won't ask because that would mean admitting he's here.

'Where've you been?' she asks.

'With Leonard.'

She spots a spider crawling along the floor and frantically sweeps it out the door. 'I'm sick to death of all the noise in this house.'

'It's quiet now.'

'I can't sleep now.'

196

'Why not?'

'Was Mandy here?'

'You know she was.'

She squints at him. 'If I knew I wouldn't be asking, would I?'

'She was here then she left.'

'Is she coming back?'

'They're moving here.'

'They're what?'

'They're moving here.'

'Who says?' Holding the broom she looks like a witch about to take off.

'They're being evicted so they're moving here.'

'Where am I supposed to go?'

'You'll stay here, too.'

'I'm not staying here with those boys.'

'Don't you ever think of anybody besides yourself?'

He can't believe he's bothering to argue with her.

She peers at him. 'What are you talking about?'

'All you ever think about is yourself; you never think about anybody else.'

'I looked after your father for sixteen years.'

'Right. Forget I said anything.'

'You don't know what you're talking about. You had it easy. You never had to go begging for …'

He slams his hand on the table. 'Forget about it!'

Her lizard eyes pop open, and he sees that he has frightened her. 'Ma, just go to bed, I'm tired.'

'Quit telling me to go to bed. All you want me to do is go to bed. I might as well be dead.'

It disturbs him that he still doesn't like her, even though she's dying, even though he knows that horrible things have happened to her.

'You wait till you're old,' she warns him, 'and people start pushing you around. You see how you like it.'

'I didn't mean to push you around. I'm tired.'

'They taped the jeweller's mouth and tied his hands and feet. That's what they do now.'

'What jeweller?'

'Nobody's doing that to me.'

Connie limps in the back door wearing her wrap-around sunglasses. Milton stares at her, unsure how to react.

'Can I stay here?' she asks. 'I sprained my ankle.'

Immediately he wonders if she's lying. As though reading his mind, she pulls up her pant leg revealing her viciously swollen ankle.

'You'd better put ice on it,' he tells her.

Mare stares at Connie. 'What makes you think you can just march in here?'

'Milton,' Connie says, 'can you talk to her? I can't talk to her.' She talks slowly, as though half asleep. Milton wonders what drugs she's on.

'Ma, I said she could stay.'

Mare's face crinkles, and to Milton's horror, she begins to sob. 'You said you'd protect me,' she tells him. 'She wants to kill me.'

'No, she doesn't.' He looks at Connie. 'Tell her you were only kidding.'

'I was only kidding.'

'You're lying,' Mare cries. 'You all lie all the time. You think I don't notice.'

'Ma, you're tired; go to bed.'

She stamps her foot. 'Quit telling me to go to bed!'

'Alright,' he says, 'then I'm going to bed.'

She grabs his arm. 'You can't leave me here with her.'

Connie holds up her hands. 'I'm not going to touch you, alright?'

Milton stares into Connie's sunglasses. 'You'll have to sleep in the living-room. Leonard's here.'

'Why?'

'He's dying, and there's nobody to look after him.' He grips his mother's bony arm. 'I'm going to take you upstairs.'

Outside her room she stops and peers at him. 'Did you have a bowel movement yet?'

He doesn't want to go back downstairs but decides he must, otherwise Connie will think he's scared of her. Street light from the window reveals her outline on the couch. 'Did you put ice on it?' he asks.

'It'll be alright. I've just got to get off it for awhile.'

'How did it happen?'

'I was running to get the subway, and I tripped.'

He'd expected some story about being raped or mugged, some story intended to make him feel sorry for her. 'Which subway?' He thinks that if she's lying she'll hesitate before answering.

'Fuck off, Milton.'

'Don't tell me to fuck off in my own house.'

'If you're going to start that bullshit again, I'm leaving.'

He really wants to like her and tries to imagine the horrible things that have happened to her. When she wasn't around, he'd felt badly for giving her a hard time; he'd hoped that they would meet again some day and realize that they love each other. Or anyway not hate each other. He doesn't want to hate her; he doesn't want to hate anybody anymore. He's tired of hating. It wears him down. He doesn't understand why—when he knows everybody's dying and that horrible things have happened to them—they still get up his nose. On the show about alcoholics they all said that in order to change you had to want to change. Well, Milton wants to change, but it isn't happening. The woman in the TV movie who cured herself of cancer, she changed and that was based on a true story. She started meditating, picturing waterfalls and lily-pads.

'Do you want something?' Connie asks.

'Maybe I should get you some aspirin.'

'I just want to be left alone.'

~

When his brother moans in the night, Milton tenses, hoping he'll stop. 'Fuck you!' Leonard shouts. Milton, worrying that Mare has gone into Leonard's room, hurries down the hall and pushes open the door. Leonard wrestles with his blankets. 'Fuck you!' he shouts again.

'Leonard?' Milton asks, but Leonard doesn't seem to hear him. 'Leonard, there's nobody here.'

'What?'

'There's nobody here.'

199

Leonard lies still. 'I know that.'

'Then why are you shouting?'

'Was I shouting?'

'Yes.'

'I'm sorry.'

'That's alright.' Unsure what to do, Milton collects crumpled Kleenexes from around the bed and tosses them into the wastebasket.

'I believe,' Leonard declares, 'that God gets off on our misery.'

Milton sits on a chair Mandy has placed beside the bed. 'I thought you said you didn't believe in him.'

'Everybody believes in him. Even if they say they don't. And they're all scared to hate him because he might punish them. Well, I'm not scared of the fucker. At first I thought maybe I was wrong for hating him and that was why he decided to kill me off. But the fact that he's killing me off proves my point. He can't handle opposition. If his love was all-encompassing, like the morons say, he wouldn't need to kill me off. He'd let me go on hating my stupid life. That's penance in itself. Now he's taking my life away from me so I'll feel guilty for hating it in the first place. And he's making me die just like Jerry did because he wants me to know exactly what I'm in for. Well, you know what, you fucker? I don't give a shit anymore. Do what you want with me, you crock of shit!'

Milton recognizes the old Leonard in this outburst and wonders if the new, saintly Leonard will return in the morning. 'Are you in pain?' he asks.

'Of course I'm in pain.' Leonard kicks his blankets. 'I'm always in pain. That's what the fucker wants.'

'It's been more than four hours since you had morphine.'

'Let the fucker burn me alive. I don't care anymore. Kill me off you bag of shit! You fucking ... you fuck ...' Suddenly short of breath Leonard flops back onto the pillow and closes his eyes. Milton watches him, waiting for some clue as to what to do next. Leonard groans and slowly rolls onto his side, pulling his knees into his stomach and clasping his hands under his chin. If Milton didn't know better, he'd think he was praying.

'Alright, give me some,' Leonard says wearily. Milton reaches for the bottle.

~

The light is still on in his mother's room. When he knocks on the door and gets no response he opens it. She sits hunched on the narrow bed, her curved spine forcing her head down. She doesn't look up at him, and he wonders if she's dead or asleep.

'Mother?'

'What do you want?' She still doesn't look at him.

'I just wanted to see if you were alright.'

'Why wouldn't I be alright?'

'You should be asleep.'

'I had to go to the bathroom if that's alright with you, your highness.'

He knows she's lying. He would have heard her door open and close if she'd gone to the bathroom. On Ariel's chest of drawers he sees the empty lemon loaf packet. Crumbs dot the floor between the chest of drawers and the bed. It upsets him more than he can understand that her only comfort is lemon loaf. He sees himself in her, curled into her deformed frame, sitting on the edge of a bed in a strange room waiting for something to happen, preferably not death. Suddenly he wants to make her comfortable in the cloud-covered room. Make it hers. It can't go on being Ariel's forever.

'Maybe we should paint in here,' he suggests. 'What colour would you like? Maybe tomorrow we'll pick up some paint samples, and you can see if there's something you'd like.' She doesn't move. 'Alright, Ma?'

'Whatever you say.'

'Okay, well, we'll see how you feel in the morning. Get some sleep now.'

Alone in his bed he wonders where the girl that was Teresa is: if she's killed herself or if she's asleep on some boxes in an alley somewhere. She no longer contains Ariel for him. She's just another dirty, drugged teenager to avoid on the street. He tells himself to stop thinking about her. Instead he makes plans for tomorrow. Tomorrow will be different.

SEVENTEEN

Behind her sunglasses, Connie sits in the kitchen eating a bowl of Cheerios.

'How's the ankle?' Milton asks.

'I can't walk on it.'

Milton thinks she's just saying this so he won't kick her out. Her hair looks stringy, and he wonders when she last had a shower. She shakes more Cheerios into her bowl and adds milk.

'Did you make coffee?' he asks, hoping to sound casual, as though he doesn't remember that she's had her hand on his balls or that he's seen her tits.

'I don't drink coffee.'

He fills the kettle. 'Did you hear Leonard screaming last night?'

'No.'

He waits for her to ask what happened, but she doesn't. 'He was pretty sick.'

She spoons more sugar onto her cereal.

'You should talk to him,' Milton urges. 'He'd like to see you.'

'No, he wouldn't.'

'How do you know?'

'Because he hasn't talked to me in ten years.'

'He didn't know where you were.'

'He could've found out.'

Milton hates how he bumps into walls with her, no matter which way he turns. 'Mandy says he could be dying.'

'She phoned. She's coming over.'

He spoons instant coffee into a cup. It tastes like dishwater, but he's been drinking it anyway, since Judith told him not to. Listening to Connie munching the Cheerios, he waits for the kettle to boil. 'I'm sorry your baby died,' he offers, expecting this statement to change things, open her up, make her realize that he's not just another pervert. But all she does is jerk one shoulder up in a shrug. Winnie pushes open the back door. His clothes are more crumpled than usual, his uncombed hair pokes up from his head. 'Coco killed himself,' he wails then sees Connie and turns deep red. 'Sorry,' he mutters.

'That's alright, Win,' Milton assures him. 'Sit down for a minute and tell us what happened.'

Winnie looks at Milton and jerks his head towards the back-yard. 'Can we ... you know?'

'Sure.' Milton follows him out, closing the kitchen door behind him. Winnie hops around in a desperate little dance.

'Mom's cat had babies, and Coco didn't, so he got run over.'

'Win, dogs don't kill themselves. They're not like people.'

'Coco was. He wanted babies.'

'How do you know he's dead?'

'Buzz found his body,' Winnie moans then squats on the pile of old tires Milton keeps forgetting to put out for the garbage. 'He's dead!' He starts to heave huge, jagged sobs. Milton doesn't know what to do. He wishes people would quit crying in front of him. Awkwardly he pats Winnie's shoulder, which starts a fresh cycle of tears. 'Mom says I can't bury him in the yard. She says he'll smell. She's putting him in a Glad bag on garbage day.'

'We'll bury him here,' Milton offers, although he's not too

excited about having a dead dog in his yard.

'Can we?'

'Sure.'

'I don't want to put him in a Glad bag.'

'We'll figure something out.'

'I can't believe he's dead!' Winnie howls, slamming his palms into his temples. 'I shouldn't have let him out by himself. It's just I was sick.'

'It wasn't your fault, there's no point beating yourself up about it. If he killed himself, he wanted to die anyway and maybe he's in heaven or somewhere.' He pulls a Kleenex out of his pocket and hands it to Winnie. 'You've got to respect his decision, Win. If he didn't want to live without babies that's his business.'

Winnie sniffs. 'I guess.'

~

'What was all that about?' Mandy asks.

Milton watches her putting food into his cupboards. 'What are you doing?'

'Seth tried to hit me last night. I told him if he did I'd cut his balls off in his sleep. He was drunk enough to believe it. Anyway I'm bringing the boys over here, if that's alright.'

As usual Milton feels he has no choice.

'We've got tons of canned goods,' she says. 'And macaroni and that.'

'Where's Connie?'

'In your room. She looked terrible. I told her to get some sleep. God knows what she's been up to. I swear this family is so screwed up.'

'So where's Seth going to go?'

'He's not coming here, that's for sure. I told him if he comes here I'll use Mother's gun on him, and I'm not kidding. On "Sixty Minutes", they showed these battered wives, you know these dumb cows sitting around waiting for some bastard to show his good side. And I'm thinking, that's me. I'm sitting around making excuses for this asshole. Well, forget that. He comes near me or the boys, and I'll blow his balls off. I'm not kidding. Some woman did that you know, cut them off with scissors.' She opens a packet of graham crackers and bites one.

'I've got to bury Winnie's dog,' Milton explains.

'What happened to it?'

'It got run over.'

'Oh, poor thing.'

'Yeah, well, I've got to bury it before it starts to smell.'

'Tell him to come by later and have sandwiches with us.'

'I'll see how he feels.'

~

Coco looks very strange dead. His legs stick straight out, and his ears lie flat against his head. One eye is closed but the other's half open.

'Can you close his eye?' Winnie asks quietly.

Milton bends down and tries to close the eye with his thumb as he has seen people close corpses' eyes in movies, but the lid won't go down. 'It's stuck. If I press too hard I'll poke his eye out.'

Winnie clamps his hands over his mouth as though stiffling a cry. 'So what do we put him in?'

'Well, I was thinking Ariel's pool. If we fold it in half and tape it it'll be like a sandwich. It won't crush him, and it'll keep the dirt off.' He knew he'd never be able to throw the pool out. This way it serves a purpose and can stay in his yard.

'I wanted a coffin,' Winnie says.

'That's going to cost you. Even if they make them for dogs they're probably a hundred bucks or more.'

Winnie turns and stares at the pool, which is decorated with starfish, leaning against the house.

'It's plastic,' Milton points out. 'Worms won't get through it.'

'Okay.'

Milton digs a very deep hole because he doesn't want the dog turning up in the rain. He pauses every few minutes to rest his back. The neighbour's cat sits on the fence watching him. Milton threatens it with the shovel, but it just stares at him.

'Did Connie say anything?' Winnie asks.

'About what?'

'The party.'

'No.'

'Does she think I'm retarded?'

'I haven't gotten around to asking her.'

They bind the pool closed with duct tape then Milton lays it flat in the pit. Winnie solemnly tosses the last of his dog biscuits into the grave. He closes his eyes and folds his hands in prayer. Milton waits for him to finish then shovels dirt back into the hole. Watching Ariel's pool disappear, he believes that she's really dead and that the only spirit flitting around is in his head.

'I'm going to be so lonely,' Winnie says.

Milton stares at the grave. 'You get used to it.'

~

Coming home from the hardware store, Milton sees the blind man. He's about to duck out of sight then remembers that the blind man can't see him. Instead, he leans in close to a store window filled with wedding dresses. Inside the store, past the mannequins, a fat girl in a white gown twists and turns in front of a mirror. Milton keeps still, listening to the blind man's cane tapping. Then his bent figure in the sagging duffle coat appears reflected in the store window. Milton doesn't understand why he feels guilty. It wasn't like he knocked the blind man over on purpose. He hates how he feels guilty for no reason. 'I'm sorry about what happened at Mr. Grocer,' he blurts out, startling the blind man who pulls his hands into his chest as though preparing to block blows. 'I knocked you over in the store,' Milton explains, but the blind man starts to hurry away from him. Milton follows. 'My wife wouldn't let me help you. I wanted to, but she kept kicking me.' The blind man emits horrible, high-pitched gutteral noises. He turns on Milton waving his cane like a sword. Milton hangs back. The blind man hurries on, and Milton feels worse than before he said anything. Then he thinks about how the blind man must feel, without eyes or a tongue, and he tells himself he has no right to feel bad. He remembers what Leonard said about hating his life before he found out he was dying. Milton wonders if he himself is going to have to start dying before he stops hating his life. He looks at the people passing him on the sidewalk, staring down at the pavement. They all look like they hate their lives even though they have eyes and tongues. Milton would like to know if anybody really loves their life. There's a guy at work who's always talking about what a great weekend he had. Milton would like to know if the guy's weekends are really all that great or if he justs says that so nobody will figure out what a shitbag of a life he has. Milton has a feeling that nobody's all that excited about their lives. Except maybe Bruce Willis or somebody.

~

He's about to take the paint samples upstairs to show Mare when Mandy comes in from the kitchen and grabs his arm. 'Leonard's worse, you better go see him. The homecare nurse came. She called his doctor for a prescription for parasites. She says that's why he's got diarrhea. She thinks he got it from the cat. We're supposed to keep the cat out of there.' Milton starts up the stairs. 'Also, Milton?'

'What?'

'He keeps saying he's freezing. I think a warm bath would help but I don't think he'd be too happy about me doing it.'

'Alright.'

'Also, Milton?'

'What?'

'There's some latex gloves up there. The nurse said we should wear them because he's got open sores, and we're handling bodily fluids.'

This upsets Milton more than he'd expect. He can't imagine how Leonard's going to feel with everybody wearing gloves around him.

'I'm not kidding, Milt, this is serious. We have to wear them.'

'Alright.'

'If you don't want to, we can take him to the hospital.'

'I said alright.'

Milton sits on the chair by the bed and touches Leonard's arm so he'll know he's there. There's no sign of the raging Leonard, just a very sick, weak man.

'Hi, Milton,' he mutters, and Milton wonders how he knew it

was him. 'I didn't know where I was this morning,' Leonard continues. 'I spent the longest time trying to figure out where I was.' He rubs his eyes. 'I thought someone was trying to kill me.'

Last night Milton dreamed that he'd killed somebody. He didn't know who or how, just that he'd done it and that he'd be found out. He tried to act normal while the people around him talked about the murder. He felt no remorse for killing the person, only distress at the prospect of being arrested and put in jail. When he woke and realized he hadn't killed anybody, he felt enormous relief. 'Who did you think was trying to kill you?' he asks.

'I have no idea.'

Milton tries to slip the gloves on noiselessly, but they squeak. 'Do you want a bath?'

'You don't have to do that.'

'It'll warm you up, and Mandy'll want to change the sheets anyway.'

Carrying his brother he doesn't think about who Leonard is or what he's done to him. Lowering him into the tub his only concern is that Leonard's head doesn't bump into the porcelain. He has no feelings for him other than that he doesn't want to see him get hurt. Milton wonders if this feeling is related to love. He tells himself not to care one way or the other since every time he tries to love somebody it doesn't work out.

'I understand about the gloves,' Leonard says.

~

'I think it's awesome,' Mandy comments, 'how you've turned around. I mean, who would've thought you'd turn out to be this awesome nurse.' She stuffs the sheets and towels into the washer then shakes Tide over them. 'Anyways I wanted to ask you about Rory. Did you talk to him?'

'I was going to, but you were there.' Milton sprays bug killer in the area where Mandy said she saw the cockroach.

'Right, well there's something really weird going on. I mean he won't press charges.'

'So?'

She turns the dial; the washer rumbles into action. 'See I'm scared he's gay.'

'What if he is?'

'Oh, come on, Milton. Look what happened to Leonard.'

'They do things differently now.' He squirts under the stairwell. 'Tell him to wear a raincoat or whatever.'

'You tell him. As soon as I tell him, he won't do it.'

'So don't tell him.'

'Somebody has to tell him, and his dad certainly won't.'

Milton is beginning to realize that whenever she says 'somebody' she means him. 'I never even see him.'

'Yeah well, now that he's staying here, you will.' She pulls T-shirts out of the dryer and starts to fold them. 'Did you hear about that little girl that's missing? That's the third child this year. It makes you sick. I swear if they ever catch these perverts, they should cut their balls off.' She shakes out a shirt. 'Spray under the dryer, they're always under appliances.' Milton gets down on his hands and knees and sprays under the dryer. The fumes from the insecticide are making him nauseous.

'Do you think I'm a bad mother?' Mandy asks suddenly.

He knows that, if he tells her what he really thinks, she won't talk to him for days. 'No,' he says.

'I try really hard, you know; it's not easy raising two kids on your own.'

Seth stumbles over the step into the laundry room then steadies himself against the washer. 'I thought I heard voices.'

'I told you not to come here,' Mandy tells him.

Already Milton can smell the beer.

'I'm sorry, babe,' Seth mumbles. 'I'm really sorry. Please come home.'

Mandy stares at him. 'There is no home, understand? There is no home.'

'I want to see my boys.'

'Since when are you interested in your boys? Get out of here, I mean it.'

Still on his hands and knees, Milton wonders how he's going to stop Seth from killing Mandy.

'You've got no right,' Seth argues.

Milton knows he'd lose in hand-to-hand combat.

'Don't talk to me about rights,' Mandy says.

In some movie they tied the bad guy's shoe laces together, tripping him. Milton tries to reach Seth's Kodiaks, but he keeps moving around.

Seth holds out his arms as though he were about to start singing. 'I love you, babe.'

Mandy shakes her head. 'Forget it.' She tries to push past him, but he blocks her.

'You turn them against me,' he persists.

'I do no such thing.' She tries again to pass him, but he grabs her shoulders. Milton jumps up and shoves the bug killer in Seth's face. 'Leave her alone, or I'll spray.' Seth swipes at the insecticide just as Milton squirts. Seth covers his face with his hands. 'Jesus,' he cries. Mandy slips past him and runs upstairs.

'I'm calling the cops,' she calls back.

'Jesus, Milton,' Seth says. 'What'd you do that for?'

Milton guides him to the sink. 'Rinse it off.'

'It fucking burns.'

'Rinse it off.'

'All she wants is for me to get some shit job.' Seth splashes water on his face.

'You better get going before the cops get here.'

'I could be a fucking busboy for all she cares. A fucking street cleaner. It makes no difference.'

'So let her go.' Milton hands Seth a towel.

Milton can't understand why people who complain about each other stay together.

Seth leans against the sink patting his face with the towel. 'I love her.'

Milton doesn't believe him. He has a feeling Seth goes around telling Mandy he loves her so she won't leave him. She probably considers herself lucky to be loved, probably thinks she couldn't do any better. Which may be true. Not too many men want a fat lady wearing them down. 'Well ...' Milton starts for the door, hoping Seth will follow.

Seth sits on Leonard's boxes of books and stares at the bug killer. 'You got roaches?'

'Mandy thinks so.'

'Don't listen to her. She's got bug phobia.' He tosses the towel into the laundry basket. 'So where's your wife?'

'She left.'

'What happened?'

'I hit her.'

Surprised, Seth looks at him. 'Why?'

'She wouldn't do what I wanted.'

Seth nods, looking grim.

'It would have been smarter to smash my own head. Maybe then she'd've felt sorry for me.'

'I don't know about that.' Seth opens his hands and stares at his palms. 'So what am I supposed to do now?'

'You could go home.'

'You heard her; there is no home.'

'There must be some bar you can go to.'

'I don't want to go to a bar. I miss my boys.'

When he starts to sob, Milton can't believe another person is crying in front of him. This never used to happen when people thought he was mean. He considers calling Mandy then realizes that this will only start the scene over again. 'Come on,' he urges. 'I'll give you a ride somewhere.' Gently he tugs on Seth's arm, and like a scolded child, the big man complies.

~

Mandy sets a plate of sandwiches on the table. 'Where'd you take him?'

Milton pulls out a chair. 'Back to your place.' He left Seth sitting on the front steps, looking as though he had no idea where he was. In the car he'd said repeatedly that he didn't know what to do and Milton couldn't think of what to tell him. He tried talking about the documentary he watched last night about killer whales; he described them playing around in the open sea, staying close together, talking, not fighting or killing each other. He said he thought humans could learn a lot from whales. He admitted that he'd felt lonely watching them and that he'd wanted to be a whale. He'd hoped that hearing about the whales would make Seth realize that he shouldn't hit his wife. But all Seth said was that he saw some whales in an aquarium once and thought they were no big deal.

Morty skids into the kitchen and grabs one of the sandwiches. 'Some guy shot a whole bunch of people in a mall, then blew his own head off.'

'What guy?' Mandy asks.

'Some guy on the news.'

'I swear,' Mandy says, 'you'd think something nice could happen once in a while.'

'He raped a girl first,' Morty explains with his mouth full, 'and hacked her to bits with a machete then killed like twelve other people. A whole lot more were wounded.'

Mandy stares at him. 'Do you think this is good dinner conversation?'

'Sorry.' Morty swallows. Mandy holds the plate out to Milton but he's thinking about the transient killer whales, different from the regular killer whales because they eat sea-lion pups, snap them off the beach while the pups' mothers are getting food. The transient whale in the documentary didn't kill the pup right away but batted it around in the water, allowing it to try frantically to escape. Each time the pup managed to swim close to the beach, the whale would snap it back in its jaws then bat it around again before letting it try to escape. Milton was furious and couldn't understand why God or whoever would create such harmony among the regular killer whales, then let this asshole transient whale go around torturing sea-lion pups. When the sea-lion mother showed up and stood on the shore crying out in despair, Milton had to change the channel.

'They should cut his balls off,' Mandy declares. 'All they'll do is stick him in prison for a few years and us taxpayers will have to pay for his room and board. It makes you sick.'

'You don't pay taxes,' Morty points out. 'You're on welfare.'

'Maybe there's supposed to be assholes,' Milton offers.

Mandy looks at him. 'What?'

'Maybe we're supposed to learn something from these assholes who go around killing people.'

'Like what?'

'I don't know. It's just, in nature animals kill each other, and they're not always too nice about it. So maybe it's supposed to happen.' He thinks about the assholes who tortured Jesus. God let them go ahead and hammer nails into his hands. Maybe all this killing is going on for a reason. He can't think of one, though.

'We're supposed to be smarter than animals,' Mandy says.

Morty grabs another sandwich. 'Animals just have instincts. We've got brains.'

Connie hobbles in and sits at the table.

'Did you sleep?' Mandy asks.

'It's impossible with Leonard moaning.'

'Milton rescued me today,' Mandy tells her. 'Seth came over, and Milton scared him off with bug killer.'

'How appropriate,' Connie comments.

Mandy opens her sandwich and pours ketchup on the baloney. 'Seriously, Milt, I thought you were awesome. I mean I really felt like I had a big brother.'

When he sprayed Seth he felt like he was doing the right thing. Now he's not so sure. He hates how he never feels certain that he's done the right thing. Which is why for a long time he didn't do anything. At least then he didn't have to worry that maybe he did the wrong thing. 'He seemed pretty upset,' he tells them. 'He even cried.'

'Oh, he always does that.' Mandy spreads the ketchup with her knife. 'And you think, oh, what a sweetheart; maybe I was wrong about him. Then he goes and gets shit-faced again.'

Connie opens a sandwich and inspects the ingredients. 'Who was Leonard screaming at?'

'Nobody in particular,' Mandy says. 'When I was trying to give him his pills, he called me a bitch and said I was trying to kill him. I think he thought I was a nurse.'

Milton considers explaining that Leonard is yelling at God but decides not to; they might think this means that Leonard is demented and should go to the hospital.

Mandy sighs heavily. 'I wish we had a religion. Then we could get a priest in here, and he could do whatever it is they do.'

'Priests rape little boys,' Morty informs her.

'Pardon?' Mandy glares at him.

'It's true. It's on the news all the time.'

'Since when do you watch the news?'

'Oh, Mum, everybody knows about priests.'

'Just because some priests do it, doesn't mean all priests are bad. Don't you ever say all priests are bad.'

Morty shrugs and wipes his hands on his jeans.

'Use a napkin,' Mandy tells him.

Morty picks up a napkin off the table and wipes his hands vaguely. 'Uncle Milton, can I watch TV in your room?'

'Sure.' Morty takes off up the stairs. 'I should probably set it up in the living-room,' Milton offers. The problem is he'd have to put it where Ariel died because that's where the cable outlet is.

Mandy starts clearing plates from the table. 'Don't worry about it. He watches too much TV anyway.'

Milton finds Leonard asleep when he goes in to check on him. He sits by the bed and studies him trying to imagine what it would be like to be inside Leonard's body. If he could be inside Leonard's body for a day he has a feeling it would change his life, and he would become a positive person.

'Is he dead or asleep?' Connie asks, startling Milton.

'Asleep,' he says, although he's not sure.

'He looks dead.' Connie grips Leonard's wrist, feeling for a pulse. Milton waits nervously for her verdict. Suddenly the reality of Leonard's impending death horrifies him. Connie narrows her eyes. 'What?' Milton asks.

'He's alive.' She drops Leonard's wrist and sits on the edge of the bed, staring at him. 'He looks pretty repulsive.' She pulls the covers back, exposing his skeletal chest. 'I'd shoot myself before I'd let this happen.' Milton takes the covers from her and lays them back over Leonard.

'So are you two best buddies now or what?' she asks.

'What do you mean?'

'Now that he's dying, do you forgive him all his sins?'

'No.'

'He sodomized my friend Arnie when he was eight.'

Again Milton doesn't know whether to believe her, thinks maybe she's on something. 'When?' he asks.

'After school. He said he had Lego in his room so Arnie went up.'

'How do you know what happened?'

'Arnie's anus was bleeding. That's usually a pretty good indication.'

'I don't believe you.'

'So don't.'

'Why do you say stuff like that?'

'Like what?'

'Even if it's true you don't have to say it.'

'I think rupturing little boys' sphincters is a pretty major offense,' Connie says. 'Just because he's dying, you all want to believe he's some kind of saint.'

'I don't.'

'No, you like cleaning up his shit and vomit.'

'Are you jealous or something?' Milton asks. 'The way you're going, you'll be dead pretty soon yourself.'

Connie picks up one of the bottles of morphine and studies it. 'I wonder how much it takes.' He tries to snatch the bottle from her, but she holds it out of his reach. 'You think he wants to lie around in shit and vomit?'

'He doesn't want to die.'

She shakes her head. 'Milton, you're such an innocent.' She slides the morphine into her jean jacket. He knows the only way to get it would be to wrestle with her—meaning he'd have to touch her—which scares him. She scrutinizes the collection of drugs on the side table. 'So what is all this shit anyway?' She picks up a bottle of pills.

'Don't touch them.'

'A fat lot of good they're doing him.' She picks up another bottle. 'They probably cost a fucking fortune. The AIDS racket. Somebody's making some dough.'

Milton manages to grab the bottles from her. 'Just leave them alone, alright?' He hates how he has to plead with her.

'We could fuck right here,' she says abruptly, lightly. 'At Leonard's feet. It might give him a buzz.'

215

Only now is Milton convinced that there is something seriously, dangerously, irreversibly wrong with his sister. He has a feeling that horrible things happen to her because she wants them to, needs them to; because without them she feels without value. As a victim she feels needed by the victimiser. As a victim she has cause for suffering. She wants him to fornicate with her so that she can say she was raped by her brother. 'Why did you masturbate Winnie?' he asks.

'Because he wanted it.'

'Are you telling people you got raped by a retard?'

'No.'

'Leave him alone.'

'Is that a threat?'

He realizes that this is what she wants. 'Forget it.' He feels like crying because at one time he carried her on his shoulders; at one time he read stories to her about princesses; at one time maybe he could have done something. What was he doing all those years? As she has said, he's had his head up his own asshole. He feels like crying because, just like with Ariel and Judith and the girl, he's too late.

~

Winnie won't leave Coco. His mother is so angry with him, she has locked him out. Milton takes the sleeping bags that he and Judith bought, for camping trips they never made, out to the backyard. He and Winnie sit in the bags on either side of Coco's grave.

'I couldn't leave him alone tonight,' Winnie insists.

'Of course not.' Milton remembers the cold of Ariel on the hospital cot. Still in her Big Bird sweatshirt, she'd looked normal although very pale. Blood had leaked from her mouth, but the hospital staff must have wiped it off. He tried to pick her up but her rib cage crumbled under his hands, and he was afraid of breaking her. So he leaned over her, resting his forehead on the cot between her shoulder and neck, trying to inhale her smell. But it was gone, overcome by a sickly, sweet hospital odour. He remained bent over her, determined to shield her from strangers while Judith, hysterical, slammed her hands into the walls.

216

Winnie fingers the end of his nose. 'Do you believe in heaven?'

'I don't know.'

'There has to be one. Otherwise there's no point in being good.'

'Sure there is. You have to live with yourself.'

'Do you think I'm good?'

Milton nods.

'Even after what happened with Connie?'

Milton nods again.

'Mum doesn't think so.'

'She's just worried about you.'

'She says she thinks my soul's tainted.' He pulls the sleeping bag up to his chin.

'She just doesn't want to see you get hurt.' Milton isn't sure that this is true. Lindsay Wagner wouldn't let her retarded boy join scouts because she said she didn't want to see him get hurt. In the end he joined anyway and made all kinds of friends. Milton couldn't see this happening in real life. When people see Winnie coming they look the other way.

'Did you ask Connie if she thinks I'm retarded?' Winnie hands Milton a caramel.

'She doesn't think you're retarded.'

'Really?'

Milton nods, uncomfortable about lying.

Winnie unwraps a caramel for himself. 'Do you think she'd go out with me?' Milton shrugs. 'Would you mind if I asked her?'

'Do what you want.'

Winnie pops the caramel in his mouth and lies back in the grass, staring up at the sky. 'I saw this show on near-death experiences. When you almost die, you see this dark tunnel with this light at the end, and all your dead friends are floating around in it. And there's flowers and stuff. It's supposed to be really pretty. Anyways, then you have to decide if you want to be with your dead friends or back in real life. I hope that happened to Coco. I mean I hope he decided to stay. I hope he's not lonely.'

Milton wonders if this is true, and if Ariel made the decision while the TV was squeezing the breath out of her. It makes sense, otherwise why didn't she cry out? He wonders what it was in the tunnel that convinced her to stay.

It grows cold and damp, and Winnie starts to cough so Milton insists he go home. Winnie agrees only after Milton calls his mother and asks her to unlock the door.

~

Rory has his feet up on Milton's bed.

'What's on?' Milton asks.

'The news. There's been another oil spill.'

On the screen, birds covered in oil struggle to fly. 'Why the fuck can't they fix those boats so they don't leak?' Milton asks.

'Too much money.'

Milton can't stand to watch the seals drowning in oil so he starts down the hall to brush his teeth.

'Uncle Milton,' Rory cries. 'That's you!'

Milton hurries back and sees what must be himself because he's wearing the plaid shirt and jeans and the girl is sitting beside him. It doesn't look like him. He isn't that bald or that fat. His lips are moving, but he can't hear himself. The newscaster is talking over him about a tearful reunion and how some stories have happy endings. Then there's a close-up of a McDonald's bacon-double-cheeseburger.

'Wow,' Rory comments. 'You're famous Uncle Milt. Now everybody knows about it.'

They took his picture and made up a story. He feels violated. He wanted the world to know the truth, and all they did was make it look like a TV movie.

'Did you know it was going to be on?' Rory asks. 'We should have taped it.'

Milton remembers all the times they've shown people's faces but cut out their voices and talked over them. He's always assumed they were summarizing what the people were saying, but now he knows they lie. This shocks him. For years he has watched the news believing that a responsible citizen should stay tuned to world events. But now he knows it's all lies. Except for the animals dying in oil. The whales dying in oil. Why don't they destroy humans? Why don't they smash the boats whose propellers scar their backs?

Why don't they chew up human's legs like Jaws? What makes them able to forgive?

'Mom says you wanted to talk to me about something important,' Rory says. 'If it's about Ryan I've made my decision.'

Milton kicks off his sneakers. 'She's concerned about you, that's all.' He can't stand to say, 'She doesn't want to see you get hurt.'

'Why?'

Milton's tired of lies. 'She thinks you're gay.'

'I'm not.'

'So tell her.'

'She won't believe me.'

'That's her problem.' He has a feeling Rory is gay because he was so quick to deny it and because when he said, 'I've made my decision,' he sounded like his mouth was frozen. 'Don't worry about it.'

'Do you think I'm gay?'

'No.'

'She's so paranoid.'

Milton nods, staring at an ad for pantyhose. A redhead runs her hands over her legs like she's getting off on it. 'Just practise safe sex,' he advises. He's never said these words before, and the 's's take forever.

'I do,' Rory insists.

'Good.'

Rory stands. 'Okay, well, I guess I'll hit the sack. Goodnight, I think it's great what you did. With the girl.'

Milton nods vaguely and lies back on his bed. He pulls the paint samples from his back pocket and flips through them. After a few minutes he gets up to see if his mother's light is on. It isn't. Back in his own room, he sits down on the bed studying the samples. He has no idea what her favourite colour is. It seems to him that a son should know what his mother's favourite colour is. Mandy always asks him if he has remembered to call their mother on her birthday. He never has and he always feels guilty about it. Once he phoned, and Mare gave him such a hard time about never phoning that he never phoned again. The whales stay with their mothers for her lifetime. A mother whale can live for as many as eighty years and have five babies, and they'll all stay together. Milton can't imagine this.

They must not hold grudges. Judith says he holds grudges, and he agrees with her. He used to think it was normal, but now he has a feeling it's a waste of time. Like why should he bother to think about assholes like Munroe and Aiken or the Goof? They shouldn't even be inside his head. They don't deserve to be inside his head.

From now on he's going to try to be more like a whale.

EIGHTEEN

Milton dreams he has a heart condition. Doctors surround his bed, insisting that he has to have an operation. He becomes angry and tells them they've made a mistake. Then he's in the subway with Judith. She's pregnant and pulls her sweater up to show him it's 'real'. He waits for her to tell him it's not his, but she doesn't, and he's afraid to ask. Suddenly a man who looks like Geraldo Rivera has a knife and is going to slice open Judith's belly. She doesn't notice him, and Milton can't decide if he should warn her, since it might not be his baby.

The smoke wakes him up. He puts his pants on and goes downstairs, passing the sleeping bodies of Connie and the boys on the couch and the floor. The basement light is on. He finds Mandy, cigarette in hand, sitting on Leonard's boxes of books.

'I couldn't sleep,' she explains. 'I'm sorry, I can't quit now. I mean, I get so tight in my chest, you know. It's like, there's this fucking monster sitting on my chest, and I can't breathe. I'm really sorry,

I mean you've been so great and everything ...'

'It's okay.'

'I will quit, it's just I can't go cold turkey.'

He nods knowing she won't.

'Mother snores,' she adds, 'unevenly so you think maybe she's dead. You lie there waiting for the next snore wondering how you'll deal with her being really dead. I mean can you imagine it?'

'No.'

She flicks her cigarette ash into the sink. 'Next it's us, you know. I mean that's what's so weird about it. Once she's gone, there's nobody.' She shakes her head. 'I'm so scared. You know you always read about those middle-aged women who leave their husbands and start careers, become social workers and that. I can't do that.'

'Why not?'

'Because I don't have the smarts.'

'Who says?'

'Oh, come on, Milton. Everybody knows I'm not exactly super intelligent.'

'I don't know that.' He remembers Mare referring to Mandy as dumb, but he doesn't know this for a fact. Connie and Leonard were supposed to be smart, and look what happened to them. 'Maybe you should go back to school,' he suggests.

'How am I supposed to afford it?'

'You can stay here.' He's not sure this is such a great idea, but then he remembers the whales sticking together no matter what.

'I don't even have grade thirteen. Besides there's no jobs for women over thirty-five. We might as well be dead. Nobody even wants to look at us. I couldn't even get a decent waitressing job. They all want girls in mini-skirts.'

Milton can see her point. You never see pudgy older women waitressing in fancy restaurants or nice bars. The older women are always behind department store counters.

'Maybe you can learn about computers,' he offers. 'There's night courses you can take.' He doesn't know why he's saying this since he hates it when people give him advice. He always wonders if the people who give advice ever notice that nobody takes it.

Mandy inhales on her cigarette, holding the smoke deep in her lungs before exhaling. 'There's a woman in the projects who's got eleven kids. You should see the size of her welfare check. She's always telling me I should have more kids so I'll get more money.'

Milton knows that if he doesn't change the subject she'll go on about how hard her life is. It's not that he doesn't believe her; it's just that he has a feeling if something good happened to her she wouldn't notice. 'What's with Mother and Connie?' he asks.

'What do you mean?'

'Mother thinks Connie wants to kill her.'

Mandy nods. 'She went at her with scissors once.'

'Connie did?'

Mandy nods again.

'Why?'

'Mother used to make her kneel on gravel and stuff. Sometimes she locked her in her closet.'

'What were we doing?'

'I don't know about you, but I was just glad she wasn't doing it to me. Which is pretty sick. I mean I felt sorry for Connie, but she was a brat. I think they're identical to tell you the truth. They deserve each other.'

Milton realizes how safe he has been in his ignorance. And it seems to him that this might not have been a bad thing; it's not like his knowing would have changed anything. It's like, all the shit that's going on in the world, his knowing about it doesn't change anything. The politicians and corporation heads could change things, but they go around saying they don't know about it. It seems to Milton that they would know about it if they were doing their jobs right. Which makes him think that if he was what Connie calls a 'decent brother' he would have known about Mare abusing her. Maybe he forced himself not to think about it because he didn't want to know. Knowing about it would mean he'd have to do something.

'They found that little girl.' Mandy stubs her cigarette out in the sink. 'Cut to pieces in a fridge.' She shakes her head. 'It just makes you not want to live. I mean I can't even look at men without wondering if they're perverts. I must know at least one, there are so many of them. The girl was three years old. How do you rape a three-year-old?'

Milton doesn't want to think about it, doesn't want to know.

'The poor mother,' Mandy adds. 'They showed her on the news. She was crying and that.'

He wonders if he should ask Mandy if she knows anything about Leonard sodomizing Arnie. But then he decides that once he's said it, there's no taking it back. Once it's said, it's as good as done.

'Did Rory talk to you?' Mandy asks.

Milton nods.

'Do you think he's gay?'

Milton shakes his head but, uncomfortable with the lie, pretends to be checking for dead roaches under the stairwell.

'That's a relief.' She pulls out another cigarette, lights it and stares at the floor. 'I so badly wanted him to go to college and that, but his grades are as bad as mine were, so there's no way he'd get a scholarship. For a while there I was putting away fifty bucks a month for his education, but that didn't last.' She smokes, still staring at the floor. Milton can hear rain tapping against the window.

'It's funny, you know,' Mandy continues, 'you have kids, and you really think they're special. You have this feeling things are going to be different for them. You really believe that. Then they get older and start acting like all the other kids. Or like you, which is worse. They start repeating things you didn't think they'd heard in the first place. I mean they're like sponges; they suck up everything. There's no way you can hide stuff from them. You want to protect them, you don't want them to know, but there's no way.' She covers her eyes with her hands, and Milton knows she's trying not to cry. 'This is going to sound weird, but in a way, you're lucky you lost Ariel. I mean at least you'll always think of her as special.' Outside, tires screech and a car radio blares then fades away. Mandy stands and yanks laundry out of the dryer then begins pairing socks. 'Leonard's diarrhea isn't getting any better. I put a garbage bag over the mattress but we're going to have to start putting diapers on him. I can't keep cleaning sheets every hour.' She shakes out a sheet and starts to fold it. 'And he's getting bed sores. I keep trying to patch them up, but his skin just won't heal.'

Milton doesn't know what she expects him to say so he grabs

some clean underwear he recognizes to be his. 'I'll check in on him,' he offers. 'You should try to get some sleep.'

'I'll be alright.'

Leonard is moaning again. Milton shakes him gently. 'It's me. Milton.' Leonard doesn't seem to hear him.

Mandy comes in with clean sheets and hands Milton a pair of latex gloves. 'Can you lift him up while I change them?' Milton puts on the gloves and slides his arms under his brother, trying not to gag from the smell of shit. He watches Mandy remove the soiled sheets and make the bed. She grabs a damp cloth and wipes Leonard's behind. 'Wait a second,' she tells Milton. She opens a jar of Vaseline then carefully but speedily applies it to her brother's anus. 'Okay put him down.' She gathers up the dirty sheets and goes downstairs. Milton arranges Leonard on the bed, wondering if he did sodomize Arnie. It disturbs him that a piece of information can change how you look at a person, even if the information comes from an unreliable source. If Leonard did sodomize Arnie, Milton wonders if he still thinks about it, or if his suffering has obliterated his past. On TV, dying people reminisce about their past, but Milton can't see how, when you're in pain, you'd want to talk about the old days. The old days can't matter much when you don't know if you're going to be here tomorrow. Milton has a feeling Leonard isn't too concerned about sodomizing Arnie. And standing on the outskirts of his brother's hell, Milton isn't too concerned either. He wonders if this means he forgives him.

He can't sleep, so he turns on the TV and flicks past a half-hour commercial for a weight-loss program, a talk show he's never seen before, a Chinese man telling him how to make millions in real estate and Bobby Hull advertising hair replacement. He stops on a 'Bonanza' episode. Two bad guys argue about crossing into Ben Cartwright's land. The first bad guy insists he'd never cross Ben Cartwright's land without his permission. The second bad guy, with a gold tooth, says he'd better go with him, or there's going to be trouble. The first bad guy pulls out a gun and says they'll have to part company because he ain't gonna mess with Ben Cartwright. The gold-toothed bad guy says suit yourself. When the first bad guy slides his gun back in his holster and turns to his horse, the gold-toothed bad guy shoots him in the back. Milton changes channels and sees penguins leaping off rocks into the sea. The narrator explains that some of the baby penguins aren't strong enough to escape the sea lions. A sea lion pokes its head out of the water and sinks its tusks into a baby penguin. It doesn't kill it right away but chomps on it, then bats it about before chomping on it again. The narrator explains that this is play for the sea lion, that it doesn't actually eat baby penguins it just likes to torture them. Milton can't understand why the sea lion, who has seen its own babies mangled by transient killer whales, would go around killing baby penguins when it doesn't even eat them. At least the whales eat the baby sea lions. The sea lions have no reason to kill the baby penguins, except to make someone suffer as they have suffered. Judith says that the persecuted persecute, and that's why there will always be wars. The sea lion swims away and the dead baby penguin is left floating with its little webbed feet poking out of the water. Milton switches back to the talk show. A blonde starlet he doesn't recognize is talking earnestly about a benefit for the homeless. She says it should be a really great night: Robin Williams will be there. Her mini-skirt rides up her thighs as she swings her leg. Gold glints from her earlobes and cleavage. Then she announces that wearing a fur coat is a crime. She says she has a whole bunch of fake fur coats at home, and they're truly fabulous.

~

The gunshot wakes him. At first he thinks it's part of a dream but then he recognizes Leonard's screams. As he hurries out of bed he can already picture the blood gushing from his brother's head.

'Are you fucking crazy?' he hears Mandy shout. He rushes into the room and sees her picking up the gun. His mother is on the floor, recovering from a fall. Leonard, whimpering, struggles to get out of bed.

'She tried to shoot him.' Mandy holds the gun away from her as though she's afraid it will fire. Milton sees the bullet hole in the ceiling. 'It must have jumped out of her hand,' Mandy explains. 'I don't think she's ever fired it before.'

Leonard, exhausted, cringes in the bed holding his arms over his head as though shielding himself from blows. His cat darts from under the bed and out the doorway where Connie stands wearing her sunglasses. 'Call the cops,' she says.

'What for?' Mandy asks. 'Nobody's hurt.'

'You alright, Ma?' Milton asks since she hasn't moved. When she doesn't respond, he crouches beside her. 'You alright?' She's cradling her right wrist in her left hand and he wonders if it's broken. 'Your wrist okay?'

'I thought you took the gun from her,' Mandy says.

'She took it back.'

'And you didn't get it from her?'

He tries putting his hands under his mother's arms to help her up, but she shakes him off. Mandy puts the gun on the dresser then sits beside Leonard and tries to pull his arms away from his face. 'It's alright, Len; she's just crazy. Milton, can you get her out of here?'

'She won't go.'

The boys, sleepy-eyed, stand in the hall looking in.

'Go back to bed,' Mandy commands.

'What happened?' Rory asks.

'The gun went off by accident,' Mandy lies.

'Did anybody get shot?' Morty asks excitedly.

'No, go back to bed. Right now!'

'It's morning,' Morty protests, 'can't we have breakfast?'

'Downstairs now!' Mandy shouts. Morty scurries downstairs and Rory reluctantly follows.

Milton notices that Mare's wrist is swelling. 'I think I'd better take her to the hospital.'

'I'm not going anywhere,' Mare grumbles.

'You really are nuts, you know that?' Mandy tells her. 'You should be in a home. Milton, get her out of here. I don't care if you break her bones. I've had it with her.' She pulls the covers up around Leonard. 'It's alright Len. Everything's going to be alright.' But Leonard continues holding his arms over his head.

'Hey, guys,' Connie says, pointing the gun at her temple. 'How about it?' The fake gold bangles on her wrist jangle.

'Don't be stupid,' Mandy cautions.

'Who's stupid?' Connie points the gun at Mandy.

Milton tries to remember how the hero knocks the gun out of the bad guy's hand. Usually they squeeze the bad guy's wrist forcing the gun out of his grip. Or sometimes they kick the gun out of his hand. Or tackle him from behind so he drops it.

'Good,' Mandy taunts, 'go ahead and kill me. Then you can look after Leonard and Mother.' She turns back to Leonard and strokes the back of his head.

'Put the gun down,' Milton orders. The words don't feel like his own, more like Bruce Willis's or somebody's.

'Ignore her,' Mandy tells him. 'She's just a little selfish bitch who loves doing numbers. What's the matter, Connie? Why don't you shoot all of us? Then you could be all by your own slutty self.'

'Mandy,' Milton warns.

'I'm serious. I've fucking had it with her. She goes around with her tits hanging out acting surprised when guys come on to her. Well, we all know you're a whore, dear, so you can quit acting like nobody understands you.'

'Mandy,' Milton repeats.

'She fucked my husband in my own house. I felt sorry for her because I know what Mom did to her, but forget that.'

Connie, staring at Mandy, seems to have forgotten she's holding the gun. It hangs at her side. Milton steps towards her, hoping to retrieve it.

'Just don't kill my boys, alright?' Mandy asks. 'Don't fuck them either. If you haven't already, god knows.' She looks at Mare. 'Milton, Mother's about to have an attack. Get her pills out of her sweater pocket, she can't if her wrist's broken.' While his mother gasps, Milton finds the small plastic pill-box. 'Put one under her tongue,' Mandy instructs. Milton forces Mare's jaw open and pushes the pill under her tongue. 'She'll be alright,' Mandy adds. 'Lie her flat and give her a minute.'

The gunshot and the sound of Connie's body crashing into the dresser and Mandy screaming all happen at once. Then the boys are running upstairs. 'Stay down there!' Mandy shouts. Rory slams the door on Morty but comes in himself. Morty starts to cry, Leonard moans, Mandy screams oh my god, oh my god. Rory stands beside her and pulls her face into his stomach while he stares at the blood and brains spattered across the wall. Milton, still on the floor holding his mother, is afraid to look at the body without a head. Instead he looks at his mother, her face distorted from pain as though someone were twisting a knife inside her.

'Uncle Milton?' Rory asks, his voice faint. Milton looks up at the boy, his face drained of blood, his eyes still fixed on Connie's remains. 'You'd better call 911.'

~

They sit in emergency for three and a half hours without talking. Milton has explained to the nurse that his mother broke her wrist and has angina, but she said there had just been a multi-car pile-up. An intern gave Mare some Tylenol with codeine to kill the pain. Milton suspects she's keeping quiet because she's stoned. He has called Mandy several times to find out if the police have left yet. She didn't sound like Mandy: her voice was hoarse from screaming, and she had none of her usual conviction. Rory answered the fourth time and said that the police had left with the body and the gun. When Milton told the police that it was Connie's, he could tell that the cop chewing the Clorets didn't believe him and wanted to ask more questions, but Milton insisted he had to go to the hospital with his mother. He wishes the muscles in his legs and shoulders would stop twitching. Pieces of Connie keep splintering inside his head: her bangles, her breasts, her sunglasses, her sneer. He rubs his palms into his eyes then leans his elbows on his knees and stares at a stain—coffee or maybe blood—on the floor. He picks up the *Sun* he bought earlier, hoping that forcing himself to read will stop him from thinking. He focusses hard on the words 'nurse clubbed to death'. The murderer broke in her back door. The nurse had been planning to retire to her cottage in Ireland. Her co-workers said she was always talking about it. Milton doesn't get how you could club a person to death. It must take a while. Blood must spurt while the person struggles, screams and pleads. There must be a point when you want to stop and run away from it, from yourself. Maybe not, maybe the bleeding heap turns into everybody you've ever hated, and you believe that when it stops moving you'll be free. The nurse's co-workers said she was the nicest person in the world. Milton studies her photo. She looks chubby-cheeked, jolly, like somebody's aunt. Why did the asshole kill her? Why didn't he kill another asshole? Or himself? He's probably sitting in a bar right now pleased with himself for getting away with it. He'll probably do it again. He'll crave the rush that killing gives him, the only rush he gets because he's slime and has nothing to live for.

In his head, Milton hears the gunshot again and Mandy's screams and Connie's body crashing into the dresser. She must have spent the last ten years surrounded by slime. She must have felt like slime. A drunk with a nose bleed stumbles through the sliding doors and says he's dying, then he asks if anybody can spare some change. People deadened from waiting and pain ignore him. He approaches Milton, his eyes blood-shot, his nose a mass of broken capillaries. Blood leaks from his nostrils. Milton wants to kick his face in, wants to tell him he's a fucking waste of space. But his muscles become rigid, restraining him. He looks at the floor, hoping the drunk will go away. Instead, he leans into him, breathing Lysol and cheap sherry. Milton tries to think of the whales but instead he says, 'Get out of my face, or I'll break your fucking nose.' A freckled orderly grabs the drunk's arm. 'Okay, buddy,' he says. 'This isn't a shelter. You know where the shelter is.'

'I'm bleeding,' the drunk protests, but Milton can see that he has already given up the fight and will allow himself to be propelled out of the hospital.

When Mare's name is finally called she doesn't move. She looks shriveled and squashed. Milton nudges her. 'It's time to see the doctor.' The orderly helps Milton lift her into a wheelchair. It would be good if she died now, Milton thinks, in the hospital, with nurses and doctors around her. A woman with straw-coloured hair and heavy makeup stands by the fire extinguisher wavering on her stiletto heels. She's not wearing underwear, and her skin-tight white leggings are soiled down one side. Milton wonders if she fell down or was pushed. As she zigzags towards admitting her cellulite jiggles. She is past her prime, and Milton wonders what she has to do now to make a living, how much abuse she has to endure. She speaks with the nurse who pushes forms at her. The hooker starts to swear and call the nurse a bitch. The nurse doesn't flinch, only closes the sliding window. The hooker slams her palm into the window then stumbles backwards. After regaining her balance she begins weaving her way back through the doors. Milton thinks of Connie getting older, losing her power as her breasts started to sag and her thighs to pucker. Maybe she wanted to die. Maybe he saved her from a life worse than death.

He takes a coffee outside and sits on a bench facing the street. People walk past carrying briefcases, and Milton wishes he was any one of them. He wonders how they got to be normal, what makes them different from himself. They can't all have smarts. Some of them must have made mistakes. What separates him from them? It can't be just that he had a hag of a mother and a vegetable for a father. He thinks of Teresa, how she didn't blame the father who raped her or the mother who let him. He wonders if she blamed them before she blew her brains out with glue. Connie blamed everybody. And blew her brains out.

A puppy prances towards him and sniffs his pants. Its owner, a girl dressed like a hippie in a flowing skirt and beads, pulls gently on the leash. But the puppy continues to hop around Milton, throwing his paws up on his knees, knocking his coffee-cup.

'Fred,' the girl chides. 'This way, Fred.'

'It's okay.' Milton strokes Fred's floppy ears.

'He wants to know everything,' the girl explains.

'He's young.' Milton knows that Fred will grow up to be just like all the other dogs.

The girl lifts Fred off Milton and plops him back on the sidewalk. 'Come on, puppy.' Fred glances back at Milton only briefly, then he speeds ahead to discover new wonders. Watching his tail wag ceaselessly, Milton thinks maybe Mandy has a point about him being lucky to remember Ariel as special.

~

'She won't come to the phone,' Rory says. 'She doesn't want to talk to anybody.'

'Did you tell her it was me?' Milton asks.

'Yeah, she said to tell you that if you bring Gramma back here she'll kill her. She's acting really weird. We had to clean everything up, like the blood and everything. It made her sick, then she was crying. Now she's just sitting with Leonard. She told me to go to school, but I'm not leaving her like this.'

The thought of sponging up his sister's brains makes Milton dizzy and hot. He leans against the wall. 'How's Leonard?'

'I don't know. The same.'

'Did anybody phone? The cops?' He has a feeling they won't believe it's suicide, and he'll have somebody like Columbo crawling all over his house. Already they dusted for prints and marked down exactly where everybody said they were standing in relation to the body. When Milton explained that everybody's prints would be on the gun—since they'd all been trying to get it away from Connie— the cop chewing the Clorets didn't say anything, just scribbled something on a pad.

'A retarded guy came by,' Rory adds. 'He wanted to know what happened, so I told him. He seemed pretty upset about it.'

'Did he say anything?'

'No. He sat in the backyard for a while. Then he left.'

Mare sits in the wheelchair staring at her cast in its sling. Milton notices that she smells of urine. He tries to think of where to take her since they can't go home. He doesn't want to have to talk to her, look at her, listen to her. They could go to a movie, but that would only use up two hours. They could go to the zoo, but then she'd have to walk.

'So are you going to walk again or what?' he asks.

'Don't use that tone with me.'

'Well, your legs aren't broken.'

'I'm sick to death of moving around. All you people do is move me around.'

Her fingers still look swollen. 'Does it hurt?' he asks, but she only grimaces at the sling. 'Maybe you should take some more Tylenol.'

'I'm not taking any more pills.'

His muscles start twitching again. 'If it hurts, you should

take them.'

'They bung you right up. I'm not taking any.' She starts to pull her wrist out of the sling.

'What are you doing?'

'I'm not wearing this.'

'You have to.'

'Who says?'

'It's the only way the blood will drain out of it.'

She starts to pull the sling over her head.

'Mother, I'm not taking you out of the hospital unless you wear it. Please, just wear it.'

'I can't do anything with it.'

'You're not supposed to. You're supposed to rest it.'

Her eyes shift around the waiting-room. 'You're going to put me in a home.'

'No, I'm not.' He pulls out his car keys, thinking they'll have to drive somewhere so they can stay in the car and he won't have to look at her. 'I was thinking maybe we could go for a drive. Do you want to go for a drive?'

'Why would I want to do that?'

He wouldn't mind driving out into the country, where there are cows and trees and birds. In the country maybe his muscles would stop twitching. 'We could go for a drive in the country.'

'What country?'

'This country. Outside the city.'

'What if the car breaks down? That's what happens. Your car breaks down and hooligans rob you.'

'We could go to Niagara Falls.' This makes perfect sense. It will take them a couple of hours to get there and later he can tell Judith about it, let her know he saw the Falls without her. 'So get out of the chair, and we'll go,' he says. 'I just have to stop by and see somebody first.'

'What about my room?'

'What about it?'

'You said you'd paint it.'

'I will when we come back.'

She rubs her abdomen. 'You think I don't know what's going on.'

'I promise I'm not putting you in a home.'

'You say that now.'

Things will be different once they get on the road, he thinks. They'll be safe in the car, far from Connie's body and the cops. 'You've never seen Niagara Falls,' he reminds her. 'It's one of the wonders of the world; you should see it.' He grips her good arm. 'Come on, Ma. We can't hang around the hospital all day.'

'You kick me around like old shoes.'

~

Mr. Huang tells him that Winnie is cleaning the eighth-floor wash-rooms. Milton sits his mother down in the waiting area by the security desk and asks the doorman to keep an eye on her.

Winnie's mopping behind a cubicle and doesn't notice Milton right away.

'Hey, Win,' Milton says.

Winnie glances at him then continues cleaning. 'What are you doing here?'

'I just wanted to make sure you're alright.'

'I'm alright.'

'You heard about Connie?'

Winnie nods and mops around the toilet base. 'Did you see it?'

'I was there, but I didn't look.'

'Must've been gross.' Winnie drops his mop in the bucket then wrings it out. 'Did you say something to her?' he asks, moving into the next cubicle.

'What do you mean?'

'She said none of you even cared if she was alive or dead.'

'She told you that?'

'She said not one person on the entire planet would notice if she died. She said a lady died, and nobody found out until she started to smell.'

Milton can't argue with this. If she'd disappeared, nobody would have been too concerned. They wouldn't have even been notified unless she had ID on her. Maybe this is why she chose to blow her head off right in front of them. That way they'd have to know about it.

Winnie starts mopping in the next cubicle. 'I don't get how she could do that. I mean how could you do that?'

'I guess she didn't want to live any more.'

'Why not, though?'

'I guess she couldn't see any point in it.'

'That's no reason to go killing yourself. You only kill yourself if you're starving or have some disease or something.' He dunks the mop in the bucket again and wrings it out. 'When Mom was a nurse, an eighteen-year-old boy got totally paralyzed from a car crash and asked her to kill him. His parents were putting him in a home with old people, and he didn't want to go. Mom would've killed him, but she'd have gotten arrested. I'd want to die if I was paralyzed.'

Milton wonders if he should explain that Connie took drugs, but he decides this will only upset Winnie further. Instead he says, 'Maybe she felt paralyzed. Maybe she felt like she couldn't move. Maybe she felt like she was going to sleep on cardboard boxes forever.'

'I told her I could get her a job. Mr. Huang's always looking for people.'

'Maybe she didn't want a job.'

Winnie stares down at his mop, furrowing his brow. Milton wants more than anything to lift the sadness from him. 'Maybe she saw that tunnel,' he suggests, 'with all her friends in it.'

'That's only when you nearly die.'

Milton nods then catches sight of himself in the mirror and is shocked at how desperate he looks with his slept-on hair and unshaven face. The fluorescent lights accentuate the bags under his eyes and make his skin look grey. 'Well, she must have really wanted to do it. She made sure she couldn't miss.'

Winnie looks at him. 'How did she do that?'

'She put it in her mouth.' Milton is telling him this because he doesn't want him hearing it from anybody else. Winnie's crossed eyes open wider, and he leans against the cubicle.

'I just think,' Milton continues, 'it's okay to not want to live and to do something about it. Most people just sit around complaining. I think if somebody has the guts to kill themselves, they should be allowed to do it.' He's not sure he means this; he wonders if, had he known Teresa intended to die in the fire, he would have let her. He remembers telling her she was too young to kill herself, that she couldn't know what would happen. He's not sure about that either. He has a feeling Connie knew what would happen.

Winnie drops his mop in the bucket. 'She said all she wanted was for you to believe in her.'

It surprises Milton that even in death Connie continues to manipulate. He has this idea that when people die he'll be free of them. When his mother was getting her third by-pass he wanted her to die so he'd be free of her. He has a feeling he'll never be free of her. Or Connie. Being dead they have even more power over him, because he feels guilty for letting them die. But maybe, now that he's taking his mother to Niagara Falls, he can make peace with her and be free. He thinks again about the Japs taking the old people up the mountain to die, putting them in sacks and slinging them over their shoulders. The old people didn't mind. They wanted to die because they could no longer help around the farm. Dying up in the mountains was noble. Maybe at the foot of the Falls his mother will find inner peace and want to die. He'll get her a hotel room, and she'll die peacefully in her sleep.

'If I'd had a sister,' Winnie tells him, 'there's no way I would've let her kill herself.'

'I didn't let her. I didn't even see her.'

'You were there. You could've done something.'

'The gun was loaded. She was waving it around.' This is a lie. She'd dropped the gun to her side. He doesn't like how he's defending himself, doesn't like how Winnie is no longer his ally; now he's Connie's ally. Even though she's dead. 'I'd better get going,' he says. 'I'm taking my mother to Niagara Falls.' He expects Winnie to ask when he's coming back, but he doesn't. 'So I'll see you when I get back.'

Winnie flips a toilet seat. 'Sure.' He doesn't look at him, and Milton feels angry because he doesn't think he deserves this kind of treatment. Especially after burying Coco. He's been a good friend to Winnie, and now he's turning against him because his slut of a sister went and killed herself. Then he remembers that when he gets mad it's because he's done something stupid, like letting his mother have the gun. Then he pictures Connie when she was four years old, when he carried her on his shoulders and she called ambulances 'ambliances'. He has a feeling that this picture will stay with him long after the drug addict fades. This picture will freshen his guilt and despair. Already, reaching for the elevator button, he feels like scum. 'Fuck her,' he mumbles, realizing that she's more dangerous dead than alive. He has a feeling dead people will be hiding in closets in his brain his entire life, ready to jump out at him when he least expects it.

His mother's asleep or dead in the chair. Milton gently shakes her. 'Ma, let's get going.'

She blinks her lizard eyes. 'Where?'

'Niagara Falls.'

NINETEEN

Industrial park chases him down the highway. Each time he accelerates, Mare tells him to slow down. Cars whip past, seeming to
swerve dangerously close. Milton imagines the Volare spinning out
of control, bouncing off concrete into another car then into concrete
again. He hears the silence after the crash, pictures the wrecked car
smoking, blood dripping from its doors. He doesn't want his mother to die this way so he drives carefully, constantly checking his side
and rearview mirrors to see if some drunk bastard is coming at him.
Mare has been very quiet; he wonders if she's grieving. He doesn't
think so, since she keeps sucking on her candies. He wonders if she's
in what the shrink with the hairy mole would call 'denial' about
Connie's death. Or if part of her brain is damaged. Mandy explained
that it's the tumours on Leonard's brain that are affecting his eyes
and memory. Maybe his mother has brain tumours. Or maybe the
blood is bunged up in certain arteries that feed her brain.

It bothers him that she doesn't seem to mind that Connie's dead.

'I've got to go,' she says.

'You just went.'

'I did not.'

'Can't you hold it?'

'If I could I wouldn't have said anything, would I?'

A long time ago, before his dad became a vegetable, they were all driving to his aunt's wedding. Milton needed to go, but Mare told him to hold it. He couldn't and peed in his Sunday clothes. Afraid the other kids would smell it, he sat alone on the church steps pretending to be engrossed in a *Thor* comic. He can now take his revenge on his mother by making her pee in the car. But then he'd have to smell it. 'We'll get off at the next exit,' he tells her.

They stop at a Tim Horton's. While she uses the ladies room, he sits at the counter and orders a coffee. A man has his wheelchair pushed up to a table. His rolls of flab spread as he leans forward to reach for his eclair donut. Milton notices his legs move and wonders why he's sitting in a wheelchair. His thin wife sits at the table nibbling on Timbits. Her cheeks sag as though she no longer has the muscles needed to smile. She pulls nervously at her eyebrows while she watches her husband wolf down the eclair then an apple fritter. When he drains his coffee-cup and holds it out to her, she takes it to the counter for a refill. The man sits back and stretches his legs. Milton has a feeling he's in the wheelchair because he's too fat to walk; he has crippled himself with fat so he can sit in a wheelchair and boss his wife around. Milton thinks about Connie relating stories of abuse and expecting people to feel sorry for her and to do things for her. It occurs to Milton that most people cripple themselves so they don't have to do certain things. His mother is crippling her brain so she won't have to think about Connie or Leonard. And Mandy's smoking, and Seth's drinking, and Teresa's sniffing glue. They all say they can't quit. It seems to Milton the people who say they 'can't' are the ones to avoid. They keep saying they 'can't' so other people will do things for them. Then he remembers Judith wearing him down about improving his reading skills. He kept saying he couldn't when the truth of it was that he just didn't want to sit in a class with a bunch of Chinese or whatever. It seems to him that nobody has to know he can't read properly. Before, it bothered him because he couldn't read to Ariel. He even got Judith to look up 'reading disabilities' in the yellow pages and wrote the number down, but then Ariel died.

The thin woman hands the fat man the coffee-cup and sits back at the table, pulling at her eyebrows, watching him load the cup with sugar. Milton wants to tell her that she doesn't have to live chained to this man: she can walk out of Tim Horton's and leave him to choke on his fritter. But Milton has a feeling she needs to be in chains, that without them she wouldn't know where to put her hands and feet. At least, with the fat man, she knows what's coming to her. Milton doesn't know what's coming to him, and it scares him. Judith says he shouldn't be afraid of the unknown. He argues that he isn't afraid, he just doesn't want to waste time thinking about what he doesn't need to know: her dreams, for example. One time she told him that in her dream he was dressed like a clown with a painted face and orange hair. She explained that he wanted her to go with him, but she hesitated because he looked like a clown. Milton said he wasn't interested in her dreams and suggested she keep them to herself. Judith accused him of being afraid of her unconscious mind. She said the only thing that interested him was the TV; that he was a TV addict. He argued that watching TV was a lot better then running around wasting money on shrinks, or taking drugs or drinking or killing or hitting people. This was before he hit her.

His mother shuffles towards him. 'What are you thinking about?'

'Nothing.'

'You're thinking about something.'

'I was thinking, too bad it's raining.' He remembers the girl with the puppy saying Fred 'wants to know everything' and himself saying, 'He's young.' On a documentary about owls, the baby owls were wide awake and looking around, cocking their heads upside down then side to side. The mother owl was just sitting there, blending in with the bark. Milton has a feeling he's blending in with the bark. He's scared he'll be blending in with the bark then suddenly he'll be dead.

'You'd think they could clean the toilet at least,' Mare grumbles. 'There's pee all over the seat.'

Milton can't remember wanting to learn. All he can remember is being scared people would find out that he couldn't.

~

In front of him an old man in a hat, gripping the steering wheel with both hands, drives very slowly in the middle of the road. Each time Milton prepares to pass, the man swerves further into the oncoming lane.

'There's something rattling,' Mare tells him.

'It always does that.'

'It didn't used to.'

'Well, it's been rattling ever since I've had it.'

'You should get it tuned up.'

'I've had it tuned up. It keeps rattling.'

'You didn't go to a good mechanic.' She unwraps one of her candies. 'Most of them don't know anything. You should go see Nick on Gerrard Street. He knows about cars.'

She hasn't stopped talking since they left the Tim Horton's. Milton is glad he's driving. Otherwise he'd want to tape her mouth shut. A guy taped his hostages' mouths with duct tape. It seemed to work pretty well, better than gagging them with rags or whatever.

'And he doesn't keep you waiting,' she adds. 'You take your car in, he fixes it, and he doesn't charge you hundreds of dollars.' She stuffs the cellophane wrapping into the ash tray then slams it shut. 'Most of those mechanics charge you a hundred dollars just to look at it.'

The cows and trees and birds aren't stopping Milton from feeling like scum for letting his sister die. It seems to him that his mother should be feeling like scum since it was her gun. He hates it that she doesn't even care. What kind of mother doesn't notice her daughter kill herself? He almost wants to stop the car and tell her to get out, leave her there by the roadside for hooligans to rob.

He sees the squirrel a split second before it thuds against his tire. 'Jesus christ,' he says, slamming on the brakes.

'Don't swear.'

'I hit a squirrel.'

241

'It shouldn't have been in the road anyway.'

'It was crossing the road.'

'What are you stopping for?'

'I want to see if it's dead.'

'Of course it's dead.'

'It might be suffering.' Long ago they were walking in a park and saw a baby chipmunk suffering. Mare said it must have fallen out of the nest. She assured Milton that its mother would come down for it. But he couldn't see how the mother chipmunk would be able to carry the baby chipmunk back up the tree. The baby couldn't move. Milton could see its little chest heaving. He wanted to pick it up and take it home and feed it with an eye dropper. But Mare told him it would bite him, and he'd get rabies. He begged to at least stay with the chipmunk, but she told him they had to get their father's dinner. She and Leonard continued walking, leaving Milton staring at the chipmunk. He hated her for this. She never waited for him; when he wanted to look at comics at the drugstore, or ride the pony at the IGA, she'd continue walking as though she didn't care what he did.

'What are you worrying about a squirrel for?' she asks. 'They're just rats with bushy tails.'

He gets out of the car and walks back to where he thinks he hit the squirrel. He doesn't see it right away but then suddenly it jumps six inches, twitching and twisting in the air, then falls back hard on the road. Then again it leaps up, twisting, trying to right itself but again crashes into the asphalt. Milton realizes that he is scaring it and steps back. It does another aborted jump. Milton can't stand it, can't stand that he has damaged this animal who has never hurt anybody. The squirrel leaps and twitches in the air once more then lies quivering. Milton knows that he will have to put it out of its misery and wishes he had his mother's gun. He looks around for rocks to smash its head but only grassy banks and orchards line the road. He considers wringing its little neck then realizes that he could run it over and crush it completely. The inevitability of this solution devastates him.

'Is it dead?' she asks.

'No.'

She peers at it, clutching her hands in front of her. 'It looks dead.'

'It's breathing.'

'No, it isn't.'

He looks back at it. Its eyes are open, its little paws curled under its chin. Blood oozes from its tiny snout but no breath. Milton thanks God or whoever. 'I have to move it.'

'Why?'

'I don't want it to get run over.'

'It's dead. It won't know the difference.'

'I want to give it a decent burial.'

'What for? There's dead squirrels on the road all the time,'

'I don't want this one on the road.'

'Why not?'

He squats down to pick it up. A car honks then swerves around them.

'You'll get us killed,' she says.

He can't figure out how to pick up the squirrel, remembers trying to pick up Ariel, how she no longer had solid bones in her.

'Don't touch it,' Mare tells him. 'It'll roll over and bite you, and you'll get rabies.'

'You said it was dead.' He has a feeling she doesn't even realize that she lies.

'You can't be too sure. Sometimes they act dead then turn around and bite you. Where are you going?'

'To get some cardboard.' Back at the car he empties a Kleenex box and tears open one side thinking it's not fair that, now that he's old enough to tell his mother what he thinks of her, she's an old lady who'll die if she gets too excited. Kneeling beside the squirrel, he places the flat of his hand against its back remembering the times he and Ariel fed squirrels peanuts. She wanted to pet them, but they ran away. Milton explained that they were wild, that you weren't meant to pet wild animals. It feels criminal to be touching the squirrel's soft fur. He slides it onto the cardboard then gently rolls it into the box. He'd like to tape it closed but has no tape then realizes that he should leave it open so that the squirrel's family can see it. Otherwise they won't know what happened to it.

'You're acting like a six-year-old,' his mother says.

As he lays the squirrel under a tree he tells it that he's sorry. He'd like to close its eyes but is afraid he'll poke them out. With his index finger he strokes its head and tiny ears.

'You care more about that squirrel than your own mother. You have no idea how you treat me. You think I have no feelings.'

'Shut up,' he says quietly but firmly, and she starts to cry. He has never told her to shut up before, never made her cry before. This new-found power sends electricity through him, and he wonders if now would be a good time to rip her apart. Except that she looks so pathetic under the apple trees in the rain. And then she farts; a garbage fart. 'Just get in the car,' he tells her. 'I'll be there in a minute.'

~

'I have to do number two,' she says. He doesn't respond, only stares out at the rain blurring the windshield; he wishes they'd just gone to a movie or something. He feels hung-over even though he didn't drink last night.

'I haven't gone today,' Mare explains. 'It's that food your sister buys. No roughage. She takes pills for it. I tell her she keeps taking those pills, and her bowels won't work at all. That's what happens, you take those pills, and your bowels get lazy.'

He has a feeling that, when they get there, his mother isn't going to look at the Falls, find inner peace and want to die.

'That's how Norm Glerup got cancer,' she informs him. 'They cleaned him right up. Cut everything off. Now he has to use a bag.'

Milton would like to be a good son; he remembers an old lady and a Charlie's Angel crying together, saying they didn't have much time left. Milton had thought that he and his mother didn't have much time left. But looking at her hunched in her seat, sucking her candies, he suspects she'll live another twenty years. The shrink with the hairy mole said that Milton will never feel at ease with himself if she dies with unfinished business between them. He advised Milton to tell his mother that he loves her but that he must take charge of his own life. Milton argued that he didn't love his mother, that he wouldn't mind if he never saw her again. 'There's still a lot of anger there,' the shrink cautioned, shaking his head. On 'Geraldo', three people came on who thought they hated their parents. Then the parents showed up, and Geraldo made them all talk to each other. At the end of the show Geraldo said, 'Everybody hug.' They did, and Geraldo said, 'That's beautiful.' But Milton doesn't want to hug his mother, particularly since she smells bad. All he wants is to lie on his bed and watch TV, even though he knows this means that he's an addict. At least then he doesn't have to hear about bowel movements.

'Maybe we should go back,' he suggests.

'What?'

'Maybe we should go back.'

'What for?'

'It's raining.'

'You're going to put me in a home.'

'No, I'm not.'

'I want to go to Niagara Falls.'

Leaning forward in her seat with her hands on the dash, staring at him, her eyes wide and anxious, she reminds him of Ariel when he left her with the babysitter. Always she clung to him as though she was afraid he would never return. Seeing his daughter in his mother shocks him. 'Alright,' he says and pulls in to a gas station.

While he pumps air into the tire with the slow leak, he thinks about the people on 'Sixty Minutes' who'd had lobotomies. Before the operation they'd been crazy or depressed or violent. Afterwards they acted more like cattle. Milton thought it was interesting that you could alter your brain by poking around in it, and he wondered if, in the future, surgeons could become precise and eliminate certain parts of people's brains just like they eliminate certain parts of people's bodies. Milton wouldn't mind going to a surgeon and telling him he would like to stop thinking about certain things: could they cut them out of his brain? Maybe they could poke around in the brains of rapists and serial killers. They're always researching how to save dying people, but Milton thinks they should start thinking about the living. Instead of sticking them in prisons maybe they can do something to their brains to make them law-abiding citizens. He suspects people would get upset at this idea, just like people get upset about capital punishment. But Milton thinks that if you kill

245

somebody, you should be donated to science. He's sick of animals being tortured to find out how to cure humans. He can't believe he's thinking about this while Connie's body is turning cold in the morgue. He suspects he should be thinking about something else. He doesn't know what, though.

'They haven't cleaned the toilet in a hundred years,' Mare informs him.

He wants to know how she has managed to live her entire life believing that she's right and everybody else is wrong. She must have this idea of herself that is totally different from who she really is. 'You alright?' he asks. Only now does it occur to him how difficult it must be to wipe your butt with your left hand.

'Why wouldn't I be alright?'

Milton wonders if his idea of himself is totally different from who he really is.

'Did you ask the man to look at the car?' She peers at him.

'Why?'

'Because of the rattle.'

'There's no problem with the rattle.'

'Harry Gouthro got a garbage bag caught in his engine, and it blew up.' She prods the shoulder of the attendant who's pumping gas into a Ford van. 'There's something wrong with my car,' she tells him. The attendant straightens up revealing that half of his face is badly scarred. Milton thinks he must have been in a fire.

'We don't service cars here, Ma'am.'

'Why not?'

Milton notices that the attendant's ear has been burned off and that there's no hair growing around it. He wonders if, under the Blue Jays cap, the attendant has any hair at all.

'We just pump gas here, Ma'am.'

'What kind of gas station doesn't fix cars?' Mare demands. Milton can't believe she's harassing a man without an ear.

'Sorry,' the attendant says. 'We're just a gas station.'

'A gas station without a mechanic,' Mare comments. Milton thinks of *Phantom of the Opera*. He couldn't afford to go, but he's seen the commercials. He doesn't get how a guy with half his face burnt off is supposed to be sexy. 'Let's go, Mother,' he says trying to sound in charge.

'I'm not getting into a car that rattles,' she insists. Milton can see that the attendant doesn't know what to do; he would like to help, but he can't.

'Mother,' Milton repeats.

She stares at the attendant. 'You're just too lazy to do anything about it.'

'Honestly, Ma'am, I don't know how to fix cars.'

'I want to talk to the manager,' she announces, and Milton remembers the many times she has demanded 'to talk to the manager'. Always Milton has gazed into the distance, hoping to appear unrelated to her.

'I'm leaving now.' He gets into the car and revs the engine hoping she'll think he's leaving without her. But she continues grilling the attendant who shakes his head then pulls the gas nozzle from the van and hooks it on the pump. Milton accelerates almost ramming into a bleached blonde in a Mercedes. Her painted lips move as she swears at him, but he can't hear because her windows are closed. He pulls around her wondering who she had to screw to get the Mercedes, then he hears Judith saying maybe the blonde bought the Mercedes herself, maybe she's a high-powered career woman. The attendant takes a credit card from the van and walks back to the service station. In the rearview mirror, Milton watches his mother looking around, suddenly lost. He backs up and pushes open the passenger door. 'Get in.'

'Where do you think you're going?'

'Just get in the car.'

'I want him to fix it.'

'He can't fix it.'

'He shouldn't be working here if he can't fix it. I want to talk to the manager.'

'The manager isn't here,' Milton explains.

'How do you know?'

'There's nobody in the office.' He points to the office where the attendant is filling out a credit-card slip. 'Mother, please get in the car.'

'Nobody wants to work anymore.'

'Half his face is burnt off.'

'What's that got to do with anything?'

'I just don't think you should give a guy a hard time when half his face is burnt off.'

'Your grandfather lost his hand, and he didn't complain about it.'

'He didn't get a job though, did he? There must've been something he could've done. Be a doorman or something.' Never before has he suggested that, rather than being a saint, her father was a layabout. He waits for her to throw a fit, tell him that he's had it easy, doesn't know what it was like during the war.

'You don't know anything,' she mutters.

'I'm leaving now.' He revs the engine.

She gets in. 'I don't see you finding a job.'

He's been waiting for her to bring this up; he'd hoped that maybe she was too senile to remember. 'I've only been off two weeks.'

'I don't know why you can't keep a job. Leonard always has a job.'

'Leonard's a fag and is dying.'

'What?'

'Leonard, your son, who you tried to shoot this morning.'

She says nothing, only stares fiercely at the attendant returning to the van.

'Are you going to keep pretending you don't remember?' Milton asks. Suddenly he's convinced that she remembers everything, and this revolts him. He would prefer to think of her as senile; unable to comprehend that her daughter has commited suicide and that her son is dying of AIDS. Now she seems only cunning to him, disguising her malice with dementia. 'Did you want to put him out of his misery?' he asks, believing that if she says yes he can forgive her. If she says yes, even the gun can be forgiven. He wants her to say yes.

She doesn't look at him. 'You don't know anything.'

~

He considers shoving her over the Falls, imagines her somersaulting in the air then vanishing into the froth. Gone forever. He'd be put in prison, but at least he wouldn't have to listen to her. From what he's seen on TV, prison isn't all that bad. You get to watch TV and work out. Maybe nobody would rape him since he's fat and bald.

'A mother threw her baby over,' Milton tells her. 'Imagine doing that.' He can imagine his mother doing it. He thinks of Judith saying 'at some point you're going to have to start saying what you really mean'. Maybe he should tell his mother that she might as well have thrown her babies over Niagara Falls, considering how they turned out. He wonders if this is his inner child speaking. Judith read a book about 'the inner child in you' and told Milton that she was facing her own inner child. Wounds she didn't know existed were surfacing, she said. Wounds that she'd blocked out. The only way to recover from the wounds was to embrace her inner child. Milton knew that she wanted him to read the book and embrace his inner child because she kept asking him questions about his childhood, if he was spanked or whatever. He told her he couldn't remember. He does, though. Certain things, like his mother catching him showing his penis to Wanda Zemeski. Wanda asked to see it; it wasn't like he forced it on her. But Mare never let him play with Wanda again, insisted that he only play with boys. Milton didn't like playing with boys because they forced him to be the Indian and get shot.

He points to a boat. 'That must be *The Maid of the Mist*. We could go on that if you want.'

'Why would I want to do that?'

'I don't know. All kinds of famous people have been on it.'

She grimaces at the boat, and Milton has a feeling the wonder of the Falls has had no effect on her. It has on him, though. He'd always expected Niagara Falls to look like a huge fountain. He hadn't expected it to look so wild and for there to be so much water and mist. On postcards Niagara Falls looks man-made. But standing up close to them he feels a force of nature; even though he's standing on concrete, he feels a current running through him. The rushing river hypnotizes him, urging him to hurdle the barrier.

'What are you thinking about?' she asks.

He shifts his stare to the swirling foam at the base of the falls. 'Marilyn Monroe contemplated suicide on *The Maid of the Mist*.'

'How do you know that?'

'I read it somewhere.' This isn't true. Judith told him. He

doesn't say this because he doesn't want his mother to know he can't read. The only person besides Mandy who knows he can't read is Judith. He told her on their sixth date because he wanted her to know the worst about him. She didn't laugh or stare at him but took his hand and held it in both of hers. 'Well, you'll just have to learn then,' she said, and at that moment, he agreed with her, believed it was possible, pictured himself sitting in front of a fireplace reading Winston Churchill. But then he got busy with work. When Judith suggested that maybe his inner child was afraid to read, Milton went out to clean the eavestroughs.

But he can feel himself small, in flannel shorts, at his desk, his knees scabby from being pushed over by Bobby Mullan. Terrified the teacher will ask him to read, he slumps down in his chair and holds his head low over *Dick and Jane* so the teacher can't meet his eyes. She asks anyway. And he can hear his classmates snicker. He hates them, wants them all to be hit by cars, eat apples filled with razor blades.

'What's the matter with you?' his mother demands.

'Nothing.'

In grade six the principal phoned and asked to see his mother. Mare said she couldn't leave her sick husband. At dinner she told Milton that his teachers thought he was mentally handicapped and what did he have to say about it. 'Nothing,' Milton answered. Then his father started drooling, and his mother went to get a cloth to wipe his face.

Judith said, 'How could your mother not know you couldn't read?' But Milton understands it, can see how his mother didn't want to know because then she'd have to do something about it.

A Japanese man taps Milton's shoulder and pushes a camera at him. 'Take picture, please?' he asks.

'I don't know much about cameras,' Milton tells him. But the Japanese man only nods and continues pushing the camera at him. Milton notices a red button that he suspects he must press to take the picture. He looks through the lense at the Japanese man, leaning against the railing smiling widely, and he wishes he was the Japanese man. He probably knows about computers, probably has an important job with some big corporation. Milton presses the red button.

'Thank you,' the Japanese man says, nodding and retrieving the camera.

'No problem.' Milton looks around for his mother. She stands staring at a group of Amish people all in black, excepting middle-aged twins dressed identically in navy blue. Both men wear toques pulled low over their foreheads and keep their hands in the pockets of their wool jackets. They seem unable to straighten their legs and stand awkwardly on permanently bent knees. Their mouths hang open, and their eyelids droop. They don't interact but stand on the outskirts of the group. When the group moves, the twins follow but with their heads bowed, dragging their feet, still keeping their hands in their pockets.

'Too much inbreeding,' Mare comments.

Milton was disappointed when Harrison Ford and the Amish girl didn't get it on. He thought Harrison Ford should have converted to Amish. Even though they didn't have cars, the Amish seemed to have a pretty good life. Milton thinks the retarded twins are lucky to be Amish. They'll be looked after. Milton doesn't know who's going to look after Winnie. Even though he has been trying not to think about him, and telling himself that the end of their friendship is Winnie's loss, Milton already misses him and wonders who's going to sit at the kitchen table with him now, be his friend now.

'Some guy keeps going over in a barrel,' he says.

'What?'

'Some guy keeps going over in a barrel, breaks his arms but keeps going over. He's got a world record.' Milton wonders if every time he makes it the man feels lucky to be alive and becomes a positive person. Maybe that's why the man does it. Every time he starts feeling numb and thinking that his life is pointless, he climbs into a barrel and goes over Niagara Falls. Maybe it's like a drug to him. Maybe he's addicted.

'I'm cold,' Mare grumbles.

'Too bad there's no sun. You're supposed to be able to see a rainbow when there's sun.' He looks at her. 'They're pretty great though, don't you think?'

She stares grimly at the Falls.

Milton's mouth twitches. He feels that, if he weren't pinned down by his mother, he might be having a good experience. Even though Connie killed herself and Leonard's dying there's something about being in the open air, feeling the Falls' mist and hearing its roar that makes him feel unimportant. He doesn't understand why he likes this feeling when before he wanted to be a hero.

Mare crosses her arms. 'Only crazy people come out here in this weather.'

'You wanted to come.' The shrink told Milton he had to let out his anger towards his mother otherwise he'd 'act out' his anger with other people. Milton wonders if this is true, if he hit Judith because he was angry with his mother.

'There's places we can go,' he suggests, studying a flyer he picked up while waiting for her to pee. 'There's wax museums and the Houdini Hall of Fame. Or maybe we could go up the Skylar Tower, do you want to do that?'

'I want to see the Elvis museum. The lady who cleans the toilets says it has things that belonged to Elvis personally.'

'Since when do you like Elvis?'

'He loved his mother.'

The girl selling the tickets to the Elvis museum is cute. Milton wishes his mother weren't here so he could ask the girl out. Then he remembers that he's never had the guts to ask a complete stranger out. She's hooking a rug and barely looks up when Milton buys the tickets. The pattern on the rug is of a rainbow, and Milton considers asking about it or telling her it's pretty. But he's afraid his mother will embarrass him, tell him she has to 'go' or whatever. He imagines that the girl is thinking what kind of loser goes to Niagara Falls with his mother. Milton has noticed that most of the tourists are couples holding hands; in the park there was a couple necking on a bench. Driving through town all the signs outside the hotels advertised Jacuzzis, some of them heart-shaped. Outside the mall containing the Elvis museum, Milton looked up at one of the hotels and noticed a bare-chested man pulling back the curtains and opening the window. Milton wondered if the woman in the room behind him was naked and horny.

'This isn't his car,' Mare declares.

'It isn't?'

'His was pink.'

They look at items that Elvis is said to have used; a hair dryer, scarves, guitars, a flashlight, a book by JFK.

'He killed himself because his mother died,' Mare explains.

He considers telling her that some people say Elvis slept with his mother until he was sixteen. But he decides this might get her too excited.

She stares at one of Elvis' white studded costumes. 'He was a good son.' Milton knows she's saying this to remind him that he isn't a 'good son'. He considers reminding her that she isn't a good mother, but he's afraid to, afraid of what might happen. The shrink often asked 'what are you afraid of?' Milton couldn't say exactly. He knew that Judith and the shrink thought that he was withholding information, but the truth of it was that he really didn't know.

On the way out Milton glances at the girl, but she doesn't look up from the rug. He hopes he'll dream about her. Sometimes he dreams that women he hardly knows desire him. Last week he dreamed about the girl in shipping and receiving. They were standing at opposite ends of a bar like in the beer commercials. From the way she was looking at him, he knew she wanted him.

'Where are we going now?' Mare asks.

'We could get our picture taken and put on a plate.'

'Why would we do that?'

'As a souvenir.' He'd thought that maybe, if she had a picture of the two of them smiling on a plate, she'd realize that he was a good son.

'Nobody's taking my picture,' she says.

'Okay, well, are you hungry? Maybe we should get something to eat.'

'Whatever you want.'

They take a bus up Clifton Hill. The abundance of flashing neon signs reminds Milton of Las Vegas even though he's never been there. They pass the Guinness world of Records, the Houdini Hall of Fame and Ripley's Believe It or Not Museum. It amazes Milton that people actually pay money to go to these places. They look shabby, and he regrets bringing his mother here. He so badly wants her to be happy, so badly wants things to be different between them.

'What do you feel like eating?' he asks.

'Whatever you want.'

A boy standing outside Mama Leone's Italian Restaurant shoves a flyer at Milton and explains that they're offering a ten percent discount. Milton decides they might as well go in since he knows his mother likes spaghetti. They both order lasagne and stare out the window at the Ferris wheel looming over the street. It bothers him that he can't please her, so he tries to hurt her. 'Connie must be in the morgue by now.' He wants to remind her that Connie's dead; dead because of her gun. But his mother only spreads her napkin over her lap. 'I guess we can't afford much of a funeral,' Milton adds. 'Mandy said she'll get her cremated.' He watches her take a piece of bread from the basket and butter it. 'Was it expensive getting Dad cremated? All I remember is you taking the ashes somewhere. Where did you take them?'

'The lake.'

On the day the urn disappeared nobody said anything. Milton imagines her driving down to the beach in the Volare with the urn rolling around on the seat beside her. He pictures her walking down to the boardwalk then onto one of the piers like Meryl Streep in *The French Lieutenant's Woman*.

'I couldn't get it open,' she tells him. 'I had to ask a man walking his dog to open it.'

'Then what happened?'

'What do you think happened? I put them in the lake. Maddie Colbert put hers in the ocean. They kept washing back onto the beach, and people stepped on them. She hated Florida, said there were floods all the time. She only stayed because of him, but then he died, and she couldn't get a decent price for the house. Now she's got Lou Gehrig's disease. They stuck a tube in her belly so they can pour food into her.' She bites her bread and glowers at him. 'Her son put her in a home.'

'Nobody's putting you in a home.'

'You say that now.' While the waitress serves the lasagne, Milton notices that her bra straps dig into her flesh under her blouse. Mare grips her fork awkwardly in her left hand. 'They stick you in a room with a bunch of old people waiting to be dead.' She pokes at the lasagne. 'That's all they do. They tie the old people to the beds so they get sores full of maggots.'

'They do not.'

'They had hidden cameras that showed how they left the old people to lie in their own dirt and fed them watery potato soup. One nurse strangled an old lady. Called her a bitch and strangled her.'

'Where was this?'

'On TV.'

'It must have been a movie. They always show stuff like that in movies.'

'It happens all the time. You give me back my gun before putting me in a home.'

A guy at work put his mother in a home. They couldn't have tied her to the bed because she wandered into the city. Completely disoriented, she stood on a street-corner and cried until a Filipino nanny tried to help her. The old lady couldn't remember where she lived or her phone number. The nanny notified the police who had already been contacted by the home. The old lady never tried to escape again. The guy at work said she realized how lucky she was to be in a home. Milton wondered if this was true, or if the old lady was just scared of getting lost again. Maybe he should let his mother get lost in Niagara Falls, scare her so she'll appreciate how he's looking after her.

He has this idea that if she says he's a good son he'll feel like one.

The second time Milton told the shrink he didn't love his mother, the shrink didn't say anything, just pulled on his mole hairs.

'They had hidden cameras,' Mare explains, 'and all the old people had bed sores so big you could put your fist in them.'

'Nobody's putting you in a home.'

'You say that now.'

Watching his mother shake parmesan on her lasagne, he knows he'll never put her in a home. He'll be one of those balding middle-aged men who live with their mothers. If he ever meets another woman and she asks to go to his place, he'll have to say he lives with his mother. Like the thin woman is chained to the fat man, Milton feels chained to his mother. As much as this depresses him, at least he knows what's coming to him.

She takes another piece of bread from the basket. 'I'd never live in Florida. The pollution never clears. You can get things cheap, though. They don't tax the life out of you like they do here.'

The Charlie's Angel and the dying mother shouted at each other then cried. The mother was in a wheelchair. The daughter fell to her knees, burying her face in her mother's lap. Milton wonders if he should shout at his mother, tell her that Connie killed herself because she locked her in a closet and made her kneel on gravel. Or that Leonard fucked little boys.

She shakes her head. 'This country's going down the toilet. Where do you think you're going to find a job these days without an education?'

Milton shrugs. Maybe he should tell her that all her children hate her, even Leonard.

'There's kids graduating who can't find jobs,' she warns him.

Long ago he asked her to come and see his science project at the school fair. She didn't, even though he reminded her in the morning. When he got home, she was feeding his father. Milton didn't remind her that she'd missed his science project. He just hated her for it. Mandy told him about a man in Scarborough who shot his mother and sisters then himself. It comforts Milton that he doesn't want to kill his mother. When he was a teenager he wanted her dead, imagined pouring kerosene into her gas tank so she'd blow up. When he was a teenager she made him feel worthless because he couldn't live up to her standards, Leonard's standards. But now he tells himself she's a scared old lady who pisses herself, and Leonard's dying, so she shouldn't be able to make him feel worthless.

She does though.

'You should get into a job re-training program,' she tells him. 'That's what Maddie's daughter did, before she put her in a home. She learned how to be a medical steno.'

'You said her son put her in a home.'

'They both did. They both have houses and cars, and they put her in a home.'

'Nobody's putting you in a home.'

'You say that now.' She puts her fork down and pats her mouth with the napkin. Milton looks out the window at a couple necking across the street. The woman's butt is twice the size of the man's, and she only stands as tall as his shoulder. The man slides one hand down to her bum. Milton wonders what a butt like that feels like, if it's spongey or firm.

'You think I haven't been nice to you,' Mare says.

'What?'

'If I haven't always been nice to you, there was a reason for it.'

It disturbs him that she knew she wasn't being nice to him. He'd prefer to think she just happened to neglect him because of Leonard and their father.

'You don't know what it was like,' she continues. 'With your father sick and no money.'

Milton wonders if this is the moment he's been waiting for, the confrontation, the reconciliation. But suddenly he doesn't want to hear about it; understands that she's only bringing this up because she's scared he'll put her in a home.

'Forget about it,' he tells her.

The waitress, carrying dirty plates, passes their table. 'Everything alright here?' she asks.

'Alright,' Milton says.

Mare stares hard at her plate. Milton wonders if she's spotted a hair or a piece of bone. 'What is it?' he asks.

'Are you going to paint my room?'

'Yes.'

'When?'

'I don't know. When we get back.'

She looks very small against the high-backed chair. There's tomato sauce on her cardigan. 'We'll go to the paint store,' he assures her, 'and pick something out. What colour do you want?'

'Rose.'

'Okay.'

'Can we go tomorrow?'

Again he sees the fragility of Ariel in her. 'Sure.'

She shoves lettuce around on her plate. 'They put too much dressing on so you won't notice it's rotten.'

If she stayed like Ariel, maybe he could love her.

~

He waits twenty minutes before knocking on the ladies' room door. When she doesn't respond, he tries the handle then gets a spare key from the attendant. Even after unlocking the door, he can't push it open. He looks down and sees her leg. 'Mother?' He doesn't want to push harder on the door because it will crush her. He reaches down and shakes her leg. 'Mother?' He crouchs and tries to ease her away from the door so he can open it, but she's wedged against the toilet. He kneels and carefully pushes on the door, wincing as he feels it press into her. When he has it open a foot wide, he squeezes inside and steps over her. Her eyes are open, the skin on her face drawn, her mouth puckered as though she's been crying out in agony. Blue tinges the skin around her lips and nose. Her stockings and panties are down around her knees and there is shit on the toilet seat and floor. Her cast is tangled in the sling. The plastic pill box lies open beside her, the pills dotting the concrete floor. He should have known she'd have trouble opening them with her left hand. He grips her wrist waiting for a pulse. The smell of shit is making him sick. Outside the pump dings as someone fills their tires.

She cried out, and he didn't hear. He had his head up his own asshole.

He pulls toilet paper from the roll and wipes her small and withered behind then tries to pull up her stockings. He wraps one arm around her waist and pulls with the other, trying not to hurt her, even though she's dead. He wipes the floor and the toilet seat then flushes the soiled tissue away. After washing his hands, he tries to lay her out as flat as possible. He straightens her skirt and cardigan then tries to wipe off the tomato sauce with toilet paper, but it shreds. Carefully he crosses her arms over her chest, covering the stain. He kneels beside her, wanting to close her eyes but fearing he'll pop them out. Then he imagines a stranger doing it and forces himself to gently close one lid then the other. He sits back, leaning against the wall, waiting to feel something. All he knows is that he doesn't want strangers handling her, strangers who'll treat her like a corpse. He wants to protect her.

He wonders if this means he forgives her.

TWENTY

He sits in the Volare outside Mr. Grocer, watching Judith check out the last customers. Finally the cementhead manager locks the doors, and Judith cashes out. Milton knows she'll be another fifteen minutes because, after Ariel died, he couldn't stand being home alone and would pick Judith up when she worked nights. He'd leave early and watch her as he is now, hoping she'd get in the car and kiss him and that everything would be all right between them. But Judith would complain about her bunion or about some customer who'd demanded last week's sale price on a can of corn. Eventually she'd ask Milton what had happened to him at work. He'd say nothing, and she'd say something must have happened. He'd shrug, and they'd drive on in silence. At home he'd watch TV, and she'd do laundry. Sometimes she'd curl up beside him, but then she would annoy him by commenting on the shows, saying things like 'How come Jaclyn Smith doesn't age?' or 'Those aren't real boobs' or 'She must never eat anything.'

He doesn't understand why he keeps wanting to see her when he knows they don't get along.

A young man with bags under his eyes warned Milton that he couldn't leave his mother for an indeterminate length of time in the hospital morgue. Arrangements would have to be made. Milton knows that transporting her to Toronto will be expensive, and he wonders what would happen if he did just leave her there, what they'd do with the body. He pictures raging furnaces in the bowels of the hospital filled with charred corpses, diseased organs, amputated arms and legs.

The cementhead unlocks the glass doors for Judith. She steps out and looks up and down the street. Only now does it occur to Milton that the Goof might be picking her up. He considers waiting to see but then realizes that, if the Goof gets to her first, he won't see her at all; he'll be left alone in his car feeling as though his hands don't belong to him. He keeps shaking them, hoping to feel attached to them. All the way back from Hamilton he didn't have to read signs or decide when to pass other cars because someone else's hands were on the wheel.

The void on the seat beside him won't fill. He dreads emptying her candy wrappings from the ashtray.

'Judith,' he calls, getting out. She looks at him but says nothing, only stares. 'Can you come here for a minute?' he asks. She shoves her hands deep into her coat pockets. 'Please?' He knows he shouldn't have come here; he should get back in the car, slam the door and drive off leaving her wondering about him. As she approaches, he tries to think of something to say that will soften her towards him. He knows she won't believe him if he says he loves her. He could try 'I miss you'. In *Die Hard,* Bruce Willis' wife said she missed him, and you could see that he regretted giving her a hard time.

'What is it?' she asks.

'Do you think we could maybe go for a coffee?'

'Terry's picking me up.'

'He's a little late, isn't he?' Milton asks, glancing at his watch before remembering that he isn't wearing one.

'He had a sales meeting in Mississauga.' She looks around.

'He said he might be late.'

'I can give you a ride.'

'What do you want, Milton? You can't keep following me around.'

'My mother died.'

This stops her. 'When?'

'Today. We went to Niagara Falls.' He waits for her to make some comment about how he never took her to Niagara Falls.

'I'm sorry.'

'That's alright.'

She brushes some leaves off the hood of the car. 'Do you feel okay about it? I mean you didn't exactly love her.'

'It just feels weird. Like there's this hole. I don't know.' He leans his elbows on the car door and stares down at a piece of chewing gum flattened onto the road. 'I don't know what to do with the body.'

'Where is it?'

'Hamilton.'

'You could bury it locally. You don't have to bring it back here.'

Judith doesn't believe in burying corpses. She thinks cremation frees the spirit. She wanted to burn Ariel, but Milton wouldn't let her. It was the only time he screamed at her, so loud it felt as though his throat were bleeding.

'My sister shot herself this morning,' he says.

'What?'

'Connie shot herself.'

She slumps against the car, and he knows she's upset. This pleases him. 'I miss you,' he adds, but the words don't sound like his. He knows she doesn't believe him because she buttons up her coat and pulls out her gloves.

'What do you want from me, Milton?'

'Nothing.'

'Yes, you do. What is it? You don't want me back so why are you doing this?'

'I don't know.' He really doesn't. She sighs and looks up at the street-lamp. The wind blows a sheet of old newspaper around her legs. She kicks it away and pulls her collar tight around her neck. 'It's warmer in the car,' he tells her.

'The heater doesn't work.'

'Yeah, but at least there's no wind.' He gently takes her elbow, guides her to the passenger side and opens the door. Back behind the wheel he feels more in control. 'You sure you don't want a coffee?'

'You have to say whatever it is you want to say, and then you have to leave me alone.' She turns in her seat and stares at him. He wishes he smoked and could spend time lighting a cigarette. People always look pensive when they smoke, and he knows she expects him to be pensive. He tries to think of something to say about their relationship, or about his mother or Connie. Or his inner child. 'How do you know I don't want you back?' he asks.

'Because you hated having me around.'

'No, I didn't.'

Abruptly she flips the sun visor down then up again. She stares down the street. He wonders if he should try to hold her hand.

'I turn into a bitch around you.' She shakes her head. 'And I'm not a bitch.'

'I never said you were a bitch.'

'You didn't have to say it.' She pulls a Kleenex from her pocket, blows her nose then stares down at the tissue. 'We're too different.'

He wonders if he should argue that, according to Mandy and Leonard, he has changed.

'There's Terry,' she says, and Milton sees the Jap car. If he had a gun, he'd shoot at it. Maybe he hasn't changed.

'I'm so lonely,' he offers quickly, startling himself. He shouldn't have said this, knows that feeling sorry for himself won't bring her back. He tries to turn away from her, but she lays a hand on the back of his neck and pulls his face into her shoulder. He presses his forehead into her wool coat and inhales the perfume he smelled at the party. It's not a bad smell, just not hers.

'It's okay to cry,' she assures him.

He can't, although he'd like to so she'll know he has feelings, but the Goof is already knocking on the windshield. She rolls the window down. 'It's alright, Terry. I'll be there in a second.' She rolls the window back up, and Milton feels the softness of her cheek against his head. Tentatively he places an arm across her lap.

'Why do you think your sister killed herself?'

'She said nobody cared if she was alive or dead.'

'Did she care about anybody?'

'I don't know. I don't think so.' His nose is squashed against her arm making breathing difficult, but he doesn't want to move and disturb the peace between them.

'I don't think,' she says, 'that you can expect anybody to care about you if you don't care about anybody.'

A street-car rumbles by, sending vibrations through them. 'Do you care about Terry?' Milton asks.

'I like him.'

'Are you going to have his baby?'

'With my mucus, that's unlikely.'

'It could happen.' What he wants to know is if they're using contraceptives.

'I'm really glad you came by. I don't want us to be mad at each other.'

He knows he has to keep talking, or she'll let him go. 'Have you stopped thinking about her?' he asks.

'No.'

'If you have another baby you might.'

'No.' She pulls away from him, and he has no choice but to sit up. He looks at her, but she won't meet his eyes. She crosses her arms and stares at the dash. She looks scared to him, and he wonders what has frightened her. Guilt for having it off with the Goof? Trying to make babies with the Goof?

'Milton, I'm not going to spend my life hanging onto her. I know you want me to, but I can't.'

'I don't want you to.'

'You don't want us to recover. We have to try to recover.'

'I know that.'

'No, you don't. You're hanging onto me because of her.' Now she looks at him, but he's afraid to look at her so he stares at his hands on the wheel. They still don't belong to him.

'I had this dream,' she continues, 'and I know you don't want to hear about it, but I'm telling you anyway because I think it's significant.' She blows her nose again. 'I was holding this baby inside my coat. It was really cold, and I wanted to protect it from the wind.

It kept pushing its face into my boob like it wanted to nurse. The thing is, it wasn't my baby. I didn't know whose it was. I just kept walking with it, wishing I had milk to give it. I knew if I had milk the baby would think I was its mother, and I could keep it. I really wanted to keep it.'

He waits, staring at the Goof's car, knowing that momentarily she will explain the significance of the dream.

'Remember,' she says, 'before we had Ariel I always dreamed that the baby died? I forgot to feed it or left it behind or something. Well, this baby was alive. Only it wasn't mine. Anyway I just have this feeling that it was Ariel saying it's okay. Before, I felt guilty even thinking about it.'

'It wasn't your baby, though,' Milton points out.

'That's the part I can't figure out. Maybe because of my mucus I'm supposed to adopt or something.'

Terry gets out of the Honda again and stands with his hands on his hips. Judith waves at him.

'I don't want you to go,' Milton blurts out, disgusted by his feeble tone.

'Sweetheart,' she murmurs. She hasn't called him sweetheart in months. He wants her to say it again, feels that if she doesn't say it again he'll die. 'We don't even know each other anymore,' she tells him. Out of the corner of his eye he sees her grip the door handle. In seconds she will be gone. He freezes like the deer in the middle of the road. 'Look,' she adds, 'I don't want us to fight, okay? Please, can we just call a truce here? I'm sorry about your mother and sister, but I can't help you with that; I really can't. I'm sorry.'

She speaks quickly as though she's afraid that if she doesn't, she'll fall apart. He knows that she's trying to hold herself together with words.

His hands on the wheel don't move.

'Milton, tell me it's alright to leave. Please?'

He tries to send a message from his head to his hands to stop her, but they won't move. 'It's alright.'

'Okay.' She gets out of the car but leans on the door looking in at him. 'Are you going to be alright?'

He nods telling himself that he must make plans, start a new life. Tomorrow is Hallowe'en, he'll buy a pumpkin.

'Say hi to Winnie for me.'

He nods, suddenly wanting her to go, to leave now before he hits her, strangles her.

'I'll see you later then,' she says, but he knows she won't, knows he'll never see her again. She'll marry the Goof and move to Mississauga and have babies and forget about Ariel, and himself.

~

The serial killer kept the woman in his basement and played rock music to drown her screams. He stripped her, raped her then hand-cuffed her wrists and ankles to a chair. He videotaped himself cutting her and burning her so that he could watch the tape later. When she bled to death, he couldn't figure out what to do with the body so he chopped it up and cooked it in the oven and on the stove. The FBI agents say serial killers are nobodys who want power and control.

Milton wants to know how he's different from the serial killers since he's a nobody who wants power and control. He sees their faces over and over again on the news. They get interviewed on TV. Nobody tells them they're scum, that they should get their hands and balls cut off. Everybody talks nicely to them. Nobodys like Milton just get laid off, stepped on, forgotten. Until they kill somebody.

He let Judith go. This comforts him.

He sets the pumpkin by Ariel's headstone. They couldn't afford a fancy one, just a short, squat piece of pink granite that already had 'Beloved Daughter' carved into it. He hasn't visited the grave because he didn't want to think about her small body rotting beneath him. But now it soothes him to know where she is: in a safe place where nobody can hurt her. It feels peaceful here with dead people all around him, people who used up their lives worrying about being rich or famous, or fat or bald, or loved or hated. They all ended up dead. Equal. When Milton's dead he'll be no different from Bruce Willis or somebody.

It seems to him that he should feel worse with his family dying all around him. He wonders if he's in shock. One of the survivors of the mass murder in the mall watched her parents get shot. Afterwards, her brother and sister kept asking if she was all right. When she said she was, they shook their heads and insisted that she was 'in denial'. Milton suspects that he's 'in denial' and he doesn't understand why the shrink and Judith claim that being 'in denial' is bad for a person. It seems to Milton that if being in denial protects a person, there can't be anything wrong with it. If the mind plays tricks to stop a person from despairing, they should count themselves lucky. He suspects it's the people who can't deny any longer who end up on the streets talking to themselves. Or killing people, or themselves.

His hands feel cold. This pleases him. He blows on them then rubs them together.

~

In the car, looking at the house, all he wants is to go to a Holiday Inn and stay in a room that looks exactly like hundreds of other rooms; a room without a history, with no blood or shit or vomit in it.

Rory comes out and opens the car door. 'Everything alright, Uncle Milton?'

'Sure.'

'You coming inside?'

'In a minute.'

Rory gets in the car and closes the door. 'Leonard's at the hospital.'

'Why?'

'He couldn't breathe. Mom's really upset. She won't talk to us about it. She got dinner and everything then told Morty to go to bed. He usually stays up to watch "The Simpsons" so he was pretty upset. Where's Gramma?'

'She had an attack.'

'Is she okay?'

'She's dead,' he says carefully, trying to read Rory's expression in the street-light.

'She's dead, really?'

Milton nods. Rory slouches down in the seat. 'Wow. This

could be on that show about unbelievable events. Last night they showed this couple having a New Year's Eve party—they're like this perfectly normal couple—then he goes upstairs and overdoses. He's a doctor. So she finds him and freaks out and falls downstairs skewering herself on this sculpture they bought in Africa. By the time they get her to the hospital she bleeds to death. It's a true story. I bet if we wrote and told them what happened to us, they'd put it on the show.'

Milton nods as if considering this information. He has never heard Rory chatter in this way, and Milton wonders if Rory's talking ceaselessly because he's in denial.

'Then they showed a depressed lady committing suicide by holding a plastic bag over her head.'

Blocks away, dogs bark. 'How's Morty?' Milton asks.

'Mom screamed at him. He's not used to her screaming at him so he was bawling. He's okay now. I promised to fix his bike tomorrow.'

'Okay, well, I guess we better go in.'

'Uncle Milton?'

'Yeah?'

'You're not going to leave right away, are you? I mean I almost wish Dad was here. At least then it would be more normal.'

Only now does Milton see the fear in the boy, and it upsets him that he has been expecting him to behave as an adult. 'I'm not going anywhere. You relax now. You've already done more than your share.'

Outside the front door, Rory pauses. 'The cops said people don't usually shoot themselves in front of other people. They said usually they plan it. They do it on their own and leave a note.'

Milton nods, wondering what Rory needs him to say, what would console him.

'I know she screwed my dad.'

'Well, if she did, your dad had something to do with it.'

Rory nods. 'I know.' He kicks dead leaves off the steps. 'I just don't think it's fair to kill yourself in front of other people.'

'No.'

~

267

Mandy lies on Milton's bed watching 'Rescue 911'. She points to the screen. 'His parachute won't open. He's just got that little orange one.'

Milton watches the skydiver plummeting towards an open field. 'Why won't it open?'

'It's tangled or something.' Sirens sound, the skydivers' wife and friends run across a used-car lot predicting where he will land. 'There's no way he can live,' Mandy comments.

'They always live on "Rescue 911".'

'Yeah, but this time there's no way.' The skydiver crashes feet first into the ground, and the rescue team swarms him. Next he's in a hospital with his legs in traction and his arms in casts. Then it's a year later, and he's sitting on his couch beside his wife talking about how he thought he was going to die until he landed and realized he was still alive. He really appreciated life after that, he says. Then they show him jumping out of a plane with his wife.

'If he appreciates life, why's he jumping out of planes again?' Mandy demands.

'Maybe that's the only way he remembers to appreciate it.'

'I think that's sick. I bet it's expensive too. I bet it's like a hundred bucks a jump or something.' A Burger King commercial comes on, and Milton turns down the volume.

'So are you okay?' he asks.

'Oh yeah. I think she's a bitch for doing it. There's no way my boys are going to get over it. Any chance of being normal. Forget that.'

'Worse things have happened to people.'

'Mopping up your aunt's brains isn't something you forget.'

'I think he's dealing with it pretty well. I think he's a pretty amazing kid.'

She covers her face with her hands the way she does when she's trying not to cry.

'I do,' Milton insists. 'I know you think there's nothing special about him, but I think he's a decent human being, and that's special.'

She sniffs, wiping her eyes. He can't see how he's supposed to tell her about their mother.

'Where's mother?' she asks. 'I'm sorry about this morning, but I just couldn't face her. I mean, senile or not, she brought that gun into this house, and I'll never forgive her for that.' She stares back at the TV where a blonde is getting into the passenger side of a sleek Buick. Inside she kisses a man in a suit as he shifts gears.

'So what happened with Leonard?' Milton asks.

'He's in a coma. He was drowning from the crap in his lungs. They had to stick a needle in his back to drain it out. I'm sorry, I know you didn't want him to go to hospital, but I couldn't deal with it.'

'Well, if he's in a coma he won't know the difference.'

She stares at smiling children chewing on pizza slices. 'They don't expect him to come out of it. I get the feeling they can't figure out why he doesn't die. They've got tubes up his nose and in his arm and in his penis for god's sakes. I swear, take me out and shoot me before that happens. Holy shit.' She turns up the volume with the converter. On TV, a station wagon is sinking into a lake. A hysterical woman rushes after it, trying to free her baby from the car-seat before the vehicle becomes completely submerged.

'Do you really want to watch this?' Milton asks. The mother screams to her young son on the shore to call 911. He does but, in his distress, becomes incoherent. Two men rush out from neighbouring cottages and dive into the lake. One of them climbs into the rear of the station wagon and pulls out the baby. The mother grabs the infant and weeps with joy.

'I shouldn't have called her a slut,' Mandy admits.

'You didn't.'

'I called her a whore.'

'Maybe she was one.'

'I shouldn't have said it to her face.' An ad for IDA Drugs comes on; the pharmacist smiles as he hands a package to an old lady who smiles.

'I shouldn't have let Mother have the gun,' Milton says.

'There wasn't supposed to be any bullets in it. Seth took her bullets. She must've had some stashed somewhere. I swear she's so sneaky; she's like the worst child.'

'She died today.' He wants to stop her before she says something she'll regret. She stares at him. 'We went to Niagara Falls, and on the way back she had an attack.'

269

Mandy covers her face with her hands again.

'Maybe it was too much excitement for her,' he suggests. On TV, a fluffy white cat is being served its dinner by a butler. Milton switches it off.

'You try to do the right thing,' Mandy says, 'and it's a fucking disaster. I've fucking had it. I don't want to do this anymore.' She gets up and starts for the door, but Milton grabs her arm.

'What are you doing?' he asks.

'I don't know. I just don't want to be here anymore.'

'Where are you going to go?'

'I don't know.'

'Stop for a second. Let's talk about this.'

'What's to talk about? I hit my mother and made my sister shoot herself. I have to live with that.'

'Don't go blaming yourself.'

'You think Connie would have done it if I'd played her little game? No way. You think Mother would have died if I'd let her come home from the hospital?'

'I just don't think there's any point in blaming anybody. I mean, maybe they're better off dead. What's so great about being alive anyway? All that happens is you get older and more scared of being dead. You said yourself that just when you think things can't get shittier, something shittier happens. Maybe we did them a favour.' Leonard's cat comes in and jumps on the bed.

'Shit, I forgot to feed it,' Mandy says.

'It's pretty fat. I wouldn't worry about it.'

Mandy sits on the bed beside the cat. 'I can't believe she's dead.'

'Who?'

'Mother. It doesn't feel like she's dead.'

Milton nods vaguely, picks some socks off the floor and drops them on the dresser.

'On the news,' Mandy tells him, 'they showed this father and daughter. The daughter had some blood disease that ruined her kidneys so she needed a transplant. Both her brothers and her father offered her one of theirs. They were all willing to cut themselves open to save her life. I don't think I'd do that. I mean if I could save somebody in my family by giving a kidney, I wouldn't do it. I'd be too scared. They said the dad was smiling on the way to the operating room.'

'You'd give one of your boys a kidney.'

'I don't know. I think I'd try to find a donor first.'

'So what's wrong with that?'

'Seth says I don't know how to love.'

'He should talk.'

Morty stands in the doorway rubbing his eyes. 'Mum?'

'What is it, honey?'

'I can't sleep.'

'You want to curl up with me?'

Morty nods. Mandy takes his hand. 'I'm sorry I shouted at you before.'

Morty hikes up his pajama bottoms. 'That's okay.'

She kisses the top of his head. 'So Milton, we'll talk more in the morning, okay?'

'Sure.' He watches them walk down the hall, feeling sad that his sister will never really understand how much she loves her boys. Unless they die.

~

Leonard shares his room with a man who has been paralyzed by AIDS. He tells Milton about the fife he plays and the band he wants to put together. Milton wonders how he got AIDS since he doesn't seem gay; he wonders if the man's a drug addict or if he got it from a blood transfusion or from heterosexual sex. 'I need a drummer,' the man informs him. 'My buddy moved to Vancouver. He keeps telling me I should move there, but I don't know. It rains all the time, right?'

'I've never been,' Milton admits.

'I heard it rains.'

Milton wonders what kind of drugs the man is on, if he's hallucinating or if normally he mouths off to complete strangers. 'We built a hockey rink for the kids,' the man continues. 'It was a lot of fun. Hard work, though.' Milton wonders if the man is aware that he is paralyzed or if, when the drugs wear off, he'll reach down to scratch and won't feel anything. Even though Milton doesn't know the man, he would like to protect him from this discovery.

Mandy pulls the curtain. 'Excuse us,' she says to the man.

He grins. 'No problem.'

Leonard is asleep in a tangle of tubes.

'They say he can hear us,' Mandy tells Milton. 'Sometimes people who come out of comas remember stuff people said to them.' She leans close to Leonard's ear. 'Hi, Len. Milton's here.' She turns to Milton and whispers, 'Don't tell him about Mother.'

Milton doesn't know what to tell him, would like to ask why he doesn't die, what he's hanging on for. He has a feeling, if Leonard could explain this to him, he'd have a better understanding of the meaning of life.

Mandy nudges him and mouths, 'Say something.'

Milton leans over Leonard's ear. 'Hi, Leonard. How's it going?'

'We're all waiting for you to come home,' Mandy explains loudly. 'We want you home for Christmas.'

Milton has a feeling that, even if Leonard can hear, he isn't interested. He's probably in the tunnel looking at dead friends and trying to decide if he wants to live or die. Maybe he doesn't want to die because Mare's with him and so is their father. Maybe he's arguing with Mare, and that's why his eyeballs are rolling around under his lids.

'At least he's not in pain,' Mandy comments. The fife player starts humming an Irish tune. Mandy looks at Milton and rolls her eyes.

'So what do we do now?' he whispers.

'I just think it's important that he knows we haven't deserted him.' She leans over Leonard again. 'The cat's fine, and I'm watering the plants. The Hibiscus got another flower, which is pretty awesome considering it's almost winter.' She signals to Milton to say something, but he can't think of what.

'I went to Niagara Falls,' he offers. 'It really is one of the wonders of the world. Maybe, when you get better, we'll go there.' He doesn't like the way his voice sounds, like the voice people who don't like kids use when they talk to them. It's not that he doesn't like Leonard. It's just that he feels left behind, inconsequential. Leonard is experiencing something only dying people get to experience.

Milton doesn't think he wants living people standing around staring at him.

The coffee in the hospital cafeteria tastes worse than instant. Mandy adds sugar. 'That guy in the room with Leonard, he's homeless. The nurse told me they don't know what to do with him. They can't just put him back on the street.'

'He seems pretty cheerful for a homeless person.'

'He's wacko.'

Milton thinks being wacko when you're paralyzed and homeless is probably a good thing.

Mandy sighs heavily. 'So there's just you and me now.'

Milton nods, watching a girl eating french fries and reading what must be a romance novel because it has a man and a woman kissing on the cover. Milton feels sorry for the girl because she's plump and pimply with buck teeth, and he can't imagine any guy romancing her. Then it occurs to him that maybe she's better off getting it in a book. At least with the book she won't be disappointed. Maybe she imagines she's the heroine and, while she's reading, feels beautiful and desired.

'I wish I felt sad or something,' Mandy says. 'But all I feel is guilty.'

It seems to Milton that the people who go around feeling guilty think they're pretty important, as if things wouldn't have happened without them. 'She might've died anyway,' he points out, 'even if we'd come home.'

'I doubt it.'

'Anyway, the daughter who watched her parents get shot in the mall said at least they didn't have to die from cancer. It's the same with Mother. It was over pretty quick.'

'There's no way Connie would have done it if I wasn't screaming at her.'

Milton sees no point in arguing with her; he understands that she needs to feel guilty, that it makes her feel special.

Keeping her eyes on the page, the girl fondles an oatmeal cookie. Milton wonders what she's reading at this particular moment, maybe something about a handsome man cupping his hands over her breasts or stroking her thighs.

'So what do we do about Mother?' Mandy asks.

'I thought I'd call a funeral home in Hamilton and ask them to cremate her. Then I can go pick up the ashes. Unless you want to see her first.'

Mandy shakes her head. 'How are we going to pay for it?'

'They've got a payment plan.'

Milton suspects she wants to smoke because she keeps fidgeting. She starts to shred the empty sugar packets. 'Some male nurse at a hospital killed a patient by putting sugar in her IV. It was in the paper this morning. They had a close relationship. I guess he couldn't stand to see her suffer.'

'Leonard's not suffering. He's in a coma.'

'I guess.' She grips the salt and pepper shakers with one hand and squeezes them together. 'Before he went into it he did this weird breathing, like he was panting or something. It scared the shit out of me. Then it seemed like he stopped breathing. I thought he was dead. I've never seen anybody die. Did you see Mom die?'

'No.' He doesn't want to tell her she died in a toilet.

'Where did she die?'

He looks down at his cup and swishes the coffee around. 'In the car. I went to buy some chips.'

'That's so weird. I mean that she'd die just like that.'

'Maybe she wanted to. Maybe she knew about Leonard and just didn't want to live anymore.'

'I can't understand that, you know, having a favourite kid and treating the rest of us like shit. I swear I'll never forgive her for that.'

Milton thinks about the whales again and how they don't hold grudges. It seems to him Mandy's carrying around all this blame and resentment, and it's weighing her down. He'd say this, but he doesn't want to upset her. Also he understands that she needs it, that without the weight pinning her down she would have no reason to live. He remembers Judith saying it felt like they were hanging onto the planet by a tiny thread. Without her problems, Mandy must feel as if she'd fall off the planet. Like he'd feel if he let go of Ariel.

'Shit.' Mandy pulls at something on her sweater.

'What is it?'

Judith said they have to try to recover.

'I really appreciate you helping out with the laundry,' Mandy tells him, 'but you've got to take the Kleenex out of your pockets. It was all over everything this morning.'

'Sorry.'

'That's okay.'

Maybe he'll paint the room anyway. Rose.

TWENTY-ONE

He knocks on the door many times before Winnie's mother answers. 'What do you want?' she asks.

'Can I talk to Winnie?'

'He's out.'

Milton thinks she's lying. 'Okay, well, can you tell him I dropped by?' He hears movement behind the door then Winnie whispering. 'Win,' Milton says, 'I need to talk to you. I thought maybe we'd go for a donut and check out the trick-or-treaters.'

Winnie opens the door. 'We can go out for half an hour.'

'Okay.'

They pass ferocious pumpkins with jagged mouths and squinty eyes. They pass houses with fake cobwebs covering their porches and skeletons dangling from their windows. Milton can't think of what to say since usually Winnie does the talking. A speaker on the porch of one house blares out spooky music and bloodcurdling screams. 'Imagine listening to that all night,' Milton remarks,

276

expecting Winnie to comment, but he doesn't. Teenagers dressed as tramps saunter past. 'Some costume,' he adds. 'All they do is put on an old hat and expect you to hand over candy.' Still Winnie says nothing. A small boy wearing a box, that Milton supposes is meant to look like a computer, walks by with his dad. 'That's original,' Milton observes, but Winnie doesn't respond.

They sit at a table by the window. Winnie fingers his Bavarian Cream.

'So, when are you going to quit being mad at me?' Milton asks.

'I'm not mad at you.'

'Then why aren't you talking to me?'

Winnie shrugs. Outside on the pavement a man dressed as a bumblebee hops up and down then gets into a sports car with a woman dressed as an alien.

'You think it's my fault,' Milton says.

'I do not.'

'Things happen sometimes, and you think you're doing the right thing but then it doesn't work out. That doesn't mean you were wrong to do it in the first place. At the time it seemed like the right thing to do.'

'Mom says you should always think ahead. She says nobody thinks ahead anymore. Everybody's greedy.'

'She's got a point,' Milton agrees. 'It's just I don't see how you can know what's going to happen. I mean you can get pretty worked up about it—prepare and all that—then something else happens, and you feel like a jerk. I mean, maybe if I tried to stop her she would've killed all of us. Maybe she was just looking for an excuse to die. People do that: try to find a way out, jump in front of a subway car or whatever. Maybe I made it easy for her.' Milton doesn't like the way he's justifying himself; he wants to stop justifying himself, wants to believe it wasn't his fault.

Winnie bites his donut and chews thoughtfully. 'Do you think her soul was tainted?'

'I don't know. I don't know if she was born like that or if something happened to her. I mean I can't figure out if people change, or if we just stop trying to please other people.'

'Mom says her soul must've been tainted, since she killed

herself. She says she'll suffer eternal damnation.' He stares hard at a German Shepherd peeing on a parking sign. 'I don't like anybody anymore.'

'What do you mean?'

'I don't like anybody. Even Angelo and Maria.'

'Why not?'

Still staring at the dog, Winnie shrugs and rubs some icing sugar off his chin.

'Did something happen at work?' Milton asks.

'Nobody tells you the truth.'

'Sure they do.' Milton realizes that this in itself is a lie. 'Maybe telling the truth isn't such a great idea anyway. I mean if people went around telling the truth all the time other people would get hurt.'

'They get hurt anyway.'

'Maybe more people would get hurt if everybody told the truth.'

Winnie pokes his finger back and forth through the handle of his coffee-cup. 'I don't trust anybody any more.'

'You've got to trust people.' Milton doesn't know why he's saying this, since he doesn't trust anybody.

'People call me names behind my back.'

'What's it matter to you what they say?'

'You didn't like it when those guys called you a rat.'

'Which guys?'

'The guys that got you fired.'

'Yeah, but that was before. Now I don't give a damn.'

'You do, too.'

'It's all inside your head.' Milton taps his temple. 'If inside your head you don't let those people get to you, they won't get to you.'

'They still get to you.'

'I try not to let them.'

'They still do. Connie got to you. That's why you let her kill herself.'

'That's not true.'

Winnie finishes his donut and wipes his hands on his pants. 'Mom says evil people suffer eternal damnation, but I don't believe her. I don't believe there's a heaven or a hell. I think Coco's just dead and Connie's just dead.'

'Is that so bad?'

Winnie shrugs and crumples the wax paper from his donut. 'There's no point to anything.'

Milton would like to tell him there's a point in loving people and in being decent, but nothing in his life has proved this to be true. And he doesn't want to lie.

'The way I see it you don't have any choice, Win. I mean you're a good person. You couldn't be evil.'

Two little boys dressed in hockey outfits, clutching shopping bags filled with candy, hover by the door. 'Go pee,' their mother tells them, then she orders a coffee to go.

'I'm tired,' Winnie says.

'Do you want to go home?'

Winnie nods.

They walk back in silence. Milton searches for something to say that will bring back the old Winnie. Judith could think of something, or anyway she'd be able to distract Winnie from his pain. Milton wonders if that's what it's all about in the end: distraction. Since you can't change it. 'Maybe,' he suggests, 'we could go to a hockey game when the season starts.'

'Sure,' Winnie agrees, without enthusiasm.

'I'll book some tickets.'

'Sure.'

~

They each carry a tin. Mandy carries Connie, and Milton holds Mare. 'This is illegal you know,' Mandy warns him.

'Not if it goes in the lake. Only if you dump it on somebody's property.'

'I didn't expect them to weigh so much. I mean I thought it would be like cigarette ash or something.'

'It's the bones,' Milton explains.

'Somebody told me you can't even be sure if it's your loved ones' ashes. They could be somebody else's. They just scrape the oven. You might have somebody else's left-overs in your tin.'

'I don't think it matters all that much, do you?'

'I guess not.'

They waited until dark so nobody would see them. But now Milton has trouble determining where the sand ends and the water begins. 'I guess we should walk out onto one of those piers.'

'I'm not going out there. How are we supposed to see the edge?'

'If we dump them here, it'll just wash up on the shore.'

'It'll probably do that anyway.'

'I'm going out on the pier.'

'I'm coming with you then.'

It has been raining again, and his sneakers slip on the concrete. He reaches back for Mandy's hand and is surprised by her grip. He has a feeling if he falls into the water she won't let go, even if it means she drowns with him. This surprises and comforts him.

'I think we're coming close to the edge,' he cautions.

'Be careful.'

'I am.'

Suddenly the water laps below him. 'Okay stop. I'm going to throw Mother in first. Do you want to say a prayer or something?'

'I can't think of anything. Can you?'

Milton stares at a ship far off; he pictures the sailors sitting behind the lit port-holes, safe and secure, without dead people around them. 'May she rest in peace?' he asks.

'That's good. Say that.'

He pries open the tin then holds it over the water. 'May you rest in peace.' He shakes it empty. Some ash blows back onto his jeans and he quickly brushes them off. 'What do we do with the tin?'

'I don't want it, do you want it?'

'We can't toss it in the lake.'

'Why not?' Mandy asks.

'That's polluting.'

'Okay, fine. Give it to me. I'll stick it in the garbage. Here.' She hands him the second tin.

'Should I say the same thing?'

'Unless you can think of something better.'

He tries to think of something better. Something that will make Connie's spirit forgive him, leave him alone and find another body to inhabit, in another country. His mind goes blank. 'May you rest in peace,' he says and empties the tin.

'Okay let's go back, this is scary.' She takes his hand again and doesn't let go, even when they're on dry land. They drop the tins in a garbage-can.

'Let's sit for a second,' he suggests.

'It's freezing.'

'Just for a second.'

'There's ash on your shoe,' she points out. He wipes it on the grass.

They sit close to each other on the bench. Milton feels the damp seeping through his jeans, but he doesn't care. He looks at Mandy. 'You okay?'

'I guess. I mean this is weird, don't you think?'

'People probably do it all the time. I mean people die everyday.'

'I guess.' She sighs. Milton stares up at the half moon and listens to the wind in the trees. It was under one of these trees that he found the baby chipmunk. These trees were here before he was born and will stand long after he's dead.

'Are you sad?' Mandy asks.

'I don't know. I mean something had to happen. It couldn't go on like that.' He's glad the trees will outlive him.

'Morty wanted to know what your favourite colour is.'

'Why?' Milton asks.

'He's making all his Christmas presents in art class.'

'He doesn't have to give me a Christmas present.'

'He wants to.'

This warms Milton, inflates him like a balloon. 'Orange,' he says.

'I'll tell him.' She pulls out a cigarette, and he cups his hands around her Bic so she can light it. 'Thanks for talking to Rory last night. I was so out of it.'

'Don't worry about it.'

'He really likes you for some reason. He says he trusts you.'

This pleases and yet frightens Milton, the responsibility of it.

'It'll be good for him,' Mandy adds, 'to have a man around who isn't a shit.'

Who isn't a shit.

It scares Milton that suddenly he's looking forward to

Christmas, already thinking about what to get for the boys. It scares him because he might be disappointed.

'I'll quit smoking,' Mandy offers, 'if you get a grip on this reading thing.'

'Where'd that come from?'

'You said yourself there's special classes for it. Maybe you could take Rory. He'll go if you go.'

'I thought you said he wasn't reading disabled.'

'Okay, so I made a mistake. I'm allowed to make a mistake, aren't I?'

'The deal was,' Milton reminds her, 'you could come live with me if you quit smoking.'

'That was before.'

'Before what?'

Mandy inhales on her cigarette and stares at the lake. 'I just think it's dumb to go through your whole life scared of words. They're just words.'

The wind picks up, and Milton hears waves. He pictures the ashes, specks spreading in the black water, fish food.

'There's no chance you'll get a decent job,' Mandy warns him, 'if you don't learn to read properly. I think half the problem is you're so sure you can't, you freak yourself out before you even start. I bet if you just calmly applied yourself you could do it.'

He remembers a gorilla he saw on 'Sixty Minutes' who spent his entire life in a concrete room in a shopping mall. He sat listless, enduring the stares and comments of shoppers staring at him through the glass. An anthropologist began to visit him and taught him how to finger paint. The gorilla was eager to learn, the anthropologist said; he would learn if he was allowed out of his cage. It upset Milton that assholes were keeping the gorilla stupid, boxing him up, robbing him of a life.

Mandy tosses her butt into the grass and pulls out another cigarette. 'We don't have to start until next week, though. I've still got a couple of packs left.'

Finally, animal-rights activists made it possible for the gorilla to go outside. At first, he was frightened and only peeked out the open door. Then cautiously he moved onto the grass and sat waiting, as though expecting something horrible to happen. When nothing did, his eyes lit up, and he scampered across the grass and stared up at the sky.

Milton thinks going to the reading class might not be so bad if Rory is with him. He likes Rory; he imagines them driving in the Volare, stopping for a donut afterwards. Maybe they can do homework together, at the kitchen table.

Mandy nudges him. 'Alright?'

'Alright.'